THE INVISIBLE MAN

THE ISLAND OF DR. MOREAU

H. G. WELLS

Reader's Library *Classics*

Contents

THE INVISIBLE MAN

CHAPTER I

THE STRANGE MAN'S ARRIVAL

The stranger came early in February, one wintry day, through a biting wind and a driving snow, the last snowfall of the year, over the down, walking from Bramblehurst railway station, and carrying a little black portmanteau in his thickly gloved hand. He was wrapped up from head to foot, and the brim of his soft felt hat hid every inch of his face but the shiny tip of his nose; the snow had piled itself against his shoulders and chest, and added a white crest to the burden he carried. He staggered into the "Coach and Horses" more dead than alive, and flung his portmanteau down. "A fire," he cried, "in the name of human charity! A room and a fire!" He stamped and shook the snow from off himself in the bar, and followed Mrs. Hall into her guest parlour to strike his bargain. And with that much introduction, that and a couple of sovereigns flung upon the table, he took up his quarters in the inn.

Mrs. Hall lit the fire and left him there while she went to prepare him a meal with her own hands. A guest to stop at Iping in the wintertime was an unheard-of piece of luck, let alone a guest who was no "haggler," and she was resolved to show herself worthy of her good fortune. As soon as the bacon was well under way, and Millie, her lymphatic maid, had been brisked up a bit by a few deftly chosen expressions of contempt, she carried the cloth, plates, and glasses into the parlour and began to lay them with the utmost *éclat*. Although the fire was burning up briskly, she was surprised to see that her visitor still wore his hat and coat, standing with his back to her and staring out of the window at the falling snow in the yard. His gloved hands were clasped behind him, and he seemed to be lost in thought. She noticed that the melting snow that still sprinkled his shoulders dripped upon her carpet. "Can I take your hat and coat, sir?" she said, "and give them a good dry in the kitchen?"

"No," he said without turning.

She was not sure she had heard him, and was about to repeat her question.

He turned his head and looked at her over his shoulder. "I prefer to keep them on," he said with emphasis, and she noticed that he wore big blue spectacles with sidelights, and had a bush side-whisker over his coat-collar that completely hid his cheeks and face.

"Very well, sir," she said. *As* you like. In a bit the room will be warmer."

He made no answer, and had turned his face away from her again, and Mrs. Hall, feeling that her conversational advances were ill-timed, laid the rest of the table things in a quick staccato and whisked out of the room. When she returned he was still standing there, like a man of stone, his back hunched, his collar turned up, his dripping hat-brim turned down, hiding his face and ears completely. She put down the eggs and bacon with considerable emphasis, and called rather than said to him, "Your lunch is served, sir."

"Thank you," he said at the same time, and did not stir until she was closing the door. Then he swung round and approached the table with a certain eager quickness.

As she went behind the bar to the kitchen she heard a sound repeated at regular intervals. Chirk, chirk, chirk, it went, the sound of a spoon being rapidly whisked round a basin. "That girl!" she said. "There! I clean forgot it. It's her being so long!" And while she herself finished mixing the mustard, she gave Millie a few verbal stabs for her excessive slowness. She had cooked the ham and eggs, laid the table, and done everything, while Millie (help indeed!) had only succeeded in delaying the mustard. And him a new guest and wanting to stay! Then she filled the mustard pot, and, putting it with a certain stateliness upon a gold and black tea-tray, carried it into the parlour.

She rapped and entered promptly. As she did so her visitor moved quickly, so that she got but a glimpse of a white object disappearing behind the table. It would seem he was picking something from the floor. She rapped down the mustard pot on the table, and then she noticed the overcoat and hat had been taken off and put over a chair in front of the fire, and a pair of wet boots threatened rust to her steel fender. She went to these things resolutely. "I suppose I may have them to dry now," she said in a voice that brooked no denial.

"Leave the hat," said her visitor, in a muffled voice, and turning she saw he had raised his head and was sitting and looking at her.

For a moment she stood gaping at him, too surprised to speak.

He held a white cloth—it was a serviette he had brought with him—over the lower part of his face, so that his mouth and jaws were completely hidden, and that was the reason of his muffled voice. But it was not that which startled Mrs. Hall. It was the fact that all his forehead above his blue glasses was covered by a white bandage, and that another covered his ears, leaving not a scrap of his face exposed excepting only his pink, peaked nose. It was bright, pink, and shiny just as it had been at first. He wore a dark-brown velvet jacket with a high, black, linen-lined collar turned up about his neck. The thick black hair, escaping as it could below and between the cross bandages, projected in curious tails and horns, giving him the strangest appearance conceivable. This muffled and bandaged head was so unlike what she had anticipated, that for a moment she was rigid.

He did not remove the serviette, but remained holding it, as she saw now, with a brown gloved hand, and regarding her with his inscrutable blue glasses. "Leave the hat," he said, speaking very distinctly through the white cloth.

Her nerves began to recover from the shock they had received. She placed the hat on the chair again by the fire. "I didn't know, sir," she began, "that—" and she stopped embarrassed.

"Thank you," he said drily, glancing from her to the door and then at her again.

"I'll have them nicely dried, sir, at once," she said, and carried his clothes out of the room. She glanced at his white-swathed head and blue goggles again as she was going out of the door; but his napkin was still in front of his face. She shivered a little as she closed the door behind her, and her face was eloquent of her surprise and perplexity. "I *never*," she whispered. "There!" She went quite softly to the kitchen, and was too preoccupied to ask Millie what she was messing about with *now*, when she got there.

The visitor sat and listened to her retreating feet. He glanced inquiringly at the window before he removed his serviette, and resumed his meal. He took a mouthful, glanced suspiciously at the window, took another mouthful, then rose and, taking the serviette in his hand, walked across the room and pulled the blind down to the top of the white muslin that obscured the lower panes. This left the room in a twilight. This done, he returned with an easier air to the table and his meal.

"The poor soul's had an accident or an op'ration or somethin'," said Mrs. Hall. "What a turn them bandages did give me, to be sure!"

She put on some more coal, unfolded the clothes-horse, and extended the traveller's coat upon this. "And they goggles! Why, he looked more like a divin' helmet than a human man!" She hung his muffler on a corner of the horse. "And holding that handkerchief over his mouth all the time. Talkin' through it! ... Perhaps his mouth was hurt too—maybe."

She turned round, as one who suddenly remembers. "Bless my soul alive!" she said, going off at a tangent; "ain't you done them taters *yet*, Millie?"

When Mrs. Hall went to clear away the stranger's lunch, her idea that his mouth must also have been cut or disfigured in the accident she supposed him to have suffered, was confirmed, for he was smoking a pipe, and all the time that she was in the room he never loosened the silk muffler he had wrapped round the lower part of his face to put the mouthpiece to his lips. Yet it was not forgetfulness, for she saw he glanced at it as it smouldered out. He sat in the corner with his back to the window-blind and spoke now, having eaten and drunk and being comfortably warmed through, with less aggressive brevity than before. The reflection of the fire lent a kind of red animation to his big spectacles they had lacked hitherto.

"I have some luggage," he said, "at Bramblehurst station," and he asked her how he could have it sent. He bowed his bandaged head quite politely in acknowledgment of her explanation. "Tomorrow?" he said. "There is no speedier delivery?" and seemed quite disappointed when she answered, "No." Was she quite sure? No man with a trap who would go over?

Mrs. Hall, nothing loath, answered his questions and developed a conversation. "It's a steep road by the down, sir," she said in answer to the question about a trap; and then, snatching at an opening, said, "It was there a carriage was upsettled, a year ago and more. A gentleman killed, besides his coachman. Accidents, sir, happen in a moment, don't they?"

But the visitor was not to be drawn so easily. "They do," he said through his muffler, eyeing her quietly through his impenetrable glasses.

"But they take long enough to get well, don't they? ... There was my sister's son, Tom, jest cut his arm with a scythe, tumbled on it in the 'ayfield, and, bless me! he was three months tied up sir. You'd hardly believe it. It's regular given me a dread of a scythe, sir."

"I can quite understand that," said the visitor.

"He was afraid, one time, that he'd have to have an op'ration—he was that bad, sir."

The visitor laughed abruptly, a bark of a laugh that he seemed to bite and kill in his mouth. *"Was* he?" he said.

"He was, sir. And no laughing matter to them as had the doing for him, as I had—my sister being took up with her little ones so much. There was bandages to do, sir, and bandages to undo. So that if I may make so bold as to say it, sir—"

"Will you get me some matches?" said the visitor, quite abruptly. "My pipe is out."

Mrs. Hall was pulled up suddenly. It was certainly rude of him, after telling him all she had done. She gasped at him for a moment, and remembered the two sovereigns. She went for the matches.

"Thanks," he said concisely, as she put them down, and turned his shoulder upon her and stared out of the window again. It was altogether too discouraging. Evidently he was sensitive on the topic of operations and bandages. She did not "make so bold as to say," however, after all. But his snubbing way had irritated her, and Millie had a hot time of it that afternoon.

The visitor remained in the parlour until four o'clock, without giving the ghost of an excuse for an intrusion. For the most part he was quite still during that time; it would seem he sat in the growing darkness smoking in the firelight—perhaps dozing.

Once or twice a curious listener might have heard him at the coals, and for the space of five minutes he was audible pacing the room. He seemed to be talking to himself. Then the armchair creaked as he sat down again.

CHAPTER II

MR. TEDDY HENFREY'S FIRST IMPRESSIONS

At four o'clock, when it was fairly dark and Mrs. Hall was screwing up her courage to go in and ask her visitor if he would take some tea, Teddy Henfrey, the clock-jobber, came into the bar. "My sakes! Mrs. Hall," said he, "but this is terrible weather for thin boots!" The snow outside was falling faster.

Mrs. Hall agreed, and then noticed he had his bag with him. "Now you're here, Mr. Teddy," said she, "I'd be glad if you'd give th' old clock in the parlour a bit of a look. 'Tis going, and it strikes well and hearty; but the hour-hand won't do nuthin' but point at six."

And leading the way, she went across to the parlour door and rapped and entered.

Her visitor, she saw as she opened the door, was seated in the armchair before the fire, dozing it would seem, with his bandaged head drooping on one side. The only light in the room was the red glow from the fire—which lit his eyes like adverse railway signals, but left his downcast face in darkness—and the scanty vestiges of the day that came in through the open door. Everything was ruddy, shadowy, and indistinct to her, the more so since she had just been lighting the bar lamp, and her eyes were dazzled. But for a second it seemed to her that the man she looked at had an enormous mouth wide open—a vast and incredible mouth that swallowed the whole of the lower portion of his face. It was the sensation of a moment: the white-bound head, the monstrous goggle eyes, and this huge yawn below it. Then he stirred, started up in his chair, put up his hand. She opened the door wide, so that the room was lighter, and she saw him more clearly, with the muffler held up to his face just as she had seen him hold the serviette before. The shadows, she fancied, had tricked her.

"Would you mind, sir, this man a-coming to look at the clock, sir?" she said, recovering from the momentary shock.

"Look at the clock?" he said, staring round in a drowsy manner, and speaking over his hand, and then, getting more fully awake, "certainly."

Mrs. Hall went away to get a lamp, and he rose and stretched himself. Then came the light, and Mr. Teddy Henfrey, entering, was confronted by this bandaged person. He was, he says, "taken aback."

"Good afternoon," said the stranger, regarding him—as Mr. Henfrey says, with a vivid sense of the dark spectacles—"like a lobster."

"I hope," said Mr. Henfrey, "that it's no intrusion."

"None whatever," said the stranger. "Though, I understand," he said turning to Mrs. Hall, "that this room is really to be mine for my own private use."

"I thought, sir," said Mrs. Hall, "you'd prefer the clock—"

"Certainly," said the stranger, "certainly—but, as a rule, I like to be alone and undisturbed.

"But I'm really glad to have the clock seen to," he said, seeing a certain hesitation in Mr. Henfrey's manner. "Very glad." Mr. Henfrey had intended to apologise and withdraw, but this anticipation reassured him. The stranger turned round with his back to the fireplace and put his hands behind his back. "And presently," he said, "when the clock-mending is over, I think I should like to have some tea. But not till the clock-mending is over."

Mrs. Hall was about to leave the room—she made no conversational advances this time, because she did not want to be snubbed in front of Mr. Henfrey—when her visitor asked her if she had made any arrangements about his boxes at Bramblehurst. She told him she had mentioned the matter to the postman, and that the carrier could bring them over on the morrow. "You are certain that is the earliest?" he said.

She was certain, with a marked coldness.

"I should explain," he added, "what I was really too cold and fatigued to do before, that I am an experimental investigator."

"Indeed, sir," said Mrs. Hall, much impressed.

"And my baggage contains apparatus and appliances."

"Very useful things indeed they are, sir," said Mrs. Hall.

"And I'm very naturally anxious to get on with my inquiries."

"Of course, sir."

"My reason for coming to Iping," he proceeded, with a certain deliberation of manner, "was ... a desire for solitude. I do not wish to be disturbed in my work. In addition to my work, an accident—"

"I thought as much," said Mrs. Hall to herself.

"—necessitates a certain retirement. My eyes—are sometimes so weak and painful that I have to shut myself up in the dark for hours together. Lock myself up. Sometimes—now and then. Not at present, certainly. At such times the slightest disturbance, the entry of a stranger into the room, is a source of excruciating annoyance to me—it is well these things should be understood."

"Certainly, sir," said Mrs. Hall. "And if I might make so bold as to ask—"

"That I think, is all," said the stranger, with that quietly irresistible air of finality he could assume at will. Mrs. Hall reserved her question and sympathy for a better occasion.

After Mrs. Hall had left the room, he remained standing in front of the fire, glaring, so Mr. Henfrey puts it, at the clock-mending. Mr. Henfrey not only took off the hands of the clock, and the face, but extracted the works; and he tried to work in as slow and quiet and unassuming a manner as possible. He worked with the lamp close to him, and the green shade threw a brilliant light upon his hands, and upon the frame and wheels, and left the rest of the room shadowy. When he looked up, coloured patches swam in his eyes. Being constitutionally of a curious nature, he had removed the works—a quite unnecessary proceeding—with the idea of delaying his departure and perhaps falling into conversation with the stranger. But the stranger stood there, perfectly silent and still. So still, it got on Henfrey's nerves. He felt alone in the room and looked up, and there, grey and dim, was the bandaged head and huge blue lenses staring fixedly, with a mist of green spots drifting in front of them. It was so uncanny to Henfrey that for a minute they remained staring blankly at one another. Then Henfrey looked down again. Very uncomfortable position! One would like to say something. Should he remark that the weather was very cold for the time of year?

He looked up as if to take aim with that introductory shot. "The weather—" he began.

"Why don't you finish and go?" said the rigid figure, evidently in a state of painfully suppressed rage. "All you've got to do is to fix the hour-hand on its axle. You're simply humbugging—"

"Certainly, sir—one minute more. I overlooked—" and Mr. Henfrey finished and went.

But he went feeling excessively annoyed. "Damn it!" said Mr. Henfrey to himself, trudging down the village through the thawing snow; "a man must do a clock at times, surely."

And again, "Can't a man look at you?—Ugly!"

And yet again, "Seemingly not. If the police was wanting you you couldn't be more wropped and bandaged."

At Gleeson's corner he saw Hall, who had recently married the stranger's hostess at the "Coach and Horses," and who now drove the Iping conveyance, when occasional people required it, to Sidderbridge Junction, coming towards him on his return from that place. Hall had evidently been "stopping a bit" at Sidderbridge, to judge by his driving. "'Ow do, Teddy?" he said, passing.

"You got a rum un up home!" said Teddy.

Hall very sociably pulled up. "What's that?" he asked.

"Rum-looking customer stopping at the 'Coach and Horses,'" said Teddy. "My sakes!"

And he proceeded to give Hall a vivid description of his grotesque guest. "Looks a bit like a disguise, don't it? I'd like to see a man's face if I had him stopping in *my* place," said Henfrey. "But women are that trustful—where strangers are concerned. He's took your rooms and he ain't even given a name, Hall."

"You don't say so!" said Hall, who was a man of sluggish apprehension.

"Yes," said Teddy. "By the week. Whatever he is, you can't get rid of him under the week. And he's got a lot of luggage coming tomorrow, so he says. Let's hope it won't be stones in boxes, Hall."

He told Hall how his aunt at Hastings had been swindled by a stranger with empty portmanteaux. Altogether he left Hall vaguely suspicious. "Get up, old girl," said Hall. "I s'pose I must see 'bout this."

Teddy trudged on his way with his mind considerably relieved.

Instead of "seeing 'bout it," however, Hall on his return was severely rated by his wife on the length of time he had spent in Sidderbridge, and his mild inquiries were answered snappishly and in a manner not to the point. But the seed of suspicion Teddy had sown germinated in the mind of Mr. Hall in spite of these discouragements. "You wim' don't know everything," said Mr. Hall, resolved to ascertain more about the personality of his guest at the earliest possible opportunity. And after the stranger had gone to bed, which he did about half-past nine, Mr. Hall went very aggressively into the parlour and looked very hard at his wife's furniture, just to show that the stranger wasn't master there, and scrutinised closely and a little contemptuously a sheet of mathematical computations the stranger had left. When retiring for the night he instructed Mrs. Hall to look very closely at the stranger's luggage when it came next day.

"You mind your own business, Hall," said Mrs. Hall, "and I'll mind mine."

She was all the more inclined to snap at Hall because the stranger was undoubtedly an unusually strange sort of stranger, and she was by no means assured about him in her own mind. In the middle of the night she woke up dreaming of huge white heads like turnips, that came trailing after her, at the end of interminable necks, and with vast black eyes. But being a sensible woman, she subdued her terrors and turned over and went to sleep again.

CHAPTER III

THE THOUSAND AND ONE BOTTLES

So it was that on the twenty-ninth day of February, at the beginning of the thaw, this singular person fell out of infinity into Iping village. Next day his luggage arrived through the slush—and very remarkable luggage it was. There were a couple of trunks indeed, such as a rational man might need, but in addition there were a box of books—big, fat books, of which some were just in an incomprehensible handwriting—and a dozen or more crates, boxes, and cases, containing objects packed in straw, as it seemed to Hall, tugging with a casual curiosity at the straw—glass bottles. The stranger, muffled in hat, coat, gloves, and wrapper, came out impatiently to meet Fearenside's cart, while Hall was having a word or so of gossip preparatory to helping bring them in. Out he came, not noticing Fearenside's dog, who was sniffing in a *dilettante* spirit at Hall's legs. "Come along with those boxes," he said. "I've been waiting long enough."

And he came down the steps towards the tail of the cart as if to lay hands on the smaller crate.

No sooner had Fearenside's dog caught sight of him, however, than it began to bristle and growl savagely, and when he rushed down the steps it gave an undecided hop, and then sprang straight at his hand. "Whup!" cried Hall, jumping back, for he was no hero with dogs, and Fearenside howled, "Lie down!" and snatched his whip.

They saw the dog's teeth had slipped the hand, heard a kick, saw the dog execute a flanking jump and get home on the stranger's leg, and heard the rip of his trousering. Then the finer end of Fearenside's whip reached his property, and the dog, yelping with dismay, retreated under the wheels of the waggon. It was all the business of a swift half-minute. No one spoke, everyone shouted. The stranger glanced swiftly at his torn glove and at his leg, made as if he would stoop to the latter, then turned and rushed swiftly up the steps into the inn. They heard him go headlong across the passage and up the uncarpeted stairs to his bedroom.

"You brute, you!" said Fearenside, climbing off the waggon with his whip in his hand, while the dog watched him through the wheel. "Come here," said Fearenside—"You'd better."

Hall had stood gaping. "He wuz bit," said Hall. "I'd better go and see to en," and he trotted after the stranger. He met Mrs. Hall in the passage. "Carrier's darg," he said "bit en."

He went straight upstairs, and the stranger's door being ajar, he pushed it open and was entering without any ceremony, being of a naturally sympathetic turn of mind.

The blind was down and the room dim. He caught a glimpse of a most singular thing, what seemed a handless arm waving towards him, and a face of three huge indeterminate spots on white, very like the face of a pale pansy. Then he was struck violently in the chest, hurled back, and the door slammed in his face and locked. It was so rapid that it gave him no time to observe. A waving of indecipherable shapes, a blow, and a concussion. There he stood on the dark little landing, wondering what it might be that he had seen.

A couple of minutes after, he rejoined the little group that had formed outside the "Coach and Horses." There was Fearenside telling about it all over again for the second time; there was Mrs. Hall saying his dog didn't have no business to bite her guests; there was Huxter, the general dealer from over the road, interrogative; and Sandy Wadgers from the forge, judicial; besides women and children, all of them saying fatuities: "Wouldn't let en bite *me*, I knows"; "'Tasn't right *have* such dargs"; "Whad *'e* bite 'n for, then?" and so forth.

Mr. Hall, staring at them from the steps and listening, found it incredible that he had seen anything so very remarkable happen upstairs. Besides, his vocabulary was altogether too limited to express his impressions.

"He don't want no help, he says," he said in answer to his wife's inquiry. "We'd better be a-takin' of his luggage in."

"He ought to have it cauterised at once," said Mr. Huxter; "especially if it's at all inflamed."

"I'd shoot en, that's what I'd do," said a lady in the group.

Suddenly the dog began growling again.

"Come along," cried an angry voice in the doorway, and there stood the muffled stranger with his collar turned up, and his hat-brim bent down. "The sooner you get those things in the better I'll be pleased." It is stated by an anonymous bystander that his trousers and gloves had been changed.

"Was you hurt, sir?" said Fearenside. "I'm rare sorry the darg—"

"Not a bit," said the stranger. "Never broke the skin. Hurry up with those things."

He then swore to himself, so Mr. Hall asserts.

Directly the first crate was, in accordance with his directions, carried into the parlour, the stranger flung himself upon it with extraordinary eagerness, and began to unpack it, scattering the straw with an utter disregard of Mrs. Hall's carpet. And from it he began to produce bottles—little fat bottles containing powders, small and slender bottles containing coloured and white fluids, fluted blue bottles labeled Poison, bottles with round bodies and slender necks, large green-glass bottles, large white-glass bottles, bottles with glass stoppers and frosted labels, bottles with fine corks, bottles with bungs, bottles with wooden caps, wine bottles, salad-oil bottles—putting them in rows on the chiffonnier, on the mantel, on the table under the window, round the floor, on the bookshelf—everywhere. The chemist's shop in Bramblehurst could not boast half so many. Quite a sight it was. Crate after crate yielded bottles, until all six were empty and the table high with straw; the only things that came out of these crates besides the bottles were a number of test-tubes and a carefully packed balance.

And directly the crates were unpacked, the stranger went to the window and set to work, not troubling in the least about the litter of straw, the fire which had gone out, the box of books outside, nor for the trunks and other luggage that had gone upstairs.

When Mrs. Hall took his dinner in to him, he was already so absorbed in his work, pouring little drops out of the bottles into test-tubes, that he did not hear her until she had swept away the bulk of the straw and put the tray on the table, with some little emphasis perhaps, seeing the state that the floor was in. Then he half turned his head and immediately turned it away again. But she saw he had removed his glasses; they were beside him on the table, and it seemed to her that his eye sockets were extraordinarily hollow. He put on his spectacles again, and then turned and faced her. She was about to complain of the straw on the floor when he anticipated her.

"I wish you wouldn't come in without knocking," he said in the tone of abnormal exasperation that seemed so characteristic of him.

"I knocked, but seemingly—"

"Perhaps you did. But in my investigations—my really very urgent and necessary investigations—the slightest disturbance, the jar of a door—I must ask you—"

"Certainly, sir. You can turn the lock if you're like that, you know. Any time."

"A very good idea," said the stranger.

"This stror, sir, if I might make so bold as to remark—"

"Don't. If the straw makes trouble put it down in the bill." And he mumbled at her—words suspiciously like curses.

He was so odd, standing there, so aggressive and explosive, bottle in one hand and test-tube in the other, that Mrs. Hall was quite alarmed. But she was a resolute woman. "In which case, I should like to know, sir, what you consider—"

"A shilling—put down a shilling. Surely a shilling's enough?"

"So be it," said Mrs. Hall, taking up the table-cloth and beginning to spread it over the table. "If you're satisfied, of course—"

He turned and sat down, with his coat-collar toward her.

All the afternoon he worked with the door locked and, as Mrs. Hall testifies, for the most part in silence. But once there was a concussion and a sound of bottles ringing together as though the table had been hit, and the smash of a bottle flung violently down, and then a rapid pacing athwart the room. Fearing "something was the matter," she went to the door and listened, not caring to knock.

"I can't go on," he was raving. "I *can't* go on. Three hundred thousand, four hundred thousand! The huge multitude! Cheated! All my life it may take me! ... Patience! Patience indeed! ... Fool! fool!"

There was a noise of hobnails on the bricks in the bar, and Mrs. Hall had very reluctantly to leave the rest of his soliloquy. When she returned the room was silent again, save for the faint crepitation of his chair and the occasional clink of a bottle. It was all over; the stranger had resumed work.

When she took in his tea she saw broken glass in the corner of the room under the concave mirror, and a golden stain that had been carelessly wiped. She called attention to it.

"Put it down in the bill," snapped her visitor. "For God's sake don't worry me. If there's damage done, put it down in the bill," and he went on ticking a list in the exercise book before him.

"I'll tell you something," said Fearenside, mysteriously. It was late in the afternoon, and they were in the little beer-shop of Iping Hanger.

"Well?" said Teddy Henfrey.

"This chap you're speaking of, what my dog bit. Well—he's black. Leastways, his legs are. I seed through the tear of his trousers and the tear of his glove. You'd have expected a sort of pinky to show, wouldn't you? Well—there wasn't none. Just blackness. I tell you, he's as black as my hat."

"My sakes!" said Henfrey. "It's a rummy case altogether. Why, his nose is as pink as paint!"

"That's true," said Fearenside. "I knows that. And I tell 'ee what I'm thinking. That marn's a piebald, Teddy. Black here and white there—in patches. And he's ashamed of it. He's a kind of half-breed, and the colour's come off patchy instead of mixing. I've heard of such things before. And it's the common way with horses, as any one can see."

CHAPTER IV

MR. CUSS INTERVIEWS THE STRANGER

I have told the circumstances of the stranger's arrival in Iping with a certain fulness of detail, in order that the curious impression he created may be understood by the reader. But excepting two odd incidents, the circumstances of his stay until the extraordinary day of the club festival may be passed over very cursorily. There were a number of skirmishes with Mrs. Hall on matters of domestic discipline, but in every case until late April, when the first signs of penury began, he over-rode her by the easy expedient of an extra payment. Hall did not like him, and whenever he dared he talked of the advisability of getting rid of him; but he showed his dislike chiefly by concealing it ostentatiously, and avoiding his visitor as much as possible. "Wait till the summer," said Mrs. Hall sagely, "when the artisks are beginning to come. Then we'll see. He may be a bit overbearing, but bills settled punctual is bills settled punctual, whatever you'd like to say."

The stranger did not go to church, and indeed made no difference between Sunday and the irreligious days, even in costume. He worked, as Mrs. Hall thought, very fitfully. Some days he would come down early and be continuously busy. On others he would rise late, pace his room, fretting audibly for hours together, smoke, sleep in the armchair by the fire. Communication with the world beyond the village he had none. His temper continued very uncertain; for the most part his manner was that of a man suffering under almost unendurable provocation, and once or twice things were snapped, torn, crushed, or broken in spasmodic gusts of violence. He seemed under a chronic irritation of the greatest intensity. His habit of talking to himself in a low voice grew steadily upon him, but though Mrs. Hall listened conscientiously she could make neither head nor tail of what she heard.

He rarely went abroad by daylight, but at twilight he would go out muffled up invisibly, whether the weather were cold or not, and he chose the loneliest paths and those most overshadowed by trees and banks. His goggling spectacles and ghastly bandaged face under the penthouse of his hat, came with a disagreeable suddenness out of the darkness upon one or two home-going labourers, and Teddy Henfrey, tumbling out of the "Scarlet Coat" one night, at half-past nine, was scared shamefully by the stranger's skull-like head (he was walking hat in hand) lit by the sudden light of the opened inn door. Such children as saw him at nightfall dreamt of bogies, and it seemed doubtful whether he disliked boys more than they disliked him, or the reverse; but there was certainly a vivid enough dislike on either side.

It was inevitable that a person of so remarkable an appearance and bearing should form a frequent topic in such a village as Iping. Opinion was greatly divided about his occupation. Mrs. Hall was sensitive on the point. When questioned, she explained very carefully that he was an "experimental investigator," going gingerly over the syllables as one who dreads pitfalls. When asked what an experimental investigator was, she would say with a touch of superiority that most educated people knew such things as that, and would thus explain that he "discovered things." Her visitor had had an accident, she said, which temporarily discoloured his face and hands, and being of a sensitive disposition, he was averse to any public notice of the fact.

Out of her hearing there was a view largely entertained that he was a criminal trying to escape from justice by wrapping himself up so as to conceal himself altogether from the eye of the police. This idea sprang from the brain of Mr. Teddy Henfrey. No crime of any magnitude dating from the middle or end of February was known to have occurred. Elaborated in the imagination of Mr. Gould, the probationary assistant in the National

School, this theory took the form that the stranger was an Anarchist in disguise, preparing explosives, and he resolved to undertake such detective operations as his time permitted. These consisted for the most part in looking very hard at the stranger whenever they met, or in asking people who had never seen the stranger, leading questions about him. But he detected nothing.

Another school of opinion followed Mr. Fearenside, and either accepted the piebald view or some modification of it; as, for instance, Silas Durgan, who was heard to assert that "if he chooses to show enself at fairs he'd make his fortune in no time," and being a bit of a theologian, compared the stranger to the man with the one talent. Yet another view explained the entire matter by regarding the stranger as a harmless lunatic. That had the advantage of accounting for everything straight away.

Between these main groups there were waverers and compromisers. Sussex folk have few superstitions, and it was only after the events of early April that the thought of the supernatural was first whispered in the village. Even then it was only credited among the women folk.

But whatever they thought of him, people in Iping, on the whole, agreed in disliking him. His irritability, though it might have been comprehensible to an urban brain-worker, was an amazing thing to these quiet Sussex villagers. The frantic gesticulations they surprised now and then, the headlong pace after nightfall that swept him upon them round quiet corners, the inhuman bludgeoning of all tentative advances of curiosity, the taste for twilight that led to the closing of doors, the pulling down of blinds, the extinction of candles and lamps—who could agree with such goings on? They drew aside as he passed down the village, and when he had gone by, young humourists would up with coat-collars and down with hat-brims, and go pacing nervously after him in imitation of his occult bearing. There was a song popular at that time called "The Bogey Man". Miss Statchell sang it at the schoolroom concert (in aid of the church lamps), and thereafter whenever one or two of the villagers were gathered together and the stranger appeared, a bar or so of this tune, more or less sharp or flat, was whistled in the midst of them. Also belated little children would call "Bogey Man!" after him, and make off tremulously elated.

Cuss, the general practitioner, was devoured by curiosity. The bandages excited his professional interest, the report of the thousand and one bottles aroused his jealous regard. All through April and May he coveted an opportunity of talking to the stranger, and at last, towards Whitsuntide, he could stand it no longer, but hit upon the subscription-list for a village nurse as an excuse. He was surprised to find that Mr. Hall did not know his guest's name. "He give a name," said Mrs. Hall—an assertion which was quite unfounded—"but I didn't rightly hear it." She thought it seemed so silly not to know the man's name.

Cuss rapped at the parlour door and entered. There was a fairly audible imprecation from within. "Pardon my intrusion," said Cuss, and then the door closed and cut Mrs. Hall off from the rest of the conversation.

She could hear the murmur of voices for the next ten minutes, then a cry of surprise, a stirring of feet, a chair flung aside, a bark of laughter, quick steps to the door, and Cuss appeared, his face white, his eyes staring over his shoulder. He left the door open behind him, and without looking at her strode across the hall and went down the steps, and she heard his feet hurrying along the road. He carried his hat in his hand. She stood behind the door, looking at the open door of the parlour. Then she heard the stranger laughing quietly, and then his footsteps came across the room. She could not see his face where she stood. The parlour door slammed, and the place was silent again.

Cuss went straight up the village to Bunting the vicar. "Am I mad?" Cuss began abruptly, as he entered the shabby little study. "Do I look like an insane person?"

"What's happened?" said the vicar, putting the ammonite on the loose sheets of his forth-coming sermon.

"That chap at the inn—"

"Well?"

"Give me something to drink," said Cuss, and he sat down.

When his nerves had been steadied by a glass of cheap sherry—the only drink the good vicar had available—he told him of the interview he had just had. "Went in," he gasped, "and began to demand a subscription for that Nurse Fund. He'd stuck his hands in his pockets as I came in, and he sat down lumpily in his chair. Sniffed. I told him I'd heard he took an

interest in scientific things. He said yes. Sniffed again. Kept on sniffing all
the time; evidently recently caught an infernal cold. No wonder, wrapped
up like that! I developed the nurse idea, and all the while kept my eyes
open. Bottles—chemicals—everywhere. Balance, test-tubes in stands, and
a smell of—evening primrose. Would he subscribe? Said he'd consider it.
Asked him, point-blank, was he researching. Said he was. A long research?
Got quite cross. 'A damnable long research,' said he, blowing the cork out,
so to speak. 'Oh,' said I. And out came the grievance. The man was just on
the boil, and my question boiled him over. He had been given a prescription, most valuable prescription—what for he wouldn't say. Was it medical?
'Damn you! What are you fishing after?' I apologised. Dignified sniff and
cough. He resumed. He'd read it. Five ingredients. Put it down; turned his
head. Draught of air from window lifted the paper. Swish, rustle. He was
working in a room with an open fireplace, he said. Saw a flicker, and there
was the prescription burning and lifting chimneyward. Rushed towards it
just as it whisked up the chimney. So! Just at that point, to illustrate his
story, out came his arm."

"Well?"

"No hand—just an empty sleeve. Lord! I thought, *that's* a deformity!
Got a cork arm, I suppose, and has taken it off. Then, I thought, there's
something odd in that. What the devil keeps that sleeve up and open, if
there's nothing in it? There was nothing in it, I tell you. Nothing down it,
right down to the joint. I could see right down it to the elbow, and there was
a glimmer of light shining through a tear of the cloth. 'Good God!' I said.
Then he stopped. Stared at me with those black goggles of his, and then at
his sleeve."

"Well?"

"That's all. He never said a word; just glared, and put his sleeve back in
his pocket quickly. 'I was saying,' said he, 'that there was the prescription
burning, wasn't I?' Interrogative cough. 'How the devil,' said I, 'can you
move an empty sleeve like that?' 'Empty sleeve?' 'Yes,' said I, 'an empty
sleeve.'

"'It's an empty sleeve, is it? You saw it was an empty sleeve?' He stood
up right away. I stood up too. He came towards me in three very slow

steps, and stood quite close. Sniffed venomously. I didn't flinch, though I'm hanged if that bandaged knob of his, and those blinkers, aren't enough to unnerve any one, coming quietly up to you.

"'You said it was an empty sleeve?' he said. 'Certainly,' I said. At staring and saying nothing a barefaced man, unspectacled, starts scratch. Then very quietly he pulled his sleeve out of his pocket again, and raised his arm towards me as though he would show it to me again. He did it very, very slowly. I looked at it. Seemed an age. 'Well?' said I, clearing my throat, 'there's nothing in it.'

"Had to say something. I was beginning to feel frightened. I could see right down it. He extended it straight towards me, slowly, slowly—just like that—until the cuff was six inches from my face. Queer thing to see an empty sleeve come at you like that! And then—"

"Well?"

"Something—exactly like a finger and thumb it felt—nipped my nose."

Bunting began to laugh.

"There wasn't anything there!" said Cuss, his voice running up into a shriek at the "there." "It's all very well for you to laugh, but I tell you I was so startled, I hit his cuff hard, and turned around, and cut out of the room—I left him—"

Cuss stopped. There was no mistaking the sincerity of his panic. He turned round in a helpless way and took a second glass of the excellent vicar's very inferior sherry. "When I hit his cuff," said Cuss, "I tell you, it felt exactly like hitting an arm. And there wasn't an arm! There wasn't the ghost of an arm!"

Mr. Bunting thought it over. He looked suspiciously at Cuss. "It's a most remarkable story," he said. He looked very wise and grave indeed. "It's really," said Mr. Bunting with judicial emphasis, "a most remarkable story."

CHAPTER V

THE BURGLARY AT THE VICARAGE

The facts of the burglary at the vicarage came to us chiefly through the medium of the vicar and his wife. It occurred in the small hours of Whit Monday, the day devoted in Iping to the Club festivities. Mrs. Bunting, it seems, woke up suddenly in the stillness that comes before the dawn, with the strong impression that the door of their bedroom had opened and closed. She did not arouse her husband at first, but sat up in bed listening. She then distinctly heard the pad, pad, pad of bare feet coming out of the adjoining dressing-room and walking along the passage towards the staircase. As soon as she felt assured of this, she aroused the Rev. Mr. Bunting as quietly as possible. He did not strike a light, but putting on his spectacles, her dressing-gown and his bath slippers, he went out on the landing to listen. He heard quite distinctly a fumbling going on at his study desk down-stairs, and then a violent sneeze.

At that he returned to his bedroom, armed himself with the most obvious weapon, the poker, and descended the staircase as noiselessly as possible. Mrs. Bunting came out on the landing.

The hour was about four, and the ultimate darkness of the night was past. There was a faint shimmer of light in the hall, but the study doorway yawned impenetrably black. Everything was still except the faint creaking of the stairs under Mr. Bunting's tread, and the slight movements in the study. Then something snapped, the drawer was opened, and there was a rustle of papers. Then came an imprecation, and a match was struck and the study was flooded with yellow light. Mr. Bunting was now in the hall, and through the crack of the door he could see the desk and the open drawer and a candle burning on the desk. But the robber he could not see. He stood there in the hall undecided what to do, and Mrs. Bunting, her face white and intent, crept slowly downstairs after him. One thing kept Mr. Bunting's courage; the persuasion that this burglar was a resident in the village.

They heard the chink of money, and realised that the robber had found the housekeeping reserve of gold—two pounds ten in half sovereigns altogether. At that sound Mr. Bunting was nerved to abrupt action. Gripping the poker firmly, he rushed into the room, closely followed by Mrs. Bunting. "Surrender!" cried Mr. Bunting, fiercely, and then stooped amazed. Apparently the room was perfectly empty.

Yet their conviction that they had, that very moment, heard somebody moving in the room had amounted to a certainty. For half a minute, perhaps, they stood gaping, then Mrs. Bunting went across the room and looked behind the screen, while Mr. Bunting, by a kindred impulse, peered under the desk. Then Mrs. Bunting turned back the window-curtains, and Mr. Bunting looked up the chimney and probed it with the poker. Then Mrs. Bunting scrutinised the waste-paper basket and Mr. Bunting opened the lid of the coal-scuttle. Then they came to a stop and stood with eyes interrogating each other.

"I could have sworn—" said Mr. Bunting.

"The candle!" said Mr. Bunting. "Who lit the candle?"

"The drawer!" said Mrs. Bunting. "And the money's gone!"

She went hastily to the doorway.

"Of all the strange occurrences—"

There was a violent sneeze in the passage. They rushed out, and as they did so the kitchen door slammed. "Bring the candle," said Mr. Bunting, and led the way. They both heard a sound of bolts being hastily shot back.

As he opened the kitchen door he saw through the scullery that the back door was just opening, and the faint light of early dawn displayed the dark masses of the garden beyond. He is certain that nothing went out of the door. It opened, stood open for a moment, and then closed with a slam.

As it did so, the candle Mrs. Bunting was carrying from the study flickered and flared. It was a minute or more before they entered the kitchen.

The place was empty. They refastened the back door, examined the kitchen, pantry, and scullery thoroughly, and at last went down into the cellar. There was not a soul to be found in the house, search as they would.

Daylight found the vicar and his wife, a quaintly-costumed little couple, still marvelling about on their own ground floor by the unnecessary light of a guttering candle.

CHAPTER VI

THE FURNITURE THAT WENT MAD

Now it happened that in the early hours of Whit Monday, before Millie was hunted out for the day, Mr. Hall and Mrs. Hall both rose and went noiselessly down into the cellar. Their business there was of a private nature, and had something to do with the specific gravity of their beer. They had hardly entered the cellar when Mrs. Hall found she had forgotten to bring down a bottle of sarsaparilla from their joint-room. As she was the expert and principal operator in this affair, Hall very properly went upstairs for it.

On the landing he was surprised to see that the stranger's door was ajar. He went on into his own room and found the bottle as he had been directed.

But returning with the bottle, he noticed that the bolts of the front door had been shot back, that the door was in fact simply on the latch. And with a flash of inspiration he connected this with the stranger's room upstairs and the suggestions of Mr. Teddy Henfrey. He distinctly remembered holding the candle while Mrs. Hall shot these bolts overnight. At the sight he stopped, gaping, then with the bottle still in his hand went upstairs again. He rapped at the stranger's door. There was no answer. He rapped again; then pushed the door wide open and entered.

It was as he expected. The bed, the room also, was empty. And what was stranger, even to his heavy intelligence, on the bedroom chair and along the rail of the bed were scattered the garments, the only garments so far as he knew, and the bandages of their guest. His big slouch hat even was cocked jauntily over the bed-post.

As Hall stood there he heard his wife's voice coming out of the depth of the cellar, with that rapid telescoping of the syllables and interrogative cocking up of the final words to a high note, by which the West Sussex villager is wont to indicate a brisk impatience. "George! You gart whad a wand?"

At that he turned and hurried down to her. "Janny," he said, over the rail of the cellar steps, "'tas the truth what Henfrey sez. 'E's not in uz room, 'e en't. And the front door's onbolted."

At first Mrs. Hall did not understand, and as soon as she did she re-solved to see the empty room for herself. Hall, still holding the bottle, went first. "If 'e en't there," he said, "'is close are. And what's 'e doin' 'ithout 'is close, then? 'Tas a most curious business."

As they came up the cellar steps they both, it was afterwards ascertained, fancied they heard the front door open and shut, but seeing it closed and nothing there, neither said a word to the other about it at the time. Mrs. Hall passed her husband in the passage and ran on first upstairs. Someone sneezed on the staircase. Hall, following six steps behind, thought that he heard her sneeze. She, going on first, was under the impression that Hall was sneezing. She flung open the door and stood regarding the room. "Of all the curious!" she said.

She heard a sniff close behind her head as it seemed, and turning, was surprised to see Hall a dozen feet off on the topmost stair. But in another moment he was beside her. She bent forward and put her hand on the pil-low and then under the clothes.

"Cold," she said. "He's been up this hour or more."

As she did so, a most extraordinary thing happened. The bed-clothes gathered themselves together, leapt up suddenly into a sort of peak, and then jumped headlong over the bottom rail. It was exactly as if a hand had clutched them in the centre and flung them aside. Immediately after, the stranger's hat hopped off the bed-post, described a whirling flight in the air through the better part of a circle, and then dashed straight at Mrs. Hall's face. Then as swiftly came the sponge from the washstand; and then the chair, flinging the stranger's coat and trousers carelessly aside, and laughing drily in a voice singularly like the stranger's, turned itself up with its four legs at Mrs. Hall, seemed to take aim at her for a moment, and charged at her. She screamed and turned, and then the chair legs came gently but firmly against her back and impelled her and Hall out of the room. The door slammed violently and was locked. The chair and bed seemed to be executing a dance of triumph for a moment, and then abruptly everything was still.

Mrs. Hall was left almost in a fainting condition in Mr. Hall's arms on the landing. It was with the greatest difficulty that Mr. Hall and Millie, who had been roused by her scream of alarm, succeeded in getting her downstairs, and applying the restoratives customary in such cases.

"'Tas sperits," said Mrs. Hall. "I know 'tas sperits. I've read in papers of en. Tables and chairs leaping and dancing..."

"Take a drop more, Janny," said Hall. "'Twill steady ye."

"Lock him out," said Mrs. Hall. "Don't let him come in again. I half guessed—I might ha' known. With them goggling eyes and bandaged head, and never going to church of a Sunday. And all they bottles—more'n it's right for any one to have. He's put the sperits into the furniture.... My good old furniture! 'Twas in that very chair my poor dear mother used to sit when I was a little girl. To think it should rise up against me now!"

"Just a drop more, Janny," said Hall. "Your nerves is all upset."

They sent Millie across the street through the golden five o'clock sunshine to rouse up Mr. Sandy Wadgers, the blacksmith. Mr. Hall's compliments and the furniture upstairs was behaving most extraordinary. Would Mr. Wadgers come round? He was a knowing man, was Mr. Wadgers, and very resourceful. He took quite a grave view of the case. "Arm darmed if thet ent witchcraft," was the view of Mr. Sandy Wadgers. "You warnt horseshoes for such gentry as he."

He came round greatly concerned. They wanted him to lead the way upstairs to the room, but he didn't seem to be in any hurry. He preferred to talk in the passage. Over the way Huxter's apprentice came out and began taking down the shutters of the tobacco window. He was called over to join the discussion. Mr. Huxter naturally followed over in the course of a few minutes. The Anglo-Saxon genius for parliamentary government asserted itself; there was a great deal of talk and no decisive action. "Let's have the facts first," insisted Mr. Sandy Wadgers. "Let's be sure we'd be acting perfectly right in bustin' that there door open. A door onbust is always open to bustin', but ye can't onbust a door once you've busted en."

And suddenly and most wonderfully the door of the room upstairs opened of its own accord, and as they looked up in amazement, they saw descending the stairs the muffled figure of the stranger staring more blackly and blankly than ever with those unreasonably large blue glass eyes of his. He came down stiffly and slowly, staring all the time; he walked across the passage staring, then stopped.

"Look there!" he said, and their eyes followed the direction of his gloved finger and saw a bottle of sarsaparilla hard by the cellar door. Then he entered the parlour, and suddenly, swiftly, viciously, slammed the door in their faces.

Not a word was spoken until the last echoes of the slam had died away. They stared at one another. "Well, if that don't lick everything!" said Mr. Wadgers, and left the alternative unsaid.

"I'd go in and ask'n 'bout it," said Wadgers, to Mr. Hall. "I'd d'mand an explanation."

It took some time to bring the landlady's husband up to that pitch. At last he rapped, opened the door, and got as far as, "Excuse me—"

"Go to the devil!" said the stranger in a tremendous voice, and "Shut that door after you." So that brief interview terminated.

CHAPTER VII

THE UNVEILING OF THE STRANGER

The stranger went into the little parlour of the "Coach and Horses" about half-past five in the morning, and there he remained until near midday, the blinds down, the door shut, and none, after Hall's repulse, venturing near him.

All that time he must have fasted. Thrice he rang his bell, the third time furiously and continuously, but no one answered him. "Him and his 'go to the devil' indeed!" said Mrs. Hall. Presently came an imperfect rumour of the burglary at the vicarage, and two and two were put together. Hall, assisted by Wadgers, went off to find Mr. Shuckleforth, the magistrate, and take his advice. No one ventured upstairs. How the stranger occupied himself is unknown. Now and then he would stride violently up and down, and twice came an outburst of curses, a tearing of paper, and a violent smashing of bottles.

The little group of scared but curious people increased. Mrs. Huxter came over; some gay young fellows resplendent in black ready-made jackets and *piqué* paper ties—for it was Whit Monday—joined the group with confused interrogations. Young Archie Harker distinguished himself by going up the yard and trying to peep under the window-blinds. He could see nothing, but gave reason for supposing that he did, and others of the Iping youth presently joined him.

It was the finest of all possible Whit Mondays, and down the village street stood a row of nearly a dozen booths, a shooting gallery, and on the grass by the forge were three yellow and chocolate waggons and some picturesque strangers of both sexes putting up a cocoanut shy. The gentlemen wore blue jerseys, the ladies white aprons and quite fashionable hats with heavy plumes. Wodger, of the "Purple Fawn," and Mr. Jaggers, the cobbler, who also sold old second-hand ordinary bicycles, were stretching a string of union-jacks and royal ensigns (which had originally celebrated the first Victorian Jubilee) across the road.

And inside, in the artificial darkness of the parlour, into which only one thin jet of sunlight penetrated, the stranger, hungry we must suppose, and fearful, hidden in his uncomfortable hot wrappings, pored through his dark glasses upon his paper or chinked his dirty little bottles, and occasionally swore savagely at the boys, audible if invisible, outside the windows. In the corner by the fireplace lay the fragments of half a dozen smashed bottles, and a pungent twang of chlorine tainted the air. So much we know from what was heard at the time and from what was subsequently seen in the room.

About noon he suddenly opened his parlour door and stood glaring fixedly at the three or four people in the bar. "Mrs. Hall," he said. Somebody went sheepishly and called for Mrs. Hall.

Mrs. Hall appeared after an interval, a little short of breath, but all the fiercer for that. Hall was still out. She had deliberated over this scene, and she came holding a little tray with an unsettled bill upon it. "Is it your bill you're wanting, sir?" she said.

"Why wasn't my breakfast laid? Why haven't you prepared my meals and answered my bell? Do you think I live without eating?"

"Why isn't my bill paid?" said Mrs. Hall. "That's what I want to know."

"I told you three days ago I was awaiting a remittance—"

"I told you two days ago I wasn't going to await no remittances. You can't grumble if your breakfast waits a bit, if my bill's been waiting these five days, can you?"

The stranger swore briefly but vividly.

"Nar, nar!" from the bar.

"And I'd thank you kindly, sir, if you'd keep your swearing to yourself, sir," said Mrs. Hall.

The stranger stood looking more like an angry diving-helmet than ever. It was universally felt in the bar that Mrs. Hall had the better of him. His next words showed as much.

"Look here, my good woman——" he began.

"Don't 'good woman' *me*," said Mrs. Hall.

"I've told you my remittance hasn't come."

"Remittance indeed!" said Mrs. Hall.

"Still, I daresay in my pocket——"

"You told me three days ago that you hadn't anything but a sovereign's worth of silver upon you."

"Well, I've found some more——"

"'Ul-lo!" from the bar.

"I wonder where you found it," said Mrs. Hall.

That seemed to annoy the stranger very much. He stamped his foot. "What do you mean?" he said.

"That I wonder where you found it," said Mrs. Hall. "And before I take any bills or get any breakfasts, or do any such things whatsoever, you got to tell me one or two things I don't understand, and what nobody don't understand, and what everybody is very anxious to understand. I want to know what you been doing t'my chair upstairs, and I want to know how 'tis your room was empty, and how you got in again. Them as stops in this house comes in by the doors—that's the rule of the house, and that you *didn't* do, and what I want to know is how you *did* come in. And I want to know——"

Suddenly the stranger raised his gloved hands clenched, stamped his foot, and said, "Stop!" with such extraordinary violence that he silenced her instantly.

"You don't understand," he said, "who I am or what I am. I'll show you. By Heaven! I'll show you." Then he put his open palm over his face and withdrew it. The centre of his face became a black cavity. "Here," he said. He stepped forward and handed Mrs. Hall something which she, staring at his metamorphosed face, accepted automatically. Then, when she saw what it was, she screamed loudly, dropped it, and staggered back. The nose—it was the stranger's nose! pink and shining—rolled on the floor.

Then he removed his spectacles, and everyone in the bar gasped. He took off his hat, and with a violent gesture tore at his whiskers and bandages. For a moment they resisted him. A flash of horrible anticipation passed through the bar. "Oh, my Gard!" said some one. Then off they came.

It was worse than anything. Mrs. Hall, standing open-mouthed and horror-struck, shrieked at what she saw, and made for the door of the house. Everyone began to move. They were prepared for scars, disfigurements, tangible horrors, but nothing! The bandages and false hair flew across the passage into the bar, making a hobbledehoy jump to avoid them. Everyone tumbled on everyone else down the steps. For the man who stood there shouting some incoherent explanation, was a solid gesticulating figure up to the coat-collar of him, and then—nothingness, no visible thing at all!

People down the village heard shouts and shrieks, and looking up the street saw the "Coach and Horses" violently firing out its humanity. They saw Mrs. Hall fall down and Mr. Teddy Henfrey jump to avoid tumbling over her, and then they heard the frightful screams of Millie, who, emerging suddenly from the kitchen at the noise of the tumult, had come upon the headless stranger from behind. These increased suddenly.

Forthwith everyone all down the street, the sweetstuff seller, cocoanut shy proprietor and his assistant, the swing man, little boys and girls, rustic dandies, smart wenches, smocked elders and aproned gipsies—began running towards the inn, and in a miraculously short space of time a crowd of perhaps forty people, and rapidly increasing, swayed and hooted and inquired and exclaimed and suggested, in front of Mrs. Hall's establishment. Everyone seemed eager to talk at once, and the result was Babel. A small group supported Mrs. Hall, who was picked up in a state of collapse. There was a conference, and the incredible evidence of a vociferous eye-witness. "O Bogey!" "What's he been doin', then?" "Ain't hurt the girl, 'as 'e?" "Run at en with a knife, I believe." "No 'ed, I tell ye. I don't mean no manner of speaking. I mean *marn 'ithout a 'ed!*" "Narnsense! 'tis some conjuring trick." "Fetched off 'is wrapping, 'e did—"

In its struggles to see in through the open door, the crowd formed itself into a straggling wedge, with the more adventurous apex nearest the inn. "He stood for a moment, I heerd the gal scream, and he turned. I saw her skirts whisk, and he went after her. Didn't take ten seconds. Back he comes with a knife in uz hand and a loaf; stood just as if he was staring. Not a moment ago. Went in that there door. I tell 'e, 'e ain't gart no 'ed at all. You just missed en—"

There was a disturbance behind, and the speaker stopped to step aside for a little procession that was marching very resolutely towards the house; first Mr. Hall, very red and determined, then Mr. Bobby Jaffers, the village constable, and then the wary Mr. Wadgers. They had come now armed with a warrant.

People shouted conflicting information of the recent circumstances. "'Ed or no 'ed," said Jaffers, "I got to 'rest en, and 'rest en I *will*."

Mr. Hall marched up the steps, marched straight to the door of the parlour and flung it open. "Constable," he said, "do your duty."

Jaffers marched in. Hall next, Wadgers last. They saw in the dim light the headless figure facing them, with a gnawed crust of bread in one gloved hand and a chunk of cheese in the other.

"That's him!" said Hall.

"What the devil's this?" came in a tone of angry expostulation from above the collar of the figure.

"You're a damned rum customer, mister," said Mr. Jaffers. "But 'ed or no 'ed, the warrant says 'body,' and duty's duty—"

"Keep off!" said the figure, starting back.

Abruptly he whipped down the bread and cheese, and Mr. Hall just grasped the knife on the table in time to save it. Off came the stranger's left glove and was slapped in Jaffers' face. In another moment Jaffers, cutting short some statement concerning a warrant, had gripped him by the handless wrist and caught his invisible throat. He got a sounding kick on the shin that made him shout, but he kept his grip. Hall sent the knife sliding along the table to Wadgers, who acted as goal-keeper for the offensive, so to speak, and then stepped forward as Jaffers and the stranger swayed and staggered towards him, clutching and hitting in. A chair stood in the way, and went aside with a crash as they came down together.

"Get the feet," said Jaffers between his teeth.

Mr. Hall, endeavouring to act on instructions, received a sounding kick in the ribs that disposed of him for a moment, and Mr. Wadgers, seeing the decapitated stranger had rolled over and got the upper side of Jaffers, retreated towards the door, knife in hand, and so collided with Mr. Huxter and the Sidderbridge carter coming to the rescue of law and order. At the same moment down came three or four bottles from the chiffonnier and shot a web of pungency into the air of the room.

"I'll surrender," cried the stranger, though he had Jaffers down, and in another moment he stood up panting, a strange figure, headless and hand-less—for he had pulled off his right glove now as well as his left. "It's no good," he said, as if sobbing for breath.

It was the strangest thing in the world to hear that voice coming as if out of empty space, but the Sussex peasants are perhaps the most matter-of-fact people under the sun. Jaffers got up also and produced a pair of handcuffs. Then he stared.

"I say!" said Jaffers, brought up short by a dim realization of the incongruity of the whole business, "Darn it! Can't use 'em as I can see."

The stranger ran his arm down his waistcoat, and as if by a miracle the buttons to which his empty sleeve pointed became undone. Then he said something about his shin, and stooped down. He seemed to be fumbling with his shoes and socks.

"Why!" said Huxter, suddenly, "that's not a man at all. It's just empty clothes. Look! You can see down his collar and the linings of his clothes. I could put my arm—"

He extended his hand; it seemed to meet something in mid-air, and he drew it back with a sharp exclamation. "I wish you'd keep your fingers out of my eye," said the aerial voice, in a tone of savage expostulation. "The fact is, I'm all here—head, hands, legs, and all the rest of it, but it happens I'm invisible. It's a confounded nuisance, but I am. That's no reason why I should be poked to pieces by every stupid bumpkin in Iping, is it?"

The suit of clothes, now all unbuttoned and hanging loosely upon its unseen supports, stood up, arms akimbo.

Several other of the men folks had now entered the room, so that it was closely crowded. "Invisible, eh?" said Huxter, ignoring the stranger's abuse. "Who ever heard the likes of that?"

"It's strange, perhaps, but it's not a crime. Why am I assaulted by a po-liceman in this fashion?"

"Ah! that's a different matter," said Jaffers. "No doubt you are a bit difficult to see in this light, but I got a warrant and it's all correct. What I'm after ain't no invisibility,—it's burglary. There's a house been broke into and money took."

"Well?"

"And circumstances certainly point—"

"Stuff and nonsense!" said the Invisible Man.

"I hope so, sir; but I've got my instructions."

"Well," said the stranger, "I'll come. I'll *come*. But no handcuffs."

"It's the regular thing," said Jaffers.

"No handcuffs," stipulated the stranger.

"Pardon me," said Jaffers.

Abruptly the figure sat down, and before any one could realise was was being done, the slippers, socks, and trousers had been kicked off under the table. Then he sprang up again and flung off his coat.

"Here, stop that," said Jaffers, suddenly realising what was happening. He gripped at the waistcoat; it struggled, and the shirt slipped out of it and left it limp and empty in his hand. "Hold him!" said Jaffers, loudly. "Once he gets the things off—"

"Hold him!" cried everyone, and there was a rush at the fluttering white shirt which was now all that was visible of the stranger.

The shirt-sleeve planted a shrewd blow in Hall's face that stopped his open-armed advance, and sent him backward into old Toothsome the sexton, and in another moment the garment was lifted up and became convulsed and vacantly flapping about the arms, even as a shirt that is being thrust over a man's head. Jaffers clutched at it, and only helped to pull it off; he was struck in the mouth out of the air, and incontinently threw his truncheon and smote Teddy Henfrey savagely upon the crown of his head.

"Look out!" said everybody, fencing at random and hitting at nothing. "Hold him! Shut the door! Don't let him loose! I got something! Here he is!" A perfect Babel of noises they made. Everybody, it seemed, was being hit all at once, and Sandy Wadgers, knowing as ever and his wits sharpened by a frightful blow in the nose, reopened the door and led the rout. The others, following incontinently, were jammed for a moment in the corner by the doorway. The hitting continued. Phipps, the Unitarian, had a front tooth broken, and Henfrey was injured in the cartilage of his ear. Jaffers was struck under the jaw, and, turning, caught at something that intervened between him and Huxter in the mêlée, and prevented their coming together. He felt a muscular chest, and in another moment the whole mass of struggling, excited men shot out into the crowded hall.

"I got him!" shouted Jaffers, choking and reeling through them all, and wrestling with purple face and swelling veins against his unseen enemy.

Men staggered right and left as the extraordinary conflict swayed swiftly towards the house door, and went spinning down the half-dozen steps of the inn. Jaffers cried in a strangled voice—holding tight, nevertheless, and making play with his knee—spun around, and fell heavily undermost with his head on the gravel. Only then did his fingers relax.

There were excited cries of "Hold him!" "Invisible!" and so forth, and a young fellow, a stranger in the place whose name did not come to light, rushed in at once, caught something, missed his hold, and fell over the constable's prostrate body. Half-way across the road a woman screamed as something pushed by her; a dog, kicked apparently, yelped and ran howling into Huxter's yard, and with that the transit of the Invisible Man was accomplished. For a space people stood amazed and gesticulating, and then came panic, and scattered them abroad through the village as a gust scatters dead leaves.

But Jaffers lay quite still, face upward and knees bent, at the foot of the steps of the inn.

CHAPTER VIII

IN TRANSIT

The eighth chapter is exceedingly brief, and relates that Gibbons, the amateur naturalist of the district, while lying out on the spacious open downs without a soul within a couple of miles of him, as he thought, and almost dozing, heard close to him the sound as of a man coughing, sneezing, and then swearing savagely to himself; and looking, beheld nothing. Yet the voice was indisputable. It continued to swear with that breadth and variety that distinguishes the swearing of a cultivated man. It grew to a climax, diminished again, and died away in the distance, going as it seemed to him in the direction of Adderdean. It lifted to a spasmodic sneeze and ended. Gibbons had heard nothing of the morning's occurrences, but the phenomenon was so striking and disturbing that his philosophical tranquillity vanished; he got up hastily, and hurried down the steepness of the hill towards the village, as fast as he could go.

CHAPTER IX

MR. THOMAS MARVEL

You must picture Mr. Thomas Marvel as a person of copious, flexible visage, a nose of cylindrical protrusion, a liquorish, ample, fluctuating mouth, and a beard of bristling eccentricity. His figure inclined to embonpoint; his short limbs accentuated this inclination. He wore a furry silk hat, and the frequent substitution of twine and shoe-laces for buttons, apparent at critical points of his costume, marked a man essentially bachelor.

Mr. Thomas Marvel was sitting with his feet in a ditch by the roadside over the down towards Adderdean, about a mile and a half out of Iping. His feet, save for socks of irregular open-work, were bare, his big toes were broad, and pricked like the ears of a watchful dog. In a leisurely manner—he did everything in a leisurely manner—he was contemplating trying on a pair of boots. They were the soundest boots he had come across for a long time, but too large for him; whereas the ones he had were, in dry weather, a very comfortable fit, but too thin-soled for damp. Mr. Thomas Marvel hated roomy shoes, but then he hated damp. He had never properly thought out which he hated most, and it was a pleasant day, and there was nothing better to do. So he put the four shoes in a graceful group on the turf and looked at them. And seeing them there among the grass and springing agrimony, it suddenly occurred to him that both pairs were exceedingly ugly to see. He was not at all startled by a voice behind him.

"They're boots, anyhow," said the Voice.

"They are—charity boots," said Mr. Thomas Marvel, with his head on one side regarding them distastefully; "and which is the ugliest pair in the whole blessed universe, I'm darned if I know!"

"H'm," said the Voice.

"I've worn worse—in fact, I've worn none. But none so owdacious ugly—if you'll allow the expression. I've been cadging boots—in particular—for days. Because I was sick of *them*. They're sound enough, of course. But a gentleman on tramp sees such a thundering lot of his boots. And if you'll believe me, I've raised nothing in the whole blessed country, try as I would, but *them*. Look at 'em! And a good country for boots, too, in a general way. But it's just my promiscuous luck. I've got my boots in this country ten years or more. And then they treat you like this."

"It's a beast of a country," said the Voice. "And pigs for people."

"Ain't it?" said Mr. Thomas Marvel. "Lord! But them boots! It beats it."

He turned his head over his shoulder to the right, to look at the boots of his interlocutor with a view to comparisons, and lo! where the boots of his interlocutor should have been were neither legs nor boots. He was irradiated by the dawn of a great amazement. "Where *are* yer?" said Mr. Thomas Marvel over his shoulder and coming on all fours. He saw a stretch of empty downs with the wind swaying the remote green-pointed furze bushes.

"Am I drunk?" said Mr. Marvel. "Have I had visions? Was I talking to myself? What the—"

"Don't be alarmed," said a Voice.

"None of your ventriloquising *me*," said Mr. Thomas Marvel, rising sharply to his feet. "Where *are* yer? Alarmed, indeed!"

"Don't be alarmed," repeated the Voice.

"*You'll* be alarmed in a minute, you silly fool," said Mr. Thomas Marvel. "Where *are* yer? Lemme get my mark on yer…

"Are yer *buried?*" said Mr. Thomas Marvel, after an interval.

There was no answer. Mr. Thomas Marvel stood bootless and amazed, his jacket nearly thrown off.

"Peewit," said a peewit, very remote.

"Peewit, indeed!" said Mr. Thomas Marvel. "This ain't no time for foolery." The down was desolate, east and west, north and south; the road with its shallow ditches and white bordering stakes, ran smooth and empty north and south, and, save for that peewit, the blue sky was empty too. "So help me," said Mr. Thomas Marvel, shuffling his coat on to his shoulders again. "It's the drink! I might ha' known."

"It's not the drink," said the Voice. "You keep your nerves steady."

"Ow!" said Mr. Marvel, and his face grew white amidst its patches. "It's the drink!" his lips repeated noiselessly. He remained staring about him, rotating slowly backwards. "I could have *swore* I heard a voice," he whispered.

"Of course you did."

"It's there again," said Mr. Marvel, closing his eyes and clasping his hand on his brow with a tragic gesture. He was suddenly taken by the collar and shaken violently, and left more dazed than ever. "Don't be a fool," said the Voice.

"I'm—off—my—blooming—chump," said Mr. Marvel. "It's no good. It's fretting about them blarsted boots. I'm off my blessed blooming chump. Or it's spirits."

"Neither one thing nor the other," said the Voice. "Listen!"

"Chump," said Mr. Marvel.

"One minute," said the Voice, penetratingly, tremulous with self-control.

"Well?" said Mr. Thomas Marvel, with a strange feeling of having been dug in the chest by a finger.

"You think I'm just imagination? Just imagination?"

"What else *can* you be?" said Mr. Thomas Marvel, rubbing the back of his neck.

"Very well," said the Voice, in a tone of relief. "Then I'm going to throw flints at you till you think differently."

"But where *are* yer?"

The Voice made no answer. Whizz came a flint, apparently out of the air, and missed Mr. Marvel's shoulder by a hair's-breadth. Mr. Marvel, turning, saw a flint jerk up into the air, trace a complicated path, hang for a moment, and then fling at his feet with almost invisible rapidity. He was too amazed to dodge. Whizz it came, and ricochetted from a bare toe into the ditch. Mr. Thomas Marvel jumped a foot and howled aloud. Then he started to run, tripped over an unseen obstacle, and came head over heels into a sitting position.

"Now," said the Voice, as a third stone curved upward and hung in the air above the tramp. "Am I imagination?"

Mr. Marvel by way of reply struggled to his feet, and was immediately rolled over again. He lay quiet for a moment. "If you struggle any more," said the Voice, "I shall throw the flint at your head."

"It's a fair do," said Mr. Thomas Marvel, sitting up, taking his wounded toe in hand and fixing his eye on the third missile. "I don't understand it. Stones flinging themselves. Stones talking. Put yourself down. Rot away. I'm done."

The third flint fell.

"It's very simple," said the Voice. "I'm an invisible man."

"Tell us something I don't know," said Mr. Marvel, gasping with pain. "Where you've hid—how you do it—I *don't* know. I'm beat."

"That's all," said the Voice. "I'm invisible. That's what I want you to understand."

"Anyone could see that. There is no need for you to be so confounded impatient, mister. *Now* then. Give us a notion. How are you hid?"

"I'm invisible. That's the great point. And what I want you to understand is this—"

"But whereabouts?" interrupted Mr. Marvel.

"Here! Six yards in front of you."

"Oh, *come!* I ain't blind. You'll be telling me next you're just thin air. I'm not one of your ignorant tramps—"

"Yes, I am—thin air. You're looking through me."

"What! Ain't there any stuff to you. *Vox et*—what is it?—jabber. Is it that?"

"I am just a human being—solid, needing food and drink, needing covering too—But I'm invisible. You see? Invisible. Simple idea. Invisible."

"What, real like?"

"Yes, real."

"Let's have a hand of you," said Marvel, "if you *are* real. It won't be so darn out-of-the-way like, then—*Lord!*" he said, "how you made me jump!—gripping me like that!"

He felt the hand that had closed round his wrist with his disengaged fingers, and his fingers went timorously up the arm, patted a muscular chest, and explored a bearded face. Marvel's face was astonishment.

"I'm dashed!" he said. "If this don't beat cock-fighting! Most remarkable!—And there I can see a rabbit clean through you, 'arf a mile away! Not a bit of you visible—except—"

He scrutinised the apparently empty space keenly. "You 'aven't been eatin' bread and cheese?" he asked, holding the invisible arm.

"You're quite right, and it's not quite assimilated into the system."

"Ah!" said Mr. Marvel. "Sort of ghostly, though."

"Of course, all this isn't half so wonderful as you think."

"It's quite wonderful enough for *my* modest wants," said Mr. Thomas Marvel. "Howjer manage it! How the dooce is it done?"

"It's too long a story. And besides—"

"I tell you, the whole business fairly beats me," said Mr. Marvel.

"What I want to say at present is this: I need help. I have come to that—I came upon you suddenly. I was wandering, mad with rage, naked, impotent. I could have murdered. And I saw you—"

"Lord!" said Mr. Marvel.

"I came up behind you—hesitated—went on—"

Mr. Marvel's expression was eloquent.

"—then stopped. 'Here,' I said, 'is an outcast like myself. This is the man for me.' So I turned back and came to you—you. And—"

"Lord!" said Mr. Marvel. "But I'm all in a tizzy. May I ask—How is it? And what you may be requiring in the way of help?—Invisible!"

"I want you to help me get clothes—and shelter—and then, with other things. I've left them long enough. If you won't—well! But you *will—must.*"

"Look here," said Mr. Marvel. "I'm too flabbergasted. Don't knock me about any more. And leave me go. I must get steady a bit. And you've pretty near broken my toe. It's all so unreasonable. Empty downs, empty sky. Nothing visible for miles except the bosom of Nature. And then comes a voice. A voice out of heaven! And stones! And a fist—Lord!"

"Pull yourself together," said the Voice, "for you have to do the job I've chosen for you."

Mr. Marvel blew out his cheeks, and his eyes were round.

"I've chosen you," said the Voice. "You are the only man except some of those fools down there, who knows there is such a thing as an invisible man. You have to be my helper. Help me—and I will do great things for you. An invisible man is a man of power." He stopped for a moment to sneeze violently.

"But if you betray me," he said, "if you fail to do as I direct you—" He paused and tapped Mr. Marvel's shoulder smartly. Mr. Marvel gave a yelp of terror at the touch. "I don't want to betray you," said Mr. Marvel, edging away from the direction of the fingers. "Don't you go a-thinking that, whatever you do. All I want to do is to help you—just tell me what I got to do. (Lord!) Whatever you want done, that I'm most willing to do."

CHAPTER X

MR. MARVEL'S VISIT TO IPING

After the first gusty panic had spent itself Iping became argumentative. Scepticism suddenly reared its head—rather nervous scepticism, not at all assured of its back, but scepticism nevertheless. It is so much easier not to believe in an invisible man; and those who had actually seen him dissolve into air, or felt the strength of his arm, could be counted on the fingers of two hands. And of these witnesses Mr. Wadgers was presently missing, having retired impregnably behind the bolts and bars of his own house, and Jaffers was lying stunned in the parlour of the "Coach and Horses." Great and strange ideas transcending experience often have less effect upon men and women than smaller, more tangible considerations. Iping was gay with bunting, and everybody was in gala dress. Whit Monday had been looked forward to for a month or more. By the afternoon even those who believed in the Unseen were beginning to resume their little amusements in a tentative fashion, on the supposition that he had quite gone away, and with the sceptics he was already a jest. But people, sceptics and believers alike, were remarkably sociable all that day.

Haysman's meadow was gay with a tent, in which Mrs. Bunting and other ladies were preparing tea, while, without, the Sunday-school children ran races and played games under the noisy guidance of the curate and the Misses Cuss and Sackbut. No doubt there was a slight uneasiness in the air, but people for the most part had the sense to conceal whatever imaginative qualms they experienced. On the village green an inclined strong [rope?], down which, clinging the while to a pulley-swung handle, one could be hurled violently against a sack at the other end, came in for considerable favour among the adolescents, as also did the swings and the cocoanut shies. There was also promenading, and the steam organ attached to a small roundabout filled the air with a pungent flavour of oil and with equally pungent music. Members of the club, who had attended church in the morning, were splendid in badges of pink and green, and some of the gayer-minded had also adorned their bowler hats with brilliant-coloured favours of ribbon. Old Fletcher, whose conceptions of holiday-making were severe, was visible through the jasmine about his window or through the open door (whichever way you chose to look), poised delicately on a plank supported on two chairs, and whitewashing the ceiling of his front room.

About four o'clock a stranger entered the village from the direction of the downs. He was a short, stout person in an extraordinarily shabby top hat, and he appeared to be very much out of breath. His cheeks were alternately limp and tightly puffed. His mottled face was apprehensive, and he moved with a sort of reluctant alacrity. He turned the corner of the church, and directed his way to the "Coach and Horses." Among others old Fletcher remembers seeing him, and indeed the old gentleman was so struck by his peculiar agitation that he inadvertently allowed a quantity of white-wash to run down the brush into the sleeve of his coat while regarding him.

This stranger, to the perceptions of the proprietor of the cocoanut shy, appeared to be talking to himself, and Mr. Huxter remarked the same thing. He stopped at the foot of the "Coach and Horses" steps, and, according to Mr. Huxter, appeared to undergo a severe internal struggle before he could induce himself to enter the house. Finally he marched up the steps, and was seen by Mr. Huxter to turn to the left and open the door of the parlour. Mr. Huxter heard voices from within the room and from the bar apprising the man of his error. "That room's private!" said Hall, and the stranger shut the door clumsily and went into the bar.

In the course of a few minutes he reappeared, wiping his lips with the back of his hand with an air of quiet satisfaction that somehow impressed Mr. Huxter as assumed. He stood looking about him for some moments, and then Mr. Huxter saw him walk in an oddly furtive manner towards the gates of the yard, upon which the parlour window opened. The stranger, after some hesitation, leant against one of the gate-posts, produced a short clay pipe, and prepared to fill it. His fingers trembled while doing so. He lit it clumsily, and folding his arms began to smoke in a languid attitude, an attitude which his occasional glances up the yard altogether belied.

All this Mr. Huxter saw over the canisters of the tobacco window, and the singularity of the man's behaviour prompted him to maintain his observation.

Presently the stranger stood up abruptly and put his pipe in his pocket. Then he vanished into the yard. Forthwith Mr. Huxter, conceiving he was witness of some petty larceny, leapt round his counter and ran out into the road to intercept the thief. As he did so, Mr. Marvel reappeared, his hat askew, a big bundle in a blue table-cloth in one hand, and three books tied together—as it proved afterwards with the Vicar's braces—in the other. Directly he saw Huxter he gave a sort of gasp, and turning sharply to the left, began to run. "Stop, thief!" cried Huxter, and set off after him. Mr. Huxter's sensations were vivid but brief. He saw the man just before him and spurting briskly for the church corner and the hill road. He saw the village flags and festivities beyond, and a face or so turned towards him. He bawled, "Stop!" again. He had hardly gone ten strides before his shin was caught in some mysterious fashion, and he was no longer running, but flying with inconceivable rapidity through the air. He saw the ground suddenly close to his face. The world seemed to splash into a million whirling specks of light, and subsequent proceedings interested him no more.

CHAPTER XI

IN THE "COACH AND HORSES"

Now in order clearly to understand what had happened in the inn, it is necessary to go back to the moment when Mr. Marvel first came into view of Mr. Huxter's window.

At that precise moment Mr. Cuss and Mr. Bunting were in the parlour. They were seriously investigating the strange occurrences of the morning, and were, with Mr. Hall's permission, making a thorough examination of the Invisible Man's belongings. Jaffers had partially recovered from his fall and had gone home in the charge of his sympathetic friends. The stranger's scattered garments had been removed by Mrs. Hall and the room tidied up. And on the table under the window where the stranger had been wont to work, Cuss had hit almost at once on three big books in manuscript labelled "Diary."

"Diary!" said Cuss, putting the three books on the table. "Now, at any rate, we shall learn something." The Vicar stood with his hands on the table.

"Diary," repeated Cuss, sitting down, putting two volumes to support the third, and opening it. "H'm—no name on the fly-leaf. Bother!—cypher. And figures."

The vicar came round to look over his shoulder.

Cuss turned the pages over with a face suddenly disappointed. "I'm—dear me! It's all cypher, Bunting."

"There are no diagrams?" asked Mr. Bunting. "No illustrations throwing light—"

"See for yourself," said Mr. Cuss. "Some of it's mathematical and some of it's Russian or some such language (to judge by the letters), and some of it's Greek. Now the Greek I thought *you*—"

"Of course," said Mr. Bunting, taking out and wiping his spectacles and feeling suddenly very uncomfortable—for he had no Greek left in his mind worth talking about; "yes—the Greek, of course, may furnish a clue."

"I'll find you a place."

"I'd rather glance through the volumes first," said Mr. Bunting, still wiping. "A general impression first, Cuss, and *then*, you know, we can go looking for clues."

He coughed, put on his glasses, arranged them fastidiously, coughed again, and wished something would happen to avert the seemingly inevitable exposure. Then he took the volume Cuss handed him in a leisurely manner. And then something did happen.

The door opened suddenly.

Both gentlemen started violently, looked round, and were relieved to see a sporadically rosy face beneath a furry silk hat. "Tap?" asked the face, and stood staring.

"No," said both gentlemen at once.

"Over the other side, my man," said Mr. Bunting. And "Please shut that door," said Mr. Cuss, irritably.

"All right," said the intruder, as it seemed in a low voice curiously different from the huskiness of its first inquiry. "Right you are," said the intruder in the former voice. "Stand clear!" and he vanished and closed the door.

"A sailor, I should judge," said Mr. Bunting. "Amusing fellows, they are. Stand clear! indeed. A nautical term, referring to his getting back out of the room, I suppose."

"I daresay so," said Cuss. "My nerves are all loose today. It quite made me jump—the door opening like that."

Mr. Bunting smiled as if he had not jumped. "And now," he said with a sigh, "these books."

Someone sniffed as he did so.

"One thing is indisputable," said Bunting, drawing up a chair next to that of Cuss. "There certainly have been very strange things happen in Iping during the last few days—very strange. I cannot of course believe in this absurd invisibility story—"

"It's incredible," said Cuss—"incredible. But the fact remains that I saw—I certainly saw right down his sleeve—"

"But did you—are you sure? Suppose a mirror, for instance— hallucinations are so easily produced. I don't know if you have ever seen a really good conjuror—"

"I won't argue again," said Cuss. "We've thrashed that out, Bunting. And just now there's these books—Ah! here's some of what I take to be Greek! Greek letters certainly."

He pointed to the middle of the page. Mr. Bunting flushed slightly and brought his face nearer, apparently finding some difficulty with his glasses. Suddenly he became aware of a strange feeling at the nape of his neck. He tried to raise his head, and encountered an immovable resistance. The feeling was a curious pressure, the grip of a heavy, firm hand, and it bore his chin irresistibly to the table. "Don't move, little men," whispered a voice, "or I'll brain you both!" He looked into the face of Cuss, close to his own, and each saw a horrified reflection of his own sickly astonishment.

"I'm sorry to handle you so roughly," said the Voice, "but it's unavoidable."

"Since when did you learn to pry into an investigator's private memoranda," said the Voice; and two chins struck the table simultaneously, and two sets of teeth rattled.

"Since when did you learn to invade the private rooms of a man in misfortune?" and the concussion was repeated.

"Where have they put my clothes?"

"Listen," said the Voice. "The windows are fastened and I've taken the key out of the door. I am a fairly strong man, and I have the poker handy— besides being invisible. There's not the slightest doubt that I could kill you both and get away quite easily if I wanted to—do you understand? Very well. If I let you go will you promise not to try any nonsense and do what I tell you?"

The vicar and the doctor looked at one another, and the doctor pulled a face. "Yes," said Mr. Bunting, and the doctor repeated it. Then the pressure on the necks relaxed, and the doctor and the vicar sat up, both very red in the face and wriggling their heads.

"Please keep sitting where you are," said the Invisible Man. "Here's the poker, you see."

"When I came into this room," continued the Invisible Man, after presenting the poker to the tip of the nose of each of his visitors, "I did not expect to find it occupied, and I expected to find, in addition to my books of memoranda, an outfit of clothing. Where is it? No—don't rise. I can see it's gone. Now, just at present, though the days are quite warm enough for an invisible man to run about stark, the evenings are quite chilly. I want clothing—and other accommodation; and I must also have those three books."

CHAPTER XII

THE INVISIBLE MAN LOSES HIS TEMPER

It is unavoidable that at this point the narrative should break off again, for a certain very painful reason that will presently be apparent. While these things were going on in the parlour, and while Mr. Huxter was watching Mr. Marvel smoking his pipe against the gate, not a dozen yards away were Mr. Hall and Teddy Henfrey discussing in a state of cloudy puzzlement the one Iping topic.

Suddenly there came a violent thud against the door of the parlour, a sharp cry, and then—silence.

"Hul-lo!" said Teddy Henfrey.

"Hul-lo!" from the Tap.

Mr. Hall took things in slowly but surely. "That ain't right," he said, and came round from behind the bar towards the parlour door.

He and Teddy approached the door together, with intent faces. Their eyes considered. "Summat wrong," said Hall, and Henfrey nodded agreement. Whiffs of an unpleasant chemical odour met them, and there was a muffled sound of conversation, very rapid and subdued.

"You all right thur?" asked Hall, rapping.

The muttered conversation ceased abruptly, for a moment silence, then the conversation was resumed, in hissing whispers, then a sharp cry of "No! no, you don't!" There came a sudden motion and the oversetting of a chair, a brief struggle. Silence again.

"What the dooce?" exclaimed Henfrey, *sotto voce.*

"You—all—right thur?" asked Mr. Hall, sharply, again.

The Vicar's voice answered with a curious jerking intonation: "Quite ri-right. Please don't—interrupt."

"Odd!" said Mr. Henfrey.

"Odd!" said Mr. Hall.

"Says, 'Don't interrupt,'" said Henfrey.

"I heerd'n," said Hall.

"And a sniff," said Henfrey.

They remained listening. The conversation was rapid and subdued. "I *can't,*" said Mr. Bunting, his voice rising; "I tell you, sir, I *will* not."

"What was that?" asked Henfrey.

"Says he wi' nart," said Hall. "Warn't speaking to us, wuz he?"

"Disgraceful!" said Mr. Bunting, within.

"'Disgraceful,'" said Mr. Henfrey. "I heard it—distinct."

"Who's that speaking now?" asked Henfrey.

"Mr. Cuss, I s'pose," said Hall. "Can you hear—anything?"

Silence. The sounds within indistinct and perplexing.

"Sounds like throwing the table-cloth about," said Hall.

Mrs. Hall appeared behind the bar. Hall made gestures of silence and invitation. This aroused Mrs. Hall's wifely opposition. "What yer listenin' there for, Hall?" she asked. "Ain't you nothin' better to do—busy day like this?"

Hall tried to convey everything by grimaces and dumb show, but Mrs. Hall was obdurate. She raised her voice. So Hall and Henfrey, rather crestfallen, tiptoed back to the bar, gesticulating to explain to her.

At first she refused to see anything in what they had heard at all. Then she insisted on Hall keeping silence, while Henfrey told her his story. She was inclined to think the whole business nonsense—perhaps they were just moving the furniture about. "I heerd'n say 'disgraceful'; *that* I did," said Hall.

"*I* heerd that, Mrs. Hall," said Henfrey.

"Like as not—" began Mrs. Hall.

"Hsh!" said Mr. Teddy Henfrey. "Didn't I hear the window?"

"What window?" asked Mrs. Hall.

"Parlour window," said Henfrey.

Everyone stood listening intently. Mrs. Hall's eyes, directed straight before her, saw without seeing the brilliant oblong of the inn door, the road white and vivid, and Huxter's shop-front blistering in the June sun. Abruptly Huxter's door opened and Huxter appeared, eyes staring with excitement, arms gesticulating. "Yap!" cried Huxter. "Stop thief!" and he ran obliquely across the oblong towards the yard gates, and vanished.

Simultaneously came a tumult from the parlour, and a sound of windows being closed.

Hall, Henfrey, and the human contents of the tap rushed out at once pell-mell into the street. They saw someone whisk round the corner towards the road, and Mr. Huxter executing a complicated leap in the air that ended on his face and shoulder. Down the street people were standing astonished or running towards them.

Mr. Huxter was stunned. Henfrey stopped to discover this, but Hall and the two labourers from the Tap rushed at once to the corner, shouting incoherent things, and saw Mr. Marvel vanishing by the corner of the church wall. They appear to have jumped to the impossible conclusion that this was the Invisible Man suddenly become visible, and set off at once along the lane in pursuit. But Hall had hardly run a dozen yards before he gave a loud shout of astonishment and went flying headlong sideways, clutching one of the labourers and bringing him to the ground. He had been charged just as one charges a man at football. The second labourer came round in a circle, stared, and conceiving that Hall had tumbled over of his own accord, turned to resume the pursuit, only to be tripped by the ankle just as Huxter had been. Then, as the first labourer struggled to his feet, he was kicked sideways by a blow that might have felled an ox.

As he went down, the rush from the direction of the village green came round the corner. The first to appear was the proprietor of the cocoanut shy, a burly man in a blue jersey. He was astonished to see the lane empty save for three men sprawling absurdly on the ground. And then something happened to his rear-most foot, and he went headlong and rolled sideways just in time to graze the feet of his brother and partner, following headlong. The two were then kicked, knelt on, fallen over, and cursed by quite a number of over-hasty people.

Now when Hall and Henfrey and the labourers ran out of the house, Mrs. Hall, who had been disciplined by years of experience, remained in the bar next the till. And suddenly the parlour door was opened, and Mr. Cuss appeared, and without glancing at her rushed at once down the steps toward the corner. "Hold him!" he cried. "Don't let him drop that parcel."

He knew nothing of the existence of Marvel. For the Invisible Man had handed over the books and bundle in the yard. The face of Mr. Cuss was angry and resolute, but his costume was defective, a sort of limp white kilt that could only have passed muster in Greece. "Hold him!" he bawled. "He's got my trousers! And every stitch of the Vicar's clothes!"

"'Tend to him in a minute!" he cried to Henfrey as he passed the prostrate Huxter, and, coming round the corner to join the tumult, was promptly knocked off his feet into an indecorous sprawl. Somebody in full flight trod heavily on his finger. He yelled, struggled to regain his feet, was knocked against and thrown on all fours again, and became aware that he was involved not in a capture, but a rout. Everyone was running back to the village. He rose again and was hit severely behind the ear. He staggered and set off back to the "Coach and Horses" forthwith, leaping over the deserted Huxter, who was now sitting up, on his way.

Behind him as he was halfway up the inn steps he heard a sudden yell of rage, rising sharply out of the confusion of cries, and a sounding smack in someone's face. He recognised the voice as that of the Invisible Man, and the note was that of a man suddenly infuriated by a painful blow.

In another moment Mr. Cuss was back in the parlour. "He's coming back, Bunting!" he said, rushing in. "Save yourself!"

Mr. Bunting was standing in the window engaged in an attempt to clothe himself in the hearth-rug and a *West Surrey Gazette.* "Who's coming?" he said, so startled that his costume narrowly escaped disintegration.

"Invisible Man," said Cuss, and rushed on to the window. "We'd better clear out from here! He's fighting mad! Mad!"

In another moment he was out in the yard.

"Good heavens!" said Mr. Bunting, hesitating between two horrible alternatives. He heard a frightful struggle in the passage of the inn, and his decision was made. He clambered out of the window, adjusted his costume hastily, and fled up the village as fast as his fat little legs would carry him.

From the moment when the Invisible Man screamed with rage and Mr. Bunting made his memorable flight up the village, it became impossible to give a consecutive account of affairs in Iping. Possibly the Invisible Man's original intention was simply to cover Marvel's retreat with the clothes and books. But his temper, at no time very good, seems to have gone completely at some chance blow, and forthwith he set to smiting and overthrowing, for the mere satisfaction of hurting.

You must figure the street full of running figures, of doors slamming and fights for hiding-places. You must figure the tumult suddenly striking on the unstable equilibrium of old Fletcher's planks and two chairs—with cataclysmic results. You must figure an appalled couple caught dismally in a swing. And then the whole tumultuous rush has passed and the Iping street with its gauds and flags is deserted save for the still raging unseen, and littered with cocoanuts, overthrown canvas screens, and the scattered stock in trade of a sweetstuff stall. Everywhere there is a sound of closing shutters and shoving bolts, and the only visible humanity is an occasional flitting eye under a raised eyebrow in the corner of a window pane.

The Invisible Man amused himself for a little while by breaking all the windows in the "Coach and Horses," and then he thrust a street lamp through the parlour window of Mrs. Gribble. He it must have been who cut the telegraph wire to Adderdean just beyond Higgins' cottage on the Adderdean road. And after that, as his peculiar qualities allowed, he passed out of human perceptions altogether, and he was neither heard, seen, nor felt in Iping any more. He vanished absolutely.

But it was the best part of two hours before any human being ventured out again into the desolation of Iping street.

CHAPTER XIII

MR. MARVEL DISCUSSES HIS RESIGNATION

When the dusk was gathering and Iping was just beginning to peep timorously forth again upon the shattered wreckage of its Bank Holiday, a short, thick-set man in a shabby silk hat was marching painfully through the twilight behind the beechwoods on the road to Bramblehurst. He carried three books bound together by some sort of ornamental elastic ligature, and a bundle wrapped in a blue table-cloth. His rubicund face expressed consternation and fatigue; he appeared to be in a spasmodic sort of hurry. He was accompanied by a voice other than his own, and ever and again he winced under the touch of unseen hands.

"If you give me the slip again," said the Voice, "if you attempt to give me the slip again—"

"Lord!" said Mr. Marvel. "That shoulder's a mass of bruises as it is."

"On my honour," said the Voice, "I will kill you."

"I didn't try to give you the slip," said Marvel, in a voice that was not far remote from tears. "I swear I didn't. I didn't know the blessed turning, that was all! How the devil was I to know the blessed turning? As it is, I've been knocked about—"

"You'll get knocked about a great deal more if you don't mind," said the Voice, and Mr. Marvel abruptly became silent. He blew out his cheeks, and his eyes were eloquent of despair.

"It's bad enough to let these floundering yokels explode my little secret, without *your* cutting off with my books. It's lucky for some of them they cut and ran when they did! Here am I ... No one knew I was invisible! And now what am I to do?"

"What am *I* to do?" asked Marvel, *sotto voce*.

"It's all about. It will be in the papers! Everybody will be looking for me; everyone on their guard—" The Voice broke off into vivid curses and ceased.

The despair of Mr. Marvel's face deepened, and his pace slackened.

"Go on!" said the Voice.

Mr. Marvel's face assumed a greyish tint between the ruddier patches.

"Don't drop those books, stupid," said the Voice, sharply—overtaking him.

"The fact is," said the Voice, "I shall have to make use of you.... You're a poor tool, but I must."

"I'm a *miserable* tool," said Marvel.

"You are," said the Voice.

"I'm the worst possible tool you could have," said Marvel.

"I'm not strong," he said after a discouraging silence.

"I'm not over strong," he repeated.

"No?"

"And my heart's weak. That little business—I pulled it through, of course—but bless you! I could have dropped."

"Well?"

"I haven't the nerve and strength for the sort of thing you want."

"I'll stimulate you."

"I wish you wouldn't. I wouldn't like to mess up your plans, you know. But I might—out of sheer funk and misery."

"You'd better not," said the Voice, with quiet emphasis.

"I wish I was dead," said Marvel.

"It ain't justice," he said; "you must admit.... It seems to me I've a perfect right—"

"Get on!" said the Voice.

Mr. Marvel mended his pace, and for a time they went in silence again.

"It's devilish hard," said Mr. Marvel.

This was quite ineffectual. He tried another tack.

"What do I make by it?" he began again in a tone of unendurable wrong.

"Oh! *shut up!*" said the Voice, with sudden amazing vigour. "I'll see to you all right. You do what you're told. You'll do it all right. You're a fool and all that, but you'll do—"

"I tell you, sir, I'm not the man for it. Respectfully—but it *is* so—"

"If you don't shut up I shall twist your wrist again," said the Invisible Man. "I want to think."

Presently two oblongs of yellow light appeared through the trees, and the square tower of a church loomed through the gloaming. "I shall keep my hand on your shoulder," said the Voice, "all through the village. Go straight through and try no foolery. It will be the worse for you if you do."

"I know that," sighed Mr. Marvel, "I know all that."

The unhappy-looking figure in the obsolete silk hat passed up the street of the little village with his burdens, and vanished into the gathering darkness beyond the lights of the windows.

CHAPTER XIV

AT PORT STOWE

Ten o'clock the next morning found Mr. Marvel, unshaven, dirty, and travel-stained, sitting with the books beside him and his hands deep in his pockets, looking very weary, nervous, and uncomfortable, and inflating his cheeks at infrequent intervals, on the bench outside a little inn on the outskirts of Port Stowe. Beside him were the books, but now they were tied with string. The bundle had been abandoned in the pine-woods beyond Bramblehurst, in accordance with a change in the plans of the Invisible Man. Mr. Marvel sat on the bench, and although no one took the slightest notice of him, his agitation remained at fever heat. His hands would go ever and again to his various pockets with a curious nervous fumbling.

When he had been sitting for the best part of an hour, however, an elderly mariner, carrying a newspaper, came out of the inn and sat down beside him. "Pleasant day," said the mariner.

Mr. Marvel glanced about him with something very like terror. "Very," he said.

"Just seasonable weather for the time of year," said the mariner, taking no denial.

"Quite," said Mr. Marvel.

The mariner produced a toothpick, and (saving his regard) was engrossed thereby for some minutes. His eyes meanwhile were at liberty to examine Mr. Marvel's dusty figure, and the books beside him. As he had approached Mr. Marvel he had heard a sound like the dropping of coins into a pocket. He was struck by the contrast of Mr. Marvel's appearance with this suggestion of opulence. Thence his mind wandered back again to a topic that had taken a curiously firm hold of his imagination.

"Books?" he said suddenly, noisily finishing with the toothpick.

Mr. Marvel started and looked at them. "Oh, yes," he said. "Yes, they're books."

"There's some extra-ordinary things in books," said the mariner.

"I believe you," said Mr. Marvel.

"And some extra-ordinary things out of 'em," said the mariner.

"True likewise," said Mr. Marvel. He eyed his interlocutor, and then glanced about him.

"There's some extra-ordinary things in newspapers, for example," said the mariner.

"There are."

"In *this* newspaper," said the mariner.

"Ah!" said Mr. Marvel.

"There's a story," said the mariner, fixing Mr. Marvel with an eye that was firm and deliberate; "there's a story about an Invisible Man, for instance."

Mr. Marvel pulled his mouth askew and scratched his cheek and felt his ears glowing. "What will they be writing next?" he asked faintly. "Ostria, or America?"

"Neither," said the mariner. *"Here."*

"Lord!" said Mr. Marvel, starting.

"When I say *here,"* said the mariner, to Mr. Marvel's intense relief, "I don't of course mean here in this place, I mean hereabouts."

"An Invisible Man!" said Mr. Marvel. "And what's *he* been up to?"

"Everything," said the mariner, controlling Marvel with his eye, and then amplifying, "every—blessed—thing."

"I ain't seen a paper these four days," said Marvel.

"Iping's the place he started at," said the mariner.

"In-*deed!"* said Mr. Marvel.

"He started there. And where he came from, nobody don't seem to know. Here it is: 'Pe-culiar Story from Iping.' And it says in this paper that the evidence is extra-ordinary strong—extra-ordinary."

"Lord!" said Mr. Marvel.

"But then, it's an extra-ordinary story. There is a clergyman and a medical gent witnesses—saw 'im all right and proper—or leastways didn't see 'im. He was staying, it says, at the 'Coach an' Horses,' and no one don't seem to have been aware of his misfortune, it says, aware of his misfortune, until in an Altercation in the inn, it says, his bandages on his head was torn off. It was then ob-served that his head was invisible. Attempts were At Once made to secure him, but casting off his garments, it says, he succeeded in escaping, but not until after a desperate struggle, in which he had inflicted serious injuries, it says, on our worthy and able constable, Mr. J. A. Jaffers. Pretty straight story, eh? Names and everything."

"Lord!" said Mr. Marvel, looking nervously about him, trying to count the money in his pockets by his unaided sense of touch, and full of a strange and novel idea. "It sounds most astonishing."

"Don't it? Extra-ordinary, *I* call it. Never heard tell of Invisible Men before, I haven't, but nowadays one hears such a lot of extra-ordinary things—that—"

"That all he did?" asked Marvel, trying to seem at his ease.

"It's enough, ain't it?" said the mariner.

"Didn't go Back by any chance?" asked Marvel. "Just escaped and that's all, eh?"

"All!" said the mariner. "Why!—ain't it enough?"

"Quite enough," said Marvel.

"I should think it was enough," said the mariner. "I should think it was enough."

"He didn't have any pals—it don't say he had any pals, does it?" asked Mr. Marvel, anxious.

"Ain't one of a sort enough for you?" asked the mariner. "No, thank Heaven, as one might say, he didn't."

He nodded his head slowly. "It makes me regular uncomfortable, the bare thought of that chap running about the country! He is at present At Large, and from certain evidence it is supposed that he has—taken—*took*, I suppose they mean—the road to Port Stowe. You see we're right *in* it!

None of your American wonders, this time. And just think of the things he might do! Where'd you be, if he took a drop over and above, and had a fancy to go for you? Suppose he wants to rob—who can prevent him? He can trespass, he can burgle, he could walk through a cordon of policemen as easy as me or you could give the slip to a blind man! Easier! For these here blind chaps hear uncommon sharp, I'm told. And wherever there was liquor he fancied—"

"He's got a tremenjous advantage, certainly," said Mr. Marvel. "And—well..."

"You're right," said the mariner. "He *has.*"

All this time Mr. Marvel had been glancing about him intently, listening for faint footfalls, trying to detect imperceptible movements. He seemed on the point of some great resolution. He coughed behind his hand.

He looked about him again, listened, bent towards the mariner, and lowered his voice: "The fact of it is—I happen—to know just a thing or two about this Invisible Man. From private sources."

"Oh!" said the mariner, interested. *"You?"*

"Yes," said Mr. Marvel. "Me."

"Indeed!" said the mariner. "And may I ask—"

"You'll be astonished," said Mr. Marvel behind his hand. "It's tremenjous."

"Indeed!" said the mariner.

"The fact is," began Mr. Marvel eagerly in a confidential undertone. Suddenly his expression changed marvellously. "Ow!" he said. He rose stiffly in his seat. His face was eloquent of physical suffering. "Wow!" he said.

"What's up?" said the mariner, concerned.

"Toothache," said Mr. Marvel, and put his hand to his ear. He caught hold of his books. "I must be getting on, I think," he said. He edged in a curious way along the seat away from his interlocutor. "But you was just a-going to tell me about this here Invisible Man!" protested the mariner. Mr. Marvel seemed to consult with himself. "Hoax," said a Voice. "It's a hoax," said Mr. Marvel.

"But it's in the paper," said the mariner.

"Hoax all the same," said Marvel. "I know the chap that started the lie. There ain't no Invisible Man whatsoever—Blimey."

"But how 'bout this paper? D'you mean to say—?"

"Not a word of it," said Marvel, stoutly.

The mariner stared, paper in hand. Mr. Marvel jerkily faced about. "Wait a bit," said the mariner, rising and speaking slowly, "D'you mean to say—?"

"I do," said Mr. Marvel.

"Then why did you let me go on and tell you all this blarsted stuff, then? What d'yer mean by letting a man make a fool of himself like that for? Eh?"

Mr. Marvel blew out his cheeks. The mariner was suddenly very red indeed; he clenched his hands. "I been talking here this ten minutes," he said; "and you, you little pot-bellied, leathery-faced son of an old boot, couldn't have the elementary manners—"

"Don't you come bandying words with *me,*" said Mr. Marvel.

"Bandying words! I'm a jolly good mind—"

"Come up," said a Voice, and Mr. Marvel was suddenly whirled about and started marching off in a curious spasmodic manner. "You'd better move on," said the mariner. "Who's moving on?" said Mr. Marvel. He was receding obliquely with a curious hurrying gait, with occasional violent jerks forward. Some way along the road he began a muttered monologue, protests and recriminations.

"Silly devil!" said the mariner, legs wide apart, elbows akimbo, watching the receding figure. "I'll show you, you silly ass—hoaxing *me!* It's here—on the paper!"

Mr. Marvel retorted incoherently and, receding, was hidden by a bend in the road, but the mariner still stood magnificent in the midst of the way, until the approach of a butcher's cart dislodged him. Then he turned himself towards Port Stowe. "Full of extra-ordinary asses," he said softly to himself. "Just to take me down a bit—that was his silly game—It's on the paper!"

And there was another extraordinary thing he was presently to hear, that had happened quite close to him. And that was a vision of a "fist full of money" (no less) travelling without visible agency, along by the wall at the corner of St. Michael's Lane. A brother mariner had seen this wonderful sight that very morning. He had snatched at the money forthwith and had been knocked headlong, and when he had got to his feet the butterfly money had vanished. Our mariner was in the mood to believe anything, he declared, but that was a bit *too* stiff. Afterwards, however, he began to think things over.

The story of the flying money was true. And all about that neighbourhood, even from the august London and Country Banking Company, from the tills of shops and inns—doors standing that sunny weather entirely open—money had been quietly and dexterously making off that day in handfuls and rouleaux, floating quietly along by walls and shady places, dodging quickly from the approaching eyes of men. And it had, though no man had traced it, invariably ended its mysterious flight in the pocket of that agitated gentleman in the obsolete silk hat, sitting outside the little inn on the outskirts of Port Stowe.

It was ten days after—and indeed only when the Burdock story was already old—that the mariner collated these facts and began to understand how near he had been to the wonderful Invisible Man.

CHAPTER XV

THE MAN WHO WAS RUNNING

In the early evening time Dr. Kemp was sitting in his study in the belvedere on the hill overlooking Burdock. It was a pleasant little room, with three windows—north, west, and south—and bookshelves covered with books and scientific publications, and a broad writing-table, and, under the north window, a microscope, glass slips, minute instruments, some cultures, and scattered bottles of reagents. Dr. Kemp's solar lamp was lit, albeit the sky was still bright with the sunset light, and his blinds were up because there was no offence of peering outsiders to require them pulled down. Dr. Kemp was a tall and slender young man, with flaxen hair and a moustache almost white, and the work he was upon would earn him, he hoped, the fellowship of the Royal Society, so highly did he think of it.

And his eye, presently wandering from his work, caught the sunset blazing at the back of the hill that is over against his own. For a minute perhaps he sat, pen in mouth, admiring the rich golden colour above the crest, and then his attention was attracted by the little figure of a man, inky black, running over the hill-brow towards him. He was a shortish little man, and he wore a high hat, and he was running so fast that his legs verily twinkled.

"Another of those fools," said Dr. Kemp. "Like that ass who ran into me this morning round a corner, with the ''Visible Man a-coming, sir!' I can't imagine what possesses people. One might think we were in the thirteenth century."

He got up, went to the window, and stared at the dusky hillside, and the dark little figure tearing down it. "He seems in a confounded hurry," said Dr. Kemp, "but he doesn't seem to be getting on. If his pockets were full of lead, he couldn't run heavier."

"Spurted, sir," said Dr. Kemp.

In another moment the higher of the villas that had clambered up the hill from Burdock had occulted the running figure. He was visible again for a moment, and again, and then again, three times between the three detached houses that came next, and then the terrace hid him.

"Asses!" said Dr. Kemp, swinging round on his heel and walking back to his writing-table.

But those who saw the fugitive nearer, and perceived the abject terror on his perspiring face, being themselves in the open roadway, did not share in the doctor's contempt. By the man pounded, and as he ran he chinked like a well-filled purse that is tossed to and fro. He looked neither to the right nor the left, but his dilated eyes stared straight downhill to where the lamps were being lit, and the people were crowded in the street. And his ill-shaped mouth fell apart, and a glairy foam lay on his lips, and his breath came hoarse and noisy. All he passed stopped and began staring up the road and down, and interrogating one another with an inkling of discomfort for the reason of his haste.

And then presently, far up the hill, a dog playing in the road yelped and ran under a gate, and as they still wondered something—a wind—a pad, pad, pad,—a sound like a panting breathing, rushed by.

People screamed. People sprang off the pavement: It passed in shouts, it passed by instinct down the hill. They were shouting in the street before Marvel was halfway there. They were bolting into houses and slamming the doors behind them, with the news. He heard it and made one last desperate spurt. Fear came striding by, rushed ahead of him, and in a moment had seized the town.

"The Invisible Man is coming! The Invisible Man!"

CHAPTER XVI

IN THE JOLLY "CRICKETERS"

The "Jolly Cricketers" is just at the bottom of the hill, where the tram-lines begin. The barman leant his fat red arms on the counter and talked of horses with an anaemic cabman, while a black-bearded man in grey snapped up biscuit and cheese, drank Burton, and conversed in American with a policeman off duty.

"What's the shouting about!" said the anaemic cabman, going off at a tangent, trying to see up the hill over the dirty yellow blind in the low window of the inn. Somebody ran by outside. "Fire, perhaps," said the barman.

Footsteps approached, running heavily, the door was pushed open violently, and Marvel, weeping and dishevelled, his hat gone, the neck of his coat torn open, rushed in, made a convulsive turn, and attempted to shut the door. It was held half open by a strap.

"Coming!" he bawled, his voice shrieking with terror. "He's coming. The 'Visible Man! After me! For Gawd's sake! 'Elp! 'Elp! 'Elp!"

"Shut the doors," said the policeman. "Who's coming? What's the row?" He went to the door, released the strap, and it slammed. The American closed the other door.

"Lemme go inside," said Marvel, staggering and weeping, but still clutching the books. "Lemme go inside. Lock me in—somewhere. I tell you he's after me. I give him the slip. He said he'd kill me and he will."

"*You're* safe," said the man with the black beard. "The door's shut. What's it all about?"

"Lemme go inside," said Marvel, and shrieked aloud as a blow suddenly made the fastened door shiver and was followed by a hurried rapping and a shouting outside. "Hullo," cried the policeman, "who's there?" Mr. Marvel began to make frantic dives at panels that looked like doors. "He'll kill me—he's got a knife or something. For Gawd's sake—!"

"Here you are," said the barman. "Come in here." And he held up the flap of the bar.

Mr. Marvel rushed behind the bar as the summons outside was repeated. "Don't open the door," he screamed. *"Please* don't open the door. *Where* shall I hide?"

"This, this Invisible Man, then?" asked the man with the black beard, with one hand behind him. "I guess it's about time we saw him."

The window of the inn was suddenly smashed in, and there was a screaming and running to and fro in the street. The policeman had been standing on the settee staring out, craning to see who was at the door. He got down with raised eyebrows. "It's that," he said. The barman stood in front of the bar-parlour door which was now locked on Mr. Marvel, stared at the smashed window, and came round to the two other men.

Everything was suddenly quiet. "I wish I had my truncheon," said the policeman, going irresolutely to the door. "Once we open, in he comes. There's no stopping him."

"Don't you be in too much hurry about that door," said the anaemic cabman, anxiously.

"Draw the bolts," said the man with the black beard, "and if he comes—" He showed a revolver in his hand.

"That won't do," said the policeman; "that's murder."

"I know what country I'm in," said the man with the beard. "I'm going to let off at his legs. Draw the bolts."

"Not with that blinking thing going off behind me," said the barman, craning over the blind.

"Very well," said the man with the black beard, and stooping down, revolver ready, drew them himself. Barman, cabman, and policeman faced about.

"Come in," said the bearded man in an undertone, standing back and facing the unbolted doors with his pistol behind him. No one came in, the door remained closed. Five minutes afterwards when a second cabman pushed his head in cautiously, they were still waiting, and an anxious face peered out of the bar-parlour and supplied information. "Are all the doors of the house shut?" asked Marvel. "He's going round—prowling round. He's as artful as the devil."

"Good Lord!" said the burly barman. "There's the back! Just watch them doors! I say—!" He looked about him helplessly. The bar-parlour door slammed and they heard the key turn. "There's the yard door and the private door. The yard door—"

He rushed out of the bar.

In a minute he reappeared with a carving-knife in his hand. "The yard door was open!" he said, and his fat underlip dropped. "He may be in the house now!" said the first cabman.

"He's not in the kitchen," said the barman. "There's two women there, and I've stabbed every inch of it with this little beef slicer. And they don't think he's come in. They haven't noticed—"

"Have you fastened it?" asked the first cabman.

"I'm out of frocks," said the barman.

The man with the beard replaced his revolver. And even as he did so the flap of the bar was shut down and the bolt clicked, and then with a tremendous thud the catch of the door snapped and the bar-parlour door burst open. They heard Marvel squeal like a caught leveret, and forthwith they were clambering over the bar to his rescue. The bearded man's revolver cracked and the looking-glass at the back of the parlour starred and came smashing and tinkling down.

As the barman entered the room he saw Marvel, curiously crumpled up and struggling against the door that led to the yard and kitchen. The door flew open while the barman hesitated, and Marvel was dragged into the kitchen. There was a scream and a clatter of pans. Marvel, head down, and lugging back obstinately, was forced to the kitchen door, and the bolts were drawn.

Then the policeman, who had been trying to pass the barman, rushed in, followed by one of the cabmen, gripped the wrist of the invisible hand that collared Marvel, was hit in the face and went reeling back. The door opened, and Marvel made a frantic effort to obtain a lodgment behind it. Then the cabman collared something. "I got him," said the cabman. The barman's red hands came clawing at the unseen. "Here he is!" said the barman.

Mr. Marvel, released, suddenly dropped to the ground and made an attempt to crawl behind the legs of the fighting men. The struggle blundered round the edge of the door. The voice of the Invisible Man was heard for the first time, yelling out sharply, as the policeman trod on his foot. Then he cried out passionately and his fists flew round like flails. The cabman suddenly whooped and doubled up, kicked under the diaphragm. The door into the bar-parlour from the kitchen slammed and covered Mr. Marvel's retreat. The men in the kitchen found themselves clutching at and struggling with empty air.

"Where's he gone?" cried the man with the beard. "Out?"

"This way," said the policeman, stepping into the yard and stopping.

A piece of tile whizzed by his head and smashed among the crockery on the kitchen table.

"I'll show him," shouted the man with the black beard, and suddenly a steel barrel shone over the policeman's shoulder, and five bullets had followed one another into the twilight whence the missile had come. As he fired, the man with the beard moved his hand in a horizontal curve, so that his shots radiated out into the narrow yard like spokes from a wheel.

A silence followed. "Five cartridges," said the man with the black beard. "That's the best of all. Four aces and a joker. Get a lantern, someone, and come and feel about for his body."

CHAPTER XVII

DR. KEMP'S VISITOR

Dr. Kemp had continued writing in his study until the shots aroused him. Crack, crack, crack, they came one after the other.

"Hullo!" said Dr. Kemp, putting his pen into his mouth again and listening. "Who's letting off revolvers in Burdock? What are the asses at now?"

He went to the south window, threw it up, and leaning out stared down on the network of windows, beaded gas-lamps and shops, with its black interstices of roof and yard that made up the town at night. "Looks like a crowd down the hill," he said, "by 'The Cricketers,'" and remained watching. Thence his eyes wandered over the town to far away where the ships' lights shone, and the pier glowed—a little illuminated, facetted pavilion like a gem of yellow light. The moon in its first quarter hung over the westward hill, and the stars were clear and almost tropically bright.

After five minutes, during which his mind had travelled into a remote speculation of social conditions of the future, and lost itself at last over the time dimension, Dr. Kemp roused himself with a sigh, pulled down the window again, and returned to his writing desk.

It must have been about an hour after this that the front-door bell rang. He had been writing slackly, and with intervals of abstraction, since the shots. He sat listening. He heard the servant answer the door, and waited for her feet on the staircase, but she did not come. "Wonder what that was," said Dr. Kemp.

He tried to resume his work, failed, got up, went downstairs from his study to the landing, rang, and called over the balustrade to the housemaid as she appeared in the hall below. "Was that a letter?" he asked.

"Only a runaway ring, sir," she answered.

"I'm restless tonight," he said to himself. He went back to his study, and this time attacked his work resolutely. In a little while he was hard at work again, and the only sounds in the room were the ticking of the clock and the subdued shrillness of his quill, hurrying in the very centre of the circle of light his lampshade threw on his table.

It was two o'clock before Dr. Kemp had finished his work for the night. He rose, yawned, and went downstairs to bed. He had already removed his coat and vest, when he noticed that he was thirsty. He took a candle and went down to the dining-room in search of a syphon and whiskey.

Dr. Kemp's scientific pursuits have made him a very observant man, and as he recrossed the hall, he noticed a dark spot on the linoleum near the mat at the foot of the stairs. He went on upstairs, and then it suddenly occurred to him to ask himself what the spot on the linoleum might be. Apparently some subconscious element was at work. At any rate, he turned with his burden, went back to the hall, put down the syphon and whiskey, and bending down, touched the spot. Without any great surprise he found it had the stickiness and colour of drying blood.

He took up his burden again, and returned upstairs, looking about him and trying to account for the blood-spot. On the landing he saw something and stopped astonished. The door-handle of his own room was blood-stained.

He looked at his own hand. It was quite clean, and then he remembered that the door of his room had been open when he came down from his study, and that consequently he had not touched the handle at all. He went straight into his room, his face quite calm—perhaps a trifle more resolute than usual. His glance, wandering inquisitively, fell on the bed. On the counterpane was a mess of blood, and the sheet had been torn. He had not noticed this before because he had walked straight to the dressing-table. On the further side the bedclothes were depressed as if someone had been recently sitting there.

Then he had an odd impression that he had heard a low voice say, "Good

Heavens!—Kemp!" But Dr. Kemp was no believer in voices.

He stood staring at the tumbled sheets. Was that really a voice? He looked about again, but noticed nothing further than the disordered and blood-stained bed. Then he distinctly heard a movement across the room, near the wash-hand stand. All men, however highly educated, retain some superstitious inklings. The feeling that is called "eerie" came upon him. He closed the door of the room, came forward to the dressing-table, and put down his burdens. Suddenly, with a start, he perceived a coiled and blood-stained bandage of linen rag hanging in mid-air, between him and the wash-hand stand.

He stared at this in amazement. It was an empty bandage, a bandage properly tied but quite empty. He would have advanced to grasp it, but a touch arrested him, and a voice speaking quite close to him.

"Kemp!" said the Voice.

"Eh?" said Kemp, with his mouth open.

"Keep your nerve," said the Voice. "I'm an Invisible Man."

Kemp made no answer for a space, simply stared at the bandage. "Invisible Man," he said.

"I am an Invisible Man," repeated the Voice.

The story he had been active to ridicule only that morning rushed through Kemp's brain. He does not appear to have been either very much frightened or very greatly surprised at the moment. Realisation came later.

"I thought it was all a lie," he said. The thought uppermost in his mind was the reiterated arguments of the morning. "Have you a bandage on?" he asked.

"Yes," said the Invisible Man.

"Oh!" said Kemp, and then roused himself. "I say!" he said. "But this is nonsense. It's some trick." He stepped forward suddenly, and his hand, extended towards the bandage, met invisible fingers.

He recoiled at the touch and his colour changed.

"Keep steady, Kemp, for God's sake! I want help badly. Stop!"

The hand gripped his arm. He struck at it.

"Kemp!" cried the Voice. "Kemp! Keep steady!" and the grip tightened.

A frantic desire to free himself took possession of Kemp. The hand of the bandaged arm gripped his shoulder, and he was suddenly tripped and flung backwards upon the bed. He opened his mouth to shout, and the corner of the sheet was thrust between his teeth. The Invisible Man had him down grimly, but his arms were free and he struck and tried to kick savagely.

"Listen to reason, will you?" said the Invisible Man, sticking to him in spite of a pounding in the ribs. "By Heaven! you'll madden me in a minute!

"Lie still, you fool!" bawled the Invisible Man in Kemp's ear.

Kemp struggled for another moment and then lay still.

"If you shout, I'll smash your face," said the Invisible Man, relieving his mouth.

"I'm an Invisible Man. It's no foolishness, and no magic. I really am an Invisible Man. And I want your help. I don't want to hurt you, but if you behave like a frantic rustic, I must. Don't you remember me, Kemp? Griffin, of University College?"

"Let me get up," said Kemp. "I'll stop where I am. And let me sit quiet for a minute."

He sat up and felt his neck.

"I am Griffin, of University College, and I have made myself invisible. I am just an ordinary man—a man you have known—made invisible."

"Griffin?" said Kemp.

"Griffin," answered the Voice. A younger student than you were, almost an albino, six feet high, and broad, with a pink and white face and red eyes, who won the medal for chemistry."

"I am confused," said Kemp. "My brain is rioting. What has this to do with Griffin?"

"I *am* Griffin."

Kemp thought. "It's horrible," he said. "But what devilry must happen to make a man invisible?"

"It's no devilry. It's a process, sane and intelligible enough—"

"It's horrible!" said Kemp. "How on earth—?"

"It's horrible enough. But I'm wounded and in pain, and tired ... Great God! Kemp, you are a man. Take it steady. Give me some food and drink, and let me sit down here."

Kemp stared at the bandage as it moved across the room, then saw a basket chair dragged across the floor and come to rest near the bed. It creaked, and the seat was depressed the quarter of an inch or so. He rubbed his eyes and felt his neck again. "This beats ghosts," he said, and laughed stupidly.

"That's better. Thank Heaven, you're getting sensible!"

"Or silly," said Kemp, and knuckled his eyes.

"Give me some whiskey. I'm near dead."

"It didn't feel so. Where are you? If I get up shall I run into you? *There!* all right. Whiskey? Here. Where shall I give it to you?"

The chair creaked and Kemp felt the glass drawn away from him. He let go by an effort; his instinct was all against it. It came to rest poised twenty inches above the front edge of the seat of the chair. He stared at it in infinite perplexity. "This is—this must be—hypnotism. You have suggested you are invisible."

"Nonsense," said the Voice.

"It's frantic."

"Listen to me."

"I demonstrated conclusively this morning," began Kemp, "that invisibility—"

"Never mind what you've demonstrated!—I'm starving," said the Voice, "and the night is chilly to a man without clothes."

"Food?" said Kemp.

The tumbler of whiskey tilted itself. "Yes," said the Invisible Man rapping it down. "Have you a dressing-gown?"

Kemp made some exclamation in an undertone. He walked to a wardrobe and produced a robe of dingy scarlet. "This do?" he asked. It was taken from him. It hung limp for a moment in mid-air, fluttered weirdly, stood full and decorous buttoning itself, and sat down in his chair. "Drawers, socks, slippers would be a comfort," said the Unseen, curtly. "And food."

"Anything. But this is the insanest thing I ever was in, in my life!"

He turned out his drawers for the articles, and then went downstairs to ransack his larder. He came back with some cold cutlets and bread, pulled up a light table, and placed them before his guest. "Never mind knives," said his visitor, and a cutlet hung in mid-air, with a sound of gnawing.

"Invisible!" said Kemp, and sat down on a bedroom chair.

"I always like to get something about me before I eat," said the Invisible Man, with a full mouth, eating greedily. "Queer fancy!"

"I suppose that wrist is all right," said Kemp.

"Trust me," said the Invisible Man.

"Of all the strange and wonderful—"

"Exactly. But it's odd I should blunder into *your* house to get my bandaging. My first stroke of luck! Anyhow I meant to sleep in this house tonight. You must stand that! It's a filthy nuisance, my blood showing, isn't it? Quite a clot over there. Gets visible as it coagulates, I see. It's only the living tissue I've changed, and only for as long as I'm alive.... I've been in the house three hours."

"But how's it done?" began Kemp, in a tone of exasperation. "Confound it! The whole business—it's unreasonable from beginning to end."

"Quite reasonable," said the Invisible Man. "Perfectly reasonable."

He reached over and secured the whiskey bottle. Kemp stared at the devouring dressing gown. A ray of candle-light penetrating a torn patch in the right shoulder, made a triangle of light under the left ribs. "What were the shots?" he asked. "How did the shooting begin?"

"There was a real fool of a man—a sort of confederate of mine—curse him!—who tried to steal my money. *Has* done so."

"Is *he* invisible too?"

"No."

"Well?"

"Can't I have some more to eat before I tell you all that? I'm hungry—in pain. And you want me to tell stories!"

Kemp got up. "*You* didn't do any shooting?" he asked.

"Not me," said his visitor. "Some fool I'd never seen fired at random. A lot of them got scared. They all got scared at me. Curse them!—I say—I want more to eat than this, Kemp."

"I'll see what there is to eat downstairs," said Kemp. "Not much, I'm afraid."

After he had done eating, and he made a heavy meal, the Invisible Man demanded a cigar. He bit the end savagely before Kemp could find a knife, and cursed when the outer leaf loosened. It was strange to see him smoking; his mouth, and throat, pharynx and nares, became visible as a sort of whirling smoke cast.

"This blessed gift of smoking!" he said, and puffed vigorously. "I'm lucky to have fallen upon you, Kemp. You must help me. Fancy tumbling on you just now! I'm in a devilish scrape—I've been mad, I think. The things I have been through! But we will do things yet. Let me tell you—"

He helped himself to more whiskey and soda. Kemp got up, looked about him, and fetched a glass from his spare room. "It's wild—but I suppose I may drink."

"You haven't changed much, Kemp, these dozen years. You fair men don't. Cool and methodical—after the first collapse. I must tell you. We will work together!"

"But how was it all done?" said Kemp, "and how did you get like this?"

"For God's sake, let me smoke in peace for a little while! And then I will begin to tell you."

But the story was not told that night. The Invisible Man's wrist was growing painful; he was feverish, exhausted, and his mind came round to brood upon his chase down the hill and the struggle about the inn. He spoke in fragments of Marvel, he smoked faster, his voice grew angry. Kemp tried to gather what he could.

"He was afraid of me, I could see that he was afraid of me," said the Invisible Man many times over. "He meant to give me the slip—he was always casting about! What a fool I was!

"The cur!

"I should have killed him!"

"Where did you get the money?" asked Kemp, abruptly.

The Invisible Man was silent for a space. "I can't tell you tonight," he said.

He groaned suddenly and leant forward, supporting his invisible head on invisible hands. "Kemp," he said, "I've had no sleep for near three days, except a couple of dozes of an hour or so. I must sleep soon."

"Well, have my room—have this room."

"But how can I sleep? If I sleep—he will get away. Ugh! What does it matter?"

"What's the shot wound?" asked Kemp, abruptly.

"Nothing—scratch and blood. Oh, God! How I want sleep!"

"Why not?"

The Invisible Man appeared to be regarding Kemp. "Because I've a particular objection to being caught by my fellow-men," he said slowly.

Kemp started.

"Fool that I am!" said the Invisible Man, striking the table smartly. "I've put the idea into your head."

CHAPTER XVIII

THE INVISIBLE MAN SLEEPS

Exhausted and wounded as the Invisible Man was, he refused to accept Kemp's word that his freedom should be respected. He examined the two windows of the bedroom, drew up the blinds and opened the sashes, to confirm Kemp's statement that a retreat by them would be possible. Outside the night was very quiet and still, and the new moon was setting over the down. Then he examined the keys of the bedroom and the two dressing-room doors, to satisfy himself that these also could be made an assurance of freedom. Finally he expressed himself satisfied. He stood on the hearth rug and Kemp heard the sound of a yawn.

"I'm sorry," said the Invisible Man, "if I cannot tell you all that I have done tonight. But I am worn out. It's grotesque, no doubt. It's horrible! But believe me, Kemp, in spite of your arguments of this morning, it is quite a possible thing. I have made a discovery. I meant to keep it to myself. I can't. I must have a partner. And you.... We can do such things ... But tomorrow. Now, Kemp, I feel as though I must sleep or perish."

Kemp stood in the middle of the room staring at the headless garment. "I suppose I must leave you," he said. "It's—incredible. Three things happening like this, overturning all my preconceptions—would make me insane. But it's real! Is there anything more that I can get you?"

"Only bid me goodnight," said Griffin.

"Goodnight," said Kemp, and shook an invisible hand. He walked sideways to the door. Suddenly the dressing-gown walked quickly towards him. "Understand me!" said the dressing-gown. "No attempts to hamper me, or capture me! Or—"

Kemp's face changed a little. "I thought I gave you my word," he said.

Kemp closed the door softly behind him, and the key was turned upon him forthwith. Then, as he stood with an expression of passive amazement on his face, the rapid feet came to the door of the dressing-room and that too was locked. Kemp slapped his brow with his hand. "Am I dreaming? Has the world gone mad—or have I?"

He laughed, and put his hand to the locked door. "Barred out of my own bedroom, by a flagrant absurdity!" he said.

He walked to the head of the staircase, turned, and stared at the locked doors. "It's fact," he said. He put his fingers to his slightly bruised neck. "Undeniable fact!

"But—"

He shook his head hopelessly, turned, and went downstairs.

He lit the dining-room lamp, got out a cigar, and began pacing the room, ejaculating. Now and then he would argue with himself.

"Invisible!" he said.

"Is there such a thing as an invisible animal? ... In the sea, yes. Thousands—millions. All the larvae, all the little nauplii and tornarias, all the microscopic things, the jelly-fish. In the sea there are more things invisible than visible! I never thought of that before. And in the ponds too! All those little pond-life things—specks of colourless translucent jelly! But in air? No!

"It can't be.

"But after all—why not?

"If a man was made of glass he would still be visible."

His meditation became profound. The bulk of three cigars had passed into the invisible or diffused as a white ash over the carpet before he spoke again. Then it was merely an exclamation. He turned aside, walked out of the room, and went into his little consulting-room and lit the gas there. It was a little room, because Dr. Kemp did not live by practice, and in it were the day's newspapers. The morning's paper lay carelessly opened and thrown aside. He caught it up, turned it over, and read the account of a

"Strange Story from Iping" that the mariner at Port Stowe had spelt over so painfully to Mr. Marvel. Kemp read it swiftly.

"Wrapped up!" said Kemp. "Disguised! Hiding it! 'No one seems to have been aware of his misfortune.' What the devil *is* his game?"

He dropped the paper, and his eye went seeking. "Ah!" he said, and caught up the *St. James' Gazette,* lying folded up as it arrived. "Now we shall get at the truth," said Dr. Kemp. He rent the paper open; a couple of columns confronted him. "An Entire Village in Sussex goes Mad" was the heading.

"Good Heavens!" said Kemp, reading eagerly an incredulous account of the events in Iping, of the previous afternoon, that have already been described. Over the leaf the report in the morning paper had been reprinted.

He re-read it. "Ran through the streets striking right and left. Jaffers insensible. Mr. Huxter in great pain—still unable to describe what he saw. Painful humiliation—vicar. Woman ill with terror! Windows smashed. This extraordinary story probably a fabrication. Too good not to print— *cum grano!*"

He dropped the paper and stared blankly in front of him. "Probably a fabrication!"

He caught up the paper again, and re-read the whole business. "But when does the Tramp come in? Why the deuce was he chasing a tramp?"

He sat down abruptly on the surgical bench. "He's not only invisible," he said, "but he's mad! Homicidal!"

When dawn came to mingle its pallor with the lamp-light and cigar smoke of the dining-room, Kemp was still pacing up and down, trying to grasp the incredible.

He was altogether too excited to sleep. His servants, descending sleepily, discovered him, and were inclined to think that over-study had worked this ill on him. He gave them extraordinary but quite explicit instructions to lay breakfast for two in the belvedere study—and then to confine themselves to the basement and ground-floor. Then he continued to pace the dining-room until the morning's paper came. That had much to say and little to tell, beyond the confirmation of the evening before, and a very badly written account of another remarkable tale from Port Burdock. This gave Kemp the essence of the happenings at the "Jolly Cricketers," and the name of Marvel. "He has made me keep with him twenty-four hours," Marvel testified. Certain minor facts were added to the Iping story, notably the cutting of the village telegraph-wire. But there was nothing to throw light on the connexion between the Invisible Man and the Tramp; for Mr. Marvel had supplied no information about the three books, or the money with which he was lined. The incredulous tone had vanished and a shoal of reporters and inquirers were already at work elaborating the matter.

Kemp read every scrap of the report and sent his housemaid out to get every one of the morning papers she could. These also he devoured.

"He is invisible!" he said. "And it reads like rage growing to mania! The things he may do! The things he may do! And he's upstairs free as the air. What on earth ought I to do?"

"For instance, would it be a breach of faith if—? No."

He went to a little untidy desk in the corner, and began a note. He tore this up half written, and wrote another. He read it over and considered it. Then he took an envelope and addressed it to "Colonel Adye, Port Burdock."

The Invisible Man awoke even as Kemp was doing this. He awoke in an evil temper, and Kemp, alert for every sound, heard his pattering feet rush suddenly across the bedroom overhead. Then a chair was flung over and the wash-hand stand tumbler smashed. Kemp hurried upstairs and rapped eagerly.

CHAPTER XIX

CERTAIN FIRST PRINCIPLES

"What's the matter?" asked Kemp, when the Invisible Man admitted him.

"Nothing," was the answer.

"But, confound it! The smash?"

"Fit of temper," said the Invisible Man. "Forgot this arm; and it's sore."

"You're rather liable to that sort of thing."

"I am."

Kemp walked across the room and picked up the fragments of broken glass. "All the facts are out about you," said Kemp, standing up with the glass in his hand; "all that happened in Iping, and down the hill. The world has become aware of its invisible citizen. But no one knows you are here."

The Invisible Man swore.

"The secret's out. I gather it was a secret. I don't know what your plans are, but of course I'm anxious to help you."

The Invisible Man sat down on the bed.

"There's breakfast upstairs," said Kemp, speaking as easily as possible, and he was delighted to find his strange guest rose willingly. Kemp led the way up the narrow staircase to the belvedere.

"Before we can do anything else," said Kemp, "I must understand a little more about this invisibility of yours." He had sat down, after one nervous glance out of the window, with the air of a man who has talking to do. His doubts of the sanity of the entire business flashed and vanished again as he looked across to where Griffin sat at the breakfast-table—a headless, handless dressing-gown, wiping unseen lips on a miraculously held serviette.

"It's simple enough—and credible enough," said Griffin, putting the serviette aside and leaning the invisible head on an invisible hand.

"No doubt, to you, but—" Kemp laughed.

"Well, yes; to me it seemed wonderful at first, no doubt. But now, great God! ... But we will do great things yet! I came on the stuff first at Chesilstowe."

"Chesilstowe?"

"I went there after I left London. You know I dropped medicine and took up physics? No; well, I did. *Light* fascinated me."

"Ah!"

"Optical density! The whole subject is a network of riddles—a network with solutions glimmering elusively through. And being but two-and-twenty and full of enthusiasm, I said, 'I will devote my life to this. This is worth while.' You know what fools we are at two-and-twenty?"

"Fools then or fools now," said Kemp.

"As though knowing could be any satisfaction to a man!

"But I went to work—like a slave. And I had hardly worked and thought about the matter six months before light came through one of the meshes suddenly—blindingly! I found a general principle of pigments and refraction—a formula, a geometrical expression involving four dimensions. Fools, common men, even common mathematicians, do not know anything of what some general expression may mean to the student of molecular physics. In the books—the books that tramp has hidden—there are marvels, miracles! But this was not a method, it was an idea, that might lead to a method by which it would be possible, without changing any other property of matter—except, in some instances colours—to lower the refractive index of a substance, solid or liquid, to that of air—so far as all practical purposes are concerned."

"Phew!" said Kemp. "That's odd! But still I don't see quite ... I can understand that thereby you could spoil a valuable stone, but personal invisibility is a far cry."

"Precisely," said Griffin. "But consider, visibility depends on the action of the visible bodies on light. Either a body absorbs light, or it reflects or refracts it, or does all these things. If it neither reflects nor refracts nor absorbs light, it cannot of itself be visible. You see an opaque red box, for instance, because the colour absorbs some of the light and reflects the rest, all the red part of the light, to you. If it did not absorb any particular part of the light, but reflected it all, then it would be a shining white box. Silver! A diamond box would neither absorb much of the light nor reflect much from the general surface, but just here and there where the surfaces were favourable the light would be reflected and refracted, so that you would get a brilliant appearance of flashing reflections and translucencies—a sort of skeleton of light. A glass box would not be so brilliant, nor so clearly visible, as a diamond box, because there would be less refraction and reflection. See that? From certain points of view you would see quite clearly through it. Some kinds of glass would be more visible than others, a box of flint glass would be brighter than a box of ordinary window glass. A box of very thin common glass would be hard to see in a bad light, because it would absorb hardly any light and refract and reflect very little. And if you put a sheet of common white glass in water, still more if you put it in some denser liquid than water, it would vanish almost altogether, because light passing from water to glass is only slightly refracted or reflected or indeed affected in any way. It is almost as invisible as a jet of coal gas or hydrogen is in air. And for precisely the same reason!"

"Yes," said Kemp, "that is pretty plain sailing."

"And here is another fact you will know to be true. If a sheet of glass is smashed, Kemp, and beaten into a powder, it becomes much more visible while it is in the air; it becomes at last an opaque white powder. This is because the powdering multiplies the surfaces of the glass at which refraction and reflection occur. In the sheet of glass there are only two surfaces; in the powder the light is reflected or refracted by each grain it passes through, and very little gets right through the powder. But if the white powdered glass is put into water, it forthwith vanishes. The powdered glass and water have much the same refractive index; that is, the light undergoes very little refraction or reflection in passing from one to the other.

"You make the glass invisible by putting it into a liquid of nearly the same refractive index; a transparent thing becomes invisible if it is put in any medium of almost the same refractive index. And if you will consider only a second, you will see also that the powder of glass might be made to vanish in air, if its refractive index could be made the same as that of air; for then there would be no refraction or reflection as the light passed from glass to air."

"Yes, yes," said Kemp. "But a man's not powdered glass!"

"No," said Griffin. "He's more transparent!"

"Nonsense!"

"That from a doctor! How one forgets! Have you already forgotten your physics, in ten years? Just think of all the things that are transparent and seem not to be so. Paper, for instance, is made up of transparent fibres, and it is white and opaque only for the same reason that a powder of glass is white and opaque. Oil white paper, fill up the interstices between the particles with oil so that there is no longer refraction or reflection except at the surfaces, and it becomes as transparent as glass. And not only paper, but cotton fibre, linen fibre, wool fibre, woody fibre, and *bone*, Kemp, *flesh*, Kemp, *hair*, Kemp, *nails* and *nerves*, Kemp, in fact the whole fabric of a man except the red of his blood and the black pigment of hair, are all made up of transparent, colourless tissue. So little suffices to make us visible one to the other. For the most part the fibres of a living creature are no more opaque than water."

"Great Heavens!" cried Kemp. "Of course, of course! I was thinking only last night of the sea larvae and all jelly-fish!"

"*Now* you have me! And all that I knew and had in mind a year after I left London—six years ago. But I kept it to myself. I had to do my work under frightful disadvantages. Oliver, my professor, was a scientific bounder, a journalist by instinct, a thief of ideas—he was always prying! And you know the knavish system of the scientific world. I simply would not publish, and let him share my credit. I went on working; I got nearer and nearer making my formula into an experiment, a reality. I told no living soul, because I meant to flash my work upon the world with crushing effect and become famous at a blow. I took up the question of pigments to fill up certain gaps. And suddenly, not by design but by accident, I made a discovery in physiology."

"Yes?"

"You know the red colouring matter of blood; it can be made white—colourless—and remain with all the functions it has now!"

Kemp gave a cry of incredulous amazement.

The Invisible Man rose and began pacing the little study. "You may well exclaim. I remember that night. It was late at night—in the daytime one was bothered with the gaping, silly students—and I worked then sometimes till dawn. It came suddenly, splendid and complete in my mind. I was alone; the laboratory was still, with the tall lights burning brightly and silently. In all my great moments I have been alone. 'One could make an animal—a tissue—transparent! One could make it invisible! All except the pigments—I could be invisible!' I said, suddenly realising what it meant to be an albino with such knowledge. It was overwhelming. I left the filtering I was doing, and went and stared out of the great window at the stars. 'I could be invisible!' I repeated.

"To do such a thing would be to transcend magic. And I beheld, unclouded by doubt, a magnificent vision of all that invisibility might mean to a man—the mystery, the power, the freedom. Drawbacks I saw none. You have only to think! And I, a shabby, poverty-struck, hemmed-in demonstrator, teaching fools in a provincial college, might suddenly become—this. I ask you, Kemp if *you* ... Anyone, I tell you, would have flung himself upon that research. And I worked three years, and every mountain of difficulty I toiled over showed another from its summit. The infinite details! And the exasperation! A professor, a provincial professor, always prying. 'When are you going to publish this work of yours?' was his everlasting question. And the students, the cramped means! Three years I had of it—

"And after three years of secrecy and exasperation, I found that to complete it was impossible—impossible."

"How?" asked Kemp.

"Money," said the Invisible Man, and went again to stare out of the window.

He turned around abruptly. "I robbed the old man—robbed my father.

"The money was not his, and he shot himself."

CHAPTER XX

AT THE HOUSE IN GREAT PORTLAND STREET

For a moment Kemp sat in silence, staring at the back of the headless figure at the window. Then he started, struck by a thought, rose, took the Invisible Man's arm, and turned him away from the outlook.

"You are tired," he said, "and while I sit, you walk about. Have my chair."

He placed himself between Griffin and the nearest window.

For a space Griffin sat silent, and then he resumed abruptly:

"I had left the Chesilstowe cottage already," he said, "when that happened. It was last December. I had taken a room in London, a large unfurnished room in a big ill-managed lodging-house in a slum near Great Portland Street. The room was soon full of the appliances I had bought with his money; the work was going on steadily, successfully, drawing near an end. I was like a man emerging from a thicket, and suddenly coming on some unmeaning tragedy. I went to bury him. My mind was still on this research, and I did not lift a finger to save his character. I remember the funeral, the cheap hearse, the scant ceremony, the windy frost-bitten hillside, and the old college friend of his who read the service over him—a shabby, black, bent old man with a snivelling cold.

"I remember walking back to the empty house, through the place that had once been a village and was now patched and tinkered by the jerry builders into the ugly likeness of a town. Every way the roads ran out at last into the desecrated fields and ended in rubble heaps and rank wet weeds. I remember myself as a gaunt black figure, going along the slippery, shiny pavement, and the strange sense of detachment I felt from the squalid respectability, the sordid commercialism of the place.

"I did not feel a bit sorry for my father. He seemed to me to be the victim of his own foolish sentimentality. The current cant required my attendance at his funeral, but it was really not my affair.

"But going along the High Street, my old life came back to me for a space, for I met the girl I had known ten years since. Our eyes met.

"Something moved me to turn back and talk to her. She was a very ordinary person.

"It was all like a dream, that visit to the old places. I did not feel then that I was lonely, that I had come out from the world into a desolate place. I appreciated my loss of sympathy, but I put it down to the general inanity of things. Re-entering my room seemed like the recovery of reality. There were the things I knew and loved. There stood the apparatus, the experiments arranged and waiting. And now there was scarcely a difficulty left, beyond the planning of details.

"I will tell you, Kemp, sooner or later, all the complicated processes. We need not go into that now. For the most part, saving certain gaps I chose to remember, they are written in cypher in those books that tramp has hidden. We must hunt him down. We must get those books again. But the essential phase was to place the transparent object whose refractive index was to be lowered between two radiating centres of a sort of ethereal vibration, of which I will tell you more fully later. No, not those Röntgen vibrations—I don't know that these others of mine have been described. Yet they are obvious enough. I needed two little dynamos, and these I worked with a cheap gas engine. My first experiment was with a bit of white wool fabric. It was the strangest thing in the world to see it in the flicker of the flashes soft and white, and then to watch it fade like a wreath of smoke and vanish.

"I could scarcely believe I had done it. I put my hand into the emptiness, and there was the thing as solid as ever. I felt it awkwardly, and threw it on the floor. I had a little trouble finding it again.

"And then came a curious experience. I heard a miaow behind me, and turning, saw a lean white cat, very dirty, on the cistern cover outside the window. A thought came into my head. 'Everything ready for you,' I said, and went to the window, opened it, and called softly. She came in, purring—the poor beast was starving—and I gave her some milk. All my food was in a cupboard in the corner of the room. After that she went smelling round the room, evidently with the idea of making herself at home. The invisible rag upset her a bit; you should have seen her spit at it! But I made her comfortable on the pillow of my truckle-bed. And I gave her butter to get her to wash."

"And you processed her?"

"I processed her. But giving drugs to a cat is no joke, Kemp! And the process failed."

"Failed!"

"In two particulars. These were the claws and the pigment stuff, what is it?—at the back of the eye in a cat. You know?"

"Tapetum."

"Yes, the *tapetum*. It didn't go. After I'd given the stuff to bleach the blood and done certain other things to her, I gave the beast opium, and put her and the pillow she was sleeping on, on the apparatus. And after all the rest had faded and vanished, there remained two little ghosts of her eyes."

"Odd!"

"I can't explain it. She was bandaged and clamped, of course—so I had her safe; but she woke while she was still misty, and miaowed dismally, and someone came knocking. It was an old woman from downstairs, who suspected me of vivisecting—a drink-sodden old creature, with only a white cat to care for in all the world. I whipped out some chloroform, applied it, and answered the door. 'Did I hear a cat?' she asked. 'My cat?' 'Not here,' said I, very politely. She was a little doubtful and tried to peer past me into the room; strange enough to her no doubt—bare walls, uncurtained windows, truckle-bed, with the gas engine vibrating, and the seethe of the radiant points, and that faint ghastly stinging of chloroform in the air. She had to be satisfied at last and went away again."

"How long did it take?" asked Kemp.

"Three or four hours—the cat. The bones and sinews and the fat were the last to go, and the tips of the coloured hairs. And, as I say, the back part of the eye, tough, iridescent stuff it is, wouldn't go at all.

"It was night outside long before the business was over, and nothing was to be seen but the dim eyes and the claws. I stopped the gas engine, felt for and stroked the beast, which was still insensible, and then, being tired, left it sleeping on the invisible pillow and went to bed. I found it hard to sleep. I lay awake thinking weak aimless stuff, going over the experiment over and over again, or dreaming feverishly of things growing misty and vanishing about me, until everything, the ground I stood on, vanished, and so I came to that sickly falling nightmare one gets. About two, the cat began miaowing about the room. I tried to hush it by talking to it, and then I decided to turn it out. I remember the shock I had when striking a light—there were just the round eyes shining green—and nothing round them. I would have given it milk, but I hadn't any. It wouldn't be quiet, it just sat down and miaowed at the door. I tried to catch it, with an idea of putting it out of the window, but it wouldn't be caught, it vanished. Then it began miaowing in different parts of the room. At last I opened the window and made a bustle. I suppose it went out at last. I never saw any more of it.

"Then—Heaven knows why—I fell thinking of my father's funeral again, and the dismal windy hillside, until the day had come. I found sleeping was hopeless, and, locking my door after me, wandered out into the morning streets."

"You don't mean to say there's an invisible cat at large!" said Kemp.

"If it hasn't been killed," said the Invisible Man. "Why not?"

"Why not?" said Kemp. "I didn't mean to interrupt."

"It's very probably been killed," said the Invisible Man. "It was alive four days after, I know, and down a grating in Great Titchfield Street; because I saw a crowd round the place, trying to see whence the miaowing came."

He was silent for the best part of a minute. Then he resumed abruptly:

"I remember that morning before the change very vividly. I must have gone up Great Portland Street. I remember the barracks in Albany Street, and the horse soldiers coming out, and at last I found the summit of Primrose Hill. It was a sunny day in January—one of those sunny, frosty days that came before the snow this year. My weary brain tried to formulate the position, to plot out a plan of action.

"I was surprised to find, now that my prize was within my grasp, how inconclusive its attainment seemed. As a matter of fact I was worked out;

the intense stress of nearly four years' continuous work left me incapable of any strength of feeling. I was apathetic, and I tried in vain to recover the enthusiasm of my first inquiries, the passion of discovery that had enabled me to compass even the downfall of my father's grey hairs. Nothing seemed to matter. I saw pretty clearly this was a transient mood, due to overwork and want of sleep, and that either by drugs or rest it would be possible to recover my energies.

"All I could think clearly was that the thing had to be carried through; the fixed idea still ruled me. And soon, for the money I had was almost exhausted. I looked about me at the hillside, with children playing and girls watching them, and tried to think of all the fantastic advantages an invisible man would have in the world. After a time I crawled home, took some food and a strong dose of strychnine, and went to sleep in my clothes on my unmade bed. Strychnine is a grand tonic, Kemp, to take the flabbiness out of a man."

"It's the devil," said Kemp. "It's the palaeolithic in a bottle."

"I awoke vastly invigorated and rather irritable. You know?"

"I know the stuff."

"And there was someone rapping at the door. It was my landlord with threats and inquiries, an old Polish Jew in a long grey coat and greasy slippers. I had been tormenting a cat in the night, he was sure—the old woman's tongue had been busy. He insisted on knowing all about it. The laws in this country against vivisection were very severe—he might be liable. I denied the cat. Then the vibration of the little gas engine could be felt all over the house, he said. That was true, certainly. He edged round me into the room, peering about over his German-silver spectacles, and a sudden dread came into my mind that he might carry away something of my secret. I tried to keep between him and the concentrating apparatus I had arranged, and that only made him more curious. What was I doing? Why was I always alone and secretive? Was it legal? Was it dangerous? I paid nothing but the usual rent. His had always been a most respectable house—in a disreputable neighbourhood. Suddenly my temper gave way. I told him to get out. He began to protest, to jabber of his right of entry. In a moment I had him by the collar; something ripped, and he went spinning out into his own passage. I slammed and locked the door and sat down quivering.

"He made a fuss outside, which I disregarded, and after a time he went away.

"But this brought matters to a crisis. I did not know what he would do, nor even what he had the power to do. To move to fresh apartments would have meant delay; altogether I had barely twenty pounds left in the world, for the most part in a bank—and I could not afford that. Vanish! It was irresistible. Then there would be an inquiry, the sacking of my room.

"At the thought of the possibility of my work being exposed or interrupted at its very climax, I became very angry and active. I hurried out with my three books of notes, my cheque-book—the tramp has them now—and directed them from the nearest Post Office to a house of call for letters and parcels in Great Portland Street. I tried to go out noiselessly. Coming in, I found my landlord going quietly upstairs; he had heard the door close, I suppose. You would have laughed to see him jump aside on the landing as I came tearing after him. He glared at me as I went by him, and I made the house quiver with the slamming of my door. I heard him come shuffling up to my floor, hesitate, and go down. I set to work upon my preparations forthwith.

"It was all done that evening and night. While I was still sitting under the sickly, drowsy influence of the drugs that decolourise blood, there came a repeated knocking at the door. It ceased, footsteps went away and returned, and the knocking was resumed. There was an attempt to push something under the door—a blue paper. Then in a fit of irritation I rose and went and flung the door wide open. 'Now then?' said I.

"It was my landlord, with a notice of ejectment or something. He held it out to me, saw something odd about my hands, I expect, and lifted his eyes to my face.

"For a moment he gaped. Then he gave a sort of inarticulate cry, dropped candle and writ together, and went blundering down the dark passage to the stairs. I shut the door, locked it, and went to the looking-glass. Then I understood his terror.... My face was white—like white stone.

"But it was all horrible. I had not expected the suffering. A night of racking anguish, sickness and fainting. I set my teeth, though my skin was presently afire, all my body afire; but I lay there like grim death. I understood now how it was the cat had howled until I chloroformed it. Lucky it was I lived alone and untended in my room. There were times when I sobbed and groaned and talked. But I stuck to it.... I became insensible and woke languid in the darkness.

"The pain had passed. I thought I was killing myself and I did not care. I shall never forget that dawn, and the strange horror of seeing that my hands had become as clouded glass, and watching them grow clearer and thinner as the day went by, until at last I could see the sickly disorder of my room through them, though I closed my transparent eyelids. My limbs became glassy, the bones and arteries faded, vanished, and the little white nerves went last. I gritted my teeth and stayed there to the end. At last only the dead tips of the fingernails remained, pallid and white, and the brown stain of some acid upon my fingers.

"I struggled up. At first I was as incapable as a swathed infant—stepping with limbs I could not see. I was weak and very hungry. I went and stared at nothing in my shaving-glass, at nothing save where an attenuated pigment still remained behind the retina of my eyes, fainter than mist. I had to hang on to the table and press my forehead against the glass.

"It was only by a frantic effort of will that I dragged myself back to the apparatus and completed the process.

"I slept during the forenoon, pulling the sheet over my eyes to shut out the light, and about midday I was awakened again by a knocking. My strength had returned. I sat up and listened and heard a whispering. I sprang to my feet and as noiselessly as possible began to detach the connections of my apparatus, and to distribute it about the room, so as to destroy the suggestions of its arrangement. Presently the knocking was renewed and voices called, first my landlord's, and then two others. To gain time I answered them. The invisible rag and pillow came to hand and I opened the window and pitched them out on to the cistern cover. As the window opened, a heavy crash came at the door. Someone had charged it with the idea of smashing the lock. But the stout bolts I had screwed up some days before stopped him. That startled me, made me angry. I began to tremble and do things hurriedly.

"I tossed together some loose paper, straw, packing paper and so forth, in the middle of the room, and turned on the gas. Heavy blows began to rain upon the door. I could not find the matches. I beat my hands on the wall with rage. I turned down the gas again, stepped out of the window on the cistern cover, very softly lowered the sash, and sat down, secure and invisible, but quivering with anger, to watch events. They split a panel, I saw, and in another moment they had broken away the staples of the bolts and stood in the open doorway. It was the landlord and his two step-sons, sturdy young men of three or four and twenty. Behind them fluttered the old hag of a woman from downstairs.

"You may imagine their astonishment to find the room empty. One of the younger men rushed to the window at once, flung it up and stared out. His staring eyes and thick-lipped bearded face came a foot from my face. I was half minded to hit his silly countenance, but I arrested my doubled fist. He stared right through me. So did the others as they joined him. The old man went and peered under the bed, and then they all made a rush for the cupboard. They had to argue about it at length in Yiddish and Cockney English. They concluded I had not answered them, that their imagination had deceived them. A feeling of extraordinary elation took the place of my anger as I sat outside the window and watched these four people—for the old lady came in, glancing suspiciously about her like a cat, trying to understand the riddle of my behaviour.

"The old man, so far as I could understand his *patois*, agreed with the old lady that I was a vivisectionist. The sons protested in garbled English that I was an electrician, and appealed to the dynamos and radiators. They were all nervous about my arrival, although I found subsequently that they had bolted the front door. The old lady peered into the cupboard and under the bed, and one of the young men pushed up the register and stared up the chimney. One of my fellow lodgers, a coster-monger who shared the opposite room with a butcher, appeared on the landing, and he was called in and told incoherent things.

"It occurred to me that the radiators, if they fell into the hands of some acute well-educated person, would give me away too much, and watching my opportunity, I came into the room and tilted one of the little dynamos off its fellow on which it was standing, and smashed both apparatus. Then, while they were trying to explain the smash, I dodged out of the room and went softly downstairs.

"I went into one of the sitting-rooms and waited until they came down, still speculating and argumentative, all a little disappointed at finding no 'horrors,' and all a little puzzled how they stood legally towards me. Then I slipped up again with a box of matches, fired my heap of paper and rubbish, put the chairs and bedding thereby, led the gas to the affair, by means of an india-rubber tube, and waving a farewell to the room left it for the last time."

"You fired the house!" exclaimed Kemp.

"Fired the house. It was the only way to cover my trail—and no doubt it was insured. I slipped the bolts of the front door quietly and went out into the street. I was invisible, and I was only just beginning to realise the extraordinary advantage my invisibility gave me. My head was already teeming with plans of all the wild and wonderful things I had now impunity to do."

CHAPTER XXI

IN OXFORD STREET

"In going downstairs the first time I found an unexpected difficulty because I could not see my feet; indeed I stumbled twice, and there was an unaccustomed clumsiness in gripping the bolt. By not looking down, however, I managed to walk on the level passably well.

"My mood, I say, was one of exaltation. I felt as a seeing man might do, with padded feet and noiseless clothes, in a city of the blind. I experienced a wild impulse to jest, to startle people, to clap men on the back, fling people's hats astray, and generally revel in my extraordinary advantage.

"But hardly had I emerged upon Great Portland Street, however (my lodging was close to the big draper's shop there), when I heard a clashing concussion and was hit violently behind, and turning saw a man carrying a basket of soda-water syphons, and looking in amazement at his burden. Although the blow had really hurt me, I found something so irresistible in his astonishment that I laughed aloud. 'The devil's in the basket,' I said, and suddenly twisted it out of his hand. He let go incontinently, and I swung the whole weight into the air.

"But a fool of a cabman, standing outside a public house, made a sudden rush for this, and his extending fingers took me with excruciating violence under the ear. I let the whole down with a smash on the cabman, and then, with shouts and the clatter of feet about me, people coming out of shops, vehicles pulling up, I realised what I had done for myself, and cursing my folly, backed against a shop window and prepared to dodge out of the confusion. In a moment I should be wedged into a crowd and inevitably discovered. I pushed by a butcher boy, who luckily did not turn to see the nothingness that shoved him aside, and dodged behind the cabman's four-wheeler. I do not know how they settled the business. I hurried straight across the road, which was happily clear, and hardly heeding which way I went, in the fright of detection the incident had given me, plunged into the afternoon throng of Oxford Street.

"I tried to get into the stream of people, but they were too thick for me, and in a moment my heels were being trodden upon. I took to the gutter, the roughness of which I found painful to my feet, and forthwith the shaft of a crawling hansom dug me forcibly under the shoulder blade, reminding me that I was already bruised severely. I staggered out of the way of the cab, avoided a perambulator by a convulsive movement, and found myself behind the hansom. A happy thought saved me, and as this drove slowly along I followed in its immediate wake, trembling and astonished at the turn of my adventure. And not only trembling, but shivering. It was a bright day in January and I was stark naked and the thin slime of mud that covered the road was freezing. Foolish as it seems to me now, I had not reckoned that, transparent or not, I was still amenable to the weather and all its consequences.

"Then suddenly a bright idea came into my head. I ran round and got into the cab. And so, shivering, scared, and sniffing with the first intimations of a cold, and with the bruises in the small of my back growing upon my attention, I drove slowly along Oxford Street and past Tottenham Court Road. My mood was as different from that in which I had sallied forth ten minutes ago as it is possible to imagine. This invisibility indeed! The one thought that possessed me was—how was I to get out of the scrape I was in.

"We crawled past Mudie's, and there a tall woman with five or six yellow-labelled books hailed my cab, and I sprang out just in time to escape her, shaving a railway van narrowly in my flight. I made off up the roadway to Bloomsbury Square, intending to strike north past the Museum and so get into the quiet district. I was now cruelly chilled, and the strangeness of my situation so unnerved me that I whimpered as I ran. At the northward corner of the Square a little white dog ran out of the Pharmaceutical Society's offices, and incontinently made for me, nose down.

"I had never realised it before, but the nose is to the mind of a dog what the eye is to the mind of a seeing man. Dogs perceive the scent of a man moving as men perceive his vision. This brute began barking and leaping, showing, as it seemed to me, only too plainly that he was aware of me. I crossed Great Russell Street, glancing over my shoulder as I did so, and went some way along Montague Street before I realised what I was running towards.

"Then I became aware of a blare of music, and looking along the street saw a number of people advancing out of Russell Square, red shirts, and the banner of the Salvation Army to the fore. Such a crowd, chanting in the roadway and scoffing on the pavement, I could not hope to penetrate, and dreading to go back and farther from home again, and deciding on the spur of the moment, I ran up the white steps of a house facing the museum railings, and stood there until the crowd should have passed. Happily the dog stopped at the noise of the band too, hesitated, and turned tail, running back to Bloomsbury Square again.

"On came the band, bawling with unconscious irony some hymn about 'When shall we see His face?' and it seemed an interminable time to me before the tide of the crowd washed along the pavement by me. Thud, thud, thud, came the drum with a vibrating resonance, and for the moment I did not notice two urchins stopping at the railings by me. 'See 'em,' said one. 'See what?' said the other. 'Why—them footmarks—bare. Like what you makes in mud.'

"I looked down and saw the youngsters had stopped and were gaping at the muddy footmarks I had left behind me up the newly whitened steps. The passing people elbowed and jostled them, but their confounded intelligence was arrested. 'Thud, thud, thud, when, thud, shall we see, thud, his face, thud, thud.' 'There's a barefoot man gone up them steps, or I don't know nothing,' said one. 'And he ain't never come down again. And his foot was a-bleeding.'

"The thick of the crowd had already passed. 'Looky there, Ted,' quoth the younger of the detectives, with the sharpness of surprise in his voice, and pointed straight to my feet. I looked down and saw at once the dim suggestion of their outline sketched in splashes of mud. For a moment I was paralysed.

"'Why, that's rum,' said the elder. 'Dashed rum! It's just like the ghost of a foot, ain't it?' He hesitated and advanced with outstretched hand. A man pulled up short to see what he was catching, and then a girl. In another moment he would have touched me. Then I saw what to do. I made a step, the boy started back with an exclamation, and with a rapid movement I swung myself over into the portico of the next house. But the smaller boy was sharp-eyed enough to follow the movement, and before I was well down the steps and upon the pavement, he had recovered from his momentary astonishment and was shouting out that the feet had gone over the wall.

"They rushed round and saw my new footmarks flash into being on the lower step and upon the pavement. 'What's up?' asked someone. 'Feet! Look! Feet running!'

"Everybody in the road, except my three pursuers, was pouring along after the Salvation Army, and this blow not only impeded me but them. There was an eddy of surprise and interrogation. At the cost of bowling over one young fellow I got through, and in another moment I was rushing headlong round the circuit of Russell Square, with six or seven astonished people following my footmarks. There was no time for explanation, or else the whole host would have been after me.

"Twice I doubled round corners, thrice I crossed the road and came back upon my tracks, and then, as my feet grew hot and dry, the damp impressions began to fade. At last I had a breathing space and rubbed my feet clean with my hands, and so got away altogether. The last I saw of the chase was a little group of a dozen people perhaps, studying with infinite perplexity a slowly drying footprint that had resulted from a puddle in Tavistock Square, a footprint as isolated and incomprehensible to them as Crusoe's solitary discovery.

"This running warmed me to a certain extent, and I went on with a better courage through the maze of less frequented roads that runs hereabouts. My back had now become very stiff and sore, my tonsils were painful from the cabman's fingers, and the skin of my neck had been scratched by his nails; my feet hurt exceedingly and I was lame from a little cut on one foot. I saw in time a blind man approaching me, and fled limping, for I feared his subtle intuitions. Once or twice accidental collisions occurred and I left people amazed, with unaccountable curses ringing in their ears. Then came something silent and quiet against my face, and across the Square fell a thin veil of slowly falling flakes of snow. I had caught a cold, and do as I would I could not avoid an occasional sneeze. And every dog that came in sight, with its pointing nose and curious sniffing, was a terror to me.

"Then came men and boys running, first one and then others, and shouting as they ran. It was a fire. They ran in the direction of my lodging, and looking back down a street I saw a mass of black smoke streaming up above the roofs and telephone wires. It was my lodging burning; my clothes, my apparatus, all my resources indeed, except my cheque-book and the three volumes of memoranda that awaited me in Great Portland Street, were there. Burning! I had burnt my boats—if ever a man did! The place was blazing."

The Invisible Man paused and thought. Kemp glanced nervously out of the window. "Yes?" he said. "Go on."

CHAPTER XXII

IN THE EMPORIUM

"So last January, with the beginning of a snowstorm in the air about me—and if it settled on me it would betray me!—weary, cold, painful, inexpressibly wretched, and still but half convinced of my invisible quality, I began this new life to which I am committed. I had no refuge, no appliances, no human being in the world in whom I could confide. To have told my secret would have given me away—made a mere show and rarity of me. Nevertheless, I was half-minded to accost some passer-by and throw myself upon his mercy. But I knew too clearly the terror and brutal cruelty my advances would evoke. I made no plans in the street. My sole object was to get shelter from the snow, to get myself covered and warm; then I might hope to plan. But even to me, an Invisible Man, the rows of London houses stood latched, barred, and bolted impregnably.

"Only one thing could I see clearly before me—the cold exposure and misery of the snowstorm and the night.

"And then I had a brilliant idea. I turned down one of the roads leading from Gower Street to Tottenham Court Road, and found myself outside Omniums, the big establishment where everything is to be bought—you know the place: meat, grocery, linen, furniture, clothing, oil paintings even—a huge meandering collection of shops rather than a shop. I had thought I should find the doors open, but they were closed, and as I stood in the wide entrance a carriage stopped outside, and a man in uniform—

you know the kind of personage with 'Omnium' on his cap—flung open the door. I contrived to enter, and walking down the shop—it was a department where they were selling ribbons and gloves and stockings and that kind of thing—came to a more spacious region devoted to picnic baskets and wicker furniture.

"I did not feel safe there, however; people were going to and fro, and I prowled restlessly about until I came upon a huge section in an upper floor containing multitudes of bedsteads, and over these I clambered, and found a resting-place at last among a huge pile of folded flock mattresses. The place was already lit up and agreeably warm, and I decided to remain where I was, keeping a cautious eye on the two or three sets of shopmen and customers who were meandering through the place, until closing time came. Then I should be able, I thought, to rob the place for food and clothing, and disguised, prowl through it and examine its resources, perhaps sleep on some of the bedding. That seemed an acceptable plan. My idea was to procure clothing to make myself a muffled but acceptable figure, to get money, and then to recover my books and parcels where they awaited me, take a lodging somewhere and elaborate plans for the complete realisation of the advantages my invisibility gave me (as I still imagined) over my fellow-men.

"Closing time arrived quickly enough. It could not have been more than an hour after I took up my position on the mattresses before I noticed the blinds of the windows being drawn, and customers being marched doorward. And then a number of brisk young men began with remarkable alacrity to tidy up the goods that remained disturbed. I left my lair as the crowds diminished, and prowled cautiously out into the less desolate parts of the shop. I was really surprised to observe how rapidly the young men and women whipped away the goods displayed for sale during the day. All the boxes of goods, the hanging fabrics, the festoons of lace, the boxes of sweets in the grocery section, the displays of this and that, were being whipped down, folded up, slapped into tidy receptacles, and everything that could not be taken down and put away had sheets of some coarse stuff like sacking flung over them. Finally all the chairs were turned up on to the counters, leaving the floor clear. Directly each of these young people had done, he or she made promptly for the door with such an expression of animation as I have rarely observed in a shop assistant before. Then came a lot of youngsters scattering sawdust and carrying pails and brooms. I had to dodge to get out of the way, and as it was, my ankle got stung with the sawdust. For some time, wandering through the swathed and darkened departments, I could hear the brooms at work. And at last a good hour or more after the shop had been closed, came a noise of locking doors. Silence came upon the place, and I found myself wandering through the vast and intricate shops, galleries, show-rooms of the place, alone. It was very still; in one place I remember passing near one of the Tottenham Court Road entrances and listening to the tapping of boot-heels of the passers-by.

"My first visit was to the place where I had seen stockings and gloves for sale. It was dark, and I had the devil of a hunt after matches, which I found at last in the drawer of the little cash desk. Then I had to get a candle. I had to tear down wrappings and ransack a number of boxes and drawers, but at last I managed to turn out what I sought; the box label called them lambswool pants, and lambswool vests. Then socks, a thick comforter, and then I went to the clothing place and got trousers, a lounge jacket, an over-coat and a slouch hat—a clerical sort of hat with the brim turned down. I began to feel a human being again, and my next thought was food.

"Upstairs was a refreshment department, and there I got cold meat. There was coffee still in the urn, and I lit the gas and warmed it up again, and altogether I did not do badly. Afterwards, prowling through the place in search of blankets—I had to put up at last with a heap of down quilts—I came upon a grocery section with a lot of chocolate and candied fruits, more than was good for me indeed—and some white burgundy. And near that was a toy department, and I had a brilliant idea. I found some arti-ficial noses—dummy noses, you know, and I thought of dark spectacles. But Omniums had no optical department. My nose had been a difficulty indeed—I had thought of paint. But the discovery set my mind running on wigs and masks and the like. Finally I went to sleep in a heap of down quilts, very warm and comfortable.

"My last thoughts before sleeping were the most agreeable I had had since the change. I was in a state of physical serenity, and that was reflected in my mind. I thought that I should be able to slip out unobserved in the morning with my clothes upon me, muffling my face with a white wrapper

I had taken, purchase, with the money I had taken, spectacles and so forth, and so complete my disguise. I lapsed into disorderly dreams of all the fantastic things that had happened during the last few days. I saw the ugly little Jew of a landlord vociferating in his rooms; I saw his two sons marvelling, and the wrinkled old woman's gnarled face as she asked for her cat. I experienced again the strange sensation of seeing the cloth disappear, and so I came round to the windy hillside and the sniffing old clergyman mumbling 'Earth to earth, ashes to ashes, dust to dust,' at my father's open grave.

"'You also,' said a voice, and suddenly I was being forced towards the grave. I struggled, shouted, appealed to the mourners, but they continued stonily following the service; the old clergyman, too, never faltered droning and sniffing through the ritual. I realised I was invisible and inaudible, that overwhelming forces had their grip on me. I struggled in vain, I was forced over the brink, the coffin rang hollow as I fell upon it, and the gravel came flying after me in spadefuls. Nobody heeded me, nobody was aware of me. I made convulsive struggles and awoke.

"The pale London dawn had come, the place was full of a chilly grey light that filtered round the edges of the window blinds. I sat up, and for a time I could not think where this ample apartment, with its counters, its piles of rolled stuff, its heap of quilts and cushions, its iron pillars, might be. Then, as recollection came back to me, I heard voices in conversation.

"Then far down the place, in the brighter light of some department which had already raised its blinds, I saw two men approaching. I scrambled to my feet, looking about me for some way of escape, and even as I did so the sound of my movement made them aware of me. I suppose they saw merely a figure moving quietly and quickly away. 'Who's that?' cried one, and 'Stop there!' shouted the other. I dashed around a corner and came full tilt—a faceless figure, mind you!—on a lanky lad of fifteen. He yelled and I bowled him over, rushed past him, turned another corner, and by a happy inspiration threw myself behind a counter. In another moment feet went running past and I heard voices shouting, 'All hands to the doors!' asking what was 'up,' and giving one another advice how to catch me.

"Lying on the ground, I felt scared out of my wits. But—odd as it may seem—it did not occur to me at the moment to take off my clothes as I should have done. I had made up my mind, I suppose, to get away in them, and that ruled me. And then down the vista of the counters came a bawling of 'Here he is!'

"I sprang to my feet, whipped a chair off the counter, and sent it whirling at the fool who had shouted, turned, came into another round a corner, sent him spinning, and rushed up the stairs. He kept his footing, gave a view hallo, and came up the staircase hot after me. Up the staircase were piled a multitude of those bright-coloured pot things—what are they?"

"Art pots," suggested Kemp.

"That's it! Art pots. Well, I turned at the top step and swung round, plucked one out of a pile and smashed it on his silly head as he came at me. The whole pile of pots went headlong, and I heard shouting and footsteps running from all parts. I made a mad rush for the refreshment place, and there was a man in white like a man cook, who took up the chase. I made one last desperate turn and found myself among lamps and ironmongery. I went behind the counter of this, and waited for my cook, and as he bolted in at the head of the chase, I doubled him up with a lamp. Down he went, and I crouched down behind the counter and began whipping off my clothes as fast as I could. Coat, jacket, trousers, shoes were all right, but a lambswool vest fits a man like a skin. I heard more men coming, my cook was lying quiet on the other side of the counter, stunned or scared speechless, and I had to make another dash for it, like a rabbit hunted out of a wood-pile.

"'This way, policeman!' I heard someone shouting. I found myself in my bedstead storeroom again, and at the end of a wilderness of wardrobes. I rushed among them, went flat, got rid of my vest after infinite wriggling, and stood a free man again, panting and scared, as the policeman and three of the shopmen came round the corner. They made a rush for the vest and pants, and collared the trousers. 'He's dropping his plunder,' said one of the young men. 'He *must* be somewhere here.'

"But they did not find me all the same.

"I stood watching them hunt for me for a time, and cursing my ill-luck in losing the clothes. Then I went into the refreshment-room, drank a little milk I found there, and sat down by the fire to consider my position.

"In a little while two assistants came in and began to talk over the business very excitedly and like the fools they were. I heard a magnified account of my depredations, and other speculations as to my whereabouts.

Then I fell to scheming again. The insurmountable difficulty of the place, especially now it was alarmed, was to get any plunder out of it. I went down into the warehouse to see if there was any chance of packing and addressing a parcel, but I could not understand the system of checking. About eleven o'clock, the snow having thawed as it fell, and the day being finer and a little warmer than the previous one, I decided that the Emporium was hopeless, and went out again, exasperated at my want of success, with only the vaguest plans of action in my mind."

CHAPTER XXIII

IN DRURY LANE

"But you begin now to realise," said the Invisible Man, "the full disadvantage of my condition. I had no shelter—no covering—to get clothing was to forego all my advantage, to make myself a strange and terrible thing. I was fasting; for to eat, to fill myself with unassimilated matter, would be to become grotesquely visible again."

"I never thought of that," said Kemp.

"Nor had I. And the snow had warned me of other dangers. I could not go abroad in snow—it would settle on me and expose me. Rain, too, would make me a watery outline, a glistening surface of a man—a bubble. And fog—I should be like a fainter bubble in a fog, a surface, a greasy glimmer of humanity. Moreover, as I went abroad—in the London air—I gathered dirt about my ankles, floating smuts and dust upon my skin. I did not know how long it would be before I should become visible from that cause also. But I saw clearly it could not be for long.

"Not in London at any rate.

"I went into the slums towards Great Portland Street, and found myself at the end of the street in which I had lodged. I did not go that way, because of the crowd halfway down it opposite to the still smoking ruins of the house I had fired. My most immediate problem was to get clothing. What to do with my face puzzled me. Then I saw in one of those little miscellaneous shops—news, sweets, toys, stationery, belated Christmas tomfoolery, and so forth—an array of masks and noses. I realised that problem was solved. In a flash I saw my course. I turned about, no longer aimless, and went—circuitously in order to avoid the busy ways, towards the back streets north of the Strand; for I remembered, though not very distinctly where, that some theatrical costumiers had shops in that district.

"The day was cold, with a nipping wind down the northward running streets. I walked fast to avoid being overtaken. Every crossing was a danger, every passenger a thing to watch alertly. One man as I was about to pass him at the top of Bedford Street, turned upon me abruptly and came into me, sending me into the road and almost under the wheel of a passing hansom. The verdict of the cab-rank was that he had had some sort of stroke. I was so unnerved by this encounter that I went into Covent Garden Market and sat down for some time in a quiet corner by a stall of violets, panting and trembling. I found I had caught a fresh cold, and had to turn out after a time lest my sneezes should attract attention.

"At last I reached the object of my quest, a dirty, fly-blown little shop in a by-way near Drury Lane, with a window full of tinsel robes, sham jewels, wigs, slippers, dominoes and theatrical photographs. The shop was old-fashioned and low and dark, and the house rose above it for four storeys, dark and dismal. I peered through the window and, seeing no one within, entered. The opening of the door set a clanking bell ringing. I left it open, and walked round a bare costume stand, into a corner behind a cheval glass. For a minute or so no one came. Then I heard heavy feet striding across a room, and a man appeared down the shop.

"My plans were now perfectly definite. I proposed to make my way into the house, secrete myself upstairs, watch my opportunity, and when everything was quiet, rummage out a wig, mask, spectacles, and costume, and go into the world, perhaps a grotesque but still a credible figure. And incidentally of course I could rob the house of any available money.

"The man who had just entered the shop was a short, slight, hunched, beetle-browed man, with long arms and very short bandy legs. Apparently I had interrupted a meal. He stared about the shop with an expression of expectation. This gave way to surprise, and then to anger, as he saw the shop empty. 'Damn the boys!' he said. He went to stare up and down the street. He came in again in a minute, kicked the door to with his foot spitefully, and went muttering back to the house door.

"I came forward to follow him, and at the noise of my movement he stopped dead. I did so too, startled by his quickness of ear. He slammed the house door in my face.

"I stood hesitating. Suddenly I heard his quick footsteps returning, and the door reopened. He stood looking about the shop like one who was still not satisfied. Then, murmuring to himself, he examined the back of the counter and peered behind some fixtures. Then he stood doubtful. He had left the house door open and I slipped into the inner room.

"It was a queer little room, poorly furnished and with a number of big masks in the corner. On the table was his belated breakfast, and it was a confoundedly exasperating thing for me, Kemp, to have to sniff his coffee and stand watching while he came in and resumed his meal. And his table manners were irritating. Three doors opened into the little room, one going upstairs and one down, but they were all shut. I could not get out of the room while he was there; I could scarcely move because of his alertness, and there was a draught down my back. Twice I strangled a sneeze just in time.

"The spectacular quality of my sensations was curious and novel, but for all that I was heartily tired and angry long before he had done his eating. But at last he made an end and putting his beggarly crockery on the black tin tray upon which he had had his teapot, and gathering all the crumbs up on the mustard stained cloth, he took the whole lot of things after him. His burden prevented his shutting the door behind him—as he would have done; I never saw such a man for shutting doors—and I followed him into a very dirty underground kitchen and scullery. I had the pleasure of seeing him begin to wash up, and then, finding no good in keeping down there, and the brick floor being cold on my feet, I returned upstairs and sat in his chair by the fire. It was burning low, and scarcely thinking, I put on a little coal. The noise of this brought him up at once, and he stood aglare. He peered about the room and was within an ace of touching me. Even after that examination, he scarcely seemed satisfied. He stopped in the doorway and took a final inspection before he went down.

"I waited in the little parlour for an age, and at last he came up and opened the upstairs door. I just managed to get by him.

"On the staircase he stopped suddenly, so that I very nearly blundered into him. He stood looking back right into my face and listening. 'I could have sworn,' he said. His long hairy hand pulled at his lower lip. His eye went up and down the staircase. Then he grunted and went on up again.

"His hand was on the handle of a door, and then he stopped again with the same puzzled anger on his face. He was becoming aware of the faint sounds of my movements about him. The man must have had diabolically acute hearing. He suddenly flashed into rage. 'If there's anyone in this house—' he cried with an oath, and left the threat unfinished. He put his hand in his pocket, failed to find what he wanted, and rushing past me went blundering noisily and pugnaciously downstairs. But I did not follow him. I sat on the head of the staircase until his return.

"Presently he came up again, still muttering. He opened the door of the room, and before I could enter, slammed it in my face.

"I resolved to explore the house, and spent some time in doing so as noiselessly as possible. The house was very old and tumble-down, damp so that the paper in the attics was peeling from the walls, and rat infested. Some of the door handles were stiff and I was afraid to turn them. Several rooms I did inspect were unfurnished, and others were littered with theatrical lumber, bought second-hand, I judged, from its appearance. In one room next to his I found a lot of old clothes. I began routing among these, and in my eagerness forgot again the evident sharpness of his ears. I heard a stealthy footstep and, looking up just in time, saw him peering in at the tumbled heap and holding an old-fashioned revolver in his hand. I stood perfectly still while he stared about open-mouthed and suspicious. 'It must have been her,' he said slowly. 'Damn her!'

"He shut the door quietly, and immediately I heard the key turn in the lock. Then his footsteps retreated. I realised abruptly that I was locked in. For a minute I did not know what to do. I walked from door to window and back, and stood perplexed. A gust of anger came upon me. But I decided to inspect the clothes before I did anything further, and my first attempt brought down a pile from an upper shelf. This brought him back, more sinister than ever. That time he actually touched me, jumped back with amazement and stood astonished in the middle of the room.

"Presently he calmed a little. 'Rats,' he said in an undertone, fingers on lips. He was evidently a little scared. I edged quietly out of the room, but a plank creaked. Then the infernal little brute started going all over the house, revolver in hand and locking door after door and pocketing the keys. When I realised what he was up to I had a fit of rage—I could hardly control myself sufficiently to watch my opportunity. By this time I knew he was alone in the house, and so I made no more ado, but knocked him on the head."

"Knocked him on the head?" exclaimed Kemp.

"Yes—stunned him—as he was going downstairs. Hit him from behind with a stool that stood on the landing. He went downstairs like a bag of old boots."

"But—I say! The common conventions of humanity—"

"Are all very well for common people. But the point was, Kemp, that I had to get out of that house in a disguise without his seeing me. I couldn't think of any other way of doing it. And then I gagged him with a Louis Quatorze vest and tied him up in a sheet."

"Tied him up in a sheet!"

"Made a sort of bag of it. It was rather a good idea to keep the idiot scared and quiet, and a devilish hard thing to get out of—head away from the string. My dear Kemp, it's no good your sitting glaring as though I was a murderer. It had to be done. He had his revolver. If once he saw me he would be able to describe me—"

"But still," said Kemp, "in England—today. And the man was in his own house, and you were—well, robbing."

"Robbing! Confound it! You'll call me a thief next! Surely, Kemp, you're not fool enough to dance on the old strings. Can't you see my position?"

"And his too," said Kemp.

The Invisible Man stood up sharply. "What do you mean to say?"

Kemp's face grew a trifle hard. He was about to speak and checked himself. "I suppose, after all," he said with a sudden change of manner, "the thing had to be done. You were in a fix. But still—"

"Of course I was in a fix—an infernal fix. And he made me wild too—hunting me about the house, fooling about with his revolver, locking and unlocking doors. He was simply exasperating. You don't blame me, do you? You don't blame me?"

"I never blame anyone," said Kemp. "It's quite out of fashion. What did you do next?"

"I was hungry. Downstairs I found a loaf and some rank cheese—more than sufficient to satisfy my hunger. I took some brandy and water, and then went up past my impromptu bag—he was lying quite still—to the room containing the old clothes. This looked out upon the street, two lace curtains brown with dirt guarding the window. I went and peered out through their interstices. Outside the day was bright—by contrast with the brown shadows of the dismal house in which I found myself, dazzlingly bright. A brisk traffic was going by, fruit carts, a hansom, a four-wheeler with a pile of boxes, a fishmonger's cart. I turned with spots of colour swimming before my eyes to the shadowy fixtures behind me. My excitement was giving place to a clear apprehension of my position again. The room was full of a faint scent of benzoline, used, I suppose, in cleaning the garments.

"I began a systematic search of the place. I should judge the hunchback had been alone in the house for some time. He was a curious person. Everything that could possibly be of service to me I collected in the clothes storeroom, and then I made a deliberate selection. I found a handbag I thought a suitable possession, and some powder, rouge, and sticking-plaster.

"I had thought of painting and powdering my face and all that there was to show of me, in order to render myself visible, but the disadvantage of this lay in the fact that I should require turpentine and other appliances and a considerable amount of time before I could vanish again. Finally I chose a mask of the better type, slightly grotesque but not more so than many human beings, dark glasses, greyish whiskers, and a wig. I could find no underclothing, but that I could buy subsequently, and for the time I swathed myself in calico dominoes and some white cashmere scarfs. I could find no socks, but the hunchback's boots were rather a loose fit and sufficed. In a desk in the shop were three sovereigns and about thirty shillings' worth of silver, and in a locked cupboard I burst in the inner room were eight pounds in gold. I could go forth into the world again, equipped.

"Then came a curious hesitation. Was my appearance really credible? I tried myself with a little bedroom looking-glass, inspecting myself from every point of view to discover any forgotten chink, but it all seemed sound. I was grotesque to the theatrical pitch, a stage miser, but I was certainly not a physical impossibility. Gathering confidence, I took my looking-glass down into the shop, pulled down the shop blinds, and surveyed myself from every point of view with the help of the cheval glass in the corner.

"I spent some minutes screwing up my courage and then unlocked the shop door and marched out into the street, leaving the little man to get out of his sheet again when he liked. In five minutes a dozen turnings intervened between me and the costumier's shop. No one appeared to notice me very pointedly. My last difficulty seemed overcome."

He stopped again.

"And you troubled no more about the hunchback?" said Kemp.

"No," said the Invisible Man. "Nor have I heard what became of him. I suppose he untied himself or kicked himself out. The knots were pretty tight."

He became silent and went to the window and stared out.

"What happened when you went out into the Strand?"

"Oh!—disillusionment again. I thought my troubles were over. Practically I thought I had impunity to do whatever I chose, everything—save to give away my secret. So I thought. Whatever I did, whatever the consequences might be, was nothing to me. I had merely to fling aside my garments and vanish. No person could hold me. I could take my money where I found it. I decided to treat myself to a sumptuous feast, and then put up at a good hotel, and accumulate a new outfit of property. I felt amazingly confident; it's not particularly pleasant recalling that I was an ass. I went into a place and was already ordering lunch, when it occurred to me that I could not eat unless I exposed my invisible face. I finished ordering the lunch, told the man I should be back in ten minutes, and went out exasperated. I don't know if you have ever been disappointed in your appetite."

"Not quite so badly," said Kemp, "but I can imagine it."

"I could have smashed the silly devils. At last, faint with the desire for tasteful food, I went into another place and demanded a private room. 'I am disfigured,' I said. 'Badly.' They looked at me curiously, but of course it was not their affair—and so at last I got my lunch. It was not particularly well served, but it sufficed; and when I had had it, I sat over a cigar, trying to plan my line of action. And outside a snowstorm was beginning.

"The more I thought it over, Kemp, the more I realised what a helpless absurdity an Invisible Man was—in a cold and dirty climate and a crowded civilised city. Before I made this mad experiment I had dreamt of a thousand advantages. That afternoon it seemed all disappointment. I went over the heads of the things a man reckons desirable. No doubt invisibility made it possible to get them, but it made it impossible to enjoy them when they are got. Ambition—what is the good of pride of place when you cannot appear there? What is the good of the love of woman when her name must needs be Delilah? I have no taste for politics, for the blackguardisms of fame, for philanthropy, for sport. What was I to do? And for this I had become a wrapped-up mystery, a swathed and bandaged caricature of a man!"

He paused, and his attitude suggested a roving glance at the window.

"But how did you get to Iping?" said Kemp, anxious to keep his guest busy talking.

"I went there to work. I had one hope. It was a half idea! I have it still. It is a full blown idea now. A way of getting back! Of restoring what I have done. When I choose. When I have done all I mean to do invisibly. And that is what I chiefly want to talk to you about now."

"You went straight to Iping?"

"Yes. I had simply to get my three volumes of memoranda and my cheque-book, my luggage and underclothing, order a quantity of chemicals to work out this idea of mine—I will show you the calculations as soon as I get my books—and then I started. Jove! I remember the snowstorm now, and the accursed bother it was to keep the snow from damping my pasteboard nose."

"At the end," said Kemp, "the day before yesterday, when they found you out, you rather—to judge by the papers—"

"I did. Rather. Did I kill that fool of a constable?"

"No," said Kemp. "He's expected to recover."

"That's his luck, then. I clean lost my temper, the fools! Why couldn't they leave me alone? And that grocer lout?"

"There are no deaths expected," said Kemp.

"I don't know about that tramp of mine," said the Invisible Man, with an unpleasant laugh.

"By Heaven, Kemp, you don't know what rage *is!* ... To have worked for years, to have planned and plotted, and then to get some fumbling purblind idiot messing across your course! ... Every conceivable sort of silly creature that has ever been created has been sent to cross me.

"If I have much more of it, I shall go wild—I shall start mowing 'em.

"As it is, they've made things a thousand times more difficult."

"No doubt it's exasperating," said Kemp, drily.

CHAPTER XXIV

THE PLAN THAT FAILED

"But now," said Kemp, with a side glance out of the window, "what are we to do?"

He moved nearer his guest as he spoke in such a manner as to prevent the possibility of a sudden glimpse of the three men who were advancing up the hill road—with an intolerable slowness, as it seemed to Kemp.

"What were you planning to do when you were heading for Port Burdock? *Had* you any plan?"

"I was going to clear out of the country. But I have altered that plan rather since seeing you. I thought it would be wise, now the weather is hot and invisibility possible, to make for the South. Especially as my secret was known, and everyone would be on the lookout for a masked and muffled man. You have a line of steamers from here to France. My idea was to get aboard one and run the risks of the passage. Thence I could go by train into Spain, or else get to Algiers. It would not be difficult. There a man might always be invisible—and yet live. And do things. I was using that tramp as a money box and luggage carrier, until I decided how to get my books and things sent over to meet me."

"That's clear."

"And then the filthy brute must needs try and rob me! He *has* hidden my books, Kemp. Hidden my books! If I can lay my hands on him!"

"Best plan to get the books out of him first."

"But where is he? Do you know?"

"He's in the town police station, locked up, by his own request, in the strongest cell in the place."

"Cur!" said the Invisible Man.

"But that hangs up your plans a little."

"We must get those books; those books are vital."

"Certainly," said Kemp, a little nervously, wondering if he heard footsteps outside. "Certainly we must get those books. But that won't be difficult, if he doesn't know they're for you."

"No," said the Invisible Man, and thought.

Kemp tried to think of something to keep the talk going, but the Invisible Man resumed of his own accord.

"Blundering into your house, Kemp," he said, "changes all my plans. For you are a man that can understand. In spite of all that has happened, in spite of this publicity, of the loss of my books, of what I have suffered, there still remain great possibilities, huge possibilities—"

"You have told no one I am here?" he asked abruptly.

Kemp hesitated. "That was implied," he said.

"No one?" insisted Griffin.

"Not a soul."

"Ah! Now—" The Invisible Man stood up, and sticking his arms akimbo began to pace the study.

"I made a mistake, Kemp, a huge mistake, in carrying this thing through alone. I have wasted strength, time, opportunities. Alone—it is wonderful how little a man can do alone! To rob a little, to hurt a little, and there is the end.

"What I want, Kemp, is a goal-keeper, a helper, and a hiding-place, an arrangement whereby I can sleep and eat and rest in peace, and unsuspected. I must have a confederate. With a confederate, with food and rest—a thousand things are possible.

"Hitherto I have gone on vague lines. We have to consider all that invisibility means, all that it does not mean. It means little advantage for eavesdropping and so forth—one makes sounds. It's of little help—a little help perhaps—in housebreaking and so forth. Once you've caught me you could easily imprison me. But on the other hand I am hard to catch. This invisibility, in fact, is only good in two cases: It's useful in getting away, it's useful in approaching. It's particularly useful, therefore, in killing. I can walk round a man, whatever weapon he has, choose my point, strike as I like. Dodge as I like. Escape as I like."

Kemp's hand went to his moustache. Was that a movement downstairs?

"And it is killing we must do, Kemp."

"It is killing we must do," repeated Kemp. "I'm listening to your plan, Griffin, but I'm not agreeing, mind. *Why* killing?"

"Not wanton killing, but a judicious slaying. The point is, they know there is an Invisible Man—as well as we know there is an Invisible Man. And that Invisible Man, Kemp, must now establish a Reign of Terror. Yes; no doubt it's startling. But I mean it. A Reign of Terror. He must take some town like your Burdock and terrify and dominate it. He must issue his orders. He can do that in a thousand ways—scraps of paper thrust under doors would suffice. And all who disobey his orders he must kill, and kill all who would defend them."

"Humph!" said Kemp, no longer listening to Griffin but to the sound of his front door opening and closing.

"It seems to me, Griffin," he said, to cover his wandering attention, "that your confederate would be in a difficult position."

"No one would know he was a confederate," said the Invisible Man, eagerly. And then suddenly, "Hush! What's that downstairs?"

"Nothing," said Kemp, and suddenly began to speak loud and fast. "I don't agree to this, Griffin," he said. "Understand me, I don't agree to this. Why dream of playing a game against the race? How can you hope to gain happiness? Don't be a lone wolf. Publish your results; take the world—take the nation at least—into your confidence. Think what you might do with a million helpers—"

The Invisible Man interrupted—arm extended. "There are footsteps coming upstairs," he said in a low voice.

"Nonsense," said Kemp.

"Let me see," said the Invisible Man, and advanced, arm extended, to the door.

And then things happened very swiftly. Kemp hesitated for a second and then moved to intercept him. The Invisible Man started and stood still.

"Traitor!" cried the Voice, and suddenly the dressing-gown opened, and sitting down the Unseen began to disrobe. Kemp made three swift steps to the door, and forthwith the Invisible Man—his legs had vanished—sprang to his feet with a shout. Kemp flung the door open.

As it opened, there came a sound of hurrying feet downstairs and voices.

With a quick movement Kemp thrust the Invisible Man back, sprang aside, and slammed the door. The key was outside and ready. In another moment Griffin would have been alone in the belvedere study, a prisoner. Save for one little thing. The key had been slipped in hastily that morning. As Kemp slammed the door it fell noisily upon the carpet.

Kemp's face became white. He tried to grip the door handle with both hands. For a moment he stood lugging. Then the door gave six inches. But he got it closed again. The second time it was jerked a foot wide, and the dressing-gown came wedging itself into the opening. His throat was gripped by invisible fingers, and he left his hold on the handle to defend himself. He was forced back, tripped and pitched heavily into the corner of the landing. The empty dressing-gown was flung on the top of him.

Halfway up the staircase was Colonel Adye, the recipient of Kemp's letter, the chief of the Burdock police. He was staring aghast at the sudden appearance of Kemp, followed by the extraordinary sight of clothing tossing empty in the air. He saw Kemp felled, and struggling to his feet. He saw him rush forward, and go down again, felled like an ox.

Then suddenly he was struck violently. By nothing! A vast weight, it seemed, leapt upon him, and he was hurled headlong down the staircase, with a grip on his throat and a knee in his groin. An invisible foot trod on his back, a ghostly patter passed downstairs, he heard the two police officers in the hall shout and run, and the front door of the house slammed violently.

He rolled over and sat up staring. He saw, staggering down the staircase, Kemp, dusty and disheveled, one side of his face white from a blow, his lip bleeding, and a pink dressing-gown and some underclothing held in his arms.

"My God!" cried Kemp, "the game's up! He's gone!"

CHAPTER XXV

THE HUNTING OF THE INVISIBLE MAN

For a space Kemp was too inarticulate to make Adye understand the swift things that had just happened. They stood on the landing, Kemp speaking swiftly, the grotesque swathings of Griffin still on his arm. But presently Adye began to grasp something of the situation.

"He is mad," said Kemp; "inhuman. He is pure selfishness. He thinks of nothing but his own advantage, his own safety. I have listened to such a story this morning of brutal self-seeking.... He has wounded men. He will kill them unless we can prevent him. He will create a panic. Nothing can stop him. He is going out now—furious!"

"He must be caught," said Adye. "That is certain."

"But how?" cried Kemp, and suddenly became full of ideas. "You must begin at once. You must set every available man to work; you must prevent his leaving this district. Once he gets away, he may go through the countryside as he wills, killing and maiming. He dreams of a reign of terror! A reign of terror, I tell you. You must set a watch on trains and roads and shipping. The garrison must help. You must wire for help. The only thing that may keep him here is the thought of recovering some books of notes he counts of value. I will tell you of that! There is a man in your police station—Marvel."

"I know," said Adye, "I know. Those books—yes. But the tramp...."

"Says he hasn't them. But he thinks the tramp has. And you must prevent him from eating or sleeping; day and night the country must be astir for him. Food must be locked up and secured, all food, so that he will have to break his way to it. The houses everywhere must be barred against him. Heaven send us cold nights and rain! The whole country-side must begin hunting and keep hunting. I tell you, Adye, he is a danger, a disaster; unless he is pinned and secured, it is frightful to think of the things that may happen."

"What else can we do?" said Adye. "I must go down at once and begin organising. But why not come? Yes—you come too! Come, and we must hold a sort of council of war—get Hopps to help—and the railway managers. By Jove! it's urgent. Come along—tell me as we go. What else is there we can do? Put that stuff down."

In another moment Adye was leading the way downstairs. They found the front door open and the policemen standing outside staring at empty air. "He's got away, sir," said one.

"We must go to the central station at once," said Adye. "One of you go on down and get a cab to come up and meet us—quickly. And now, Kemp, what else?"

"Dogs," said Kemp. "Get dogs. They don't see him, but they wind him. Get dogs."

"Good," said Adye. "It's not generally known, but the prison officials over at Halstead know a man with bloodhounds. Dogs. What else?"

"Bear in mind," said Kemp, "his food shows. After eating, his food shows until it is assimilated. So that he has to hide after eating. You must keep on beating. Every thicket, every quiet corner. And put all weapons—all implements that might be weapons, away. He can't carry such things for long. And what he can snatch up and strike men with must be hidden away."

"Good again," said Adye. "We shall have him yet!"

"And on the roads," said Kemp, and hesitated.

"Yes?" said Adye.

"Powdered glass," said Kemp. "It's cruel, I know. But think of what he may do!"

Adye drew the air in sharply between his teeth. "It's unsportsmanlike. I don't know. But I'll have powdered glass got ready. If he goes too far...."

"The man's become inhuman, I tell you," said Kemp. "I am as sure he will establish a reign of terror—so soon as he has got over the emotions of this escape—as I am sure I am talking to you. Our only chance is to be ahead. He has cut himself off from his kind. His blood be upon his own head."

CHAPTER XXVI

THE WICKSTEED MURDER

The Invisible Man seems to have rushed out of Kemp's house in a state of blind fury. A little child playing near Kemp's gateway was violently caught up and thrown aside, so that its ankle was broken, and thereafter for some hours the Invisible Man passed out of human perceptions. No one knows where he went nor what he did. But one can imagine him hurrying through the hot June forenoon, up the hill and on to the open downland behind Port Burdock, raging and despairing at his intolerable fate, and sheltering at last, heated and weary, amid the thickets of Hintondean, to piece together again his shattered schemes against his species. That seems the most probable refuge for him, for there it was he re-asserted himself in a grimly tragical manner about two in the afternoon.

One wonders what his state of mind may have been during that time, and what plans he devised. No doubt he was almost ecstatically exasperated by Kemp's treachery, and though we may be able to understand the motives that led to that deceit, we may still imagine and even sympathise a little with the fury the attempted surprise must have occasioned. Perhaps something of the stunned astonishment of his Oxford Street experiences may have returned to him, for he had evidently counted on Kemp's co-operation in his brutal dream of a terrorised world. At any rate he vanished from human ken about midday, and no living witness can tell what he did until about half-past two. It was a fortunate thing, perhaps, for humanity, but for him it was a fatal inaction.

During that time a growing multitude of men scattered over the countryside were busy. In the morning he had still been simply a legend, a terror; in the afternoon, by virtue chiefly of Kemp's drily worded proclamation, he was presented as a tangible antagonist, to be wounded, captured, or overcome, and the countryside began organising itself with inconceivable rapidity. By two o'clock even he might still have removed himself out of the district by getting aboard a train, but after two that became impossible. Every passenger train along the lines on a great parallelogram between Southampton, Manchester, Brighton and Horsham, travelled with locked doors, and the goods traffic was almost entirely suspended. And in a great circle of twenty miles round Port Burdock, men armed with guns and bludgeons were presently setting out in groups of three and four, with dogs, to beat the roads and fields.

Mounted policemen rode along the country lanes, stopping at every cottage and warning the people to lock up their houses, and keep indoors unless they were armed, and all the elementary schools had broken up by three o'clock, and the children, scared and keeping together in groups, were hurrying home. Kemp's proclamation—signed indeed by Adye—was posted over almost the whole district by four or five o'clock in the afternoon. It gave briefly but clearly all the conditions of the struggle, the necessity of keeping the Invisible Man from food and sleep, the necessity for incessant watchfulness and for a prompt attention to any evidence of his movements. And so swift and decided was the action of the authorities, so prompt and universal was the belief in this strange being, that before nightfall an area of several hundred square miles was in a stringent state of siege. And before nightfall, too, a thrill of horror went through the whole watching nervous countryside. Going from whispering mouth to mouth, swift and certain over the length and breadth of the country, passed the story of the murder of Mr. Wicksteed.

If our supposition that the Invisible Man's refuge was the Hintondean thickets, then we must suppose that in the early afternoon he sallied out again bent upon some project that involved the use of a weapon. We cannot know what the project was, but the evidence that he had the iron rod in hand before he met Wicksteed is to me at least overwhelming.

Of course we can know nothing of the details of that encounter. It occurred on the edge of a gravel pit, not two hundred yards from Lord Burdock's lodge gate. Everything points to a desperate struggle—the trampled ground, the numerous wounds Mr. Wicksteed received, his splintered walking-stick; but why the attack was made, save in a murderous frenzy, it is impossible to imagine. Indeed the theory of madness is almost unavoidable. Mr. Wicksteed was a man of forty-five or forty-six, steward to Lord Burdock, of inoffensive habits and appearance, the very last person in the world to provoke such a terrible antagonist. Against him it would seem the Invisible Man used an iron rod dragged from a broken piece of fence. He stopped this quiet man, going quietly home to his midday meal, attacked him, beat down his feeble defences, broke his arm, felled him, and smashed his head to a jelly.

Of course, he must have dragged this rod out of the fencing before he met his victim—he must have been carrying it ready in his hand. Only two details beyond what has already been stated seem to bear on the matter. One is the circumstance that the gravel pit was not in Mr. Wicksteed's direct path home, but nearly a couple of hundred yards out of his way. The other is the assertion of a little girl to the effect that, going to her afternoon school, she saw the murdered man "trotting" in a peculiar manner across a field towards the gravel pit. Her pantomime of his action suggests a man pursuing something on the ground before him and striking at it ever and again with his walking-stick. She was the last person to see him alive. He passed out of her sight to his death, the struggle being hidden from her only by a clump of beech trees and a slight depression in the ground.

Now this, to the present writer's mind at least, lifts the murder out of the realm of the absolutely wanton. We may imagine that Griffin had taken the rod as a weapon indeed, but without any deliberate intention of using it in murder. Wicksteed may then have come by and noticed this rod inexplicably moving through the air. Without any thought of the Invisible Man—for Port Burdock is ten miles away—he may have pursued it. It is quite conceivable that he may not even have heard of the Invisible Man. One can then imagine the Invisible Man making off—quietly in order to avoid discovering his presence in the neighbourhood, and Wicksteed, excited and curious, pursuing this unaccountably locomotive object—finally striking at it.

No doubt the Invisible Man could easily have distanced his middle-aged pursuer under ordinary circumstances, but the position in which Wicksteed's body was found suggests that he had the ill luck to drive his quarry into a corner between a drift of stinging nettles and the gravel pit. To those who appreciate the extraordinary irascibility of the Invisible Man, the rest of the encounter will be easy to imagine.

But this is pure hypothesis. The only undeniable facts—for stories of children are often unreliable—are the discovery of Wicksteed's body, done to death, and of the blood-stained iron rod flung among the nettles. The abandonment of the rod by Griffin, suggests that in the emotional excitement of the affair, the purpose for which he took it—if he had a purpose—was abandoned. He was certainly an intensely egotistical and unfeeling man, but the sight of his victim, his first victim, bloody and pitiful at his feet, may have released some long pent fountain of remorse which for a time may have flooded whatever scheme of action he had contrived.

After the murder of Mr. Wicksteed, he would seem to have struck across the country towards the downland. There is a story of a voice heard about sunset by a couple of men in a field near Fern Bottom. It was wailing and laughing, sobbing and groaning, and ever and again it shouted. It must have been queer hearing. It drove up across the middle of a clover field and died away towards the hills.

That afternoon the Invisible Man must have learnt something of the rapid use Kemp had made of his confidences. He must have found houses locked and secured; he may have loitered about railway stations and prowled about inns, and no doubt he read the proclamations and realised something of the nature of the campaign against him. And as the evening advanced, the fields became dotted here and there with groups of three or four men, and noisy with the yelping of dogs. These men-hunters had particular instructions in the case of an encounter as to the way they should support one another. But he avoided them all. We may understand something of his exasperation, and it could have been none the less because he himself had supplied the information that was being used so remorselessly against him.

For that day at least he lost heart; for nearly twenty-four hours, save when he turned on Wicksteed, he was a hunted man. In the night, he must have eaten and slept; for in the morning he was himself again, active, powerful, angry, and malignant, prepared for his last great struggle against the world.

CHAPTER XXVII

THE SIEGE OF KEMP'S HOUSE

Kemp read a strange missive, written in pencil on a greasy sheet of paper.

"You have been amazingly energetic and clever," this letter ran, "though what you stand to gain by it I cannot imagine. You are against me. For a whole day you have chased me; you have tried to rob me of a night's rest. But I have had food in spite of you, I have slept in spite of you, and the game is only beginning. The game is only beginning. There is nothing for it, but to start the Terror. This announces the first day of the Terror. Port Burdock is no longer under the Queen, tell your Colonel of Police, and the rest of them; it is under me—the Terror! This is day one of year one of the new epoch—the Epoch of the Invisible Man. I am Invisible Man the First. To begin with the rule will be easy. The first day there will be one execution for the sake of example—a man named Kemp. Death starts for him today. He may lock himself away, hide himself away, get guards about him, put on armour if he likes—Death, the unseen Death, is coming. Let him take precautions; it will impress my people. Death starts from the pillar box by midday. The letter will fall in as the postman comes along, then off! The game begins. Death starts. Help him not, my people, lest Death fall upon you also. Today Kemp is to die."

Kemp read this letter twice, "It's no hoax," he said. "That's his voice! And he means it."

He turned the folded sheet over and saw on the addressed side of it the postmark Hintondean, and the prosaic detail "2d. to pay."

He got up slowly, leaving his lunch unfinished—the letter had come by the one o'clock post—and went into his study. He rang for his housekeeper, and told her to go round the house at once, examine all the fastenings of the windows, and close all the shutters. He closed the shutters of his study himself. From a locked drawer in his bedroom he took a little revolver, examined it carefully, and put it into the pocket of his lounge jacket. He wrote a number of brief notes, one to Colonel Adye, gave them to his servant to take, with explicit instructions as to her way of leaving the house. "There is no danger," he said, and added a mental reservation, "to you." He remained meditative for a space after doing this, and then returned to his cooling lunch.

He ate with gaps of thought. Finally he struck the table sharply. "We will have him!" he said; "and I am the bait. He will come too far."

He went up to the belvedere, carefully shutting every door after him. "It's a game," he said, "an odd game—but the chances are all for me, Mr. Griffin, in spite of your invisibility. Griffin *contra mundum* ... with a vengeance."

He stood at the window staring at the hot hillside. "He must get food every day—and I don't envy him. Did he really sleep last night? Out in the open somewhere—secure from collisions. I wish we could get some good cold wet weather instead of the heat.

"He may be watching me now."

He went close to the window. Something rapped smartly against the brickwork over the frame, and made him start violently back.

"I'm getting nervous," said Kemp. But it was five minutes before he went to the window again. "It must have been a sparrow," he said.

Presently he heard the front-door bell ringing, and hurried downstairs. He unbolted and unlocked the door, examined the chain, put it up, and opened cautiously without showing himself. A familiar voice hailed him. It was Adye.

"Your servant's been assaulted, Kemp," he said round the door.

"What!" exclaimed Kemp.

"Had that note of yours taken away from her. He's close about here. Let me in."

Kemp released the chain, and Adye entered through as narrow an opening as possible. He stood in the hall, looking with infinite relief at Kemp refastening the door. "Note was snatched out of her hand. Scared her horribly. She's down at the station. Hysterics. He's close here. What was it about?"

Kemp swore.

"What a fool I was," said Kemp. "I might have known. It's not an hour's walk from Hintondean. Already?"

"What's up?" said Adye.

"Look here!" said Kemp, and led the way into his study. He handed Adye the Invisible Man's letter. Adye read it and whistled softly. "And you—?" said Adye.

"Proposed a trap—like a fool," said Kemp, "and sent my proposal out by a maid servant. To him."

Adye followed Kemp's profanity.

"He'll clear out," said Adye.

"Not he," said Kemp.

A resounding smash of glass came from upstairs. Adye had a silvery glimpse of a little revolver half out of Kemp's pocket. "It's a window, upstairs!" said Kemp, and led the way up. There came a second smash while they were still on the staircase. When they reached the study they found two of the three windows smashed, half the room littered with splintered glass, and one big flint lying on the writing table. The two men stopped in the doorway, contemplating the wreckage. Kemp swore again, and as he did so the third window went with a snap like a pistol, hung starred for a moment, and collapsed in jagged, shivering triangles into the room.

"What's this for?" said Adye.

"It's a beginning," said Kemp.

"There's no way of climbing up here?"

"Not for a cat," said Kemp.

"No shutters?"

"Not here. All the downstairs rooms—Hullo!"

Smash, and then whack of boards hit hard came from downstairs. "Confound him!" said Kemp. "That must be—yes—it's one of the bedrooms.

He's going to do all the house. But he's a fool. The shutters are up, and the glass will fall outside. He'll cut his feet."

Another window proclaimed its destruction. The two men stood on the landing perplexed. "I have it!" said Adye. "Let me have a stick or something, and I'll go down to the station and get the bloodhounds put on. That ought to settle him! They're hard by—not ten minutes—"

Another window went the way of its fellows.

"You haven't a revolver?" asked Adye.

Kemp's hand went to his pocket. Then he hesitated. "I haven't one—at least to spare."

"I'll bring it back," said Adye, "you'll be safe here."

Kemp, ashamed of his momentary lapse from truthfulness, handed him the weapon.

"Now for the door," said Adye.

As they stood hesitating in the hall, they heard one of the first-floor bedroom windows crack and clash. Kemp went to the door and began to slip the bolts as silently as possible. His face was a little paler than usual. "You must step straight out," said Kemp. In another moment Adye was on the doorstep and the bolts were dropping back into the staples. He hesitated for a moment, feeling more comfortable with his back against the door. Then he marched, upright and square, down the steps. He crossed the lawn and approached the gate. A little breeze seemed to ripple over the grass. Something moved near him. "Stop a bit," said a Voice, and Adye stopped dead and his hand tightened on the revolver.

"Well?" said Adye, white and grim, and every nerve tense.

"Oblige me by going back to the house," said the Voice, as tense and grim as Adye's.

"Sorry," said Adye a little hoarsely, and moistened his lips with his tongue. The Voice was on his left front, he thought. Suppose he were to take his luck with a shot?

"What are you going for?" said the Voice, and there was a quick movement of the two, and a flash of sunlight from the open lip of Adye's pocket.

Adye desisted and thought. "Where I go," he said slowly, "is my own business." The words were still on his lips, when an arm came round his neck, his back felt a knee, and he was sprawling backward. He drew clumsily and fired absurdly, and in another moment he was struck in the mouth and the revolver wrested from his grip. He made a vain clutch at a slippery limb, tried to struggle up and fell back. "Damn!" said Adye. The Voice laughed. "I'd kill you now if it wasn't the waste of a bullet," it said. He saw the revolver in mid-air, six feet off, covering him.

"Well?" said Adye, sitting up.

"Get up," said the Voice.

Adye stood up.

"Attention," said the Voice, and then fiercely, "Don't try any games. Remember I can see your face if you can't see mine. You've got to go back to the house."

"He won't let me in," said Adye.

"That's a pity," said the Invisible Man. "I've got no quarrel with you."

Adye moistened his lips again. He glanced away from the barrel of the revolver and saw the sea far off very blue and dark under the midday sun, the smooth green down, the white cliff of the Head, and the multitudinous town, and suddenly he knew that life was very sweet. His eyes came back to this little metal thing hanging between heaven and earth, six yards away. "What am I to do?" he said sullenly.

"What am *I* to do?" asked the Invisible Man. "You will get help. The only thing is for you to go back."

"I will try. If he lets me in will you promise not to rush the door?"

"I've got no quarrel with you," said the Voice.

Kemp had hurried upstairs after letting Adye out, and now crouching among the broken glass and peering cautiously over the edge of the study window sill, he saw Adye stand parleying with the Unseen. "Why doesn't he fire?" whispered Kemp to himself. Then the revolver moved a little and the glint of the sunlight flashed in Kemp's eyes. He shaded his eyes and tried to see the source of the blinding beam.

"Surely!" he said, "Adye has given up the revolver."

"Promise not to rush the door," Adye was saying. "Don't push a winning game too far. Give a man a chance."

"You go back to the house. I tell you flatly I will not promise anything."

Adye's decision seemed suddenly made. He turned towards the house, walking slowly with his hands behind him. Kemp watched him—puzzled. The revolver vanished, flashed again into sight, vanished again, and became evident on a closer scrutiny as a little dark object following Adye. Then things happened very quickly. Adye leapt backwards, swung around, clutched at this little object, missed it, threw up his hands and fell forward on his face, leaving a little puff of blue in the air. Kemp did not hear the sound of the shot. Adye writhed, raised himself on one arm, fell forward, and lay still.

For a space Kemp remained staring at the quiet carelessness of Adye's attitude. The afternoon was very hot and still, nothing seemed stirring in all the world save a couple of yellow butterflies chasing each other through the shrubbery between the house and the road gate. Adye lay on the lawn near the gate. The blinds of all the villas down the hill-road were drawn, but in one little green summer-house was a white figure, apparently an old man asleep. Kemp scrutinised the surroundings of the house for a glimpse of the revolver, but it had vanished. His eyes came back to Adye. The game was opening well.

Then came a ringing and knocking at the front door, that grew at last tumultuous, but pursuant to Kemp's instructions the servants had locked themselves into their rooms. This was followed by a silence. Kemp sat listening and then began peering cautiously out of the three windows, one after another. He went to the staircase head and stood listening uneasily. He armed himself with his bedroom poker, and went to examine the interior fastenings of the ground-floor windows again. Everything was safe and quiet. He returned to the belvedere. Adye lay motionless over the edge of the gravel just as he had fallen. Coming along the road by the villas were the housemaid and two policemen.

Everything was deadly still. The three people seemed very slow in approaching. He wondered what his antagonist was doing.

He started. There was a smash from below. He hesitated and went downstairs again. Suddenly the house resounded with heavy blows and the splintering of wood. He heard a smash and the destructive clang of the iron fastenings of the shutters. He turned the key and opened the kitchen door. As he did so, the shutters, split and splintering, came flying inward. He stood aghast. The window frame, save for one crossbar, was still intact, but only little teeth of glass remained in the frame. The shutters had been driven in with an axe, and now the axe was descending in sweeping blows upon the window frame and the iron bars defending it. Then suddenly it leapt aside and vanished. He saw the revolver lying on the path outside, and then the little weapon sprang into the air. He dodged back. The revolver cracked just too late, and a splinter from the edge of the closing door flashed over his head. He slammed and locked the door, and as he stood outside he heard Griffin shouting and laughing. Then the blows of the axe with its splitting and smashing consequences, were resumed.

Kemp stood in the passage trying to think. In a moment the Invisible Man would be in the kitchen. This door would not keep him a moment, and then—

A ringing came at the front door again. It would be the policemen. He ran into the hall, put up the chain, and drew the bolts. He made the girl speak before he dropped the chain, and the three people blundered into the house in a heap, and Kemp slammed the door again.

"The Invisible Man!" said Kemp. "He has a revolver, with two shots— left. He's killed Adye. Shot him anyhow. Didn't you see him on the lawn? He's lying there."

"Who?" said one of the policemen.

"Adye," said Kemp.

"We came in the back way," said the girl.

"What's that smashing?" asked one of the policemen.

"He's in the kitchen—or will be. He has found an axe—"

Suddenly the house was full of the Invisible Man's resounding blows on the kitchen door. The girl stared towards the kitchen, shuddered, and retreated into the dining-room. Kemp tried to explain in broken sentences. They heard the kitchen door give.

"This way," said Kemp, starting into activity, and bundled the policemen into the dining-room doorway.

"Poker," said Kemp, and rushed to the fender. He handed the poker he had carried to the policeman and the dining-room one to the other. He suddenly flung himself backward.

"Whup!" said one policeman, ducked, and caught the axe on his poker.

The pistol snapped its penultimate shot and ripped a valuable Sidney Cooper. The second policeman brought his poker down on the little weapon, as one might knock down a wasp, and sent it rattling to the floor.

At the first clash the girl screamed, stood screaming for a moment by the fireplace, and then ran to open the shutters—possibly with an idea of escaping by the shattered window.

The axe receded into the passage, and fell to a position about two feet from the ground. They could hear the Invisible Man breathing. "Stand away, you two," he said. "I want that man Kemp."

"We want you," said the first policeman, making a quick step forward and wiping with his poker at the Voice. The Invisible Man must have started back, and he blundered into the umbrella stand.

Then, as the policeman staggered with the swing of the blow he had aimed, the Invisible Man countered with the axe, the helmet crumpled like paper, and the blow sent the man spinning to the floor at the head of the kitchen stairs. But the second policeman, aiming behind the axe with his poker, hit something soft that snapped. There was a sharp exclamation of pain and then the axe fell to the ground. The policeman wiped again at vacancy and hit nothing; he put his foot on the axe, and struck again. Then he stood, poker clubbed, listening intent for the slightest movement.

He heard the dining-room window open, and a quick rush of feet within. His companion rolled over and sat up, with the blood running down between his eye and ear. "Where is he?" asked the man on the floor.

"Don't know. I've hit him. He's standing somewhere in the hall. Unless he's slipped past you. Doctor Kemp—sir."

Pause.

"Doctor Kemp," cried the policeman again.

The second policeman began struggling to his feet. He stood up. Suddenly the faint pad of bare feet on the kitchen stairs could be heard. "Yap!" cried the first policeman, and incontinently flung his poker. It smashed a little gas bracket.

He made as if he would pursue the Invisible Man downstairs. Then he thought better of it and stepped into the dining-room.

"Doctor Kemp—" he began, and stopped short.

"Doctor Kemp's a hero," he said, as his companion looked over his shoulder.

The dining-room window was wide open, and neither housemaid nor Kemp was to be seen.

The second policeman's opinion of Kemp was terse and vivid.

CHAPTER XXVIII

THE HUNTER HUNTED

Mr. Heelas, Mr. Kemp's nearest neighbour among the villa holders, was asleep in his summer house when the siege of Kemp's house began. Mr. Heelas was one of the sturdy minority who refused to believe "in all this nonsense" about an Invisible Man. His wife, however, as he was subsequently to be reminded, did. He insisted upon walking about his garden just as if nothing was the matter, and he went to sleep in the afternoon in accordance with the custom of years. He slept through the smashing of the windows, and then woke up suddenly with a curious persuasion of something wrong. He looked across at Kemp's house, rubbed his eyes and looked again. Then he put his feet to the ground, and sat listening. He said he was damned, but still the strange thing was visible. The house looked as though it had been deserted for weeks—after a violent riot. Every window was broken, and every window, save those of the belvedere study, was blinded by the internal shutters.

"I could have sworn it was all right"—he looked at his watch—"twenty minutes ago."

He became aware of a measured concussion and the clash of glass, far away in the distance. And then, as he sat open-mouthed, came a still more wonderful thing. The shutters of the drawing-room window were flung open violently, and the housemaid in her outdoor hat and garments, appeared struggling in a frantic manner to throw up the sash. Suddenly a man appeared beside her, helping her—Dr. Kemp! In another moment the window was open, and the housemaid was struggling out; she pitched forward and vanished among the shrubs. Mr. Heelas stood up, exclaiming vaguely and vehemently at all these wonderful things. He saw Kemp stand on the sill, spring from the window, and reappear almost instantaneously running along a path in the shrubbery and stooping as he ran, like a man who evades observation. He vanished behind a laburnum, and appeared again clambering over a fence that abutted on the open down. In a second he had tumbled over and was running at a tremendous pace down the slope towards Mr. Heelas.

"Lord!" cried Mr. Heelas, struck with an idea; "it's that Invisible Man brute! It's right, after all!"

With Mr. Heelas to think things like that was to act, and his cook watching him from the top window was amazed to see him come pelting towards the house at a good nine miles an hour. There was a slamming of doors, a ringing of bells, and the voice of Mr. Heelas bellowing like a bull. "Shut the doors, shut the windows, shut everything!—the Invisible Man is coming!" Instantly the house was full of screams and directions, and scurrying feet. He ran himself to shut the French windows that opened on the veranda; as he did so Kemp's head and shoulders and knee appeared over the edge of the garden fence. In another moment Kemp had ploughed through the asparagus, and was running across the tennis lawn to the house.

"You can't come in," said Mr. Heelas, shutting the bolts. "I'm very sorry if he's after you, but you can't come in!"

Kemp appeared with a face of terror close to the glass, rapping and then shaking frantically at the French window. Then, seeing his efforts were useless, he ran along the veranda, vaulted the end, and went to hammer at the side door. Then he ran round by the side gate to the front of the house, and so into the hill-road. And Mr. Heelas staring from his window—a face of horror—had scarcely witnessed Kemp vanish, ere the asparagus was being trampled this way and that by feet unseen. At that Mr. Heelas fled precipitately upstairs, and the rest of the chase is beyond his purview. But as he passed the staircase window, he heard the side gate slam.

Emerging into the hill-road, Kemp naturally took the downward direc-

tion, and so it was he came to run in his own person the very race he had
watched with such a critical eye from the belvedere study only four days
ago. He ran it well, for a man out of training, and though his face was white
and wet, his wits were cool to the last. He ran with wide strides, and wherever a patch of rough ground intervened, wherever there came a patch of
raw flints, or a bit of broken glass shone dazzling, he crossed it and left the
bare invisible feet that followed to take what line they would.

For the first time in his life Kemp discovered that the hill-road was in-
describably vast and desolate, and that the beginnings of the town far below at the hill foot were strangely remote. Never had there been a slower
or more painful method of progression than running. All the gaunt villas,
sleeping in the afternoon sun, looked locked and barred; no doubt they
were locked and barred—by his own orders. But at any rate they might
have kept a lookout for an eventuality like this! The town was rising up
now, the sea had dropped out of sight behind it, and people down below
were stirring. A tram was just arriving at the hill foot. Beyond that was the
police station. Was that footsteps he heard behind him? Spurt.

The people below were staring at him, one or two were running, and his
breath was beginning to saw in his throat. The tram was quite near now, and
the "Jolly Cricketers" was noisily barring its doors. Beyond the tram were
posts and heaps of gravel—the drainage works. He had a transitory idea
of jumping into the tram and slamming the doors, and then he resolved
to go for the police station. In another moment he had passed the door of
the "Jolly Cricketers," and was in the blistering fag end of the street, with
human beings about him. The tram driver and his helper—arrested by the
sight of his furious haste—stood staring with the tram horses unhitched.
Further on the astonished features of navvies appeared above the mounds
of gravel.

His pace broke a little, and then he heard the swift pad of his pursuer, and leapt forward again. "The Invisible Man!" he cried to the navvies,
with a vague indicative gesture, and by an inspiration leapt the excavation
and placed a burly group between him and the chase. Then abandoning
the idea of the police station he turned into a little side street, rushed by
a greengrocer's cart, hesitated for the tenth of a second at the door of a

sweetstuff shop, and then made for the mouth of an alley that ran back into the main Hill Street again. Two or three little children were playing here, and shrieked and scattered at his apparition, and forthwith doors and windows opened and excited mothers revealed their hearts. Out he shot into Hill Street again, three hundred yards from the tram-line end, and immediately he became aware of a tumultuous vociferation and running people.

He glanced up the street towards the hill. Hardly a dozen yards off ran a huge navvy, cursing in fragments and slashing viciously with a spade, and hard behind him came the tram conductor with his fists clenched. Up the street others followed these two, striking and shouting. Down towards the town, men and women were running, and he noticed clearly one man coming out of a shop-door with a stick in his hand. "Spread out! Spread out!" cried some one. Kemp suddenly grasped the altered condition of the chase. He stopped, and looked round, panting. "He's close here!" he cried. "Form a line across—"

He was hit hard under the ear, and went reeling, trying to face round towards his unseen antagonist. He just managed to keep his feet, and he struck a vain counter in the air. Then he was hit again under the jaw, and sprawled headlong on the ground. In another moment a knee compressed his diaphragm, and a couple of eager hands gripped his throat, but the grip of one was weaker than the other; he grasped the wrists, heard a cry of pain from his assailant, and then the spade of the navvy came whirling through the air above him, and struck something with a dull thud. He felt a drop of moisture on his face. The grip at his throat suddenly relaxed, and with a convulsive effort, Kemp loosed himself, grasped a limp shoulder, and rolled uppermost. He gripped the unseen elbows near the ground. "I've got him!" screamed Kemp. "Help! Help—hold! He's down! Hold his feet!"

In another second there was a simultaneous rush upon the struggle, and a stranger coming into the road suddenly might have thought an exceptionally savage game of Rugby football was in progress. And there was no shouting after Kemp's cry—only a sound of blows and feet and heavy breathing.

Then came a mighty effort, and the Invisible Man threw off a couple of his antagonists and rose to his knees. Kemp clung to him in front like a hound to a stag, and a dozen hands gripped, clutched, and tore at the Unseen. The tram conductor suddenly got the neck and shoulders and lugged him back.

Down went the heap of struggling men again and rolled over. There was, I am afraid, some savage kicking. Then suddenly a wild scream of "Mercy! Mercy!" that died down swiftly to a sound like choking.

"Get back, you fools!" cried the muffled voice of Kemp, and there was a vigorous shoving back of stalwart forms. "He's hurt, I tell you. Stand back!"

There was a brief struggle to clear a space, and then the circle of eager faces saw the doctor kneeling, as it seemed, fifteen inches in the air, and holding invisible arms to the ground. Behind him a constable gripped invisible ankles.

"Don't you leave go of en," cried the big navvy, holding a blood-stained spade; "he's shamming."

"He's not shamming," said the doctor, cautiously raising his knee; "and I'll hold him." His face was bruised and already going red; he spoke thickly because of a bleeding lip. He released one hand and seemed to be feeling at the face. "The mouth's all wet," he said. And then, "Good God!"

He stood up abruptly and then knelt down on the ground by the side of the thing unseen. There was a pushing and shuffling, a sound of heavy feet as fresh people turned up to increase the pressure of the crowd. People now were coming out of the houses. The doors of the "Jolly Cricketers" stood suddenly wide open. Very little was said.

Kemp felt about, his hand seeming to pass through empty air. "He's not breathing," he said, and then, "I can't feel his heart. His side—ugh!"

Suddenly an old woman, peering under the arm of the big navvy, screamed sharply. "Looky there!" she said, and thrust out a wrinkled finger.

And looking where she pointed, everyone saw, faint and transparent as though it was made of glass, so that veins and arteries and bones and nerves could be distinguished, the outline of a hand, a hand limp and prone. It grew clouded and opaque even as they stared.

"Hullo!" cried the constable. "Here's his feet a-showing!"

And so, slowly, beginning at his hands and feet and creeping along his limbs to the vital centres of his body, that strange change continued. It was like the slow spreading of a poison. First came the little white nerves, a hazy grey sketch of a limb, then the glassy bones and intricate arteries, then the flesh and skin, first a faint fogginess, and then growing rapidly dense and opaque. Presently they could see his crushed chest and his shoulders, and the dim outline of his drawn and battered features.

When at last the crowd made way for Kemp to stand erect, there lay, naked and pitiful on the ground, the bruised and broken body of a young man about thirty. His hair and brow were white—not grey with age, but white with the whiteness of albinism—and his eyes were like garnets. His hands were clenched, his eyes wide open, and his expression was one of anger and dismay.

"Cover his face!" said a man. "For Gawd's sake, cover that face!" and three little children, pushing forward through the crowd, were suddenly twisted round and sent packing off again.

Someone brought a sheet from the "Jolly Cricketers," and having covered him, they carried him into that house. And there it was, on a shabby bed in a tawdry, ill-lighted bedroom, surrounded by a crowd of ignorant and excited people, broken and wounded, betrayed and unpitied, that Griffin, the first of all men to make himself invisible, Griffin, the most gifted physicist the world has ever seen, ended in infinite disaster his strange and terrible career.

THE EPILOGUE

So ends the story of the strange and evil experiments of the Invisible Man. And if you would learn more of him you must go to a little inn near Port Stowe and talk to the landlord. The sign of the inn is an empty board save for a hat and boots, and the name is the title of this story. The landlord is a short and corpulent little man with a nose of cylindrical proportions, wiry hair, and a sporadic rosiness of visage. Drink generously, and he will tell you generously of all the things that happened to him after that time, and of how the lawyers tried to do him out of the treasure found upon him.

"When they found they couldn't prove whose money was which, I'm blessed," he says, "if they didn't try to make me out a blooming treasure trove! Do I *look* like a Treasure Trove? And then a gentleman gave me a guinea a night to tell the story at the Empire Music 'All—just to tell 'em in my own words—barring one."

And if you want to cut off the flow of his reminiscences abruptly, you can always do so by asking if there weren't three manuscript books in the story. He admits there were and proceeds to explain, with asseverations that everybody thinks *he* has 'em! But bless you! he hasn't. "The Invisible Man it was took 'em off to hide 'em when I cut and ran for Port Stowe. It's that Mr. Kemp put people on with the idea of *my* having 'em."

And then he subsides into a pensive state, watches you furtively, bustles nervously with glasses, and presently leaves the bar.

He is a bachelor man—his tastes were ever bachelor, and there are no women folk in the house. Outwardly he buttons—it is expected of him— but in his more vital privacies, in the matter of braces for example, he still turns to string. He conducts his house without enterprise, but with eminent decorum. His movements are slow, and he is a great thinker. But he has a reputation for wisdom and for a respectable parsimony in the village, and his knowledge of the roads of the South of England would beat Cobbett.

And on Sunday mornings, every Sunday morning, all the year round, while he is closed to the outer world, and every night after ten, he goes into his bar parlour, bearing a glass of gin faintly tinged with water, and having placed this down, he locks the door and examines the blinds, and even looks under the table. And then, being satisfied of his solitude, he unlocks the cupboard and a box in the cupboard and a drawer in that box, and pro- duces three volumes bound in brown leather, and places them solemnly in the middle of the table. The covers are weather-worn and tinged with an algal green—for once they sojourned in a ditch and some of the pages have been washed blank by dirty water. The landlord sits down in an armchair, fills a long clay pipe slowly—gloating over the books the while. Then he pulls one towards him and opens it, and begins to study it—turning over the leaves backwards and forwards.

His brows are knit and his lips move painfully. "Hex, little two up in the air, cross and a fiddle-de-dee. Lord! what a one he was for intellect!"

Presently he relaxes and leans back, and blinks through his smoke across the room at things invisible to other eyes. "Full of secrets," he says. "Wonderful secrets!"

"Once I get the haul of them—*Lord!*"

"I wouldn't do what *he* did; I'd just—well!" He pulls at his pipe.

So he lapses into a dream, the undying wonderful dream of his life. And though Kemp has fished unceasingly, no human being save the landlord knows those books are there, with the subtle secret of invisibility and a dozen other strange secrets written therein. And none other will know of them until he dies.

The Island of Dr. Moreau

INTRODUCTION

On February the First 1887, the *Lady Vain* was lost by collision with a derelict when about the latitude 1° S. and longitude 107° W.

On January the Fifth, 1888—that is eleven months and four days after—my uncle, Edward Prendick, a private gentleman, who certainly went aboard the *Lady Vain* at Callao, and who had been considered drowned, was picked up in latitude 5° 3' S. and longitude 101° W. in a small open boat of which the name was illegible, but which is supposed to have belonged to the missing schooner *Ipecacuanha*. He gave such a strange account of himself that he was supposed demented. Subsequently he alleged that his mind was a blank from the moment of his escape from the *Lady Vain*. His case was discussed among psychologists at the time as a curious instance of the lapse of memory consequent upon physical and mental stress. The following narrative was found among his papers by the undersigned, his nephew and heir, but unaccompanied by any definite request for publication.

The only island known to exist in the region in which my uncle was picked up is Noble's Isle, a small volcanic islet and uninhabited. It was visited in 1891 by *H. M. S. Scorpion*. A party of sailors then landed, but found nothing living thereon except certain curious white moths, some hogs and rabbits, and some rather peculiar rats. So that this narrative is without confirmation in its most essential particular. With that understood, there seems no harm in putting this strange story before the public in accordance, as I believe, with my uncle's intentions. There is at least this much in its behalf: my uncle passed out of human knowledge about latitude 5° S. and longitude 105° E., and reappeared in the same part of the ocean after a space of eleven months. In some way he must have lived during the interval. And it seems that a schooner called the *Ipecacuanha* with a drunken captain, John Davies, did start from Africa with a puma and certain other animals aboard in January, 1887, that the vessel was well known at several ports in the South Pacific, and that it finally disappeared from those seas (with a considerable amount of copra aboard), sailing to its unknown fate from Bayna in December, 1887, a date that tallies entirely with my uncle's story.

CHARLES EDWARD PRENDICK
(The Story written by Edward Prendick.)

I

In the Dingey of the "Lady Vain"

I do not propose to add anything to what has already been written concerning the loss of the *Lady Vain*. As everyone knows, she collided with a derelict when ten days out from Callao. The longboat, with seven of the crew, was picked up eighteen days after by H. M. gunboat *Myrtle*, and the story of their terrible privations has become quite as well known as the far more horrible *Medusa* case. But I have to add to the published story of the *Lady Vain* another, possibly as horrible and far stranger. It has hitherto been supposed that the four men who were in the dingey perished, but this is incorrect. I have the best of evidence for this assertion: I was one of the four men.

But in the first place I must state that there never were four men in the dingey,—the number was three. Constans, who was "seen by the captain to jump into the gig,"[1] luckily for us and unluckily for himself did not reach us. He came down out of the tangle of ropes under the stays of the smashed bowsprit, some small rope caught his heel as he let go, and he hung for a moment head downward, and then fell and struck a block or spar floating in the water. We pulled towards him, but he never came up.

I say luckily for us he did not reach us, and I might almost say luckily for himself; for we had only a small beaker of water and some soddened ship's biscuits with us, so sudden had been the alarm, so unprepared the ship for any disaster. We thought the people on the launch would be better provi-

[1] *Daily News,* March 17, 1887.

sioned (though it seems they were not), and we tried to hail them. They could not have heard us, and the next morning when the drizzle cleared,—which was not until past midday,—we could see nothing of them. We could not stand up to look about us, because of the pitching of the boat. The two other men who had escaped so far with me were a man named Helmar, a passenger like myself, and a seaman whose name I don't know,—a short sturdy man, with a stammer.

We drifted famishing, and, after our water had come to an end, tormented by an intolerable thirst, for eight days altogether. After the second day the sea subsided slowly to a glassy calm. It is quite impossible for the ordinary reader to imagine those eight days. He has not, luckily for himself, anything in his memory to imagine with. After the first day we said little to one another, and lay in our places in the boat and stared at the horizon, or watched, with eyes that grew larger and more haggard every day, the misery and weakness gaining upon our companions. The sun became pitiless. The water ended on the fourth day, and we were already thinking strange things and saying them with our eyes; but it was, I think, the sixth before Helmar gave voice to the thing we had all been thinking. I remember our voices were dry and thin, so that we bent towards one another and spared our words. I stood out against it with all my might, was rather for scuttling the boat and perishing together among the sharks that followed us; but when Helmar said that if his proposal was accepted we should have drink, the sailor came round to him.

I would not draw lots however, and in the night the sailor whispered to Helmar again and again, and I sat in the bows with my clasp-knife in my hand, though I doubt if I had the stuff in me to fight; and in the morning I agreed to Helmar's proposal, and we handed halfpence to find the odd man. The lot fell upon the sailor; but he was the strongest of us and would not abide by it, and attacked Helmar with his hands. They grappled together and almost stood up. I crawled along the boat to them, intending to help Helmar by grasping the sailor's leg; but the sailor stumbled with the swaying of the boat, and the two fell upon the gunwale and rolled overboard together. They sank like stones. I remember laughing at that, and wondering why I laughed. The laugh caught me suddenly like a thing from without.

I lay across one of the thwarts for I know not how long, thinking that if I had the strength I would drink sea-water and madden myself to die quickly. And even as I lay there I saw, with no more interest than if it had been a picture, a sail come up towards me over the sky-line. My mind must have been wandering, and yet I remember all that happened, quite distinctly. I remember how my head swayed with the seas, and the horizon with the sail above it danced up and down; but I also remember as distinctly that I had a persuasion that I was dead, and that I thought what a jest it was that they should come too late by such a little to catch me in my body.

For an endless period, as it seemed to me, I lay with my head on the thwart watching the schooner (she was a little ship, schooner-rigged fore and aft) come up out of the sea. She kept tacking to and fro in a widening compass, for she was sailing dead into the wind. It never entered my head to attempt to attract attention, and I do not remember anything distinctly after the sight of her side until I found myself in a little cabin aft. There's a dim half-memory of being lifted up to the gangway, and of a big round countenance covered with freckles and surrounded with red hair staring at me over the bulwarks. I also had a disconnected impression of a dark face, with extraordinary eyes, close to mine; but that I thought was a nightmare, until I met it again. I fancy I recollect some stuff being poured in between my teeth; and that is all.

II

THE MAN WHO WAS GOING NOWHERE

THE CABIN IN WHICH I FOUND MYSELF was small and rather untidy. A youngish man with flaxen hair, a bristly straw-coloured moustache, and a dropping nether lip, was sitting and holding my wrist. For a minute we stared at each other without speaking. He had watery grey eyes, oddly void of expression. Then just overhead came a sound like an iron bedstead being knocked about, and the low angry growling of some large animal. At the same time the man spoke. He repeated his question,—"How do you feel now?"

I think I said I felt all right. I could not recollect how I had got there. He must have seen the question in my face, for my voice was inaccessible to me.

"You were picked up in a boat, starving. The name on the boat was the *Lady Vain*, and there were spots of blood on the gunwale."

At the same time my eye caught my hand, so thin that it looked like a dirty skin-purse full of loose bones, and all the business of the boat came back to me.

"Have some of this," said he, and gave me a dose of some scarlet stuff, iced.

It tasted like blood, and made me feel stronger.

"You were in luck," said he, "to get picked up by a ship with a medical man aboard." He spoke with a slobbering articulation, with the ghost of a lisp.

"What ship is this?" I said slowly, hoarse from my long silence.

"It's a little trader from Arica and Callao. I never asked where she came from in the beginning,—out of the land of born fools, I guess. I'm a passenger myself, from Arica. The silly ass who owns her,—he's captain too, named Davies,—he's lost his certificate, or something. You know the kind of man,—calls the thing the *Ipecacuanha*, of all silly, infernal names; though when there's much of a sea without any wind, she certainly acts according."

(Then the noise overhead began again, a snarling growl and the voice of a human being together. Then another voice, telling some "Heaven-forsaken idiot" to desist.)

"You were nearly dead," said my interlocutor. "It was a very near thing, indeed. But I've put some stuff into you now. Notice your arm's sore? Injections. You've been insensible for nearly thirty hours."

I thought slowly. (I was distracted now by the yelping of a number of dogs.) "Am I eligible for solid food?" I asked.

"Thanks to me," he said. "Even now the mutton is boiling."

"Yes," I said with assurance; "I could eat some mutton."

"But," said he with a momentary hesitation, "you know I'm dying to hear of how you came to be alone in that boat. *Damn that howling!*" I thought I detected a certain suspicion in his eyes.

He suddenly left the cabin, and I heard him in violent controversy with some one, who seemed to me to talk gibberish in response to him. The matter sounded as though it ended in blows, but in that I thought my ears were mistaken. Then he shouted at the dogs, and returned to the cabin.

"Well?" said he in the doorway. "You were just beginning to tell me."

I told him my name, Edward Prendick, and how I had taken to Natural History as a relief from the dulness of my comfortable independence.

He seemed interested in this. "I've done some science myself. I did my Biology at University College,—getting out the ovary of the earthworm and the radula of the snail, and all that. Lord! It's ten years ago. But go on! go on! tell me about the boat."

He was evidently satisfied with the frankness of my story, which I told in concise sentences enough, for I felt horribly weak; and when it was finished he reverted at once to the topic of Natural History and his own biological studies. He began to question me closely about Tottenham Court Road and Gower Street. "Is Caplatzi still flourishing? What a shop that was!" He had evidently been a very ordinary medical student, and drifted incontinently to the topic of the music halls. He told me some anecdotes.

"Left it all," he said, "ten years ago. How jolly it all used to be! But I made a young ass of myself,—played myself out before I was twenty-one. I daresay it's all different now. But I must look up that ass of a cook, and see what he's done to your mutton."

The growling overhead was renewed, so suddenly and with so much savage anger that it startled me. "What's that?" I called after him, but the door had closed. He came back again with the boiled mutton, and I was so excited by the appetising smell of it that I forgot the noise of the beast that had troubled me.

After a day of alternate sleep and feeding I was so far recovered as to be able to get from my bunk to the scuttle, and see the green seas trying to keep pace with us. I judged the schooner was running before the wind. Montgomery—that was the name of the flaxen-haired man—came in again as I stood there, and I asked him for some clothes. He lent me some duck things of his own, for those I had worn in the boat had been thrown overboard. They were rather loose for me, for he was large and long in his limbs. He told me casually that the captain was three-parts drunk in his own cabin. As I assumed the clothes, I began asking him some questions about the destination of the ship. He said the ship was bound to Hawaii, but that it had to land him first.

"Where?" said I.

"It's an island, where I live. So far as I know, it hasn't got a name."

He stared at me with his nether lip dropping, and looked so wilfully stupid of a sudden that it came into my head that he desired to avoid my questions. I had the discretion to ask no more.

III

THE STRANGE FACE

WE LEFT THE CABIN AND FOUND A MAN at the companion obstructing our way. He was standing on the ladder with his back to us, peering over the combing of the hatchway. He was, I could see, a misshapen man, short, broad, and clumsy, with a crooked back, a hairy neck, and a head sunk between his shoulders. He was dressed in dark-blue serge, and had peculiarly thick, coarse, black hair. I heard the unseen dogs growl furiously, and forthwith he ducked back,—coming into contact with the hand I put out to fend him off from myself. He turned with animal swiftness.

In some indefinable way the black face thus flashed upon me shocked me profoundly. It was a singularly deformed one. The facial part projected, forming something dimly suggestive of a muzzle, and the huge half-open mouth showed as big white teeth as I had ever seen in a human mouth. His eyes were blood-shot at the edges, with scarcely a rim of white round the hazel pupils. There was a curious glow of excitement in his face.

"Confound you!" said Montgomery. "Why the devil don't you get out of the way?"

The black-faced man started aside without a word. I went on up the companion, staring at him instinctively as I did so. Montgomery stayed at the foot for a moment. "You have no business here, you know," he said in a deliberate tone. "Your place is forward."

The black-faced man cowered. "They—won't have me forward." He spoke slowly, with a queer, hoarse quality in his voice.

"Won't have you forward!" said Montgomery, in a menacing voice. "But I tell you to go!" He was on the brink of saying something further, then looked up at me suddenly and followed me up the ladder.

I had paused half way through the hatchway, looking back, still astonished beyond measure at the grotesque ugliness of this black-faced creature. I had never beheld such a repulsive and extraordinary face before, and yet—if the contradiction is credible—I experienced at the same time an odd feeling that in some way I *had* already encountered exactly the features and gestures that now amazed me. Afterwards it occurred to me that probably I had seen him as I was lifted aboard; and yet that scarcely satisfied my suspicion of a previous acquaintance. Yet how one could have set eyes on so singular a face and yet have forgotten the precise occasion, passed my imagination.

Montgomery's movement to follow me released my attention, and I turned and looked about me at the flush deck of the little schooner. I was already half prepared by the sounds I had heard for what I saw. Certainly I never beheld a deck so dirty. It was littered with scraps of carrot, shreds of green stuff, and indescribable filth. Fastened by chains to the mainmast were a number of grisly staghounds, who now began leaping and barking at me, and by the mizzen a huge puma was cramped in a little iron cage far too small even to give it turning room. Farther under the starboard bulwark were some big hutches containing a number of rabbits, and a solitary llama was squeezed in a mere box of a cage forward. The dogs were muzzled by leather straps. The only human being on deck was a gaunt and silent sailor at the wheel.

The patched and dirty spankers were tense before the wind, and up aloft the little ship seemed carrying every sail she had. The sky was clear, the sun midway down the western sky; long waves, capped by the breeze with froth, were running with us. We went past the steersman to the taff-rail, and saw the water come foaming under the stern and the bubbles go dancing and vanishing in her wake. I turned and surveyed the unsavoury length of the ship.

"Is this an ocean menagerie?" said I.

"Looks like it," said Montgomery.

"What are these beasts for? Merchandise, curios? Does the captain think he is going to sell them somewhere in the South Seas?"

"It looks like it, doesn't it?" said Montgomery, and turned towards the wake again.

Suddenly we heard a yelp and a volley of furious blasphemy from the companion hatchway, and the deformed man with the black face came up hurriedly. He was immediately followed by a heavy red-haired man in a white cap. At the sight of the former the staghounds, who had all tired of barking at me by this time, became furiously excited, howling and leaping against their chains. The black hesitated before them, and this gave the red-haired man time to come up with him and deliver a tremendous blow between the shoulder-blades. The poor devil went down like a felled ox, and rolled in the dirt among the furiously excited dogs. It was lucky for him that they were muzzled. The red-haired man gave a yawp of exultation and stood staggering, and as it seemed to me in serious danger of either going backwards down the companion hatchway or forwards upon his victim.

So soon as the second man had appeared, Montgomery had started forward. "Steady on there!" he cried, in a tone of remonstrance. A couple of sailors appeared on the forecastle. The black-faced man, howling in a singular voice rolled about under the feet of the dogs. No one attempted to help him. The brutes did their best to worry him, butting their muzzles at him. There was a quick dance of their lithe grey-figured bodies over the clumsy, prostrate figure. The sailors forward shouted, as though it was admirable sport. Montgomery gave an angry exclamation, and went striding down the deck, and I followed him. The black-faced man scrambled up and staggered forward, going and leaning over the bulwark by the main shrouds, where he remained, panting and glaring over his shoulder at the dogs. The red-haired man laughed a satisfied laugh.

"Look here, Captain," said Montgomery, with his lisp a little accentuated, gripping the elbows of the red-haired man, "this won't do!"

I stood behind Montgomery. The captain came half round, and regarded him with the dull and solemn eyes of a drunken man. "Wha' won't do?" he said, and added, after looking sleepily into Montgomery's face for a minute, "Blasted Sawbones!"

With a sudden movement he shook his arms free, and after two ineffectual attempts stuck his freckled fists into his side pockets.

"That man's a passenger," said Montgomery. "I'd advise you to keep your hands off him."

"Go to hell!" said the captain, loudly. He suddenly turned and staggered towards the side. "Do what I like on my own ship," he said.

I think Montgomery might have left him then, seeing the brute was drunk; but he only turned a shade paler, and followed the captain to the bulwarks.

"Look you here, Captain," he said; "that man of mine is not to be ill-treated. He has been hazed ever since he came aboard."

For a minute, alcoholic fumes kept the captain speechless. "Blasted Sawbones!" was all he considered necessary.

I could see that Montgomery had one of those slow, pertinacious tempers that will warm day after day to a white heat, and never again cool to forgiveness; and I saw too that this quarrel had been some time growing. "The man's drunk," said I, perhaps officiously; "you'll do no good."

Montgomery gave an ugly twist to his dropping lip. "He's always drunk. Do you think that excuses his assaulting his passengers?"

"My ship," began the captain, waving his hand unsteadily towards the cages, "was a clean ship. Look at it now!" It was certainly anything but clean. "Crew," continued the captain, "clean, respectable crew."

"You agreed to take the beasts."

"I wish I'd never set eyes on your infernal island. What the devil—want beasts for on an island like that? Then, that man of yours—understood he was a man. He's a lunatic; and he hadn't no business aft. Do you think the whole damned ship belongs to you?"

"Your sailors began to haze the poor devil as soon as he came aboard."

"That's just what he is—he's a devil! an ugly devil! My men can't stand him. *I* can't stand him. None of us can't stand him. Nor *you* either!"

Montgomery turned away. "*You* leave that man alone, anyhow," he said, nodding his head as he spoke.

But the captain meant to quarrel now. He raised his voice. "If he comes this end of the ship again I'll cut his insides out, I tell you. Cut out his blasted insides! Who are you, to tell me what I'm to do? I tell you I'm captain of this ship,—captain and owner. I'm the law here, I tell you,—the law and the prophets. I bargained to take a man and his attendant to and from Arica, and bring back some animals. I never bargained to carry a mad devil and a silly Sawbones, a—"

Well, never mind what he called Montgomery. I saw the latter take a step forward, and interposed. "He's drunk," said I. The captain began some abuse even fouler than the last. "Shut up!" I said, turning on him sharply, for I had seen danger in Montgomery's white face. With that I brought the downpour on myself.

However, I was glad to avert what was uncommonly near a scuffle, even at the price of the captain's drunken ill-will. I do not think I have ever heard quite so much vile language come in a continuous stream from any man's lips before, though I have frequented eccentric company enough. I found some of it hard to endure, though I am a mild-tempered man; but, certainly, when I told the captain to "shut up" I had forgotten that I was merely a bit of human flotsam, cut off from my resources and with my fare unpaid; a mere casual dependant on the bounty, or speculative enterprise, of the ship. He reminded me of it with considerable vigour; but at any rate I prevented a fight.

IV

At the Schooner's Rail

THAT NIGHT LAND WAS SIGHTED AFTER SUNDOWN, and the schooner hove to. Montgomery intimated that was his destination. It was too far to see any details; it seemed to me then simply a low-lying patch of dim blue in the uncertain blue-grey sea. An almost vertical streak of smoke went up from it into the sky. The captain was not on deck when it was sighted. After he had vented his wrath on me he had staggered below, and I understand he went to sleep on the floor of his own cabin. The mate practically assumed the command. He was the gaunt, taciturn individual we had seen at the wheel. Apparently he was in an evil temper with Montgomery. He took not the slightest notice of either of us. We dined with him in a sulky silence, after a few ineffectual efforts on my part to talk. It struck me too that the men regarded my companion and his animals in a singularly unfriendly manner. I found Montgomery very reticent about his purpose with these creatures, and about his destination; and though I was sensible of a growing curiosity as to both, I did not press him.

We remained talking on the quarter deck until the sky was thick with stars. Except for an occasional sound in the yellow-lit forecastle and a movement of the animals now and then, the night was very still. The puma lay crouched together, watching us with shining eyes, a black heap in the corner of its cage. Montgomery produced some cigars. He talked to me of London in a tone of half-painful reminiscence, asking all kinds of questions about changes that had taken place. He spoke like a man who had loved his life there, and had been suddenly and irrevocably cut off from it. I gossiped as well as I could of this and that. All the time the strangeness of him was shaping itself in my mind; and as I talked I peered at his odd, pallid face in the dim light of the binnacle lantern behind me. Then I looked out at the darkling sea, where in the dimness his little island was hidden.

This man, it seemed to me, had come out of Immensity merely to save my life. Tomorrow he would drop over the side, and vanish again out of my existence. Even had it been under commonplace circumstances, it would have made me a trifle thoughtful; but in the first place was the singularity of an educated man living on this unknown little island, and coupled with that the extraordinary nature of his luggage. I found myself repeating the captain's question. What did he want with the beasts? Why, too, had he pretended they were not his when I had remarked about them at first? Then, again, in his personal attendant there was a bizarre quality which had impressed me profoundly. These circumstances threw a haze of mystery round the man. They laid hold of my imagination, and hampered my tongue.

Towards midnight our talk of London died away, and we stood side by side leaning over the bulwarks and staring dreamily over the silent, starlit sea, each pursuing his own thoughts. It was the atmosphere for sentiment, and I began upon my gratitude.

"If I may say it," said I, after a time, "you have saved my life."

"Chance," he answered. "Just chance."

"I prefer to make my thanks to the accessible agent."

"Thank no one. You had the need, and I had the knowledge; and I injected and fed you much as I might have collected a specimen. I was bored and wanted something to do. If I'd been jaded that day, or hadn't liked your face, well—it's a curious question where you would have been now!"

This damped my mood a little. "At any rate," I began.

"It's a chance, I tell you," he interrupted, "as everything is in a man's life. Only the asses won't see it! Why am I here now, an outcast from civilisation, instead of being a happy man enjoying all the pleasures of London? Simply because eleven years ago—I lost my head for ten minutes on a foggy night."

He stopped. "Yes?" said I.

"That's all."

We relapsed into silence. Presently he laughed. "There's something in this starlight that loosens one's tongue. I'm an ass, and yet somehow I would like to tell you."

"Whatever you tell me, you may rely upon my keeping to myself—if that's it."

He was on the point of beginning, and then shook his head, doubtfully.

"Don't," said I. "It is all the same to me. After all, it is better to keep your secret. There's nothing gained but a little relief if I respect your confidence. If I don't—well?"

He grunted undecidedly. I felt I had him at a disadvantage, had caught him in the mood of indiscretion; and to tell the truth I was not curious to learn what might have driven a young medical student out of London. I have an imagination. I shrugged my shoulders and turned away. Over the taffrail leant a silent black figure, watching the stars. It was Montgomery's strange attendant. It looked over its shoulder quickly with my movement, then looked away again.

It may seem a little thing to you, perhaps, but it came like a sudden blow to me. The only light near us was a lantern at the wheel. The creature's face was turned for one brief instant out of the dimness of the stern towards this illumination, and I saw that the eyes that glanced at me shone with a pale-green light. I did not know then that a reddish luminosity, at least, is not uncommon in human eyes. The thing came to me as stark inhumanity. That black figure with its eyes of fire struck down through all my adult thoughts and feelings, and for a moment the forgotten horrors of childhood came back to my mind. Then the effect passed as it had come. An uncouth black figure of a man, a figure of no particular import, hung over the taffrail against the starlight, and I found Montgomery was speaking to me.

"I'm thinking of turning in, then," said he, "if you've had enough of this."

I answered him incongruously. We went below, and he wished me good-night at the door of my cabin.

That night I had some very unpleasant dreams. The waning moon rose late. Its light struck a ghostly white beam across my cabin, and made an ominous shape on the planking by my bunk. Then the staghounds woke, and began howling and baying; so that I dreamt fitfully, and scarcely slept until the approach of dawn.

V

The Man Who had Nowhere to Go

IN THE EARLY MORNING (it was the second morning after my recovery, and I believe the fourth after I was picked up), I awoke through an avenue of tumultuous dreams,—dreams of guns and howling mobs,—and became sensible of a hoarse shouting above me. I rubbed my eyes and lay listening to the noise, doubtful for a little while of my whereabouts. Then came a sudden pattering of bare feet, the sound of heavy objects being thrown about, a violent creaking and the rattling of chains. I heard the swish of the water as the ship was suddenly brought round, and a foamy yellow-green wave flew across the little round window and left it streaming. I jumped into my clothes and went on deck.

As I came up the ladder I saw against the flushed sky—for the sun was just rising—the broad back and red hair of the captain, and over his shoulder the puma spinning from a tackle rigged on to the mizzen spanker-boom.

The poor brute seemed horribly scared, and crouched in the bottom of its little cage.

"Overboard with 'em!" bawled the captain. "Overboard with 'em! We'll have a clean ship soon of the whole bilin' of 'em."

He stood in my way, so that I had perforce to tap his shoulder to come on deck. He came round with a start, and staggered back a few paces to stare at me. It needed no expert eye to tell that the man was still drunk.

"Hullo!" said he, stupidly; and then with a light coming into his eyes, "Why, it's Mister—Mister?"

"Prendick," said I.

"Prendick be damned!" said he. "Shut-up,—that's your name. Mister Shut-up."

It was no good answering the brute; but I certainly did not expect his next move. He held out his hand to the gangway by which Montgomery stood talking to a massive grey-haired man in dirty-blue flannels, who had apparently just come aboard.

"That way, Mister Blasted Shut-up! that way!" roared the captain.

Montgomery and his companion turned as he spoke.

"What do you mean?" I said.

"That way, Mister Blasted Shut-up,—that's what I mean! Overboard, Mister Shut-up,—and sharp! We're cleaning the ship out,—cleaning the whole blessed ship out; and overboard you go!"

I stared at him dumfounded. Then it occurred to me that it was exactly the thing I wanted. The lost prospect of a journey as sole passenger with this quarrelsome sot was not one to mourn over. I turned towards Montgomery.

"Can't have you," said Montgomery's companion, concisely.

"You can't have me!" said I, aghast. He had the squarest and most resolute face I ever set eyes upon.

"Look here," I began, turning to the captain.

"Overboard!" said the captain. "This ship aint for beasts and cannibals and worse than beasts, any more. Overboard you go, Mister Shut-up. If they can't have you, you goes overboard. But, anyhow, you go—with your friends. I've done with this blessed island for evermore, amen! I've had enough of it."

"But, Montgomery," I appealed.

He distorted his lower lip, and nodded his head hopelessly at the grey-haired man beside him, to indicate his powerlessness to help me.

"I'll see to *you*, presently," said the captain.

Then began a curious three-cornered altercation. Alternately I appealed to one and another of the three men,—first to the grey-haired man to let me land, and then to the drunken captain to keep me aboard. I even bawled entreaties to the sailors. Montgomery said never a word, only shook his head. "You're going overboard, I tell you," was the captain's refrain. "Law be damned! I'm king here." At last I must confess my voice suddenly broke in the middle of a vigorous threat. I felt a gust of hysterical petulance, and went aft and stared dismally at nothing.

Meanwhile the sailors progressed rapidly with the task of unshipping the packages and caged animals. A large launch, with two standing lugs, lay under the lee of the schooner; and into this the strange assortment of goods were swung. I did not then see the hands from the island that were receiving the packages, for the hull of the launch was hidden from me by the side of the schooner. Neither Montgomery nor his companion took the slightest notice of me, but busied themselves in assisting and directing the four or five sailors who were unloading the goods. The captain went forward interfering rather than assisting. I was alternately despairful and desperate. Once or twice as I stood waiting there for things to accomplish themselves, I could not resist an impulse to laugh at my miserable quandary. I felt all the wretcheder for the lack of a breakfast. Hunger and a lack of blood-corpuscles take all the manhood from a man. I perceived pretty clearly that I had not the stamina either to resist what the captain chose to do to expel me, or to force myself upon Montgomery and his companion. So I waited passively upon fate; and the work of transferring Montgomery's possessions to the launch went on as if I did not exist.

Presently that work was finished, and then came a struggle. I was hauled, resisting weakly enough, to the gangway. Even then I noticed the oddness of the brown faces of the men who were with Montgomery in the launch; but the launch was now fully laden, and was shoved off hastily. A broadening gap of green water appeared under me, and I pushed back with all my strength to avoid falling headlong. The hands in the launch shouted derisively, and I heard Montgomery curse at them; and then the captain, the mate, and one of the seamen helping him, ran me aft towards the stern.

The dingey of the *Lady Vain* had been towing behind; it was half full of water, had no oars, and was quite unvictualled. I refused to go aboard her, and flung myself full length on the deck. In the end, they swung me into her by a rope (for they had no stern ladder), and then they cut me adrift. I drifted slowly from the schooner. In a kind of stupor I watched all hands take to the rigging, and slowly but surely she came round to the wind; the sails fluttered, and then bellied out as the wind came into them. I stared at her weather-beaten side heeling steeply towards me; and then she passed out of my range of view.

I did not turn my head to follow her. At first I could scarcely believe what had happened. I crouched in the bottom of the dingey, stunned, and staring blankly at the vacant, oily sea. Then I realised that I was in that little hell of mine again, now half swamped; and looking back over the gunwale, I saw the schooner standing away from me, with the red-haired captain mocking at me over the taffrail, and turning towards the island saw the launch growing smaller as she approached the beach.

Abruptly the cruelty of this desertion became clear to me. I had no means of reaching the land unless I should chance to drift there. I was still weak, you must remember, from my exposure in the boat; I was empty and very faint, or I should have had more heart. But as it was I suddenly began to sob and weep, as I had never done since I was a little child. The tears ran down my face. In a passion of despair I struck with my fists at the water in the bottom of the boat, and kicked savagely at the gunwale. I prayed aloud for God to let me die.

VI

The Evil-Looking Boatmen

BUT THE ISLANDERS, SEEING THAT I WAS REALLY ADRIFT, took pity on me. I drifted very slowly to the eastward, approaching the island slantingly; and presently I saw, with hysterical relief, the launch come round and return towards me. She was heavily laden, and I could make out as she drew nearer Montgomery's white-haired, broad-shouldered companion sitting cramped up with the dogs and several packing-cases in the stern sheets. This individual stared fixedly at me without moving or speaking. The black-faced cripple was glaring at me as fixedly in the bows near the puma. There were three other men besides,—three strange brutish-looking fellows, at whom the staghounds were snarling savagely. Montgomery, who was steering, brought the boat by me, and rising, caught and fastened my painter to the tiller to tow me, for there was no room aboard.

I had recovered from my hysterical phase by this time and answered his hail, as he approached, bravely enough. I told him the dingey was nearly swamped, and he reached me a piggin. I was jerked back as the rope tightened between the boats. For some time I was busy baling.

It was not until I had got the water under (for the water in the dingey had been shipped; the boat was perfectly sound) that I had leisure to look at the people in the launch again.

The white-haired man I found was still regarding me steadfastly, but with an expression, as I now fancied, of some perplexity. When my eyes met his, he looked down at the staghound that sat between his knees. He was a powerfully-built man, as I have said, with a fine forehead and rather heavy features; but his eyes had that odd drooping of the skin above the lids which often comes with advancing years, and the fall of his heavy mouth at the corners gave him an expression of pugnacious resolution. He talked to Montgomery in a tone too low for me to hear.

From him my eyes travelled to his three men; and a strange crew they were. I saw only their faces, yet there was something in their faces—I knew not what—that gave me a queer spasm of disgust. I looked steadily at them, and the impression did not pass, though I failed to see what had occasioned it. They seemed to me then to be brown men; but their limbs were oddly swathed in some thin, dirty, white stuff down even to the fingers and feet: I have never seen men so wrapped up before, and women so only in the East. They wore turbans too, and thereunder peered out their elfin faces at me,—faces with protruding lower-jaws and bright eyes. They had lank black hair, almost like horsehair, and seemed as they sat to exceed in stature any race of men I have seen. The white-haired man, who I knew was a good six feet in height, sat a head below any one of the three. I found afterwards that really none were taller than myself; but their bodies were abnormally long, and the thigh-part of the leg short and curiously twisted. At any rate, they were an amazingly ugly gang, and over the heads of them under the forward lug peered the black face of the man whose eyes were luminous in the dark. As I stared at them, they met my gaze; and then first one and then another turned away from my direct stare, and looked at me in an odd, furtive manner. It occurred to me that I was perhaps annoying them, and I turned my attention to the island we were approaching.

It was low, and covered with thick vegetation,—chiefly a kind of palm, that was new to me. From one point a thin white thread of vapour rose slantingly to an immense height, and then frayed out like a down feather. We were now within the embrace of a broad bay flanked on either hand by a low promontory. The beach was of dull-grey sand, and sloped steeply up to a ridge, perhaps sixty or seventy feet above the sea-level, and irregularly set with trees and undergrowth. Half way up was a square enclosure of some greyish stone, which I found subsequently was built partly of coral and partly of pumiceous lava. Two thatched roofs peeped from within this enclosure. A man stood awaiting us at the water's edge. I fancied while we were still far off that I saw some other and very grotesque-looking creatures scuttle into the bushes upon the slope; but I saw nothing of these as we drew nearer. This man was of a moderate size, and with a black negroid face. He had a large, almost lipless, mouth, extraordinary lank arms, long thin feet, and bow-legs, and stood with his heavy face thrust forward staring at us. He was dressed like Montgomery and his white-haired companion, in jacket and trousers of blue serge. As we came still nearer, this individual began to run to and fro on the beach, making the most grotesque movements.

At a word of command from Montgomery, the four men in the launch sprang up, and with singularly awkward gestures struck the lugs. Montgomery steered us round and into a narrow little dock excavated in the beach. Then the man on the beach hastened towards us. This dock, as I call it, was really a mere ditch just long enough at this phase of the tide to take the longboat. I heard the bows ground in the sand, staved the dingey off the rudder of the big boat with my piggin, and freeing the painter, landed. The three muffled men, with the clumsiest movements, scrambled out upon the sand, and forthwith set to landing the cargo, assisted by the man on the beach. I was struck especially by the curious movements of the legs of the three swathed and bandaged boatmen,—not stiff they were, but distorted in some odd way, almost as if they were jointed in the wrong place. The dogs were still snarling, and strained at their chains after these men, as the white-haired man landed with them. The three big fellows spoke to one another in odd guttural tones, and the man who had waited for us on the beach began chattering to them excitedly—a foreign language, as I fancied—as they laid hands on some bales piled near the stern. Somewhere I had heard such a voice before, and I could not think where. The white-haired man stood, holding in a tumult of six dogs, and bawling orders over their din. Montgomery, having unshipped the rudder, landed likewise, and all set to work at unloading. I was too faint, what with my long fast and the sun beating down on my bare head, to offer any assistance.

Presently the white-haired man seemed to recollect my presence, and came up to me.

"You look," said he, "as though you had scarcely breakfasted." His little eyes were a brilliant black under his heavy brows. "I must apologise for that. Now you are our guest, we must make you comfortable,—though you are uninvited, you know." He looked keenly into my face. "Montgomery says you are an educated man, Mr. Prendick; says you know something of science. May I ask what that signifies?"

I told him I had spent some years at the Royal College of Science, and had done some researches in biology under Huxley. He raised his eyebrows slightly at that.

"That alters the case a little, Mr. Prendick," he said, with a trifle more respect in his manner. "As it happens, we are biologists here. This is a biological station—of a sort." His eye rested on the men in white who were busily hauling the puma, on rollers, towards the walled yard. "I and Montgomery, at least," he added. Then, "When you will be able to get away, I can't say. We're off the track to anywhere. We see a ship once in a twelve-month or so."

He left me abruptly, and went up the beach past this group, and I think entered the enclosure. The other two men were with Montgomery, erecting a pile of smaller packages on a low-wheeled truck. The llama was still on the launch with the rabbit hutches; the staghounds were still lashed to the thwarts. The pile of things completed, all three men laid hold of the truck and began shoving the ton-weight or so upon it after the puma. Presently Montgomery left them, and coming back to me held out his hand.

"I'm glad," said he, "for my own part. That captain was a silly ass. He'd have made things lively for you."

"It was you," said I, "that saved me again."

"That depends. You'll find this island an infernally rum place, I promise you. I'd watch my goings carefully, if I were you. *He*—" He hesitated, and seemed to alter his mind about what was on his lips. "I wish you'd help me with these rabbits," he said.

His procedure with the rabbits was singular. I waded in with him, and helped him lug one of the hutches ashore. No sooner was that done than he opened the door of it, and tilting the thing on one end turned its living contents out on the ground. They fell in a struggling heap one on the top of the other. He clapped his hands, and forthwith they went off with that hopping run of theirs, fifteen or twenty of them I should think, up the beach.

"Increase and multiply, my friends," said Montgomery. "Replenish the island. Hitherto we've had a certain lack of meat here."

As I watched them disappearing, the white-haired man returned with a brandy-flask and some biscuits. "Something to go on with, Prendick," said he, in a far more familiar tone than before. I made no ado, but set to work on the biscuits at once, while the white-haired man helped Montgomery to release about a score more of the rabbits. Three big hutches, however, went up to the house with the puma. The brandy I did not touch, for I have been an abstainer from my birth.

VII

The Locked Door

The reader will perhaps understand that at first everything was so strange about me, and my position was the outcome of such unexpected adventures, that I had no discernment of the relative strangeness of this or that thing. I followed the llama up the beach, and was overtaken by Montgomery, who asked me not to enter the stone enclosure. I noticed then that the puma in its cage and the pile of packages had been placed outside the entrance to this quadrangle.

I turned and saw that the launch had now been unloaded, run out again, and was being beached, and the white-haired man was walking towards us. He addressed Montgomery.

"And now comes the problem of this uninvited guest. What are we to do with him?"

"He knows something of science," said Montgomery.

"I'm itching to get to work again—with this new stuff," said the white-haired man, nodding towards the enclosure. His eyes grew brighter.

"I daresay you are," said Montgomery, in anything but a cordial tone.

"We can't send him over there, and we can't spare the time to build him a new shanty; and we certainly can't take him into our confidence just yet."

"I'm in your hands," said I. I had no idea of what he meant by "over there."

"I've been thinking of the same things," Montgomery answered. "There's my room with the outer door—"

"That's it," said the elder man, promptly, looking at Montgomery; and all three of us went towards the enclosure. "I'm sorry to make a mystery, Mr. Prendick; but you'll remember you're uninvited. Our little establishment here contains a secret or so, is a kind of Blue-Beard's chamber, in fact. Nothing very dreadful, really, to a sane man; but just now, as we don't know you—"

"Decidedly," said I, "I should be a fool to take offence at any want of confidence."

He twisted his heavy mouth into a faint smile—he was one of those saturnine people who smile with the corners of the mouth down,—and bowed his acknowledgment of my complaisance. The main entrance to the enclosure was passed; it was a heavy wooden gate, framed in iron and locked, with the cargo of the launch piled outside it, and at the corner we came to a small doorway I had not previously observed. The white-haired man produced a bundle of keys from the pocket of his greasy blue jacket, opened this door, and entered. His keys, and the elaborate locking-up of the place even while it was still under his eye, struck me as peculiar. I followed him, and found myself in a small apartment, plainly but not uncomfortably furnished and with its inner door, which was slightly ajar, opening into a paved courtyard. This inner door Montgomery at once closed. A hammock was slung across the darker corner of the room, and a small unglazed window defended by an iron bar looked out towards the sea.

This the white-haired man told me was to be my apartment; and the inner door, which "for fear of accidents," he said, he would lock on the other side, was my limit inward. He called my attention to a convenient deck-chair before the window, and to an array of old books, chiefly, I found, surgical works and editions of the Latin and Greek classics (languages I cannot read with any comfort), on a shelf near the hammock. He left the room by the outer door, as if to avoid opening the inner one again.

"We usually have our meals in here," said Montgomery, and then, as if in doubt, went out after the other. "Moreau!" I heard him call, and for the moment I do not think I noticed. Then as I handled the books on the shelf it came up in consciousness: Where had I heard the name of Moreau before? I sat down before the window, took out the biscuits that still remained to me, and ate them with an excellent appetite. Moreau!

Through the window I saw one of those unaccountable men in white, lugging a packing-case along the beach. Presently the window-frame hid him. Then I heard a key inserted and turned in the lock behind me. After a little while I heard through the locked door the noise of the staghounds, that had now been brought up from the beach. They were not barking, but sniffing and growling in a curious fashion. I could hear the rapid patter of their feet, and Montgomery's voice soothing them.

I was very much impressed by the elaborate secrecy of these two men regarding the contents of the place, and for some time I was thinking of that and of the unaccountable familiarity of the name of Moreau; but so odd is the human memory that I could not then recall that well-known name in its proper connection. From that my thoughts went to the indefinable queerness of the deformed man on the beach. I never saw such a gait, such odd motions as he pulled at the box. I recalled that none of these men had spoken to me, though most of them I had found looking at me at one time or another in a peculiarly furtive manner, quite unlike the frank stare of your unsophisticated savage. Indeed, they had all seemed remarkably taciturn, and when they did speak, endowed with very uncanny voices. What was wrong with them? Then I recalled the eyes of Montgomery's ungainly attendant.

Just as I was thinking of him he came in. He was now dressed in white, and carried a little tray with some coffee and boiled vegetables thereon. I could hardly repress a shuddering recoil as he came, bending amiably, and placed the tray before me on the table. Then astonishment paralysed me. Under his stringy black locks I saw his ear; it jumped upon me suddenly close to my face. The man had pointed ears, covered with a fine brown fur!

"Your breakfast, sair," he said.

I stared at his face without attempting to answer him. He turned and went towards the door, regarding me oddly over his shoulder. I followed him out with my eyes; and as I did so, by some odd trick of unconscious cerebration, there came surging into my head the phrase, "The Moreau Hollows"—was it? "The Moreau—" Ah! It sent my memory back ten years. "The Moreau Horrors!" The phrase drifted loose in my mind for a moment, and then I saw it in red lettering on a little buff-coloured pamphlet, to read which made one shiver and creep. Then I remembered distinctly all about it. That long-forgotten pamphlet came back with startling vividness to my mind. I had been a mere lad then, and Moreau was, I suppose, about fifty,—a prominent and masterful physiologist, well-known in scientific circles for his extraordinary imagination and his brutal directness in discussion.

Was this the same Moreau? He had published some very astonishing facts in connection with the transfusion of blood, and in addition was known to be doing valuable work on morbid growths. Then suddenly his career was closed. He had to leave England. A journalist obtained access to his laboratory in the capacity of laboratory-assistant, with the deliberate intention of making sensational exposures; and by the help of a shocking accident (if it was an accident), his gruesome pamphlet became notorious. On the day of its publication a wretched dog, flayed and otherwise mutilated, escaped from Moreau's house. It was in the silly season, and a prominent editor, a cousin of the temporary laboratory-assistant, appealed to the conscience of the nation. It was not the first time that conscience has turned against the methods of research. The doctor was simply howled out of the country. It may be that he deserved to be; but I still think that the tepid support of his fellow-investigators and his desertion by the great body of scientific workers was a shameful thing. Yet some of his experiments, by the journalist's account, were wantonly cruel. He might perhaps have purchased his social peace by abandoning his investigations; but he apparently preferred the latter, as most men would who have once fallen under the overmastering spell of research. He was unmarried, and had indeed nothing but his own interest to consider.

I felt convinced that this must be the same man. Everything pointed to it. It dawned upon me to what end the puma and the other animals—which had now been brought with other luggage into the enclosure behind the house—were destined; and a curious faint odour, the halitus of something familiar, an odour that had been in the background of my consciousness hitherto, suddenly came forward into the forefront of my thoughts. It was the antiseptic odour of the dissecting-room. I heard the puma growling through the wall, and one of the dogs yelped as though it had been struck.

Yet surely, and especially to another scientific man, there was nothing so horrible in vivisection as to account for this secrecy; and by some odd leap in my thoughts the pointed ears and luminous eyes of Montgomery's attendant came back again before me with the sharpest definition. I stared before me out at the green sea, frothing under a freshening breeze, and let these and other strange memories of the last few days chase one another through my mind.

What could it all mean? A locked enclosure on a lonely island, a notorious vivisector, and these crippled and distorted men?

VIII

The Crying of the Puma

Montgomery interrupted my tangle of mystification and suspicion about one o'clock, and his grotesque attendant followed him with a tray bearing bread, some herbs and other eatables, a flask of whiskey, a jug of water, and three glasses and knives. I glanced askance at this strange creature, and found him watching me with his queer, restless eyes. Montgomery said he would lunch with me, but that Moreau was too preoccupied with some work to come.

"Moreau!" said I. "I know that name."

"The devil you do!" said he. "What an ass I was to mention it to you! I might have thought. Anyhow, it will give you an inkling of our—mysteries. Whiskey?"

"No, thanks; I'm an abstainer."

"I wish I'd been. But it's no use locking the door after the steed is stolen. It was that infernal stuff which led to my coming here,—that, and a foggy night. I thought myself in luck at the time, when Moreau offered to get me off. It's queer—"

"Montgomery," said I, suddenly, as the outer door closed, "why has your man pointed ears?"

"Damn!" he said, over his first mouthful of food. He stared at me for a moment, and then repeated, "Pointed ears?"

"Little points to them," said I, as calmly as possible, with a catch in my breath; "and a fine black fur at the edges?"

He helped himself to whiskey and water with great deliberation. "I was under the impression—that his hair covered his ears."

"I saw them as he stooped by me to put that coffee you sent to me on the table. And his eyes shine in the dark."

By this time Montgomery had recovered from the surprise of my question. "I always thought," he said deliberately, with a certain accentuation of his flavouring of lisp, "that there *was* something the matter with his ears, from the way he covered them. What were they like?"

I was persuaded from his manner that this ignorance was a pretence. Still, I could hardly tell the man that I thought him a liar. "Pointed," I said; "rather small and furry,—distinctly furry. But the whole man is one of the strangest beings I ever set eyes on."

A sharp, hoarse cry of animal pain came from the enclosure behind us. Its depth and volume testified to the puma. I saw Montgomery wince.

"Yes?" he said.

"Where did you pick up the creature?"

"San Francisco. He's an ugly brute, I admit. Half-witted, you know. Can't remember where he came from. But I'm used to him, you know. We both are. How does he strike you?"

"He's unnatural," I said. "There's something about him—don't think me fanciful, but it gives me a nasty little sensation, a tightening of my muscles, when he comes near me. It's a touch—of the diabolical, in fact."

Montgomery had stopped eating while I told him this. "Rum!" he said. "I can't see it." He resumed his meal. "I had no idea of it," he said, and masticated. "The crew of the schooner must have felt it the same. Made a dead set at the poor devil. You saw the captain?"

Suddenly the puma howled again, this time more painfully. Montgomery swore under his breath. I had half a mind to attack him about the men on the beach. Then the poor brute within gave vent to a series of short, sharp cries.

"Your men on the beach," said I; "what race are they?"

"Excellent fellows, aren't they?" said he, absentmindedly, knitting his brows as the animal yelled out sharply.

I said no more. There was another outcry worse than the former. He looked at me with his dull grey eyes, and then took some more whiskey. He tried to draw me into a discussion about alcohol, professing to have saved my life with it. He seemed anxious to lay stress on the fact that I owed my life to him. I answered him distractedly.

Presently our meal came to an end; the misshapen monster with the pointed ears cleared the remains away, and Montgomery left me alone in the room again. All the time he had been in a state of ill-concealed irritation at the noise of the vivisected puma. He had spoken of his odd want of nerve, and left me to the obvious application.

I found myself that the cries were singularly irritating, and they grew in depth and intensity as the afternoon wore on. They were painful at first, but their constant resurgence at last altogether upset my balance. I flung aside a crib of Horace I had been reading, and began to clench my fists, to bite my lips, and to pace the room. Presently I got to stopping my ears with my fingers.

The emotional appeal of those yells grew upon me steadily, grew at last to such an exquisite expression of suffering that I could stand it in that confined room no longer. I stepped out of the door into the slumberous heat of the late afternoon, and walking past the main entrance—locked again, I noticed—turned the corner of the wall.

The crying sounded even louder out of doors. It was as if all the pain in the world had found a voice. Yet had I known such pain was in the next room, and had it been dumb, I believe—I have thought since—I could have stood it well enough. It is when suffering finds a voice and sets our nerves quivering that this pity comes troubling us. But in spite of the brilliant sunlight and the green fans of the trees waving in the soothing sea-breeze, the world was a confusion, blurred with drifting black and red phantasms, until I was out of earshot of the house in the chequered wall.

IX

The Thing in the Forest

I strode through the undergrowth that clothed the ridge behind the house, scarcely heeding whither I went; passed on through the shadow of a thick cluster of straight-stemmed trees beyond it, and so presently found myself some way on the other side of the ridge, and descending towards a streamlet that ran through a narrow valley. I paused and listened. The distance I had come, or the intervening masses of thicket, deadened any sound that might be coming from the enclosure. The air was still. Then with a rustle a rabbit emerged, and went scampering up the slope before me. I hesitated, and sat down in the edge of the shade.

The place was a pleasant one. The rivulet was hidden by the luxuriant vegetation of the banks save at one point, where I caught a triangular patch of its glittering water. On the farther side I saw through a bluish haze a tangle of trees and creepers, and above these again the luminous blue of the sky. Here and there a splash of white or crimson marked the blooming of some trailing epiphyte. I let my eyes wander over this scene for a while, and then began to turn over in my mind again the strange peculiarities of Montgomery's man. But it was too hot to think elaborately, and presently I fell into a tranquil state midway between dozing and waking.

From this I was aroused, after I know not how long, by a rustling amidst the greenery on the other side of the stream. For a moment I could see nothing but the waving summits of the ferns and reeds. Then suddenly upon the bank of the stream appeared something—at first I could not distinguish what it was. It bowed its round head to the water, and began to drink. Then I saw it was a man, going on all-fours like a beast. He was clothed in bluish cloth, and was of a copper-coloured hue, with black hair. It seemed that grotesque ugliness was an invariable character of these islanders. I could hear the suck of the water at his lips as he drank.

I leant forward to see him better, and a piece of lava, detached by my hand, went pattering down the slope. He looked up guiltily, and his eyes met mine. Forthwith he scrambled to his feet, and stood wiping his clumsy hand across his mouth and regarding me. His legs were scarcely half the length of his body. So, staring one another out of countenance, we remained for perhaps the space of a minute. Then, stopping to look back once or twice, he slunk off among the bushes to the right of me, and I heard the swish of the fronds grow faint in the distance and die away. Long after he had disappeared, I remained sitting up staring in the direction of his retreat. My drowsy tranquillity had gone.

I was startled by a noise behind me, and turning suddenly saw the flapping white tail of a rabbit vanishing up the slope. I jumped to my feet. The apparition of this grotesque, half-bestial creature had suddenly populated the stillness of the afternoon for me. I looked around me rather nervously, and regretted that I was unarmed. Then I thought that the man I had just seen had been clothed in bluish cloth, had not been naked as a savage would have been; and I tried to persuade myself from that fact that he was after all probably a peaceful character, that the dull ferocity of his countenance belied him.

Yet I was greatly disturbed at the apparition. I walked to the left along the slope, turning my head about and peering this way and that among the straight stems of the trees. Why should a man go on all-fours and drink with his lips? Presently I heard an animal wailing again, and taking it to be the puma, I turned about and walked in a direction diametrically opposite to the sound. This led me down to the stream, across which I stepped and pushed my way up through the undergrowth beyond.

I was startled by a great patch of vivid scarlet on the ground, and going up to it found it to be a peculiar fungus, branched and corrugated like a foliaceous lichen, but deliquescing into slime at the touch; and then in the shadow of some luxuriant ferns I came upon an unpleasant thing,—the dead body of a rabbit covered with shining flies, but still warm and with the head torn off. I stopped aghast at the sight of the scattered blood. Here at least was one visitor to the island disposed of! There were no traces of other violence about it. It looked as though it had been suddenly snatched up and killed; and as I stared at the little furry body came the difficulty of how the thing had been done. The vague dread that had been in my mind since I had seen the inhuman face of the man at the stream grew distincter as I stood there. I began to realise the hardihood of my expedition among these unknown people. The thicket about me became altered to my imagination. Every shadow became something more than a shadow,—became an ambush; every rustle became a threat. Invisible things seemed watching me. I resolved to go back to the enclosure on the beach. I suddenly turned away and thrust myself violently, possibly even frantically, through the bushes, anxious to get a clear space about me again.

I stopped just in time to prevent myself emerging upon an open space. It was a kind of glade in the forest, made by a fall; seedlings were already starting up to struggle for the vacant space; and beyond, the dense growth of stems and twining vines and splashes of fungus and flowers closed in again. Before me, squatting together upon the fungoid ruins of a huge fallen tree and still unaware of my approach, were three grotesque human figures. One was evidently a female; the other two were men. They were naked, save for swathings of scarlet cloth about the middle; and their skins were of a dull pinkish-drab colour, such as I had seen in no savages before. They had fat, heavy, chinless faces, retreating foreheads, and a scant bristly hair upon their heads. I never saw such bestial-looking creatures.

They were talking, or at least one of the men was talking to the other two, and all three had been too closely interested to heed the rustling of my approach. They swayed their heads and shoulders from side to side. The speaker's words came thick and sloppy, and though I could hear them distinctly I could not distinguish what he said. He seemed to me to be reciting some complicated gibberish. Presently his articulation became shriller, and spreading his hands he rose to his feet. At that the others began to gibber in unison, also rising to their feet, spreading their hands and swaying their bodies in rhythm with their chant. I noticed then the abnormal shortness of their legs, and their lank, clumsy feet. All three began slowly to circle round, raising and stamping their feet and waving their arms; a kind of tune crept into their rhythmic recitation, and a refrain,—"Aloola," or "Balloola," it sounded like. Their eyes began to sparkle, and their ugly faces to brighten, with an expression of strange pleasure. Saliva dripped from their lipless mouths.

Suddenly, as I watched their grotesque and unaccountable gestures, I perceived clearly for the first time what it was that had offended me, what had given me the two inconsistent and conflicting impressions of utter strangeness and yet of the strangest familiarity. The three creatures engaged in this mysterious rite were human in shape, and yet human beings with the strangest air about them of some familiar animal. Each of these creatures, despite its human form, its rag of clothing, and the rough humanity of its bodily form, had woven into it—into its movements, into the expression of its countenance, into its whole presence—some now irresistible suggestion of a hog, a swinish taint, the unmistakable mark of the beast.

I stood overcome by this amazing realisation and then the most horrible questionings came rushing into my mind. They began leaping in the air, first one and then the other, whooping and grunting. Then one slipped, and for a moment was on all-fours,—to recover, indeed, forthwith. But that transitory gleam of the true animalism of these monsters was enough.

I turned as noiselessly as possible, and becoming every now and then rigid with the fear of being discovered, as a branch cracked or a leaf rustled, I pushed back into the bushes. It was long before I grew bolder, and dared to move freely. My only idea for the moment was to get away from these foul beings, and I scarcely noticed that I had emerged upon a faint pathway amidst the trees. Then suddenly traversing a little glade, I saw with an unpleasant start two clumsy legs among the trees, walking with noiseless footsteps parallel with my course, and perhaps thirty yards away from me. The head and upper part of the body were hidden by a tangle of creeper. I stopped abruptly, hoping the creature did not see me. The feet stopped as I did. So nervous was I that I controlled an impulse to headlong flight with the utmost difficulty. Then looking hard, I distinguished through the interlacing network the head and body of the brute I had seen drinking. He moved his head. There was an emerald flash in his eyes as he glanced at me from the shadow of the trees, a half-luminous colour that vanished as he turned his head again. He was motionless for a moment, and then with a noiseless tread began running through the green confusion. In another moment he had vanished behind some bushes. I could not see him, but I felt that he had stopped and was watching me again.

What on earth was he,—man or beast? What did he want with me? I had no weapon, not even a stick. Flight would be madness. At any rate the Thing, whatever it was, lacked the courage to attack me. Setting my teeth hard, I walked straight towards him. I was anxious not to show the fear that seemed chilling my backbone. I pushed through a tangle of tall white-flowered bushes, and saw him twenty paces beyond, looking over his shoulder at me and hesitating. I advanced a step or two, looking steadfastly into his eyes.

"Who are you?" said I.

He tried to meet my gaze. "No!" he said suddenly, and turning went bounding away from me through the undergrowth. Then he turned and stared at me again. His eyes shone brightly out of the dusk under the trees.

My heart was in my mouth; but I felt my only chance was bluff, and walked steadily towards him. He turned again, and vanished into the dusk. Once more I thought I caught the glint of his eyes, and that was all.

For the first time I realised how the lateness of the hour might affect me. The sun had set some minutes since, the swift dusk of the tropics was already fading out of the eastern sky, and a pioneer moth fluttered silently by my head. Unless I would spend the night among the unknown dangers of the mysterious forest, I must hasten back to the enclosure. The thought of a return to that pain-haunted refuge was extremely disagreeable, but still more so was the idea of being overtaken in the open by darkness and all that darkness might conceal. I gave one more look into the blue shadows that had swallowed up this odd creature, and then retraced my way down the slope towards the stream, going as I judged in the direction from which I had come.

I walked eagerly, my mind confused with many things, and presently found myself in a level place among scattered trees. The colourless clearness that comes after the sunset flush was darkling; the blue sky above grew momentarily deeper, and the little stars one by one pierced the attenuated light; the interspaces of the trees, the gaps in the further vegetation, that had been hazy blue in the daylight, grew black and mysterious. I pushed on. The colour vanished from the world. The tree-tops rose against the luminous blue sky in inky silhouette, and all below that outline melted into one formless blackness. Presently the trees grew thinner, and the shrubby undergrowth more abundant. Then there was a desolate space covered with a white sand, and then another expanse of tangled bushes. I did not remember crossing the sand-opening before. I began to be tormented by a faint rustling upon my right hand. I thought at first it was fancy, for whenever I stopped there was silence, save for the evening breeze in the tree-tops. Then when I turned to hurry on again there was an echo to my footsteps.

I turned away from the thickets, keeping to the more open ground, and endeavouring by sudden turns now and then to surprise something in the act of creeping upon me. I saw nothing, and nevertheless my sense of another presence grew steadily. I increased my pace, and after some time came to a slight ridge, crossed it, and turned sharply, regarding it steadfastly from the further side. It came out black and clear-cut against the darkling sky; and presently a shapeless lump heaved up momentarily against the sky-line and vanished again. I felt assured now that my tawny-faced antagonist was stalking me once more; and coupled with that was another unpleasant realisation, that I had lost my way.

For a time I hurried on hopelessly perplexed, and pursued by that stealthy approach. Whatever it was, the Thing either lacked the courage to attack me, or it was waiting to take me at some disadvantage. I kept studiously to the open. At times I would turn and listen; and presently I had half persuaded myself that my pursuer had abandoned the chase, or was a mere creation of my disordered imagination. Then I heard the sound of the sea. I quickened my footsteps almost into a run, and immediately there was a stumble in my rear.

I turned suddenly, and stared at the uncertain trees behind me. One black shadow seemed to leap into another. I listened, rigid, and heard nothing but the creep of the blood in my ears. I thought that my nerves were unstrung, and that my imagination was tricking me, and turned resolutely towards the sound of the sea again.

In a minute or so the trees grew thinner, and I emerged upon a bare, low headland running out into the sombre water. The night was calm and clear, and the reflection of the growing multitude of the stars shivered in the tranquil heaving of the sea. Some way out, the wash upon an irregular band of reef shone with a pallid light of its own. Westward I saw the zodiacal light mingling with the yellow brilliance of the evening star. The coast fell away from me to the east, and westward it was hidden by the shoulder of the cape. Then I recalled the fact that Moreau's beach lay to the west.

A twig snapped behind me, and there was a rustle. I turned, and stood facing the dark trees. I could see nothing—or else I could see too much. Every dark form in the dimness had its ominous quality, its peculiar suggestion of alert watchfulness. So I stood for perhaps a minute, and then, with an eye to the trees still, turned westward to cross the headland; and as I moved, one among the lurking shadows moved to follow me.

My heart beat quickly. Presently the broad sweep of a bay to the westward became visible, and I halted again. The noiseless shadow halted a dozen yards from me. A little point of light shone on the further bend of the curve, and the grey sweep of the sandy beach lay faint under the starlight. Perhaps two miles away was that little point of light. To get to the beach I should have to go through the trees where the shadows lurked, and down a bushy slope.

I could see the Thing rather more distinctly now. It was no animal, for it stood erect. At that I opened my mouth to speak, and found a hoarse phlegm choked my voice. I tried again, and shouted, "Who is there?" There was no answer. I advanced a step. The Thing did not move, only gathered itself together. My foot struck a stone. That gave me an idea. Without taking my eyes off the black form before me, I stooped and picked up this lump of rock; but at my motion the Thing turned abruptly as a dog might have done, and slunk obliquely into the further darkness. Then I recalled a schoolboy expedient against big dogs, and twisted the rock into my handkerchief, and gave this a turn round my wrist. I heard a movement further off among the shadows, as if the Thing was in retreat. Then suddenly my tense excitement gave way; I broke into a profuse perspiration and fell a-trembling, with my adversary routed and this weapon in my hand.

It was some time before I could summon resolution to go down through the trees and bushes upon the flank of the headland to the beach. At last

I did it at a run; and as I emerged from the thicket upon the sand, I heard some other body come crashing after me. At that I completely lost my head with fear, and began running along the sand. Forthwith there came the swift patter of soft feet in pursuit. I gave a wild cry, and redoubled my pace. Some dim, black things about three or four times the size of rabbits went running or hopping up from the beach towards the bushes as I passed.

So long as I live, I shall remember the terror of that chase. I ran near the water's edge, and heard every now and then the splash of the feet that gained upon me. Far away, hopelessly far, was the yellow light. All the night about us was black and still. Splash, splash, came the pursuing feet, nearer and nearer. I felt my breath going, for I was quite out of training; it whooped as I drew it, and I felt a pain like a knife at my side. I perceived the Thing would come up with me long before I reached the enclosure, and, desperate and sobbing for my breath, I wheeled round upon it and struck at it as it came up to me,—struck with all my strength. The stone came out of the sling of the handkerchief as I did so. As I turned, the Thing, which had been running on all-fours, rose to its feet, and the missile fell fair on its left temple. The skull rang loud, and the animal-man blundered into me, thrust me back with its hands, and went staggering past me to fall headlong upon the sand with its face in the water; and there it lay still.

I could not bring myself to approach that black heap. I left it there, with the water rippling round it, under the still stars, and giving it a wide berth pursued my way towards the yellow glow of the house; and presently, with a positive effect of relief, came the pitiful moaning of the puma, the sound that had originally driven me out to explore this mysterious island. At that, though I was faint and horribly fatigued, I gathered together all my strength, and began running again towards the light. I thought I heard a voice calling me.

X

The Crying of the Man

As I drew near the house I saw that the light shone from the open door of my room; and then I heard coming from out of the darkness at the side of that orange oblong of light, the voice of Montgomery shouting, "Prendick!" I continued running. Presently I heard him again. I replied by a feeble "Hullo!" and in another moment had staggered up to him.

"Where have you been?" said he, holding me at arm's length, so that the light from the door fell on my face. "We have both been so busy that we forgot you until about half an hour ago." He led me into the room and sat me down in the deck chair. For awhile I was blinded by the light. "We did not think you would start to explore this island of ours without telling us," he said; and then, "I was afraid—But—what—Hullo!"

My last remaining strength slipped from me, and my head fell forward on my chest. I think he found a certain satisfaction in giving me brandy.

"For God's sake," said I, "fasten that door."

"You've been meeting some of our curiosities, eh?" said he.

He locked the door and turned to me again. He asked me no questions, but gave me some more brandy and water and pressed me to eat. I was in a state of collapse. He said something vague about his forgetting to warn me, and asked me briefly when I left the house and what I had seen.

I answered him as briefly, in fragmentary sentences. "Tell me what it all means," said I, in a state bordering on hysterics.

"It's nothing so very dreadful," said he. "But I think you have had about enough for one day." The puma suddenly gave a sharp yell of pain. At that he swore under his breath. "I'm damned," said he, "if this place is not as bad as Gower Street, with its cats."

"Montgomery," said I, "what was that thing that came after me? Was it a beast or was it a man?"

"If you don't sleep tonight," he said, "you'll be off your head tomorrow."

I stood up in front of him. "What was that thing that came after me?" I asked.

He looked me squarely in the eyes, and twisted his mouth askew. His eyes, which had seemed animated a minute before, went dull. "From your account," said he, "I'm thinking it was a bogle."

I felt a gust of intense irritation, which passed as quickly as it came. I flung myself into the chair again, and pressed my hands on my forehead. The puma began once more.

Montgomery came round behind me and put his hand on my shoulder. "Look here, Prendick," he said, "I had no business to let you drift out into this silly island of ours. But it's not so bad as you feel, man. Your nerves are worked to rags. Let me give you something that will make you sleep. *That*—will keep on for hours yet. You must simply get to sleep, or I won't answer for it."

I did not reply. I bowed forward, and covered my face with my hands. Presently he returned with a small measure containing a dark liquid. This he gave me. I took it unresistingly, and he helped me into the hammock.

When I awoke, it was broad day. For a little while I lay flat, staring at the roof above me. The rafters, I observed, were made out of the timbers of a ship. Then I turned my head, and saw a meal prepared for me on the table. I perceived that I was hungry, and prepared to clamber out of the hammock, which, very politely anticipating my intention, twisted round and deposited me upon all-fours on the floor.

I got up and sat down before the food. I had a heavy feeling in my head, and only the vaguest memory at first of the things that had happened over night. The morning breeze blew very pleasantly through the unglazed window, and that and the food contributed to the sense of animal comfort which I experienced. Presently the door behind me—the door inward towards the yard of the enclosure—opened. I turned and saw Montgomery's face.

"All right," said he. "I'm frightfully busy." And he shut the door.

Afterwards I discovered that he forgot to re-lock it. Then I recalled the expression of his face the previous night, and with that the memory of all I had experienced reconstructed itself before me. Even as that fear came back to me came a cry from within; but this time it was not the cry of a puma. I put down the mouthful that hesitated upon my lips, and listened. Silence, save for the whisper of the morning breeze. I began to think my ears had deceived me.

After a long pause I resumed my meal, but with my ears still vigilant. Presently I heard something else, very faint and low. I sat as if frozen in my attitude. Though it was faint and low, it moved me more profoundly than all that I had hitherto heard of the abominations behind the wall. There was no mistake this time in the quality of the dim, broken sounds; no doubt at all of their source. For it was groaning, broken by sobs and gasps of anguish. It was no brute this time; it was a human being in torment!

As I realised this I rose, and in three steps had crossed the room, seized the handle of the door into the yard, and flung it open before me.

"Prendick, man! Stop!" cried Montgomery, intervening.

A startled deerhound yelped and snarled. There was blood, I saw, in the sink,—brown, and some scarlet—and I smelt the peculiar smell of carbolic acid. Then through an open doorway beyond, in the dim light of the shadow, I saw something bound painfully upon a framework, scarred, red, and bandaged; and then blotting this out appeared the face of old Moreau, white and terrible. In a moment he had gripped me by the shoulder with a hand that was smeared red, had twisted me off my feet, and flung me headlong back into my own room. He lifted me as though I was a little child. I fell at full length upon the floor, and the door slammed and shut out the passionate intensity of his face. Then I heard the key turn in the lock, and Montgomery's voice in expostulation.

"Ruin the work of a lifetime," I heard Moreau say.

"He does not understand," said Montgomery. and other things that were inaudible.

"I can't spare the time yet," said Moreau.

The rest I did not hear. I picked myself up and stood trembling, my mind a chaos of the most horrible misgivings. Could it be possible, I thought, that such a thing as the vivisection of men was carried on here? The question shot like lightning across a tumultuous sky; and suddenly the clouded horror of my mind condensed into a vivid realisation of my own danger.

XI

The Hunting of the Man

It came before my mind with an unreasonable hope of escape that the outer door of my room was still open to me. I was convinced now, absolutely assured, that Moreau had been vivisecting a human being. All the time since I had heard his name, I had been trying to link in my mind in some way the grotesque animalism of the islanders with his abominations; and now I thought I saw it all. The memory of his work on the transfusion of blood recurred to me. These creatures I had seen were the victims of some hideous experiment. These sickening scoundrels had merely intended to keep me back, to fool me with their display of confidence, and presently to fall upon me with a fate more horrible than death,—with torture; and after torture the most hideous degradation it is possible to conceive,—to send me off a lost soul, a beast, to the rest of their Comus rout.

I looked round for some weapon. Nothing. Then with an inspiration I turned over the deck chair, put my foot on the side of it, and tore away the side rail. It happened that a nail came away with the wood, and projecting, gave a touch of danger to an otherwise petty weapon. I heard a step outside, and incontinently flung open the door and found Montgomery within a yard of it. He meant to lock the outer door! I raised this nailed stick of mine and cut at his face; but he sprang back. I hesitated a moment, then turned and fled, round the corner of the house. "Prendick, man!" I heard his astonished cry, "don't be a silly ass, man!"

Another minute, thought I, and he would have had me locked in, and as ready as a hospital rabbit for my fate. He emerged behind the corner, for I heard him shout, "Prendick!" Then he began to run after me, shouting things as he ran. This time running blindly, I went northeastward in a direction at right angles to my previous expedition. Once, as I went running headlong up the beach, I glanced over my shoulder and saw his attendant with him. I ran furiously up the slope, over it, then turning eastward along a rocky valley fringed on either side with jungle I ran for perhaps a mile altogether, my chest straining, my heart beating in my ears; and then hearing nothing of Montgomery or his man, and feeling upon the verge of exhaustion, I doubled sharply back towards the beach as I judged, and lay down in the shelter of a canebrake. There I remained for a long time, too fearful to move, and indeed too fearful even to plan a course of action. The wild scene about me lay sleeping silently under the sun, and the only sound near me was the thin hum of some small gnats that had discovered me. Presently I became aware of a drowsy breathing sound, the soughing of the sea upon the beach.

After about an hour I heard Montgomery shouting my name, far away to the north. That set me thinking of my plan of action. As I interpreted it then, this island was inhabited only by these two vivisectors and their animalised victims. Some of these no doubt they could press into their service against me if need arose. I knew both Moreau and Montgomery carried revolvers; and, save for a feeble bar of deal spiked with a small nail, the merest mockery of a mace, I was unarmed.

So I lay still there, until I began to think of food and drink; and at that thought the real hopelessness of my position came home to me. I knew no way of getting anything to eat. I was too ignorant of botany to discover any resort of root or fruit that might lie about me; I had no means of trapping the few rabbits upon the island. It grew blanker the more I turned the prospect over. At last in the desperation of my position, my mind turned to the animal men I had encountered. I tried to find some hope in what I remembered of them. In turn I recalled each one I had seen, and tried to draw some augury of assistance from my memory.

Then suddenly I heard a staghound bay, and at that realised a new danger. I took little time to think, or they would have caught me then, but snatching up my nailed stick, rushed headlong from my hiding-place to-wards the sound of the sea. I remember a growth of thorny plants, with spines that stabbed like pen-knives. I emerged bleeding and with torn clothes upon the lip of a long creek opening northward. I went straight into the water without a minute's hesitation, wading up the creek, and presently finding myself kneedeep in a little stream. I scrambled out at last on the westward bank, and with my heart beating loudly in my ears, crept into a tangle of ferns to await the issue. I heard the dog (there was only one) draw nearer, and yelp when it came to the thorns. Then I heard no more, and presently began to think I had escaped.

The minutes passed; the silence lengthened out, and at last after an hour of security my courage began to return to me. By this time I was no longer very much terrified or very miserable. I had, as it were, passed the limit of terror and despair. I felt now that my life was practically lost, and that persuasion made me capable of daring anything. I had even a certain wish to encounter Moreau face to face; and as I had waded into the water, I remembered that if I were too hard pressed at least one path of escape from torment still lay open to me,—they could not very well prevent my drowning myself. I had half a mind to drown myself then; but an odd wish to see the whole adventure out, a queer, impersonal, spectacular interest in myself, restrained me. I stretched my limbs, sore and painful from the pricks of the spiny plants, and stared around me at the trees; and, so sud-denly that it seemed to jump out of the green tracery about it, my eyes lit upon a black face watching me. I saw that it was the simian creature who had met the launch upon the beach. He was clinging to the oblique stem of a palm-tree. I gripped my stick, and stood up facing him. He began chattering. "You, you, you," was all I could distinguish at first. Suddenly he dropped from the tree, and in another moment was holding the fronds apart and staring curiously at me.

I did not feel the same repugnance towards this creature which I had ex-perienced in my encounters with the other Beast Men. "You," he said, "in the boat." He was a man, then,—at least as much of a man as Montgomery's attendant,—for he could talk.

"Yes," I said, "I came in the boat. From the ship."

"Oh!" he said, and his bright, restless eyes travelled over me, to my hands, to the stick I carried, to my feet, to the tattered places in my coat, and the cuts and scratches I had received from the thorns. He seemed puzzled at something. His eyes came back to my hands. He held his own hand out and counted his digits slowly, "One, two, three, four, five—eigh?"

I did not grasp his meaning then; afterwards I was to find that a great proportion of these Beast People had malformed hands, lacking sometimes even three digits. But guessing this was in some way a greeting, I did the same thing by way of reply. He grinned with immense satisfaction. Then his swift roving glance went round again; he made a swift movement—and vanished. The fern fronds he had stood between came swishing together.

I pushed out of the brake after him, and was astonished to find him swinging cheerfully by one lank arm from a rope of creepers that looped down from the foliage overhead. His back was to me.

"Hullo!" said I.

He came down with a twisting jump, and stood facing me.

"I say," said I, "where can I get something to eat?"

"Eat!" he said. "Eat Man's food, now." And his eye went back to the swing of ropes. "At the huts."

"But where are the huts?"

"Oh!"

"I'm new, you know."

At that he swung round, and set off at a quick walk. All his motions were curiously rapid. "Come along," said he.

I went with him to see the adventure out. I guessed the huts were some rough shelter where he and some more of these Beast People lived. I might perhaps find them friendly, find some handle in their minds to take hold of. I did not know how far they had forgotten their human heritage.

My ape-like companion trotted along by my side, with his hands hanging down and his jaw thrust forward. I wondered what memory he might have in him. "How long have you been on this island?" said I.

"How long?" he asked; and after having the question repeated, he held up three fingers.

The creature was little better than an idiot. I tried to make out what he meant by that, and it seems I bored him. After another question or two he suddenly left my side and went leaping at some fruit that hung from a tree.

He pulled down a handful of prickly husks and went on eating the contents. I noted this with satisfaction, for here at least was a hint for feeding. I tried him with some other questions, but his chattering, prompt responses were as often as not quite at cross purposes with my question. Some few were appropriate, others quite parrot-like.

I was so intent upon these peculiarities that I scarcely noticed the path we followed. Presently we came to trees, all charred and brown, and so to a bare place covered with a yellow-white incrustation, across which a drifting smoke, pungent in whiffs to nose and eyes, went drifting. On our right, over a shoulder of bare rock, I saw the level blue of the sea. The path coiled down abruptly into a narrow ravine between two tumbled and knotty masses of blackish scoriae. Into this we plunged.

It was extremely dark, this passage, after the blinding sunlight reflected from the sulphurous ground. Its walls grew steep, and approached each other. Blotches of green and crimson drifted across my eyes. My conductor stopped suddenly. "Home!" said he, and I stood in a floor of a chasm that was at first absolutely dark to me. I heard some strange noises, and thrust the knuckles of my left hand into my eyes. I became aware of a disagreeable odor, like that of a monkey's cage ill-cleaned. Beyond, the rock opened again upon a gradual slope of sunlit greenery, and on either hand the light smote down through narrow ways into the central gloom.

XII

The Sayers of the Law

Then something cold touched my hand. I started violently, and saw close to me a dim pinkish thing, looking more like a flayed child than anything else in the world. The creature had exactly the mild but repulsive features of a sloth, the same low forehead and slow gestures.

As the first shock of the change of light passed, I saw about me more distinctly. The little sloth-like creature was standing and staring at me. My conductor had vanished. The place was a narrow passage between high walls of lava, a crack in the knotted rock, and on either side interwoven heaps of sea-mat, palm-fans, and reeds leaning against the rock formed rough and impenetrably dark dens. The winding way up the ravine between these was scarcely three yards wide, and was disfigured by lumps of decaying fruit-pulp and other refuse, which accounted for the disagreeable stench of the place.

The little pink sloth-creature was still blinking at me when my Ape-man reappeared at the aperture of the nearest of these dens, and beckoned me in. As he did so a slouching monster wriggled out of one of the places, further up this strange street, and stood up in featureless silhouette against the bright green beyond, staring at me. I hesitated, having half a mind to bolt the way I had come; and then, determined to go through with the adventure, I gripped my nailed stick about the middle and crawled into the little evil-smelling lean-to after my conductor.

It was a semi-circular space, shaped like the half of a bee-hive; and against the rocky wall that formed the inner side of it was a pile of variegated fruits, cocoa-nuts among others. Some rough vessels of lava and wood stood about the floor, and one on a rough stool. There was no fire. In the darkest corner of the hut sat a shapeless mass of darkness that grunted "Hey!" as I came in, and my Ape-man stood in the dim light of the doorway and held out a split cocoa-nut to me as I crawled into the other corner and squatted down. I took it, and began gnawing it, as serenely as possible, in spite of a certain trepidation and the nearly intolerable closeness of the den. The little pink sloth-creature stood in the aperture of the hut, and something else with a drab face and bright eyes came staring over its shoulder.

"Hey!" came out of the lump of mystery opposite. "It is a man."

"It is a man," gabbled my conductor, "a man, a man, a five-man, like me."

"Shut up!" said the voice from the dark, and grunted. I gnawed my cocoa-nut amid an impressive stillness.

I peered hard into the blackness, but could distinguish nothing.

"It is a man," the voice repeated. "He comes to live with us?"

It was a thick voice, with something in it—a kind of whistling overtone—that struck me as peculiar; but the English accent was strangely good.

The Ape-man looked at me as though he expected something. I perceived the pause was interrogative. "He comes to live with you," I said.

"It is a man. He must learn the Law."

I began to distinguish now a deeper blackness in the black, a vague outline of a hunched-up figure. Then I noticed the opening of the place was darkened by two more black heads. My hand tightened on my stick.

The thing in the dark repeated in a louder tone, "Say the words." I had missed its last remark. "Not to go on all fours; that is the Law," it repeated in a kind of sing-song.

I was puzzled.

"Say the words," said the Ape-man, repeating, and the figures in the doorway echoed this, with a threat in the tone of their voices.

I realised that I had to repeat this idiotic formula; and then began the insanest ceremony. The voice in the dark began intoning a mad litany, line by line, and I and the rest to repeat it. As they did so, they swayed from side to side in the oddest way, and beat their hands upon their knees; and I followed their example. I could have imagined I was already dead and in another world. That dark hut, these grotesque dim figures, just flecked here and there by a glimmer of light, and all of them swaying in unison and chanting,

> *Not to go on all-fours; that is the Law. Are we not Men?*
> *Not to suck up Drink; that is the Law. Are we not Men?*
> *Not to eat Fish or Flesh; that is the Law. Are we not Men?*
> *Not to claw the Bark of Trees; that is the Law. Are we not Men?*
> *Not to chase other Men; that is the Law. Are we not Men?*

And so from the prohibition of these acts of folly, on to the prohibition of what I thought then were the maddest, most impossible, and most indecent things one could well imagine. A kind of rhythmic fervour fell on all of us; we gabbled and swayed faster and faster, repeating this amazing Law. Superficially the contagion of these brutes was upon me, but deep down within me the laughter and disgust struggled together. We ran through a long list of prohibitions, and then the chant swung round to a new formula.

> *His is the House of Pain.*
> *His is the Hand that makes.*
> *His is the Hand that wounds.*
> *His is the Hand that heals.*

And so on for another long series, mostly quite incomprehensible gibberish to me about *Him*, whoever he might be. I could have fancied it was a dream, but never before have I heard chanting in a dream.

"*His* is the lightning flash," we sang. "*His* is the deep, salt sea."

A horrible fancy came into my head that Moreau, after animalising these men, had infected their dwarfed brains with a kind of deification of himself. However, I was too keenly aware of white teeth and strong claws about me to stop my chanting on that account.

"*His* are the stars in the sky."

At last that song ended. I saw the Ape-man's face shining with perspiration; and my eyes being now accustomed to the darkness, I saw more distinctly the figure in the corner from which the voice came. It was the size of a man, but it seemed covered with a dull grey hair almost like a Skye-terrier. What was it? What were they all? Imagine yourself surrounded by all the most horrible cripples and maniacs it is possible to conceive, and you may understand a little of my feelings with these grotesque caricatures of humanity about me.

"He is a five-man, a five-man, a five-man—like me," said the Ape-man.

I held out my hands. The grey creature in the corner leant forward.

"Not to run on all-fours; that is the Law. Are we not Men?" he said.

He put out a strangely distorted talon and gripped my fingers. The thing was almost like the hoof of a deer produced into claws. I could have yelled with surprise and pain. His face came forward and peered at my nails, came forward into the light of the opening of the hut and I saw with a quivering disgust that it was like the face of neither man nor beast, but a mere shock of grey hair, with three shadowy over-archings to mark the eyes and mouth.

"He has little nails," said this grisly creature in his hairy beard. "It is well."

He threw my hand down, and instinctively I gripped my stick.

"Eat roots and herbs; it is His will," said the Ape-man.

"I am the Sayer of the Law," said the grey figure. "Here come all that be new to learn the Law. I sit in the darkness and say the Law."

"It is even so," said one of the beasts in the doorway.

"Evil are the punishments of those who break the Law. None escape."

"None escape," said the Beast Folk, glancing furtively at one another.

"None, none," said the Ape-man,—"none escape. See! I did a little thing, a wrong thing, once. I jabbered, jabbered, stopped talking. None could understand. I am burnt, branded in the hand. He is great. He is good!"

"None escape," said the grey creature in the corner.

"None escape," said the Beast People, looking askance at one another.

"For every one the want that is bad," said the grey Sayer of the Law. "What you will want we do not know; we shall know. Some want to follow things that move, to watch and slink and wait and spring; to kill and bite,

bite deep and rich, sucking the blood. It is bad. 'Not to chase other Men; that is the Law. Are we not Men? Not to eat Flesh or Fish; that is the Law. Are we not Men?'"

"None escape," said a dappled brute standing in the doorway.

"For every one the want is bad," said the grey Sayer of the Law. "Some want to go tearing with teeth and hands into the roots of things, snuffing into the earth. It is bad."

"None escape," said the men in the door.

"Some go clawing trees; some go scratching at the graves of the dead; some go fighting with foreheads or feet or claws; some bite suddenly, none giving occasion; some love uncleanness."

"None escape," said the Ape-man, scratching his calf.

"None escape," said the little pink sloth-creature.

"Punishment is sharp and sure. Therefore learn the Law. Say the words."

And incontinently he began again the strange litany of the Law, and again I and all these creatures began singing and swaying. My head reeled with this jabbering and the close stench of the place; but I kept on, trusting to find presently some chance of a new development.

"Not to go on all-fours; that is the Law. Are we not Men?"

We were making such a noise that I noticed nothing of a tumult outside, until some one, who I think was one of the two Swine Men I had seen, thrust his head over the little pink sloth-creature and shouted something excitedly, something that I did not catch. Incontinently those at the opening of the hut vanished; my Ape-man rushed out; the thing that had sat in the dark followed him (I only observed that it was big and clumsy, and covered with silvery hair), and I was left alone. Then before I reached the aperture I heard the yelp of a staghound.

In another moment I was standing outside the hovel, my chair-rail in my hand, every muscle of me quivering. Before me were the clumsy backs of perhaps a score of these Beast People, their misshapen heads half hidden by their shoulder-blades. They were gesticulating excitedly. Other half-animal faces glared interrogation out of the hovels. Looking in the direction in which they faced, I saw coming through the haze under the trees beyond the end of the passage of dens the dark figure and awful white face of

Moreau. He was holding the leaping staghound back, and close behind him came Montgomery revolver in hand.

For a moment I stood horror-struck. I turned and saw the passage behind me blocked by another heavy brute, with a huge grey face and twinkling little eyes, advancing towards me. I looked round and saw to the right of me and a half-dozen yards in front of me a narrow gap in the wall of rock through which a ray of light slanted into the shadows.

"Stop!" cried Moreau as I strode towards this, and then, "Hold him!"

At that, first one face turned towards me and then others. Their bestial minds were happily slow. I dashed my shoulder into a clumsy monster who was turning to see what Moreau meant, and flung him forward into another. I felt his hands fly round, clutching at me and missing me. The little pink sloth-creature dashed at me, and I gashed down its ugly face with the nail in my stick and in another minute was scrambling up a steep side pathway, a kind of sloping chimney, out of the ravine. I heard a howl behind me, and cries of "Catch him!" "Hold him!" and the grey-faced creature appeared behind me and jammed his huge bulk into the cleft. "Go on! go on!" they howled. I clambered up the narrow cleft in the rock and came out upon the sulphur on the westward side of the village of the Beast Men.

That gap was altogether fortunate for me, for the narrow chimney, slanting obliquely upward, must have impeded the nearer pursuers. I ran over the white space and down a steep slope, through a scattered growth of trees, and came to a low-lying stretch of tall reeds, through which I pushed into a dark, thick undergrowth that was black and succulent under foot. As I plunged into the reeds, my foremost pursuers emerged from the gap. I broke my way through this undergrowth for some minutes. The air behind me and about me was soon full of threatening cries. I heard the tumult of my pursuers in the gap up the slope, then the crashing of the reeds, and every now and then the crackling crash of a branch. Some of the creatures roared like excited beasts of prey. The staghound yelped to the left. I heard Moreau and Montgomery shouting in the same direction. I turned sharply to the right. It seemed to me even then that I heard Montgomery shouting for me to run for my life.

Presently the ground gave rich and oozy under my feet; but I was desperate and went headlong into it, struggled through kneedeep, and so came to a winding path among tall canes. The noise of my pursuers passed away to my left. In one place three strange, pink, hopping animals, about the size of cats, bolted before my footsteps. This pathway ran up hill, across another open space covered with white incrustation, and plunged into a canebrake again. Then suddenly it turned parallel with the edge of a steep-walled gap, which came without warning, like the ha-ha of an English park,—turned with an unexpected abruptness. I was still running with all my might, and I never saw this drop until I was flying headlong through the air.

I fell on my forearms and head, among thorns, and rose with a torn ear and bleeding face. I had fallen into a precipitous ravine, rocky and thorny, full of a hazy mist which drifted about me in wisps, and with a narrow streamlet from which this mist came meandering down the centre. I was astonished at this thin fog in the full blaze of daylight; but I had no time to stand wondering then. I turned to my right, down-stream, hoping to come to the sea in that direction, and so have my way open to drown myself. It was only later I found that I had dropped my nailed stick in my fall.

Presently the ravine grew narrower for a space, and carelessly I stepped into the stream. I jumped out again pretty quickly, for the water was almost boiling. I noticed too there was a thin sulphurous scum drifting upon its coiling water. Almost immediately came a turn in the ravine, and the in-distinct blue horizon. The nearer sea was flashing the sun from a myriad facets. I saw my death before me; but I was hot and panting, with the warm blood oozing out on my face and running pleasantly through my veins. I felt more than a touch of exultation too, at having distanced my pursuers. It was not in me then to go out and drown myself yet. I stared back the way I had come.

I listened. Save for the hum of the gnats and the chirp of some small in-sects that hopped among the thorns, the air was absolutely still. Then came the yelp of a dog, very faint, and a chattering and gibbering, the snap of a whip, and voices. They grew louder, then fainter again. The noise receded up the stream and faded away. For a while the chase was over; but I knew now how much hope of help for me lay in the Beast People.

XIII

A Parley

I turned again and went on down towards the sea. I found the hot
stream broadened out to a shallow, weedy sand, in which an abundance
of crabs and long-bodied, many-legged creatures started from my footfall. I walked to the very edge of the salt water, and then I felt I was safe. I
turned and stared, arms akimbo, at the thick green behind me, into which
the steamy ravine cut like a smoking gash. But, as I say, I was too full of
excitement and (a true saying, though those who have never known danger
may doubt it) too desperate to die.

Then it came into my head that there was one chance before me yet.
While Moreau and Montgomery and their bestial rabble chased me
through the island, might I not go round the beach until I came to their
enclosure,—make a flank march upon them, in fact, and then with a rock
lugged out of their loosely-built wall, perhaps, smash in the lock of the
smaller door and see what I could find (knife, pistol, or what not) to fight
them with when they returned? It was at any rate something to try.

So I turned to the westward and walked along by the water's edge. The
setting sun flashed his blinding heat into my eyes. The slight Pacific tide
was running in with a gentle ripple. Presently the shore fell away southward, and the sun came round upon my right hand. Then suddenly, far
in front of me, I saw first one and then several figures emerging from the

bushes,—Moreau, with his grey staghound, then Montgomery, and two others. At that I stopped.

They saw me, and began gesticulating and advancing. I stood watching them approach. The two Beast Men came running forward to cut me off from the undergrowth, inland. Montgomery came, running also, but straight towards me. Moreau followed slower with the dog.

At last I roused myself from my inaction, and turning seaward walked straight into the water. The water was very shallow at first. I was thirty yards out before the waves reached to my waist. Dimly I could see the intertidal creatures darting away from my feet.

"What are you doing, man?" cried Montgomery.

I turned, standing waist deep, and stared at them. Montgomery stood panting at the margin of the water. His face was bright-red with exertion, his long flaxen hair blown about his head, and his dropping nether lip showed his irregular teeth. Moreau was just coming up, his face pale and firm, and the dog at his hand barked at me. Both men had heavy whips. Farther up the beach stared the Beast Men.

"What am I doing? I am going to drown myself," said I.

Montgomery and Moreau looked at each other. "Why?" asked Moreau.

"Because that is better than being tortured by you."

"I told you so," said Montgomery, and Moreau said something in a low tone.

"What makes you think I shall torture you?" asked Moreau.

"What I saw," I said. "And those—yonder."

"Hush!" said Moreau, and held up his hand.

"I will not," said I. "They were men: what are they now? I at least will not be like them."

I looked past my interlocutors. Up the beach were M'ling, Montgomery's attendant, and one of the white-swathed brutes from the boat. Farther up, in the shadow of the trees, I saw my little Ape-man, and behind him some other dim figures.

"Who are these creatures?" said I, pointing to them and raising my voice more and more that it might reach them. "They were men, men like yourselves, whom you have infected with some bestial taint,—men whom you have enslaved, and whom you still fear.

"You who listen," I cried, pointing now to Moreau and shouting past him to the Beast Men,—"You who listen! Do you not see these men still fear you, go in dread of you? Why, then, do you fear them? You are many—"

"For God's sake," cried Montgomery, "stop that, Prendick!"

"Prendick!" cried Moreau.

They both shouted together, as if to drown my voice; and behind them lowered the staring faces of the Beast Men, wondering, their deformed hands hanging down, their shoulders hunched up. They seemed, as I fancied, to be trying to understand me, to remember, I thought, something of their human past.

I went on shouting, I scarcely remember what,—that Moreau and Montgomery could be killed, that they were not to be feared: that was the burden of what I put into the heads of the Beast People. I saw the green-eyed man in the dark rags, who had met me on the evening of my arrival, come out from among the trees, and others followed him, to hear me better. At last for want of breath I paused.

"Listen to me for a moment," said the steady voice of Moreau; "and then say what you will."

"Well?" said I.

He coughed, thought, then shouted: "Latin, Prendick! bad Latin, school-boy Latin; but try and understand. *Hi non sunt homines; sunt animalia qui nos habemus*—vivisected. A humanising process. I will explain. Come ashore."

I laughed. "A pretty story," said I. "They talk, build houses. They were men. It's likely I'll come ashore."

"The water just beyond where you stand is deep—and full of sharks."

"That's my way," said I. "Short and sharp. Presently."

"Wait a minute." He took something out of his pocket that flashed back the sun, and dropped the object at his feet. "That's a loaded revolver," said he. "Montgomery here will do the same. Now we are going up the beach until you are satisfied the distance is safe. Then come and take the revolvers."

"Not I! You have a third between you."

"I want you to think over things, Prendick. In the first place, I never asked you to come upon this island. If we vivisected men, we should import men, not beasts. In the next, we had you drugged last night, had we wanted to work you any mischief; and in the next, now your first panic is over and you can think a little, is Montgomery here quite up to the character you give him? We have chased you for your good. Because this island is full of inimical phenomena. Besides, why should we want to shoot you when you have just offered to drown yourself?"

"Why did you set—your people onto me when I was in the hut?"

"We felt sure of catching you, and bringing you out of danger. Afterwards we drew away from the scent, for your good."

I mused. It seemed just possible. Then I remembered something again. "But I saw," said I, "in the enclosure—"

"That was the puma."

"Look here, Prendick," said Montgomery, "you're a silly ass! Come out of the water and take these revolvers, and talk. We can't do anything more than we could do now."

I will confess that then, and indeed always, I distrusted and dreaded Moreau; but Montgomery was a man I felt I understood.

"Go up the beach," said I, after thinking, and added, "holding your hands up."

"Can't do that," said Montgomery, with an explanatory nod over his shoulder. "Undignified."

"Go up to the trees, then," said I, "as you please."

"It's a damned silly ceremony," said Montgomery.

Both turned and faced the six or seven grotesque creatures, who stood there in the sunlight, solid, casting shadows, moving, and yet so incredibly unreal. Montgomery cracked his whip at them, and forthwith they all turned and fled helter-skelter into the trees; and when Montgomery and Moreau were at a distance I judged sufficient, I waded ashore, and picked up and examined the revolvers. To satisfy myself against the subtlest trickery, I discharged one at a round lump of lava, and had the satisfaction of seeing the stone pulverised and the beach splashed with lead. Still I hesitated for a moment.

"I'll take the risk," said I, at last; and with a revolver in each hand I walked up the beach towards them.

"That's better," said Moreau, without affectation. "As it is, you have wasted the best part of my day with your confounded imagination." And with a touch of contempt which humiliated me, he and Montgomery turned and went on in silence before me.

The knot of Beast Men, still wondering, stood back among the trees. I passed them as serenely as possible. One started to follow me, but retreated again when Montgomery cracked his whip. The rest stood silent—watching. They may once have been animals; but I never before saw an animal trying to think.

XIV

Doctor Moreau Explains

"**And now, Prendick, I will explain,**" said Doctor Moreau, so soon as we had eaten and drunk. "I must confess that you are the most dictatorial guest I ever entertained. I warn you that this is the last I shall do to oblige you. The next thing you threaten to commit suicide about, I shan't do,—even at some personal inconvenience."

He sat in my deck chair, a cigar half consumed in his white, dexterous-looking fingers. The light of the swinging lamp fell on his white hair; he stared through the little window out at the starlight. I sat as far away from him as possible, the table between us and the revolvers to hand. Montgomery was not present. I did not care to be with the two of them in such a little room.

"You admit that the vivisected human being, as you called it, is, after all, only the puma?" said Moreau. He had made me visit that horror in the inner room, to assure myself of its inhumanity.

"It is the puma," I said, "still alive, but so cut and mutilated as I pray I may never see living flesh again. Of all vile—"

"Never mind that," said Moreau; "at least, spare me those youthful horrors. Montgomery used to be just the same. You admit that it is the puma. Now be quiet, while I reel off my physiological lecture to you."

And forthwith, beginning in the tone of a man supremely bored, but presently warming a little, he explained his work to me. He was very simple and convincing. Now and then there was a touch of sarcasm in his voice. Presently I found myself hot with shame at our mutual positions.

The creatures I had seen were not men, had never been men. They were animals, humanised animals,—triumphs of vivisection.

"You forget all that a skilled vivisector can do with living things," said Moreau. "For my own part, I'm puzzled why the things I have done here have not been done before. Small efforts, of course, have been made,—amputation, tongue-cutting, excisions. Of course you know a squint may be induced or cured by surgery? Then in the case of excisions you have all kinds of secondary changes, pigmentary disturbances, modifications of the passions, alterations in the secretion of fatty tissue. I have no doubt you have heard of these things?"

"Of course," said I. "But these foul creatures of yours—"

"All in good time," said he, waving his hand at me; "I am only beginning. Those are trivial cases of alteration. Surgery can do better things than that. There is building up as well as breaking down and changing. You have heard, perhaps, of a common surgical operation resorted to in cases where the nose has been destroyed: a flap of skin is cut from the forehead, turned down on the nose, and heals in the new position. This is a kind of grafting in a new position of part of an animal upon itself. Grafting of freshly obtained material from another animal is also possible,—the case of teeth, for example. The grafting of skin and bone is done to facilitate healing: the surgeon places in the middle of the wound pieces of skin snipped from another animal, or fragments of bone from a victim freshly killed. Hunter's cock-spur—possibly you have heard of that—flourished on the bull's neck; and the rhinoceros rats of the Algerian zouaves are also to be thought of,— monsters manufactured by transferring a slip from the tail of an ordinary rat to its snout, and allowing it to heal in that position."

"Monsters manufactured!" said I. "Then you mean to tell me—"

"Yes. These creatures you have seen are animals carven and wrought into new shapes. To that, to the study of the plasticity of living forms, my life has been devoted. I have studied for years, gaining in knowledge as I go. I see you look horrified, and yet I am telling you nothing new. It all lay in the surface of practical anatomy years ago, but no one had the temerity to touch it. It is not simply the outward form of an animal which I can change. The physiology, the chemical rhythm of the creature, may also be made to undergo an enduring modification,—of which vaccination and other methods of inoculation with living or dead matter are examples that will, no doubt, be familiar to you. A similar operation is the transfusion of blood,—with which subject, indeed, I began. These are all familiar cases. Less so, and probably far more extensive, were the operations of those mediaeval practitioners who made dwarfs and beggar-cripples, show-monsters,—some vestiges of whose art still remain in the preliminary manipulation of the young mountebank or contortionist. Victor Hugo gives an account of them in 'L'Homme qui Rit.'—But perhaps my meaning grows plain now. You begin to see that it is a possible thing to transplant tissue from one part of an animal to another, or from one animal to another; to alter its chemical reactions and methods of growth; to modify the articulations of its limbs; and, indeed, to change it in its most intimate structure.

"And yet this extraordinary branch of knowledge has never been sought as an end, and systematically, by modern investigators until I took it up! Some such things have been hit upon in the last resort of surgery; most of the kindred evidence that will recur to your mind has been demonstrated as it were by accident,—by tyrants, by criminals, by the breeders of horses and dogs, by all kinds of untrained clumsy-handed men working for their own immediate ends. I was the first man to take up this question armed with antiseptic surgery, and with a really scientific knowledge of the laws of growth. Yet one would imagine it must have been practised in secret before. Such creatures as the Siamese Twins—And in the vaults of the Inquisition. No doubt their chief aim was artistic torture, but some at least of the inquisitors must have had a touch of scientific curiosity."

"But," said I, "these things—these animals talk!"

He said that was so, and proceeded to point out that the possibility of vivisection does not stop at a mere physical metamorphosis. A pig may be educated. The mental structure is even less determinate than the bodily. In our growing science of hypnotism we find the promise of a possibility of superseding old inherent instincts by new suggestions, grafting upon or replacing the inherited fixed ideas. Very much indeed of what we call moral education, he said, is such an artificial modification and perversion of instinct; pugnacity is trained into courageous self-sacrifice, and suppressed sexuality into religious emotion. And the great difference between man and monkey is in the larynx, he continued,—in the incapacity to frame delicately different sound-symbols by which thought could be sustained. In this I failed to agree with him, but with a certain incivility he declined to notice my objection. He repeated that the thing was so, and continued his account of his work.

I asked him why he had taken the human form as a model. There seemed to me then, and there still seems to me now, a strange wickedness for that choice.

He confessed that he had chosen that form by chance. "I might just as well have worked to form sheep into llamas and llamas into sheep. I suppose there is something in the human form that appeals to the artistic turn of mind more powerfully than any animal shape can. But I've not confined myself to man-making. Once or twice—" He was silent, for a minute perhaps. "These years! How they have slipped by! And here I have wasted a day saving your life, and am now wasting an hour explaining myself!"

"But," said I, "I still do not understand. Where is your justification for inflicting all this pain? The only thing that could excuse vivisection to me would be some application—"

"Precisely," said he. "But, you see, I am differently constituted. We are on different platforms. You are a materialist."

"I am *not* a materialist," I began hotly.

"In my view—in my view. For it is just this question of pain that parts us. So long as visible or audible pain turns you sick; so long as your own pains drive you; so long as pain underlies your propositions about sin,—so long, I tell you, you are an animal, thinking a little less obscurely what an animal feels. This pain—"

I gave an impatient shrug at such sophistry.

"Oh, but it is such a little thing! A mind truly opened to what science has to teach must see that it is a little thing. It may be that save in this little planet, this speck of cosmic dust, invisible long before the nearest star could be attained—it may be, I say, that nowhere else does this thing called pain occur. But the laws we feel our way towards—Why, even on this earth, even among living things, what pain is there?"

As he spoke he drew a little penknife from his pocket, opened the smaller blade, and moved his chair so that I could see his thigh. Then, choosing the place deliberately, he drove the blade into his leg and withdrew it.

"No doubt," he said, "you have seen that before. It does not hurt a pin-prick. But what does it show? The capacity for pain is not needed in the muscle, and it is not placed there,—is but little needed in the skin, and only here and there over the thigh is a spot capable of feeling pain. Pain is simply our intrinsic medical adviser to warn us and stimulate us. Not all living flesh is painful; nor is all nerve, not even all sensory nerve. There's no taint of pain, real pain, in the sensations of the optic nerve. If you wound the optic nerve, you merely see flashes of light,—just as disease of the auditory nerve merely means a humming in our ears. Plants do not feel pain, nor the lower animals; it's possible that such animals as the starfish and crayfish do not feel pain at all. Then with men, the more intelligent they become, the more intelligently they will see after their own welfare, and the less they will need the goad to keep them out of danger. I never yet heard of a useless thing that was not ground out of existence by evolution sooner or later. Did you? And pain gets needless.

"Then I am a religious man, Prendick, as every sane man must be. It may be, I fancy, that I have seen more of the ways of this world's Maker than you,—for I have sought his laws, in *my* way, all my life, while you, I understand, have been collecting butterflies. And I tell you, pleasure and pain have nothing to do with heaven or hell. Pleasure and pain—bah! What is your theologian's ecstasy but Mahomet's houri in the dark? This store which men and women set on pleasure and pain, Prendick, is the mark of the beast upon them,—the mark of the beast from which they came! Pain, pain and pleasure, they are for us only so long as we wriggle in the dust.

"You see, I went on with this research just the way it led me. That is the only way I ever heard of true research going. I asked a question, devised some method of obtaining an answer, and got a fresh question. Was this possible or that possible? You cannot imagine what this means to an investigator, what an intellectual passion grows upon him! You cannot imagine the strange, colourless delight of these intellectual desires! The thing before you is no longer an animal, a fellow-creature, but a problem! Sympathetic pain,—all I know of it I remember as a thing I used to suffer from years ago. I wanted—it was the one thing I wanted—to find out the extreme limit of plasticity in a living shape."

"But," said I, "the thing is an abomination—"

"To this day I have never troubled about the ethics of the matter," he continued. "The study of Nature makes a man at last as remorseless as Nature. I have gone on, not heeding anything but the question I was pursuing; and the material has—dripped into the huts yonder. It is nearly eleven years since we came here, I and Montgomery and six Kanakas. I remember the green stillness of the island and the empty ocean about us, as though it was yesterday. The place seemed waiting for me.

"The stores were landed and the house was built. The Kanakas founded some huts near the ravine. I went to work here upon what I had brought with me. There were some disagreeable things happened at first. I began with a sheep, and killed it after a day and a half by a slip of the scalpel. I took another sheep, and made a thing of pain and fear and left it bound up to heal. It looked quite human to me when I had finished it; but when I went to it I was discontented with it. It remembered me, and was terrified beyond imagination; and it had no more than the wits of a sheep. The more I looked at it the clumsier it seemed, until at last I put the monster out of its misery. These animals without courage, these fear-haunted, pain-driven things, without a spark of pugnacious energy to face torment,—they are no good for man-making.

"Then I took a gorilla I had; and upon that, working with infinite care and mastering difficulty after difficulty, I made my first man. All the week, night and day, I moulded him. With him it was chiefly the brain that needed moulding; much had to be added, much changed. I thought him a fair specimen of the negroid type when I had finished him, and he lay bandaged, bound, and motionless before me. It was only when his life was assured that I left him and came into this room again, and found Montgomery much as you are. He had heard some of the cries as the thing grew human,—cries like those that disturbed *you* so. I didn't take him completely into my confidence at first. And the Kanakas too, had realised something of it. They were scared out of their wits by the sight of me. I got Montgomery over to me—in a way; but I and he had the hardest job to prevent the Kanakas deserting. Finally they did; and so we lost the yacht. I spent many days educating the brute,—altogether I had him for three or four months. I taught him the rudiments of English; gave him ideas of counting; even made the thing read the alphabet. But at that he was slow, though I've met with idiots slower. He began with a clean sheet, mentally; had no memories left in his mind of what he had been. When his scars were quite healed, and he was no longer anything but painful and stiff, and able to converse a little, I took him yonder and introduced him to the Kanakas as an interesting stowaway.

"They were horribly afraid of him at first, somehow,—which offended me rather, for I was conceited about him; but his ways seemed so mild, and he was so abject, that after a time they received him and took his education in hand. He was quick to learn, very imitative and adaptive, and built himself a hovel rather better, it seemed to me, than their own shanties. There was one among the boys a bit of a missionary, and he taught the thing to read, or at least to pick out letters, and gave him some rudimentary ideas of morality; but it seems the beast's habits were not all that is desirable.

"I rested from work for some days after this, and was in a mind to write an account of the whole affair to wake up English physiology. Then I came upon the creature squatting up in a tree and gibbering at two of the Kanakas who had been teasing him. I threatened him, told him the inhumanity of such a proceeding, aroused his sense of shame, and came home resolved to do better before I took my work back to England. I have been doing better. But somehow the things drift back again: the stubborn beast-flesh grows day by day back again. But I mean to do better things still. I mean to conquer that. This puma—

"But that's the story. All the Kanaka boys are dead now; one fell overboard of the launch, and one died of a wounded heel that he poisoned in some way with plant-juice. Three went away in the yacht, and I suppose and hope were drowned. The other one—was killed. Well, I have replaced them. Montgomery went on much as you are disposed to do at first, and then—

"What became of the other one?" said I, sharply,—"the other Kanaka who was killed?"

"The fact is, after I had made a number of human creatures I made a Thing—" He hesitated.

"Yes?" said I.

"It was killed."

"I don't understand," said I; "do you mean to say—"

"It killed the Kanaka—yes. It killed several other things that it caught. We chased it for a couple of days. It only got loose by accident—I never meant it to get away. It wasn't finished. It was purely an experiment. It was a limbless thing, with a horrible face, that writhed along the ground in a serpentine fashion. It was immensely strong, and in infuriating pain. It lurked in the woods for some days, until we hunted it; and then it wriggled into the northern part of the island, and we divided the party to close in upon it. Montgomery insisted upon coming with me. The man had a rifle; and when his body was found, one of the barrels was curved into the shape of an S and very nearly bitten through. Montgomery shot the thing. After that I stuck to the ideal of humanity—except for little things."

He became silent. I sat in silence watching his face.

"So for twenty years altogether—counting nine years in England—I have been going on; and there is still something in everything I do that defeats me, makes me dissatisfied, challenges me to further effort. Sometimes I rise above my level, sometimes I fall below it; but always I fall short of the things I dream. The human shape I can get now, almost with ease, so that it is lithe and graceful, or thick and strong; but often there is trouble with the hands and the claws,—painful things, that I dare not shape too freely. But it is in the subtle grafting and reshaping one must needs do to the brain that my trouble lies. The intelligence is often oddly low, with unaccountable blank ends, unexpected gaps. And least satisfactory of all is something that I cannot touch, somewhere—I cannot determine where—in the seat of the emotions. Cravings, instincts, desires that harm humanity, a strange hidden reservoir to burst forth suddenly and inundate the whole being of the creature with anger, hate, or fear. These creatures of mine seemed strange and uncanny to you so soon as you began to observe them; but to me, just after I make them, they seem to be indisputably human beings. It's afterwards, as I observe them, that the persuasion fades. First one animal trait, then another, creeps to the surface and stares out at me. But I will conquer yet! Each time I dip a living creature into the bath of burning pain, I say, 'This time I will burn out all the animal; this time I will make a rational creature of my own!' After all, what is ten years? Men have been a hundred thousand in the making." He thought darkly. "But I am drawing near the fastness. This puma of mine—" After a silence, "And they revert. As soon as my hand is taken from them the beast begins to creep back, begins to assert itself again." Another long silence.

"Then you take the things you make into those dens?" said I.

"They go. I turn them out when I begin to feel the beast in them, and presently they wander there. They all dread this house and me. There is a kind of travesty of humanity over there. Montgomery knows about it, for he interferes in their affairs. He has trained one or two of them to our service. He's ashamed of it, but I believe he half likes some of those beasts. It's his business, not mine. They only sicken me with a sense of failure. I take no interest in them. I fancy they follow in the lines the Kanaka missionary marked out, and have a kind of mockery of a rational life, poor beasts! There's something they call the Law. Sing hymns about 'all thine.' They build themselves their dens, gather fruit, and pull herbs—marry even. But I can see through it all, see into their very souls, and see there nothing but the souls of beasts, beasts that perish, anger and the lusts to live and gratify themselves.—Yet they're odd; complex, like everything else alive. There is a kind of upward striving in them, part vanity, part waste sexual emotion, part waste curiosity. It only mocks me. I have some hope of this puma. I have worked hard at her head and brain—

"And now," said he, standing up after a long gap of silence, during which we had each pursued our own thoughts, "what do you think? Are you in fear of me still?"

I looked at him, and saw but a white-faced, white-haired man, with calm eyes. Save for his serenity, the touch almost of beauty that resulted from his set tranquillity and his magnificent build, he might have passed muster among a hundred other comfortable old gentlemen. Then I shivered. By way of answer to his second question, I handed him a revolver with either hand.

"Keep them," he said, and snatched at a yawn. He stood up, stared at me for a moment, and smiled. "You have had two eventful days," said he. "I should advise some sleep. I'm glad it's all clear. Goodnight." He thought me over for a moment, then went out by the inner door.

I immediately turned the key in the outer one. I sat down again; sat for a time in a kind of stagnant mood, so weary, emotionally, mentally, and physically, that I could not think beyond the point at which he had left me. The black window stared at me like an eye. At last with an effort I put out the light and got into the hammock. Very soon I was asleep.

XV

CONCERNING THE BEAST FOLK

I WOKE EARLY. Moreau's explanation stood before my mind, clear and definite, from the moment of my awakening. I got out of the hammock and went to the door to assure myself that the key was turned. Then I tried the window-bar, and found it firmly fixed. That these man-like creatures were in truth only bestial monsters, mere grotesque travesties of men, filled me with a vague uncertainty of their possibilities which was far worse than any definite fear.

A tapping came at the door, and I heard the glutinous accents of M'ling speaking. I pocketed one of the revolvers (keeping one hand upon it), and opened to him.

"Good-morning, sair," he said, bringing in, in addition to the customary herb-breakfast, an ill-cooked rabbit. Montgomery followed him. His roving eye caught the position of my arm and he smiled askew.

The puma was resting to heal that day; but Moreau, who was singularly solitary in his habits, did not join us. I talked with Montgomery to clear my ideas of the way in which the Beast Folk lived. In particular, I was urgent to know how these inhuman monsters were kept from falling upon Moreau and Montgomery and from rending one another. He explained to me that the comparative safety of Moreau and himself was due to the limited mental scope of these monsters. In spite of their increased intelligence and the tendency of their animal instincts to reawaken, they had certain fixed ideas implanted by Moreau in their minds, which absolutely bounded their imaginations. They were really hypnotised; had been told that certain things were impossible, and that certain things were not to be done, and these prohibitions were woven into the texture of their minds beyond any possibility of disobedience or dispute.

Certain matters, however, in which old instinct was at war with Moreau's convenience, were in a less stable condition. A series of propositions called the Law (I had already heard them recited) battled in their minds with the deep-seated, ever-rebellious cravings of their animal natures. This Law they were ever repeating, I found, and ever breaking. Both Montgomery and Moreau displayed particular solicitude to keep them ignorant of the taste of blood; they feared the inevitable suggestions of that flavour. Montgomery told me that the Law, especially among the feline Beast People, became oddly weakened about nightfall; that then the animal was at its strongest; that a spirit of adventure sprang up in them at the dusk, when they would dare things they never seemed to dream about by day. To that I owed my stalking by the Leopard-man, on the night of my arrival. But during these earlier days of my stay they broke the Law only furtively and after dark; in the daylight there was a general atmosphere of respect for its multifarious prohibitions.

And here perhaps I may give a few general facts about the island and the Beast People. The island, which was of irregular outline and lay low upon the wide sea, had a total area, I suppose, of seven or eight square miles.[2] It was volcanic in origin, and was now fringed on three sides by coral reefs; some fumaroles to the northward, and a hot spring, were the only vestiges of the forces that had long since originated it. Now and then a faint quiver of earthquake would be sensible, and sometimes the ascent of the spire of smoke would be rendered tumultuous by gusts of steam; but that was all. The population of the island, Montgomery informed me, now numbered rather more than sixty of these strange creations of Moreau's art, not counting the smaller monstrosities which lived in the undergrowth and were without human form. Altogether he had made nearly a hundred and twenty; but many had died, and others—like the writhing Footless Thing of which he had told me—had come by violent ends. In answer to my question, Montgomery said that they actually bore offspring, but that

2 This description corresponds in every respect to Noble's Isle. — C. E. P.

these generally died. When they lived, Moreau took them and stamped the human form upon them. There was no evidence of the inheritance of their acquired human characteristics. The females were less numerous than the males, and liable to much furtive persecution in spite of the monogamy the Law enjoined.

It would be impossible for me to describe these Beast People in detail; my eye has had no training in details, and unhappily I cannot sketch. Most striking, perhaps, in their general appearance was the disproportion between the legs of these creatures and the length of their bodies; and yet—so relative is our idea of grace—my eye became habituated to their forms, and at last I even fell in with their persuasion that my own long thighs were ungainly. Another point was the forward carriage of the head and the clumsy and inhuman curvature of the spine. Even the Ape-man lacked that inward sinuous curve of the back which makes the human figure so graceful. Most had their shoulders hunched clumsily, and their short forearms hung weakly at their sides. Few of them were conspicuously hairy, at least until the end of my time upon the island.

The next most obvious deformity was in their faces, almost all of which were prognathous, malformed about the ears, with large and protuberant noses, very furry or very bristly hair, and often strangely-coloured or strangely-placed eyes. None could laugh, though the Ape-man had a chattering titter. Beyond these general characters their heads had little in common; each preserved the quality of its particular species: the human mark distorted but did not hide the leopard, the ox, or the sow, or other animal or animals, from which the creature had been moulded. The voices, too, varied exceedingly. The hands were always malformed; and though some surprised me by their unexpected human appearance, almost all were deficient in the number of the digits, clumsy about the finger-nails, and lacking any tactile sensibility.

The two most formidable Animal Men were my Leopard-man and a creature made of hyena and swine. Larger than these were the three bull-creatures who pulled in the boat. Then came the silvery-hairy-man, who was also the Sayer of the Law, M'ling, and a satyr-like creature of ape and goat. There were three Swine-men and a Swine-woman, a mare-rhinoceros-creature, and several other females whose sources I did not ascertain. There were several wolf-creatures, a bear-bull, and a Saint-Bernard-man. I have already described the Ape-man, and there was a particularly hateful (and evil-smelling) old woman made of vixen and bear, whom I hated from the beginning. She was said to be a passionate votary of the Law. Smaller creatures were certain dappled youths and my little sloth-creature. But enough of this catalogue.

At first I had a shivering horror of the brutes, felt all too keenly that they were still brutes; but insensibly I became a little habituated to the idea of them, and moreover I was affected by Montgomery's attitude towards them. He had been with them so long that he had come to regard them as almost normal human beings. His London days seemed a glorious, impossible past to him. Only once in a year or so did he go to Arica to deal with Moreau's agent, a trader in animals there. He hardly met the finest type of mankind in that seafaring village of Spanish mongrels. The men aboard-ship, he told me, seemed at first just as strange to him as the Beast Men seemed to me,—unnaturally long in the leg, flat in the face, prominent in the forehead, suspicious, dangerous, and cold-hearted. In fact, he did not like men: his heart had warmed to me, he thought, because he had saved my life. I fancied even then that he had a sneaking kindness for some of these metamorphosed brutes, a vicious sympathy with some of their ways, but that he attempted to veil it from me at first.

M'ling, the black-faced man, Montgomery's attendant, the first of the Beast Folk I had encountered, did not live with the others across the island, but in a small kennel at the back of the enclosure. The creature was scarcely so intelligent as the Ape-man, but far more docile, and the most human-looking of all the Beast Folk; and Montgomery had trained it to prepare food, and indeed to discharge all the trivial domestic offices that were required. It was a complex trophy of Moreau's horrible skill,—a bear, tainted with dog and ox, and one of the most elaborately made of all his creatures. It treated Montgomery with a strange tenderness and devotion. Sometimes he would notice it, pat it, call it half-mocking, half-jocular names, and so make it caper with extraordinary delight; sometimes he would ill-treat it, especially after he had been at the whiskey, kicking it, beating it, pelting it with stones or lighted fusees. But whether he treated it well or ill, it loved nothing so much as to be near him.

I say I became habituated to the Beast People, that a thousand things which had seemed unnatural and repulsive speedily became natural and ordinary to me. I suppose everything in existence takes its colour from the average hue of our surroundings. Montgomery and Moreau were too peculiar and individual to keep my general impressions of humanity well defined. I would see one of the clumsy bovine-creatures who worked the launch treading heavily through the undergrowth, and find myself asking, trying hard to recall, how he differed from some really human yokel trudging home from his mechanical labours; or I would meet the Fox-bear woman's vulpine, shifty face, strangely human in its speculative cunning, and even imagine I had met it before in some city byway.

Yet every now and then the beast would flash out upon me beyond doubt or denial. An ugly-looking man, a hunch-backed human savage to all appearance, squatting in the aperture of one of the dens, would stretch his arms and yawn, showing with startling suddenness scissor-edged incisors and sabre-like canines, keen and brilliant as knives. Or in some narrow pathway, glancing with a transitory daring into the eyes of some lithe, white-swathed female figure, I would suddenly see (with a spasmodic revulsion) that she had slit-like pupils, or glancing down note the curving nail with which she held her shapeless wrap about her. It is a curious thing, by the bye, for which I am quite unable to account, that these weird creatures—the females, I mean—had in the earlier days of my stay an instinctive sense of their own repulsive clumsiness, and displayed in consequence a more than human regard for the decency and decorum of extensive costume.

XVI

How the Beast Folk Taste Blood

My inexperience as a writer betrays me, and I wander from the thread of my story.

After I had breakfasted with Montgomery, he took me across the island to see the fumarole and the source of the hot spring into whose scalding waters I had blundered on the previous day. Both of us carried whips and loaded revolvers. While going through a leafy jungle on our road thither, we heard a rabbit squealing. We stopped and listened, but we heard no more; and presently we went on our way, and the incident dropped out of our minds. Montgomery called my attention to certain little pink animals with long hind-legs, that went leaping through the undergrowth. He told me they were creatures made of the offspring of the Beast People, that Moreau had invented. He had fancied they might serve for meat, but a rabbit-like habit of devouring their young had defeated this intention. I had already encountered some of these creatures,—once during my moonlight flight from the Leopard-man, and once during my pursuit by Moreau on the previous day. By chance, one hopping to avoid us leapt into the hole caused by the uprooting of a wind-blown tree; before it could extricate itself we managed to catch it. It spat like a cat, scratched and kicked vigorously with its hind-legs, and made an attempt to bite; but its teeth were too feeble to inflict more than a painless pinch. It seemed to me rather a pretty little creature; and as Montgomery stated that it never destroyed the turf by burrowing, and was very cleanly in its habits, I should imagine it might prove a convenient substitute for the common rabbit in gentlemen's parks.

We also saw on our way the trunk of a tree barked in long strips and splintered deeply. Montgomery called my attention to this. "Not to claw bark of trees, *that* is the Law," he said. "Much some of them care for it!" It was after this, I think, that we met the Satyr and the Ape-man. The Satyr was a gleam of classical memory on the part of Moreau,—his face ovine in expression, like the coarser Hebrew type; his voice a harsh bleat, his nether extremities Satanic. He was gnawing the husk of a pod-like fruit as he passed us. Both of them saluted Montgomery.

"Hail," said they, "to the Other with the Whip!"

"There's a Third with a Whip now," said Montgomery. "So you'd better mind!"

"Was he not made?" said the Ape-man. "He said—he said he was made."

The Satyr-man looked curiously at me. "The Third with the Whip, he that walks weeping into the sea, has a thin white face."

"He has a thin long whip," said Montgomery.

"Yesterday he bled and wept," said the Satyr. "You never bleed nor weep. The Master does not bleed or weep."

"Ollendorffian beggar!" said Montgomery, "you'll bleed and weep if you don't look out!"

"He has five fingers, he is a five-man like me," said the Ape-man.

"Come along, Prendick," said Montgomery, taking my arm; and I went on with him.

The Satyr and the Ape-man stood watching us and making other remarks to each other.

"He says nothing," said the Satyr. "Men have voices."

"Yesterday he asked me of things to eat," said the Ape-man. "He did not know."

Then they spoke inaudible things, and I heard the Satyr laughing.

It was on our way back that we came upon the dead rabbit. The red body of the wretched little beast was rent to pieces, many of the ribs stripped white, and the backbone indisputably gnawed.

At that Montgomery stopped. "Good God!" said he, stooping down, and picking up some of the crushed vertebrae to examine them more closely. "Good God!" he repeated, "what can this mean?"

"Some carnivore of yours has remembered its old habits," I said after a pause. "This backbone has been bitten through."

He stood staring, with his face white and his lip pulled askew. "I don't like this," he said slowly.

"I saw something of the same kind," said I, "the first day I came here."

"The devil you did! What was it?"

"A rabbit with its head twisted off."

"The day you came here?"

"The day I came here. In the undergrowth at the back of the enclosure, when I went out in the evening. The head was completely wrung off."

He gave a long, low whistle.

"And what is more, I have an idea which of your brutes did the thing. It's only a suspicion, you know. Before I came on the rabbit I saw one of your monsters drinking in the stream."

"Sucking his drink?"

"Yes."

"'Not to suck your drink; that is the Law.' Much the brutes care for the Law, eh? when Moreau's not about!"

"It was the brute who chased me."

"Of course," said Montgomery; "it's just the way with carnivores. After a kill, they drink. It's the taste of blood, you know.—What was the brute like?" he continued. "Would you know him again?" He glanced about us, standing astride over the mess of dead rabbit, his eyes roving among the shadows and screens of greenery, the lurking-places and ambuscades of the forest that bounded us in. "The taste of blood," he said again.

He took out his revolver, examined the cartridges in it and replaced it. Then he began to pull at his dropping lip.

"I think I should know the brute again," I said. "I stunned him. He ought to have a handsome bruise on the forehead of him."

"But then we have to *prove* that he killed the rabbit," said Montgomery. "I wish I'd never brought the things here."

I should have gone on, but he stayed there thinking over the mangled rabbit in a puzzle-headed way. As it was, I went to such a distance that the rabbit's remains were hidden.

"Come on!" I said.

Presently he woke up and came towards me. "You see," he said, almost in a whisper, "they are all supposed to have a fixed idea against eating anything that runs on land. If some brute has by any accident tasted blood—"

We went on some way in silence. "I wonder what can have happened," he said to himself. Then, after a pause again: "I did a foolish thing the other day. That servant of mine—I showed him how to skin and cook a rabbit. It's odd—I saw him licking his hands—It never occurred to me."

Then: "We must put a stop to this. I must tell Moreau."

He could think of nothing else on our homeward journey.

Moreau took the matter even more seriously than Montgomery, and I need scarcely say that I was affected by their evident consternation.

"We must make an example," said Moreau. "I've no doubt in my own mind that the Leopard-man was the sinner. But how can we prove it? I wish, Montgomery, you had kept your taste for meat in hand, and gone without these exciting novelties. We may find ourselves in a mess yet, through it."

"I was a silly ass," said Montgomery. "But the thing's done now; and you said I might have them, you know."

"We must see to the thing at once," said Moreau. "I suppose if anything should turn up, M'ling can take care of himself?"

"I'm not so sure of M'ling," said Montgomery. "I think I ought to know him."

In the afternoon, Moreau, Montgomery, myself, and M'ling went across the island to the huts in the ravine. We three were armed; M'ling carried the little hatchet he used in chopping firewood, and some coils of wire. Moreau had a huge cowherd's horn slung over his shoulder.

"You will see a gathering of the Beast People," said Montgomery. "It is a pretty sight!"

Moreau said not a word on the way, but the expression of his heavy, white-fringed face was grimly set.

We crossed the ravine down which smoked the stream of hot water, and followed the winding pathway through the canebrakes until we reached a wide area covered over with a thick, powdery yellow substance which I believe was sulphur. Above the shoulder of a weedy bank the sea glittered. We came to a kind of shallow natural amphitheatre, and here the four of us halted. Then Moreau sounded the horn, and broke the sleeping stillness of the tropical afternoon. He must have had strong lungs. The hooting note rose and rose amidst its echoes, to at last an ear-penetrating intensity.

"Ah!" said Moreau, letting the curved instrument fall to his side again.

Immediately there was a crashing through the yellow canes, and a sound of voices from the dense green jungle that marked the morass through which I had run on the previous day. Then at three or four points on the edge of the sulphurous area appeared the grotesque forms of the Beast People hurrying towards us. I could not help a creeping horror, as I perceived first one and then another trot out from the trees or reeds and come shambling along over the hot dust. But Moreau and Montgomery stood calmly enough; and, perforce, I stuck beside them.

First to arrive was the Satyr, strangely unreal for all that he cast a shadow and tossed the dust with his hoofs. After him from the brake came a monstrous lout, a thing of horse and rhinoceros, chewing a straw as it came; then appeared the Swine-woman and two Wolf-women; then the Fox-bear witch, with her red eyes in her peaked red face, and then others,—all hurrying eagerly. As they came forward they began to cringe towards Moreau and chant, quite regardless of one another, fragments of the latter half of the litany of the Law,—"His is the Hand that wounds; His is the Hand that heals," and so forth. As soon as they had approached within a distance of perhaps thirty yards they halted, and bowing on knees and elbows began flinging the white dust upon their heads.

Imagine the scene if you can! We three blue-clad men, with our misshapen black-faced attendant, standing in a wide expanse of sunlit yellow dust under the blazing blue sky, and surrounded by this circle of crouching and gesticulating monstrosities,—some almost human save in their subtle expression and gestures, some like cripples, some so strangely distorted as to resemble nothing but the denizens of our wildest dreams; and, beyond, the reedy lines of a canebrake in one direction, a dense tangle of palmtrees on the other, separating us from the ravine with the huts, and to the north the hazy horizon of the Pacific Ocean.

"Sixty-two, sixty-three," counted Moreau. "There are four more."

"I do not see the Leopard-man," said I.

Presently Moreau sounded the great horn again, and at the sound of it all the Beast People writhed and grovelled in the dust. Then, slinking out of the canebrake, stooping near the ground and trying to join the dust-throwing circle behind Moreau's back, came the Leopard-man. The last of the Beast People to arrive was the little Ape-man. The earlier animals, hot and weary with their grovelling, shot vicious glances at him.

"Cease!" said Moreau, in his firm, loud voice; and the Beast People sat back upon their hams and rested from their worshipping.

"Where is the Sayer of the Law?" said Moreau, and the hairy-grey monster bowed his face in the dust.

"Say the words!" said Moreau.

Forthwith all in the kneeling assembly, swaying from side to side and dashing up the sulphur with their hands,—first the right hand and a puff of dust, and then the left,—began once more to chant their strange litany. When they reached, "Not to eat Flesh or Fish, that is the Law," Moreau held up his lank white hand.

"Stop!" he cried, and there fell absolute silence upon them all.

I think they all knew and dreaded what was coming. I looked round at their strange faces. When I saw their wincing attitudes and the furtive dread in their bright eyes, I wondered that I had ever believed them to be men.

"That Law has been broken!" said Moreau.

"None escape," from the faceless creature with the silvery hair. "None escape," repeated the kneeling circle of Beast People.

"Who is he?" cried Moreau, and looked round at their faces, cracking his whip. I fancied the Hyena-swine looked dejected, so too did the Leopard-man. Moreau stopped, facing this creature, who cringed towards him with the memory and dread of infinite torment.

"Who is he?" repeated Moreau, in a voice of thunder.

"Evil is he who breaks the Law," chanted the Sayer of the Law.

Moreau looked into the eyes of the Leopard-man, and seemed to be dragging the very soul out of the creature.

"Who breaks the Law—" said Moreau, taking his eyes off his victim, and turning towards us (it seemed to me there was a touch of exultation in his voice).

"Goes back to the House of Pain," they all clamoured,— "goes back to the House of Pain, O Master!"

"Back to the House of Pain,—back to the House of Pain," gabbled the Ape-man, as though the idea was sweet to him.

"Do you hear?" said Moreau, turning back to the criminal, "my friend— Hullo!"

For the Leopard-man, released from Moreau's eye, had risen straight from his knees, and now, with eyes aflame and his huge feline tusks flashing out from under his curling lips, leapt towards his tormentor. I am convinced that only the madness of unendurable fear could have prompted this attack. The whole circle of threescore monsters seemed to rise about us. I drew my revolver. The two figures collided. I saw Moreau reeling back from the Leopard-man's blow. There was a furious yelling and howling all about us. Every one was moving rapidly. For a moment I thought it was a general revolt. The furious face of the Leopard-man flashed by mine, with M'ling close in pursuit. I saw the yellow eyes of the Hyena-swine blazing with excitement, his attitude as if he were half resolved to attack me. The Satyr, too, glared at me over the Hyena-swine's hunched shoulders. I heard the crack of Moreau's pistol, and saw the pink flash dart across the tumult. The whole crowd seemed to swing round in the direction of the glint of fire, and I too was swung round by the magnetism of the movement. In another second I was running, one of a tumultuous shouting crowd, in pursuit of the escaping Leopard-man.

That is all I can tell definitely. I saw the Leopard-man strike Moreau, and then everything spun about me until I was running headlong. M'ling was ahead, close in pursuit of the fugitive. Behind, their tongues already lolling out, ran the Wolf-women in great leaping strides. The Swine folk followed, squealing with excitement, and the two Bull-men in their swathings of white. Then came Moreau in a cluster of the Beast People, his wide-brimmed straw hat blown off, his revolver in hand, and his lank white hair streaming out. The Hyena-swine ran beside me, keeping pace with me and glancing furtively at me out of his feline eyes, and the others came pattering and shouting behind us.

The Leopard-man went bursting his way through the long canes, which sprang back as he passed, and rattled in M'ling's face. We others in the rear found a trampled path for us when we reached the brake. The chase lay through the brake for perhaps a quarter of a mile, and then plunged into a dense thicket, which retarded our movements exceedingly, though we went through it in a crowd together,—fronds flicking into our faces, ropy creepers catching us under the chin or gripping our ankles, thorny plants hooking into and tearing cloth and flesh together.

"He has gone on all-fours through this," panted Moreau, now just ahead of me.

"None escape," said the Wolf-bear, laughing into my face with the exultation of hunting. We burst out again among rocks, and saw the quarry ahead running lightly on all-fours and snarling at us over his shoulder. At that the Wolf Folk howled with delight. The Thing was still clothed, and at a distance its face still seemed human; but the carriage of its four limbs was feline, and the furtive droop of its shoulder was distinctly that of a hunted animal. It leapt over some thorny yellow-flowering bushes, and was hidden. M'ling was halfway across the space.

Most of us now had lost the first speed of the chase, and had fallen into a longer and steadier stride. I saw as we traversed the open that the pursuit was now spreading from a column into a line. The Hyena-swine still ran close to me, watching me as it ran, every now and then puckering its muzzle with a snarling laugh. At the edge of the rocks the Leopard-man, realising that he was making for the projecting cape upon which he had stalked me on the night of my arrival, had doubled in the undergrowth; but Montgomery had seen the manoeuvre, and turned him again. So, panting, tumbling against rocks, torn by brambles, impeded by ferns and reeds, I helped to pursue the Leopard-man who had broken the Law, and the Hyena-swine ran, laughing savagely, by my side. I staggered on, my head reeling and my heart beating against my ribs, tired almost to death, and yet not daring to lose sight of the chase lest I should be left alone with this horrible companion. I staggered on in spite of infinite fatigue and the dense heat of the tropical afternoon.

At last the fury of the hunt slackened. We had pinned the wretched brute into a corner of the island. Moreau, whip in hand, marshalled us all into an irregular line, and we advanced now slowly, shouting to one another as we advanced and tightening the cordon about our victim. He lurked noiseless and invisible in the bushes through which I had run from him during that midnight pursuit.

"Steady!" cried Moreau, "steady!" as the ends of the line crept round the tangle of undergrowth and hemmed the brute in.

"Ware a rush!" came the voice of Montgomery from beyond the thicket.

I was on the slope above the bushes; Montgomery and Moreau beat along the beach beneath. Slowly we pushed in among the fretted network of branches and leaves. The quarry was silent.

"Back to the House of Pain, the House of Pain, the House of Pain!" yelped the voice of the Ape-man, some twenty yards to the right.

When I heard that, I forgave the poor wretch all the fear he had inspired in me. I heard the twigs snap and the boughs swish aside before the heavy tread of the Horse-rhinoceros upon my right. Then suddenly through a polygon of green, in the half darkness under the luxuriant growth, I saw the creature we were hunting. I halted. He was crouched together into the smallest possible compass, his luminous green eyes turned over his shoulder regarding me.

It may seem a strange contradiction in me,—I cannot explain the fact,—but now, seeing the creature there in a perfectly animal attitude, with the light gleaming in its eyes and its imperfectly human face distorted with terror, I realised again the fact of its humanity. In another moment other of its pursuers would see it, and it would be overpowered and captured, to experience once more the horrible tortures of the enclosure. Abruptly I slipped out my revolver, aimed between its terror-struck eyes, and fired. As I did so, the Hyena-swine saw the Thing, and flung itself upon it with an eager cry, thrusting thirsty teeth into its neck. All about me the green masses of the thicket were swaying and cracking as the Beast People came rushing together. One face and then another appeared.

"Don't kill it, Prendick!" cried Moreau. "Don't kill it!" and I saw him stooping as he pushed through under the fronds of the big ferns.

In another moment he had beaten off the Hyena-swine with the handle of his whip, and he and Montgomery were keeping away the excited carnivorous Beast People, and particularly M'ling, from the still quivering body. The hairy-grey Thing came sniffing at the corpse under my arm. The other animals, in their animal ardour, jostled me to get a nearer view.

"Confound you, Prendick!" said Moreau. "I wanted him."

"I'm sorry," said I, though I was not. "It was the impulse of the moment." I felt sick with exertion and excitement. Turning, I pushed my way out of the crowding Beast People and went on alone up the slope towards the higher part of the headland. Under the shouted directions of Moreau I heard the three white-swathed Bull-men begin dragging the victim down towards the water.

It was easy now for me to be alone. The Beast People manifested a quite human curiosity about the dead body, and followed it in a thick knot, sniffing and growling at it as the Bull-men dragged it down the beach. I went to the headland and watched the bull-men, black against the evening sky as they carried the weighted dead body out to sea; and like a wave across my mind came the realisation of the unspeakable aimlessness of things upon the island. Upon the beach among the rocks beneath me were the Ape-man, the Hyena-swine, and several other of the Beast People, standing about Montgomery and Moreau. They were all still intensely excited, and all overflowing with noisy expressions of their loyalty to the Law; yet I felt an absolute assurance in my own mind that the Hyena-swine was implicated in the rabbit-killing. A strange persuasion came upon me, that, save for the grossness of the line, the grotesqueness of the forms, I had here before me the whole balance of human life in miniature, the whole interplay of instinct, reason, and fate in its simplest form. The Leopard-man had happened to go under: that was all the difference. Poor brute!

Poor brutes! I began to see the viler aspect of Moreau's cruelty. I had not thought before of the pain and trouble that came to these poor victims after they had passed from Moreau's hands. I had shivered only at the days of actual torment in the enclosure. But now that seemed to me the lesser part. Before, they had been beasts, their instincts fitly adapted to their surroundings, and happy as living things may be. Now they stumbled in the shackles of humanity, lived in a fear that never died, fretted by a law they could not understand; their mock-human existence, begun in an agony, was one long internal struggle, one long dread of Moreau—and for what? It was the wantonness of it that stirred me.

Had Moreau had any intelligible object, I could have sympathised at least a little with him. I am not so squeamish about pain as that. I could have forgiven him a little even, had his motive been only hate. But he was so irresponsible, so utterly careless! His curiosity, his mad, aimless investigations, drove him on; and the Things were thrown out to live a year or so, to struggle and blunder and suffer, and at last to die painfully. They were wretched in themselves; the old animal hate moved them to trouble one another; the Law held them back from a brief hot struggle and a decisive end to their natural animosities.

In those days my fear of the Beast People went the way of my personal fear for Moreau. I fell indeed into a morbid state, deep and enduring, and alien to fear, which has left permanent scars upon my mind. I must confess that I lost faith in the sanity of the world when I saw it suffering the painful disorder of this island. A blind Fate, a vast pitiless mechanism, seemed to cut and shape the fabric of existence and I, Moreau (by his passion for research), Montgomery (by his passion for drink), the Beast People with their instincts and mental restrictions, were torn and crushed, ruthlessly, inevitably, amid the infinite complexity of its incessant wheels. But this condition did not come all at once: I think indeed that I anticipate a little in speaking of it now.

XVII

A Catastrophe

SCARECELY SIX WEEKS PASSED before I had lost every feeling but dislike and abhorrence for this infamous experiment of Moreau's. My one idea was to get away from these horrible caricatures of my Maker's image, back to the sweet and wholesome intercourse of men. My fellow-creatures, from whom I was thus separated, began to assume idyllic virtue and beauty in my memory. My first friendship with Montgomery did not increase. His long separation from humanity, his secret vice of drunkenness, his evident sympathy with the Beast People, tainted him to me. Several times I let him go alone among them. I avoided intercourse with them in every possible way. I spent an increasing proportion of my time upon the beach, looking for some liberating sail that never appeared,—until one day there fell upon us an appalling disaster, which put an altogether different aspect upon my strange surroundings.

It was about seven or eight weeks after my landing,—rather more, I think, though I had not troubled to keep account of the time,—when this catastrophe occurred. It happened in the early morning—I should think about six. I had risen and breakfasted early, having been aroused by the noise of three Beast Men carrying wood into the enclosure.

After breakfast I went to the open gateway of the enclosure, and stood there smoking a cigarette and enjoying the freshness of the early morning. Moreau presently came round the corner of the enclosure and greeted me.

He passed by me, and I heard him behind me unlock and enter his laboratory. So indurated was I at that time to the abomination of the place, that I heard without a touch of emotion the puma victim begin another day of torture. It met its persecutor with a shriek, almost exactly like that of an angry virago.

Then suddenly something happened,—I do not know what, to this day. I heard a short, sharp cry behind me, a fall, and turning saw an awful face rushing upon me,—not human, not animal, but hellish, brown, seamed with red branching scars, red drops starting out upon it, and the lidless eyes ablaze. I threw up my arm to defend myself from the blow that flung me headlong with a broken forearm; and the great monster, swathed in lint and with red-stained bandages fluttering about it, leapt over me and passed. I rolled over and over down the beach, tried to sit up, and collapsed upon my broken arm. Then Moreau appeared, his massive white face all the more terrible for the blood that trickled from his forehead. He carried a revolver in one hand. He scarcely glanced at me, but rushed off at once in pursuit of the puma.

I tried the other arm and sat up. The muffled figure in front ran in great striding leaps along the beach, and Moreau followed her. She turned her head and saw him, then doubling abruptly made for the bushes. She gained upon him at every stride. I saw her plunge into them, and Moreau, running slantingly to intercept her, fired and missed as she disappeared. Then he too vanished in the green confusion. I stared after them, and then the pain in my arm flamed up, and with a groan I staggered to my feet. Montgomery appeared in the doorway, dressed, and with his revolver in his hand.

"Great God, Prendick!" he said, not noticing that I was hurt, "that brute's loose! Tore the fetter out of the wall! Have you seen them?" Then sharply, seeing I gripped my arm, "What's the matter?"

"I was standing in the doorway," said I.

He came forward and took my arm. "Blood on the sleeve," said he, and rolled back the flannel. He pocketed his weapon, felt my arm about painfully, and led me inside. "Your arm is broken," he said, and then, "Tell me exactly how it happened—what happened?"

I told him what I had seen; told him in broken sentences, with gasps of pain between them, and very dexterously and swiftly he bound my arm meanwhile. He slung it from my shoulder, stood back and looked at me.

"You'll do," he said. "And now?"

He thought. Then he went out and locked the gates of the enclosure. He was absent some time.

I was chiefly concerned about my arm. The incident seemed merely one more of many horrible things. I sat down in the deck chair, and I must admit swore heartily at the island. The first dull feeling of injury in my arm had already given way to a burning pain when Montgomery reappeared. His face was rather pale, and he showed more of his lower gums than ever.

"I can neither see nor hear anything of him," he said. "I've been thinking he may want my help." He stared at me with his expressionless eyes. "That was a strong brute," he said. "It simply wrenched its fetter out of the wall." He went to the window, then to the door, and there turned to me. "I shall go after him," he said. "There's another revolver I can leave with you. To tell you the truth, I feel anxious somehow."

He obtained the weapon, and put it ready to my hand on the table; then went out, leaving a restless contagion in the air. I did not sit long after he left, but took the revolver in hand and went to the doorway.

The morning was as still as death. Not a whisper of wind was stirring; the sea was like polished glass, the sky empty, the beach desolate. In my half-excited, half-feverish state, this stillness of things oppressed me. I tried to whistle, and the tune died away. I swore again,—the second time that morning. Then I went to the corner of the enclosure and stared inland at the green bush that had swallowed up Moreau and Montgomery. When would they return, and how? Then far away up the beach a little grey Beast Man appeared, ran down to the water's edge and began splashing about. I strolled back to the doorway, then to the corner again, and so began pacing to and fro like a sentinel upon duty. Once I was arrested by the distant voice of Montgomery bawling, "Coo-ee—Moreau!" My arm became less painful, but very hot. I got feverish and thirsty. My shadow grew shorter. I watched the distant figure until it went away again. Would Moreau and Montgomery never return? Three sea-birds began fighting for some stranded treasure.

Then from far away behind the enclosure I heard a pistol-shot. A long silence, and then came another. Then a yelling cry nearer, and another dismal gap of silence. My unfortunate imagination set to work to torment me. Then suddenly a shot close by. I went to the corner, startled, and saw Montgomery,—his face scarlet, his hair disordered, and the knee of his trousers torn. His face expressed profound consternation. Behind him slouched the Beast Man, M'ling, and round M'ling's jaws were some queer dark stains.

"Has he come?" said Montgomery.

"Moreau?" said I. "No."

"My God!" The man was panting, almost sobbing. "Go back in," he said, taking my arm. "They're mad. They're all rushing about mad. What can have happened? I don't know. I'll tell you, when my breath comes. Where's some brandy?"

Montgomery limped before me into the room and sat down in the deck chair. M'ling flung himself down just outside the doorway and began panting like a dog. I got Montgomery some brandy-and-water. He sat staring in front of him at nothing, recovering his breath. After some minutes he began to tell me what had happened.

He had followed their track for some way. It was plain enough at first on account of the crushed and broken bushes, white rags torn from the puma's bandages, and occasional smears of blood on the leaves of the shrubs and undergrowth. He lost the track, however, on the stony ground beyond the stream where I had seen the Beast Man drinking, and went wandering aimlessly westward shouting Moreau's name. Then M'ling had come to him carrying a light hatchet. M'ling had seen nothing of the puma affair; had been felling wood, and heard him calling. They went on shouting together. Two Beast Men came crouching and peering at them through the undergrowth, with gestures and a furtive carriage that alarmed Montgomery by their strangeness. He hailed them, and they fled guiltily. He stopped shouting after that, and after wandering some time farther in an undecided way, determined to visit the huts.

He found the ravine deserted.

Growing more alarmed every minute, he began to retrace his steps. Then it was he encountered the two Swine-men I had seen dancing on the night of my arrival; blood-stained they were about the mouth, and intensely excited. They came crashing through the ferns, and stopped with fierce faces when they saw him. He cracked his whip in some trepidation, and forthwith they rushed at him. Never before had a Beast Man dared to do that. One he shot through the head; M'ling flung himself upon the other, and the two rolled grappling. M'ling got his brute under and with his teeth in its throat, and Montgomery shot that too as it struggled in M'ling's grip. He had some difficulty in inducing M'ling to come on with him. Thence they had hurried back to me. On the way, M'ling had suddenly rushed into a thicket and driven out an under-sized Ocelot-man, also blood-stained, and lame through a wound in the foot. This brute had run a little way and then turned savagely at bay, and Montgomery—with a certain wantonness, I thought—had shot him.

"What does it all mean?" said I.

He shook his head, and turned once more to the brandy.

XVIII

THE FINDING OF MOREAU

WHEN I SAW MONTGOMERY SWALLOW a third dose of brandy, I took it upon myself to interfere. He was already more than half fuddled. I told him that some serious thing must have happened to Moreau by this time, or he would have returned before this, and that it behoved us to ascertain what that catastrophe was. Montgomery raised some feeble objections, and at last agreed. We had some food, and then all three of us started.

It is possibly due to the tension of my mind, at the time, but even now that start into the hot stillness of the tropical afternoon is a singularly vivid impression. M'ling went first, his shoulder hunched, his strange black head moving with quick starts as he peered first on this side of the way and then on that. He was unarmed; his axe he had dropped when he encountered the Swine-man. Teeth were *his* weapons, when it came to fighting. Montgomery followed with stumbling footsteps, his hands in his pockets, his face downcast; he was in a state of muddled sullenness with me on account of the brandy. My left arm was in a sling (it was lucky it was my left), and I carried my revolver in my right. Soon we traced a narrow path through the wild luxuriance of the island, going northwestward; and presently M'ling stopped, and became rigid with watchfulness. Montgomery almost staggered into him, and then stopped too. Then, listening intently, we heard coming through the trees the sound of voices and footsteps approaching us.

"He is dead," said a deep, vibrating voice.

"He is not dead; he is not dead," jabbered another.

"We saw, we saw," said several voices.

"Hullo!" suddenly shouted Montgomery, "Hullo, there!"

"Confound you!" said I, and gripped my pistol.

There was a silence, then a crashing among the interlacing vegetation, first here, then there, and then half-a-dozen faces appeared,—strange faces, lit by a strange light. M'ling made a growling noise in his throat. I recognised the Ape-man: I had indeed already identified his voice, and two of the white-swathed brown-featured creatures I had seen in Montgomery's boat. With these were the two dappled brutes and that grey, horribly crooked creature who said the Law, with grey hair streaming down its cheeks, heavy grey eyebrows, and grey locks pouring off from a central parting upon its sloping forehead,—a heavy, faceless thing, with strange red eyes, looking at us curiously from amidst the green.

For a space no one spoke. Then Montgomery hiccoughed, "Who—said he was dead?"

The Monkey-man looked guiltily at the hairy-grey Thing. "He is dead," said this monster. "They saw."

There was nothing threatening about this detachment, at any rate. They seemed awestricken and puzzled.

"Where is he?" said Montgomery.

"Beyond," and the grey creature pointed.

"Is there a Law now?" asked the Monkey-man. "Is it still to be this and that? Is he dead indeed?"

"Is there a Law?" repeated the man in white. "Is there a Law, thou Other with the Whip?"

"He is dead," said the hairy-grey Thing. And they all stood watching us.

"Prendick," said Montgomery, turning his dull eyes to me. "He's dead, evidently."

I had been standing behind him during this colloquy. I began to see how things lay with them. I suddenly stepped in front of Montgomery and lifted up my voice:—"Children of the Law," I said, "he is *not* dead!" M'ling turned his sharp eyes on me. "He has changed his shape; he has changed his body," I went on. "For a time you will not see him. He is—there," I pointed upward, "where he can watch you. You cannot see him, but he can see you. Fear the Law!"

I looked at them squarely. They flinched.

"He is great, he is good," said the Ape-man, peering fearfully upward among the dense trees.

"And the other Thing?" I demanded.

"The Thing that bled, and ran screaming and sobbing,—that is dead too," said the grey Thing, still regarding me.

"That's well," grunted Montgomery.

"The Other with the Whip—" began the grey Thing.

"Well?" said I.

"Said he was dead."

But Montgomery was still sober enough to understand my motive in denying Moreau's death. "He is not dead," he said slowly, "not dead at all. No more dead than I am."

"Some," said I, "have broken the Law: they will die. Some have died. Show us now where his old body lies,—the body he cast away because he had no more need of it."

"It is this way, Man who walked in the Sea," said the grey Thing.

And with these six creatures guiding us, we went through the tumult of ferns and creepers and tree-stems towards the northwest. Then came a yelling, a crashing among the branches, and a little pink homunculus rushed by us shrieking. Immediately after appeared a monster in headlong pursuit, blood-bedabbled, who was amongst us almost before he could stop his career. The grey Thing leapt aside. M'ling, with a snarl, flew at it, and was struck aside. Montgomery fired and missed, bowed his head, threw up his arm, and turned to run. I fired, and the Thing still came on; fired again, point-blank, into its ugly face. I saw its features vanish in a flash: its face was driven in. Yet it passed me, gripped Montgomery, and holding him, fell headlong beside him and pulled him sprawling upon itself in its death-agony.

I found myself alone with M'ling, the dead brute, and the prostrate man. Montgomery raised himself slowly and stared in a muddled way at the shattered Beast Man beside him. It more than half sobered him. He scrambled to his feet. Then I saw the grey Thing returning cautiously through the trees.

"See," said I, pointing to the dead brute, "is the Law not alive? This came of breaking the Law."

He peered at the body. "He sends the Fire that kills," said he, in his deep voice, repeating part of the Ritual. The others gathered round and stared for a space.

At last we drew near the westward extremity of the island. We came upon the gnawed and mutilated body of the puma, its shoulder-bone smashed by a bullet, and perhaps twenty yards farther found at last what we sought. Moreau lay face downward in a trampled space in a canebrake. One hand was almost severed at the wrist and his silvery hair was dabbled in blood. His head had been battered in by the fetters of the puma. The broken canes beneath him were smeared with blood. His revolver we could not find. Montgomery turned him over. Resting at intervals, and with the help of the seven Beast People (for he was a heavy man), we carried Moreau back to the enclosure. The night was darkling. Twice we heard unseen creatures howling and shrieking past our little band, and once the little pink sloth-creature appeared and stared at us, and vanished again. But we were not attacked again. At the gates of the enclosure our company of Beast People left us, M'ling going with the rest. We locked ourselves in, and then took Moreau's mangled body into the yard and laid it upon a pile of brushwood. Then we went into the laboratory and put an end to all we found living there.

XIX

Montgomery's "Bank Holiday"

WHEN THIS WAS ACCOMPLISHED, and we had washed and eaten, Montgomery and I went into my little room and seriously discussed our position for the first time. It was then near midnight. He was almost sober, but greatly disturbed in his mind. He had been strangely under the influence of Moreau's personality: I do not think it had ever occurred to him that Moreau could die. This disaster was the sudden collapse of the habits that had become part of his nature in the ten or more monotonous years he had spent on the island. He talked vaguely, answered my questions crookedly, wandered into general questions.

"This silly ass of a world," he said; "what a muddle it all is! I haven't had any life. I wonder when it's going to begin. Sixteen years being bullied by nurses and schoolmasters at their own sweet will; five in London grinding hard at medicine, bad food, shabby lodgings, shabby clothes, shabby vice, a blunder,—I didn't know any better,—and hustled off to this beastly island. Ten years here! What's it all for, Prendick? Are we bubbles blown by a baby?"

It was hard to deal with such ravings. "The thing we have to think of now," said I, "is how to get away from this island."

"What's the good of getting away? I'm an outcast. Where am *I* to join on? It's all very well for *you*, Prendick. Poor old Moreau! We can't leave him here to have his bones picked. As it is—And besides, what will become of the decent part of the Beast Folk?"

"Well," said I, "that will do tomorrow. I've been thinking we might make the brushwood into a pyre and burn his body—and those other things. Then what will happen with the Beast Folk?"

"*I* don't know. I suppose those that were made of beasts of prey will make silly asses of themselves sooner or later. We can't massacre the lot— can we? I suppose that's what *your* humanity would suggest? But they'll change. They are sure to change."

He talked thus inconclusively until at last I felt my temper going.

"Damnation!" he exclaimed at some petulance of mine; "can't you see I'm in a worse hole than you are?" And he got up, and went for the brandy. "Drink!" he said returning, "you logic-chopping, chalky-faced saint of an atheist, drink!"

"Not I," said I, and sat grimly watching his face under the yellow paraffine flare, as he drank himself into a garrulous misery.

I have a memory of infinite tedium. He wandered into a maudlin defence of the Beast People and of M'ling. M'ling, he said, was the only thing that had ever really cared for him. And suddenly an idea came to him.

"I'm damned!" said he, staggering to his feet and clutching the brandy bottle.

By some flash of intuition I knew what it was he intended. "You don't give drink to that beast!" I said, rising and facing him.

"Beast!" said he. "You're the beast. He takes his liquor like a Christian. Come out of the way, Prendick!"

"For God's sake," said I.

"Get—out of the way!" he roared, and suddenly whipped out his revolver.

"Very well," said I, and stood aside, half-minded to fall upon him as he put his hand upon the latch, but deterred by the thought of my useless arm. "You've made a beast of yourself,—to the beasts you may go."

He flung the doorway open, and stood half facing me between the yellow lamp-light and the pallid glare of the moon; his eye-sockets were blotches of black under his stubbly eyebrows.

"You're a solemn prig, Prendick, a silly ass! You're always fearing and fancying. We're on the edge of things. I'm bound to cut my throat tomorrow. I'm going to have a damned Bank Holiday tonight." He turned and went out into the moonlight. "M'ling!" he cried; "M'ling, old friend!"

Three dim creatures in the silvery light came along the edge of the wan beach,—one a white-wrapped creature, the other two blotches of blackness following it. They halted, staring. Then I saw M'ling's hunched shoulders as he came round the corner of the house.

"Drink!" cried Montgomery, "drink, you brutes! Drink and be men! Damme, I'm the cleverest. Moreau forgot this; this is the last touch. Drink, I tell you!" And waving the bottle in his hand he started off at a kind of quick trot to the westward, M'ling ranging himself between him and the three dim creatures who followed.

I went to the doorway. They were already indistinct in the mist of the moonlight before Montgomery halted. I saw him administer a dose of the raw brandy to M'ling, and saw the five figures melt into one vague patch.

"Sing!" I heard Montgomery shout,—"sing all together, 'Confound old Prendick!' That's right; now again, 'Confound old Prendick!'"

The black group broke up into five separate figures, and wound slowly away from me along the band of shining beach. Each went howling at his own sweet will, yelping insults at me, or giving whatever other vent this new inspiration of brandy demanded. Presently I heard Montgomery's voice shouting, "Right turn!" and they passed with their shouts and howls into the blackness of the landward trees. Slowly, very slowly, they receded into silence.

The peaceful splendour of the night healed again. The moon was now past the meridian and travelling down the west. It was at its full, and very bright riding through the empty blue sky. The shadow of the wall lay, a yard wide and of inky blackness, at my feet. The eastward sea was a featureless grey, dark and mysterious; and between the sea and the shadow the grey sands (of volcanic glass and crystals) flashed and shone like a beach of diamonds. Behind me the paraffine lamp flared hot and ruddy.

Then I shut the door, locked it, and went into the enclosure where Moreau lay beside his latest victims,—the staghounds and the llama and some other wretched brutes,—with his massive face calm even after his terrible death, and with the hard eyes open, staring at the dead white moon above. I sat down upon the edge of the sink, and with my eyes upon that ghastly pile of silvery light and ominous shadows began to turn over my plans. In the morning I would gather some provisions in the dingey, and after setting fire to the pyre before me, push out into the desolation of the high sea once more. I felt that for Montgomery there was no help; that he was, in truth, half akin to these Beast Folk, unfitted for human kindred.

I do not know how long I sat there scheming. It must have been an hour or so. Then my planning was interrupted by the return of Montgomery to my neighbourhood. I heard a yelling from many throats, a tumult of exultant cries passing down towards the beach, whooping and howling, and excited shrieks that seemed to come to a stop near the water's edge. The riot rose and fell; I heard heavy blows and the splintering smash of wood, but it did not trouble me then. A discordant chanting began.

My thoughts went back to my means of escape. I got up, brought the lamp, and went into a shed to look at some kegs I had seen there. Then I became interested in the contents of some biscuit-tins, and opened one. I saw something out of the tail of my eye,—a red figure,—and turned sharply.

Behind me lay the yard, vividly black-and-white in the moonlight, and the pile of wood and faggots on which Moreau and his mutilated victims lay, one over another. They seemed to be gripping one another in one last revengeful grapple. His wounds gaped, black as night, and the blood that had dripped lay in black patches upon the sand. Then I saw, without understanding, the cause of my phantom,—a ruddy glow that came and danced and went upon the wall opposite. I misinterpreted this, fancied it was a reflection of my flickering lamp, and turned again to the stores in the shed. I went on rummaging among them, as well as a one-armed man could, finding this convenient thing and that, and putting them aside for tomorrow's launch. My movements were slow, and the time passed quickly. Insensibly the daylight crept upon me.

The chanting died down, giving place to a clamour; then it began again, and suddenly broke into a tumult. I heard cries of, "More! more!" a sound like quarrelling, and a sudden wild shriek. The quality of the sounds changed so greatly that it arrested my attention. I went out into the yard and listened. Then cutting like a knife across the confusion came the crack of a revolver.

I rushed at once through my room to the little doorway. As I did so I heard some of the packing-cases behind me go sliding down and smash together with a clatter of glass on the floor of the shed. But I did not heed these. I flung the door open and looked out.

Up the beach by the boathouse a bonfire was burning, raining up sparks into the indistinctness of the dawn. Around this struggled a mass of black figures. I heard Montgomery call my name. I began to run at once towards this fire, revolver in hand. I saw the pink tongue of Montgomery's pistol lick out once, close to the ground. He was down. I shouted with all my strength and fired into the air. I heard some one cry, "The Master!" The knotted black struggle broke into scattering units, the fire leapt and sank down. The crowd of Beast People fled in sudden panic before me, up the beach. In my excitement I fired at their retreating backs as they disappeared among the bushes. Then I turned to the black heaps upon the ground.

Montgomery lay on his back, with the hairy-grey Beast-man sprawling across his body. The brute was dead, but still gripping Montgomery's throat with its curving claws. Near by lay M'ling on his face and quite still, his neck bitten open and the upper part of the smashed brandy-bottle in his hand. Two other figures lay near the fire,—the one motionless, the other groaning fitfully, every now and then raising its head slowly, then dropping it again.

I caught hold of the grey man and pulled him off Montgomery's body; his claws drew down the torn coat reluctantly as I dragged him away. Montgomery was dark in the face and scarcely breathing. I splashed sea-water on his face and pillowed his head on my rolled-up coat. M'ling was dead. The wounded creature by the fire—it was a Wolf-brute with a bearded grey face—lay, I found, with the fore part of its body upon the still glowing timber. The wretched thing was injured so dreadfully that in mercy I blew its brains out at once. The other brute was one of the Bull-men swathed in white. He too was dead. The rest of the Beast People had vanished from the beach.

I went to Montgomery again and knelt beside him, cursing my ignorance of medicine. The fire beside me had sunk down, and only charred beams of timber glowing at the central ends and mixed with a grey ash of brushwood remained. I wondered casually where Montgomery had got his wood. Then I saw that the dawn was upon us. The sky had grown brighter, the setting moon was becoming pale and opaque in the luminous blue of the day. The sky to the eastward was rimmed with red.

Suddenly I heard a thud and a hissing behind me, and, looking round, sprang to my feet with a cry of horror. Against the warm dawn great tumultuous masses of black smoke were boiling up out of the enclosure, and through their stormy darkness shot flickering threads of blood-red flame. Then the thatched roof caught. I saw the curving charge of the flames across the sloping straw. A spurt of fire jetted from the window of my room.

I knew at once what had happened. I remembered the crash I had heard. When I had rushed out to Montgomery's assistance, I had overturned the lamp.

The hopelessness of saving any of the contents of the enclosure stared me in the face. My mind came back to my plan of flight, and turning swiftly I looked to see where the two boats lay upon the beach. They were gone! Two axes lay upon the sands beside me; chips and splinters were scattered broadcast, and the ashes of the bonfire were blackening and smoking under the dawn. Montgomery had burnt the boats to revenge himself upon me and prevent our return to mankind!

A sudden convulsion of rage shook me. I was almost moved to batter his foolish head in, as he lay there helpless at my feet. Then suddenly his hand moved, so feebly, so pitifully, that my wrath vanished. He groaned, and opened his eyes for a minute. I knelt down beside him and raised his head. He opened his eyes again, staring silently at the dawn, and then they met mine. The lids fell.

"Sorry," he said presently, with an effort. He seemed trying to think. "The last," he murmured, "the last of this silly universe. What a mess—"

I listened. His head fell helplessly to one side. I thought some drink might revive him; but there was neither drink nor vessel in which to bring drink at hand. He seemed suddenly heavier. My heart went cold. I bent down to his face, put my hand through the rent in his blouse. He was dead; and even as he died a line of white heat, the limb of the sun, rose eastward beyond the projection of the bay, splashing its radiance across the sky and turning the dark sea into a weltering tumult of dazzling light. It fell like a glory upon his death-shrunken face.

I let his head fall gently upon the rough pillow I had made for him, and stood up. Before me was the glittering desolation of the sea, the awful solitude upon which I had already suffered so much; behind me the island, hushed under the dawn, its Beast People silent and unseen. The enclosure, with all its provisions and ammunition, burnt noisily, with sudden gusts of flame, a fitful crackling, and now and then a crash. The heavy smoke drove up the beach away from me, rolling low over the distant tree-tops towards the huts in the ravine. Beside me were the charred vestiges of the boats and these five dead bodies.

Then out of the bushes came three Beast People, with hunched shoulders, protruding heads, misshapen hands awkwardly held, and inquisitive, unfriendly eyes and advanced towards me with hesitating gestures.

XX

Alone with the Beast Folk

I FACED THESE PEOPLE, facing my fate in them, single-handed now,—literally single-handed, for I had a broken arm. In my pocket was a revolver with two empty chambers. Among the chips scattered about the beach lay the two axes that had been used to chop up the boats. The tide was creeping in behind me. There was nothing for it but courage. I looked squarely into the faces of the advancing monsters. They avoided my eyes, and their quivering nostrils investigated the bodies that lay beyond me on the beach. I took half-a-dozen steps, picked up the blood-stained whip that lay beneath the body of the Wolf-man, and cracked it. They stopped and stared at me.

"Salute!" said I. "Bow down!"

They hesitated. One bent his knees. I repeated my command, with my heart in my mouth, and advanced upon them. One knelt, then the other two.

I turned and walked towards the dead bodies, keeping my face towards the three kneeling Beast Men, very much as an actor passing up the stage faces the audience.

"They broke the Law," said I, putting my foot on the Sayer of the Law. "They have been slain,—even the Sayer of the Law; even the Other with the Whip. Great is the Law! Come and see."

"None escape," said one of them, advancing and peering.

"None escape," said I. "Therefore hear and do as I command." They stood up, looking questioningly at one another.

"Stand there," said I.

I picked up the hatchets and swung them by their heads from the sling of my arm; turned Montgomery over; picked up his revolver still loaded in two chambers, and bending down to rummage, found half-a-dozen cartridges in his pocket.

"Take him," said I, standing up again and pointing with the whip; "take him, and carry him out and cast him into the sea."

They came forward, evidently still afraid of Montgomery, but still more afraid of my cracking red whip-lash; and after some fumbling and hesitation, some whip-cracking and shouting, they lifted him gingerly, carried him down to the beach, and went splashing into the dazzling welter of the sea.

"On!" said I, "on! Carry him far."

They went in up to their armpits and stood regarding me.

"Let go," said I; and the body of Montgomery vanished with a splash. Something seemed to tighten across my chest.

"Good!" said I, with a break in my voice; and they came back, hurrying and fearful, to the margin of the water, leaving long wakes of black in the silver. At the water's edge they stopped, turning and glaring into the sea as though they presently expected Montgomery to arise therefrom and exact vengeance.

"Now these," said I, pointing to the other bodies.

They took care not to approach the place where they had thrown Montgomery into the water, but instead, carried the four dead Beast People slantingly along the beach for perhaps a hundred yards before they waded out and cast them away.

As I watched them disposing of the mangled remains of M'ling, I heard a light footfall behind me, and turning quickly saw the big Hyena-swine perhaps a dozen yards away. His head was bent down, his bright eyes were fixed upon me, his stumpy hands clenched and held close by his side. He stopped in this crouching attitude when I turned, his eyes a little averted.

For a moment we stood eye to eye. I dropped the whip and snatched at the pistol in my pocket; for I meant to kill this brute, the most formidable of any left now upon the island, at the first excuse. It may seem treacherous, but so I was resolved. I was far more afraid of him than of any other two of the Beast Folk. His continued life was I knew a threat against mine.

I was perhaps a dozen seconds collecting myself. Then cried I, "Salute! Bow down!"

His teeth flashed upon me in a snarl. "Who are *you* that I should—"

Perhaps a little too spasmodically I drew my revolver, aimed quickly and fired. I heard him yelp, saw him run sideways and turn, knew I had missed, and clicked back the cock with my thumb for the next shot. But he was already running headlong, jumping from side to side, and I dared not risk another miss. Every now and then he looked back at me over his shoulder. He went slanting along the beach, and vanished beneath the driving masses of dense smoke that were still pouring out from the burning enclosure. For some time I stood staring after him. I turned to my three obedient Beast Folk again and signalled them to drop the body they still carried. Then I went back to the place by the fire where the bodies had fallen and kicked the sand until all the brown blood-stains were absorbed and hidden.

I dismissed my three serfs with a wave of the hand, and went up the beach into the thickets. I carried my pistol in my hand, my whip thrust with the hatchets in the sling of my arm. I was anxious to be alone, to think out the position in which I was now placed. A dreadful thing that I was only beginning to realise was, that over all this island there was now no safe place where I could be alone and secure to rest or sleep. I had recovered strength amazingly since my landing, but I was still inclined to be nervous and to break down under any great stress. I felt that I ought to cross the island and establish myself with the Beast People, and make myself secure in their confidence. But my heart failed me. I went back to the beach, and turning eastward past the burning enclosure, made for a point where a shallow spit of coral sand ran out towards the reef. Here I could sit down and think, my back to the sea and my face against any surprise. And there I sat, chin on knees, the sun beating down upon my head and unspeakable dread in my mind, plotting how I could live on against the hour of my rescue (if ever rescue came). I tried to review the whole situation as calmly as I could, but it was difficult to clear the thing of emotion.

I began turning over in my mind the reason of Montgomery's despair.

"They will change," he said; "they are sure to change." And Moreau, what was it that Moreau had said? "The stubborn beast-flesh grows day by day back again." Then I came round to the Hyena-swine. I felt sure that if I did not kill that brute, he would kill me. The Sayer of the Law was dead: worse luck. They knew now that we of the Whips could be killed even as they themselves were killed. Were they peering at me already out of the green masses of ferns and palms over yonder, watching until I came within their spring? Were they plotting against me? What was the Hyena-swine telling them? My imagination was running away with me into a morass of unsubstantial fears.

My thoughts were disturbed by a crying of sea-birds hurrying towards some black object that had been stranded by the waves on the beach near the enclosure. I knew what that object was, but I had not the heart to go back and drive them off. I began walking along the beach in the opposite direction, designing to come round the eastward corner of the island and so approach the ravine of the huts, without traversing the possible ambuscades of the thickets.

Perhaps half a mile along the beach I became aware of one of my three Beast Folk advancing out of the landward bushes towards me. I was now so nervous with my own imaginings that I immediately drew my revolver. Even the propitiatory gestures of the creature failed to disarm me. He hesitated as he approached.

"Go away!" cried I.

There was something very suggestive of a dog in the cringing attitude of the creature. It retreated a little way, very like a dog being sent home, and stopped, looking at me imploringly with canine brown eyes.

"Go away," said I. "Do not come near me."

"May I not come near you?" it said.

"No; go away," I insisted, and snapped my whip. Then putting my whip in my teeth, I stooped for a stone, and with that threat drove the creature away.

So in solitude I came round by the ravine of the Beast People, and hiding among the weeds and reeds that separated this crevice from the sea I watched such of them as appeared, trying to judge from their gestures and appearance how the death of Moreau and Montgomery and the destruction of the House of Pain had affected them. I know now the folly of my cowardice. Had I kept my courage up to the level of the dawn, had I not allowed it to ebb away in solitary thought, I might have grasped the vacant sceptre of Moreau and ruled over the Beast People. As it was I lost the opportunity, and sank to the position of a mere leader among my fellows.

Towards noon certain of them came and squatted basking in the hot sand. The imperious voices of hunger and thirst prevailed over my dread. I came out of the bushes, and, revolver in hand, walked down towards these seated figures. One, a Wolf-woman, turned her head and stared at me, and then the others. None attempted to rise or salute me. I felt too faint and weary to insist, and I let the moment pass.

"I want food," said I, almost apologetically, and drawing near.

"There is food in the huts," said an Ox-boar-man, drowsily, and looking away from me.

I passed them, and went down into the shadow and odours of the almost deserted ravine. In an empty hut I feasted on some specked and half-decayed fruit; and then after I had propped some branches and sticks about the opening, and placed myself with my face towards it and my hand upon my revolver, the exhaustion of the last thirty hours claimed its own, and I fell into a light slumber, hoping that the flimsy barricade I had erected would cause sufficient noise in its removal to save me from surprise.

XXI

THE REVERSION OF THE BEAST FOLK

IN THIS WAY I BECAME ONE AMONG THE BEAST PEOPLE in the Island of Doctor Moreau. When I awoke, it was dark about me. My arm ached in its bandages. I sat up, wondering at first where I might be. I heard coarse voices talking outside. Then I saw that my barricade had gone, and that the opening of the hut stood clear. My revolver was still in my hand.

I heard something breathing, saw something crouched together close beside me. I held my breath, trying to see what it was. It began to move slowly, interminably. Then something soft and warm and moist passed across my hand. All my muscles contracted. I snatched my hand away. A cry of alarm began and was stifled in my throat. Then I just realised what had happened sufficiently to stay my fingers on the revolver.

"Who is that?" I said in a hoarse whisper, the revolver still pointed.

"I—Master."

"Who are you?"

"They say there is no Master now. But I know, I know. I carried the bodies into the sea, O Walker in the Sea! the bodies of those you slew. I am your slave, Master."

"Are you the one I met on the beach?" I asked.

"The same, Master."

The Thing was evidently faithful enough, for it might have fallen upon me as I slept. "It is well," I said, extending my hand for another licking kiss. I began to realise what its presence meant, and the tide of my courage flowed. "Where are the others?" I asked.

"They are mad; they are fools," said the Dog-man. "Even now they talk together beyond there. They say, 'The Master is dead. The Other with the Whip is dead. That Other who walked in the Sea is as we are. We have no Master, no Whips, no House of Pain, any more. There is an end. We love the Law, and will keep it; but there is no Pain, no Master, no Whips for ever again.' So they say. But I know, Master, I know."

I felt in the darkness, and patted the Dog-man's head. "It is well," I said again.

"Presently you will slay them all," said the Dog-man.

"Presently," I answered, "I will slay them all,—after certain days and certain things have come to pass. Every one of them save those you spare, every one of them shall be slain."

"What the Master wishes to kill, the Master kills," said the Dog-man with a certain satisfaction in his voice.

"And that their sins may grow," I said, "let them live in their folly until their time is ripe. Let them not know that I am the Master."

"The Master's will is sweet," said the Dog-man, with the ready tact of his canine blood.

"But one has sinned," said I. "Him I will kill, whenever I may meet him. When I say to you, *'That is he,'* see that you fall upon him. And now I will go to the men and women who are assembled together."

For a moment the opening of the hut was blackened by the exit of the Dog-man. Then I followed and stood up, almost in the exact spot where I had been when I had heard Moreau and his staghound pursuing me. But now it was night, and all the miasmatic ravine about me was black; and beyond, instead of a green, sunlit slope, I saw a red fire, before which hunched, grotesque figures moved to and fro. Farther were the thick trees, a bank of darkness, fringed above with the black lace of the upper branches. The moon was just riding up on the edge of the ravine, and like a bar across its face drove the spire of vapour that was for ever streaming from the fumaroles of the island.

"Walk by me," said I, nerving myself; and side by side we walked down the narrow way, taking little heed of the dim Things that peered at us out of the huts.

None about the fire attempted to salute me. Most of them disregarded me, ostentatiously. I looked round for the Hyena-swine, but he was not there. Altogether, perhaps twenty of the Beast Folk squatted, staring into the fire or talking to one another.

"He is dead, he is dead! the Master is dead!" said the voice of the Ape-man to the right of me. "The House of Pain—there is no House of Pain!"

"He is not dead," said I, in a loud voice. "Even now he watches us!"

This startled them. Twenty pairs of eyes regarded me.

"The House of Pain is gone," said I. "It will come again. The Master you cannot see; yet even now he listens among you."

"True, true!" said the Dog-man.

They were staggered at my assurance. An animal may be ferocious and cunning enough, but it takes a real man to tell a lie.

"The Man with the Bandaged Arm speaks a strange thing," said one of the Beast Folk.

"I tell you it is so," I said. "The Master and the House of Pain will come again. Woe be to him who breaks the Law!"

They looked curiously at one another. With an affectation of indifference I began to chop idly at the ground in front of me with my hatchet. They looked, I noticed, at the deep cuts I made in the turf.

Then the Satyr raised a doubt. I answered him. Then one of the dappled things objected, and an animated discussion sprang up round the fire. Every moment I began to feel more convinced of my present security. I talked now without the catching in my breath, due to the intensity of my excitement, that had troubled me at first. In the course of about an hour I had really convinced several of the Beast Folk of the truth of my assertions, and talked most of the others into a dubious state. I kept a sharp eye for my enemy the Hyena-swine, but he never appeared. Every now and then a suspicious movement would startle me, but my confidence grew rapidly. Then as the moon crept down from the zenith, one by one the listeners began to yawn (showing the oddest teeth in the light of the sinking fire), and first one and then another retired towards the dens in the ravine; and

I, dreading the silence and darkness, went with them, knowing I was safer with several of them than with one alone.

In this manner began the longer part of my sojourn upon this Island of Doctor Moreau. But from that night until the end came, there was but one thing happened to tell save a series of innumerable small unpleasant details and the fretting of an incessant uneasiness. So that I prefer to make no chronicle for that gap of time, to tell only one cardinal incident of the ten months I spent as an intimate of these half-humanised brutes. There is much that sticks in my memory that I could write,—things that I would cheerfully give my right hand to forget; but they do not help the telling of the story.

In the retrospect it is strange to remember how soon I fell in with these monsters' ways, and gained my confidence again. I had my quarrels with them of course, and could show some of their teeth-marks still; but they soon gained a wholesome respect for my trick of throwing stones and for the bite of my hatchet. And my Saint-Bernard-man's loyalty was of infinite service to me. I found their simple scale of honour was based mainly on the capacity for inflicting trenchant wounds. Indeed, I may say—without vanity, I hope—that I held something like pre-eminence among them. One or two, whom in a rare access of high spirits I had scarred rather badly, bore me a grudge; but it vented itself chiefly behind my back, and at a safe distance from my missiles, in grimaces.

The Hyena-swine avoided me, and I was always on the alert for him. My inseparable Dog-man hated and dreaded him intensely. I really believe that was at the root of the brute's attachment to me. It was soon evident to me that the former monster had tasted blood, and gone the way of the Leopard-man. He formed a lair somewhere in the forest, and became solitary. Once I tried to induce the Beast Folk to hunt him, but I lacked the authority to make them co-operate for one end. Again and again I tried to approach his den and come upon him unaware; but always he was too acute for me, and saw or winded me and got away. He too made every forest pathway dangerous to me and my ally with his lurking ambuscades. The Dog-man scarcely dared to leave my side.

In the first month or so the Beast Folk, compared with their latter condition, were human enough, and for one or two besides my canine friend

I even conceived a friendly tolerance. The little pink sloth-creature displayed an odd affection for me, and took to following me about. The Monkey-man bored me, however; he assumed, on the strength of his five digits, that he was my equal, and was for ever jabbering at me,—jabbering the most arrant nonsense. One thing about him entertained me a little: he had a fantastic trick of coining new words. He had an idea, I believe, that to gabble about names that meant nothing was the proper use of speech. He called it "Big Thinks" to distinguish it from "Little Thinks," the sane every-day interests of life. If ever I made a remark he did not understand, he would praise it very much, ask me to say it again, learn it by heart, and go off repeating it, with a word wrong here or there, to all the milder of the Beast People. He thought nothing of what was plain and comprehensible. I invented some very curious "Big Thinks" for his especial use. I think now that he was the silliest creature I ever met; he had developed in the most wonderful way the distinctive silliness of man without losing one jot of the natural folly of a monkey.

This, I say, was in the earlier weeks of my solitude among these brutes. During that time they respected the usage established by the Law, and behaved with general decorum. Once I found another rabbit torn to pieces,—by the Hyena-swine, I am assured,—but that was all. It was about May when I first distinctly perceived a growing difference in their speech and carriage, a growing coarseness of articulation, a growing disinclination to talk. My Monkey-man's jabber multiplied in volume but grew less and less comprehensible, more and more simian. Some of the others seemed altogether slipping their hold upon speech, though they still understood what I said to them at that time. (Can you imagine language, once clear-cut and exact, softening and guttering, losing shape and import, becoming mere lumps of sound again?) And they walked erect with an increasing difficulty. Though they evidently felt ashamed of themselves, every now and then I would come upon one or another running on toes and finger-tips, and quite unable to recover the vertical attitude. They held things more clumsily; drinking by suction, feeding by gnawing, grew commoner every day. I realised more keenly than ever what Moreau had told me about the "stubborn beast-flesh." They were reverting, and reverting very rapidly.

Some of them—the pioneers in this, I noticed with some surprise, were all females—began to disregard the injunction of decency, deliberately for the most part. Others even attempted public outrages upon the institution of monogamy. The tradition of the Law was clearly losing its force. I cannot pursue this disagreeable subject.

My Dog-man imperceptibly slipped back to the dog again; day by day he became dumb, quadrupedal, hairy. I scarcely noticed the transition from the companion on my right hand to the lurching dog at my side.

As the carelessness and disorganisation increased from day to day, the lane of dwelling places, at no time very sweet, became so loathsome that I left it, and going across the island made myself a hovel of boughs amid the black ruins of Moreau's enclosure. Some memory of pain, I found, still made that place the safest from the Beast Folk.

It would be impossible to detail every step of the lapsing of these monsters,—to tell how, day by day, the human semblance left them; how they gave up bandagings and wrappings, abandoned at last every stitch of clothing; how the hair began to spread over the exposed limbs; how their foreheads fell away and their faces projected; how the quasi-human intimacy I had permitted myself with some of them in the first month of my loneliness became a shuddering horror to recall.

The change was slow and inevitable. For them and for me it came without any definite shock. I still went among them in safety, because no jolt in the downward glide had released the increasing charge of explosive animalism that ousted the human day by day. But I began to fear that soon now that shock must come. My Saint-Bernard-brute followed me to the enclosure every night, and his vigilance enabled me to sleep at times in something like peace. The little pink sloth-thing became shy and left me, to crawl back to its natural life once more among the tree-branches. We were in just the state of equilibrium that would remain in one of those "Happy Family" cages which animal-tamers exhibit, if the tamer were to leave it for ever.

Of course these creatures did not decline into such beasts as the reader has seen in zoological gardens,—into ordinary bears, wolves, tigers, oxen, swine, and apes. There was still something strange about each; in each Moreau had blended this animal with that. One perhaps was ursine chiefly, another feline chiefly, another bovine chiefly; but each was tainted with other creatures,—a kind of generalised animalism appearing through the specific dispositions. And the dwindling shreds of the humanity still startled me every now and then,—a momentary recrudescence of speech perhaps, an unexpected dexterity of the fore-feet, a pitiful attempt to walk erect.

I too must have undergone strange changes. My clothes hung about me as yellow rags, through whose rents showed the tanned skin. My hair grew long, and became matted together. I am told that even now my eyes have a strange brightness, a swift alertness of movement.

At first I spent the daylight hours on the southward beach watching for a ship, hoping and praying for a ship. I counted on the *Ipecacuanha* returning as the year wore on; but she never came. Five times I saw sails, and thrice smoke; but nothing ever touched the island. I always had a bonfire ready, but no doubt the volcanic reputation of the island was taken to account for that.

It was only about September or October that I began to think of making a raft. By that time my arm had healed, and both my hands were at my service again. At first, I found my helplessness appalling. I had never done any carpentry or such-like work in my life, and I spent day after day in experimental chopping and binding among the trees. I had no ropes, and could hit on nothing wherewith to make ropes; none of the abundant creepers seemed limber or strong enough, and with all my litter of scientific education I could not devise any way of making them so. I spent more than a fortnight grubbing among the black ruins of the enclosure and on the beach where the boats had been burnt, looking for nails and other stray pieces of metal that might prove of service. Now and then some Beast-creature would watch me, and go leaping off when I called to it. There came a season of thunder-storms and heavy rain, which greatly retarded my work; but at last the raft was completed.

I was delighted with it. But with a certain lack of practical sense which has always been my bane, I had made it a mile or more from the sea; and before I had dragged it down to the beach the thing had fallen to pieces. Perhaps it is as well that I was saved from launching it; but at the time my misery at my failure was so acute that for some days I simply moped on the beach, and stared at the water and thought of death.

I did not, however, mean to die, and an incident occurred that warned me unmistakably of the folly of letting the days pass so,—for each fresh day was fraught with increasing danger from the Beast People.

I was lying in the shade of the enclosure wall, staring out to sea, when I was startled by something cold touching the skin of my heel, and starting round found the little pink sloth-creature blinking into my face. He had long since lost speech and active movement, and the lank hair of the little brute grew thicker every day and his stumpy claws more askew. He made a moaning noise when he saw he had attracted my attention, went a little way towards the bushes and looked back at me.

At first I did not understand, but presently it occurred to me that he wished me to follow him; and this I did at last,—slowly, for the day was hot. When we reached the trees he clambered into them, for he could travel better among their swinging creepers than on the ground. And suddenly in a trampled space I came upon a ghastly group. My Saint-Bernard-creature lay on the ground, dead; and near his body crouched the Hyena-swine, gripping the quivering flesh with its misshapen claws, gnawing at it, and snarling with delight. As I approached, the monster lifted its glaring eyes to mine, its lips went trembling back from its red-stained teeth, and it growled menacingly. It was not afraid and not ashamed; the last vestige of the human taint had vanished. I advanced a step farther, stopped, and pulled out my revolver. At last I had him face to face.

The brute made no sign of retreat; but its ears went back, its hair bristled, and its body crouched together. I aimed between the eyes and fired. As I did so, the Thing rose straight at me in a leap, and I was knocked over like a ninepin. It clutched at me with its crippled hand, and struck me in the face. Its spring carried it over me. I fell under the hind part of its body; but luckily I had hit as I meant, and it had died even as it leapt. I crawled out from under its unclean weight and stood up trembling, staring at its quivering body. That danger at least was over; but this, I knew was only the first of the series of relapses that must come.

I burnt both of the bodies on a pyre of brushwood; but after that I saw that unless I left the island my death was only a question of time. The Beast People by that time had, with one or two exceptions, left the ravine and made themselves lairs according to their taste among the thickets of the island. Few prowled by day, most of them slept, and the island might have seemed deserted to a new-comer; but at night the air was hideous with their calls and howling. I had half a mind to make a massacre of them; to build traps, or fight them with my knife. Had I possessed sufficient cartridges, I should not have hesitated to begin the killing. There could now be scarcely a score left of the dangerous carnivores; the braver of these were already dead. After the death of this poor dog of mine, my last friend, I too adopted to some extent the practice of slumbering in the daytime in order to be on my guard at night. I rebuilt my den in the walls of the enclosure, with such a narrow opening that anything attempting to enter must necessarily make a considerable noise. The creatures had lost the art of fire too, and recovered their fear of it. I turned once more, almost passionately now, to hammering together stakes and branches to form a raft for my escape.

I found a thousand difficulties. I am an extremely unhandy man (my schooling was over before the days of Slöjd); but most of the requirements of a raft I met at last in some clumsy, circuitous way or other, and this time I took care of the strength. The only insurmountable obstacle was that I had no vessel to contain the water I should need if I floated forth upon these untravelled seas. I would have even tried pottery, but the island contained no clay. I used to go moping about the island trying with all my might to solve this one last difficulty. Sometimes I would give way to wild outbursts of rage, and hack and splinter some unlucky tree in my intolerable vexation. But I could think of nothing.

And then came a day, a wonderful day, which I spent in ecstasy. I saw a sail to the southwest, a small sail like that of a little schooner; and forthwith I lit a great pile of brushwood, and stood by it in the heat of it, and the heat of the midday sun, watching. All day I watched that sail, eating or drinking nothing, so that my head reeled; and the Beasts came and glared at me, and seemed to wonder, and went away. It was still distant when night came and swallowed it up; and all night I toiled to keep my blaze bright and high, and the eyes of the Beasts shone out of the darkness, marvelling. In the dawn the sail was nearer, and I saw it was the dirty lug-sail of a small boat. But it sailed strangely. My eyes were weary with watching, and I peered and could not believe them. Two men were in the boat, sitting low down,—one by the bows, the other at the rudder. The head was not kept to the wind; it yawed and fell away.

As the day grew brighter, I began waving the last rag of my jacket to them; but they did not notice me, and sat still, facing each other. I went to the lowest point of the low headland, and gesticulated and shouted. There was no response, and the boat kept on her aimless course, making slowly, very slowly, for the bay. Suddenly a great white bird flew up out of the boat, and neither of the men stirred nor noticed it; it circled round, and then came sweeping overhead with its strong wings outspread.

Then I stopped shouting, and sat down on the headland and rested my chin on my hands and stared. Slowly, slowly, the boat drove past towards the west. I would have swum out to it, but something—a cold, vague fear—kept me back. In the afternoon the tide stranded the boat, and left it a hundred yards or so to the westward of the ruins of the enclosure. The men in it were dead, had been dead so long that they fell to pieces when I tilted the boat on its side and dragged them out. One had a shock of red hair, like the captain of the *Ipecacuanha*, and a dirty white cap lay in the bottom of the boat.

As I stood beside the boat, three of the Beasts came slinking out of the bushes and sniffing towards me. One of my spasms of disgust came upon me. I thrust the little boat down the beach and clambered on board her. Two of the brutes were Wolf-beasts, and came forward with quivering nostrils and glittering eyes; the third was the horrible nondescript of bear and bull. When I saw them approaching those wretched remains, heard them snarling at one another and caught the gleam of their teeth, a frantic horror succeeded my repulsion. I turned my back upon them, struck the lug and began paddling out to sea. I could not bring myself to look behind me.

I lay, however, between the reef and the island that night, and the next morning went round to the stream and filled the empty keg aboard with water. Then, with such patience as I could command, I collected a quantity of fruit, and waylaid and killed two rabbits with my last three cartridges. While I was doing this I left the boat moored to an inward projection of the reef, for fear of the Beast People.

XXII

The Man Alone

IN THE EVENING I STARTED, and drove out to sea before a gentle wind from the southwest, slowly, steadily; and the island grew smaller and smaller, and the lank spire of smoke dwindled to a finer and finer line against the hot sunset. The ocean rose up around me, hiding that low, dark patch from my eyes. The daylight, the trailing glory of the sun, went streaming out of the sky, was drawn aside like some luminous curtain, and at last I looked into the blue gulf of immensity which the sunshine hides, and saw the floating hosts of the stars. The sea was silent, the sky was silent. I was alone with the night and silence.

So I drifted for three days, eating and drinking sparingly, and meditating upon all that had happened to me,—not desiring very greatly then to see men again. One unclean rag was about me, my hair a black tangle: no doubt my discoverers thought me a madman.

It is strange, but I felt no desire to return to mankind. I was only glad to be quit of the foulness of the Beast People. And on the third day I was picked up by a brig from Apia to San Francisco. Neither the captain nor the mate would believe my story, judging that solitude and danger had made me mad; and fearing their opinion might be that of others, I refrained from telling my adventure further, and professed to recall nothing that had happened to me between the loss of the *Lady Vain* and the time when I was picked up again,—the space of a year.

I had to act with the utmost circumspection to save myself from the suspicion of insanity. My memory of the Law, of the two dead sailors, of the ambuscades of the darkness, of the body in the canebrake, haunted me; and, unnatural as it seems, with my return to mankind came, instead of that confidence and sympathy I had expected, a strange enhancement of the uncertainty and dread I had experienced during my stay upon the island. No one would believe me; I was almost as queer to men as I had been to the Beast People. I may have caught something of the natural wildness of my companions. They say that terror is a disease, and anyhow I can witness that for several years now a restless fear has dwelt in my mind,—such a restless fear as a half-tamed lion cub may feel.

My trouble took the strangest form. I could not persuade myself that the men and women I met were not also another Beast People, animals half wrought into the outward image of human souls, and that they would presently begin to revert,—to show first this bestial mark and then that. But I have confided my case to a strangely able man,—a man who had known Moreau, and seemed half to credit my story; a mental specialist,— and he has helped me mightily, though I do not expect that the terror of that island will ever altogether leave me. At most times it lies far in the back of my mind, a mere distant cloud, a memory, and a faint distrust; but there are times when the little cloud spreads until it obscures the whole sky. Then I look about me at my fellow-men; and I go in fear. I see faces, keen and bright; others dull or dangerous; others, unsteady, insincere,— none that have the calm authority of a reasonable soul. I feel as though the animal was surging up through them; that presently the degradation of the Islanders will be played over again on a larger scale. I know this is an illusion; that these seeming men and women about me are indeed men and women,—men and women for ever, perfectly reasonable creatures, full of human desires and tender solicitude, emancipated from instinct and the slaves of no fantastic Law,—beings altogether different from the Beast Folk. Yet I shrink from them, from their curious glances, their inquiries and assistance, and long to be away from them and alone. For that reason I live near the broad free downland, and can escape thither when this shadow is over my soul; and very sweet is the empty downland then, under the wind-swept sky.

When I lived in London the horror was well-nigh insupportable. I could not get away from men: their voices came through windows; locked doors were flimsy safeguards. I would go out into the streets to fight with my delusion, and prowling women would mew after me; furtive, craving men glance jealously at me; weary, pale workers go coughing by me with tired eyes and eager paces, like wounded deer dripping blood; old people, bent and dull, pass murmuring to themselves; and, all unheeding, a ragged tail of gibing children. Then I would turn aside into some chapel,—and even there, such was my disturbance, it seemed that the preacher gibbered "Big Thinks," even as the Ape-man had done; or into some library, and there the intent faces over the books seemed but patient creatures waiting for prey. Particularly nauseous were the blank, expressionless faces of people in trains and omnibuses; they seemed no more my fellow-creatures than dead bodies would be, so that I did not dare to travel unless I was assured of being alone. And even it seemed that I too was not a reasonable creature, but only an animal tormented with some strange disorder in its brain which sent it to wander alone, like a sheep stricken with gid.

This is a mood, however, that comes to me now, I thank God, more rarely. I have withdrawn myself from the confusion of cities and multitudes, and spend my days surrounded by wise books,—bright windows in this life of ours, lit by the shining souls of men. I see few strangers, and have but a small household. My days I devote to reading and to experiments in chemistry, and I spend many of the clear nights in the study of astronomy. There is—though I do not know how there is or why there is—a sense of infinite peace and protection in the glittering hosts of heaven. There it must be, I think, in the vast and eternal laws of matter, and not in the daily cares and sins and troubles of men, that whatever is more than animal within us must find its solace and its hope. I hope, or I could not live.

And so, in hope and solitude, my story ends.

EDWARD PRENDICK